"I do not want a friend of you. Lover, perhaps ... but not a friend."

He thought she looked like an earnest scholar with her arms around a book, except for that mouth that promised lush kisses and the imploring in her eyes that offered even more—a kitten to his hand, a slave to his mastery, a queen in his kingdom, a woman to his manhood.

Take her.

She was danger and mystery and warmth, all in a delectable female package. He'd not felt the warmth for so long.

"If you had any sense at all, you would run from here as if a wolf were on your scent."

"And miss the sweet devouring?"

Her smile hinted at all the answers for all the questions he'd had about her. He was compelled by lust so strong that it swallowed up all reason, leaving only need and desire.

Romances by Karen Ranney

KAREN RANNEY

My Wicked Fantasy

AVON
An Imprint of HarperCollinsPublishers

AVON BOOKS
An Imprint of HarperCollins*Publishers*
10 East 53rd Street
New York, New York 10022-5299

Copyright © 1998 by Karen Ranney
ISBN 978-0-380-79581-9
www.avonromance.com

First Avon Books mass market printing: February 1998

Avon Trademark Reg. U.S. Pat. Off. and in Other Countries, Marca Registrada, Hecho en U.S.A.
HarperCollins® is a registered trademark of HarperCollins Publishers.

Printed in the U.S.A.

10 9 8 7 6 5

To twenty years of memories
and survival

Chapter 1

"**Y**e've a gift for dreamin', lass. Don't ever lose it. The world can be a right cruel place if ye've not the knack to ignore it from time to time."

Her father's words echoed in Mary Kate's mind like the sound of a long-ago bell. What would Patrick O'Brien say about her actions? Would he understand that this journey was the culmination of a dream she'd had for so many years? Or would he simply counsel her that she was being foolish, that nothing would come of stirring up trouble?

Mary Kate would never hear his opinion. Da resided with the angels, and had for too many long years.

She knew what she was doing was probably unwise. She might not find what she wanted at the journey's end. But on the chance that she would, she'd sold every belonging she'd managed to acquire over the last four years, walked away from the small house on Bell Street, and was heading north, away from London. Memories of ten years ago provided her clues—the name of her mother's father, a tiny village called Denmouth, a dream of whispers and plans.

She'd made better time than she'd expected, being able to secure a ride here and there, when she'd planned on having to travel most of the distance on foot. This morning

1

she'd taken advantage of a farmer's kindness and now sat perched in the back of his empty wagon.

"Took my produce to London town," he'd said, bragging of the amount he'd made from the lot of it. She had smiled and congratulated him, climbing up into the back of the wagon with what grace she was still able to muster after five days on the road.

It had not been a hard journey, even though it was early November. The mornings were brisk, but the afternoons warmed so that the walk was pleasant enough. Strange, though, how the quiet had been so loud. Oh, there were the sounds of the forest, the infrequent vehicle making its way toward London. Occasionally Mary Kate would pass a farm or skirt a village. But it was the absence of conversation that had been a strange and novel experience. She had always been surrounded by people.

The wagon bed was commodious, wide enough that Mary Kate could sit and stretch her legs out before her, fold her cloak over her exposed ankles. In the corner was a crate, wrapped twice around with a length of cord, bearing the mark of the Etruria pottery works. She guessed the box was filled with cups and saucers, small plates, perhaps a gift for the farmer's wife. Her own precious hoard of creamware, lovingly collected and regretfully sold to pay for this trip, had borne the same symbol.

There had been no money left for clothing, but had there been, she would have purchased a length of linsey-woolsey and made herself a decent dress and cloak to travel in, clothing not so fine and dust-gathering, both traits apt to stir a question or two. For the most part, however, people simply looked at her with curiosity and rarely spoke what was on their minds. And she probably would not have known what to tell them.

*   *   *

There was nothing about traveling to the City that endeared itself to Archer St. John. There would be no welcome in London. Only idle gossip and whispered conjecture, the enforced alienation from those individuals Archer had disliked long before they'd decided he was not fit for their company. A curious dichotomy, that. To be refused admittance from the very place he'd always shunned.

But word had come of the arrival of a St. John ship, the *Hebrides*, and there was still the possibility of news about Alice. A hint of that would coax even St. John the Hermit from his lair.

A corner of one lip curved upward as he reflected upon his nickname. His dislike of his innumerable relatives had spawned the name at school. His boredom at those events so cherished by the ton resurrected the name. Events of the last year had made it stick. St. John the Hermit. Not so much a man withdrawing from the world as one who created his own, more preferable, existence around him.

He read prodigiously, an occupation that was not generally shared by his peers. While he rode because it was the most expeditious manner of traversing his estate, he wasn't horse-mad, a possession of temperament he found exceedingly silly in men of his age and station. He spent his time in pursuits that would not interest any of the people who spent their days lolling about in the salons of the day. Still, it was odd to be so aptly named by those who had no deeper interest in him than the cut of his coat.

One tanned hand reached out and gripped the leather handle above the door as the carriage careened around the corner. Another small smile, in deference to his coachman's absolute interpretation of his employer's every wish.

Archer had indicated the *Hebrides* would be coming in from the Space Islands and he wanted to be present at the interview with its captain; therefore, Jeremy would see that such a feat was accomplished.

With any luck, the captain would bring word of Alice.

Mary Kate peeked her head up above the high walls of the wagon. The sound of hooves approaching was growing louder, a warning of noise. The road was narrow, little more than an overgrown lane, barely able to accommodate two vehicles at once, and the turn that loomed a short distance ahead was surely one that urged caution.

Mary Kate had, after several abortive attempts at conversation, realized the farmer was nearly deaf. Surely that was the reason and not sheer foolhardiness, for his stubborn refusal to pull off on the side of the road and wait for the other vehicle to pass. The steady drone of hoofbeats seemed oddly portentous, a rhythmic melody, a low and tuneless echo that announced the sight of flashing bridles and deep-breasted horses.

A coach and four bore down on top of them, headed in the opposite direction toward London, the ebony blackness of both conveyance and horses indicating, perhaps, that this was not an ordinary brougham, nor were these everyday hacks.

Still, the farmer did not urge his stolid dray horses to a halt, nor did he seem overly concerned about the sharp turn in the road just ahead. Was it that he had not seen the carriage, or somehow misjudged its size?

Wasn't it odd how time seemed to slow until it played itself out a trickle, a drop, at a time? Mary Kate saw the coachman stand, burly arms straining in an effort to slow his horses around the curve of road, his foot planted hard against a brake that squealed in protest. A second later, the lead team of horses was upon the farmer's wagon, the narrow road and treacherous curve leaving no place for the horses to go. The frightened screams of the Thoroughbreds, the answering animal terror from the farmer's draft horses, all merged into a high-pitched keening sound. The wagon rocked from the impact, then seemed to slowly turn over.

Mary Kate felt the hot breath exhaled from flaring nostrils, saw the great straining breasts, could almost feel the harness gouging into the horses' sweat-sheened skin. The air was filled with muscled legs and sharp, iron-shod hooves, the smell of leather, splintering wood, shouts and screams, and a curious feeling of pain that was hers and yet didn't belong to her at all.

And then there was nothing.

Chapter 2

"Is she waking, then?'' Archer asked.

'It is to be hoped for, Lord St. John. The poor woman has been devoid of sensibility for some time.''

"Should she be tossing about so much, though?''

"Merely the body's way of lessening the effects of ill humors.''

Archer St. John looked askance at the physician, certain that it was not so much the body's ill humors as it was pain that caused the patient on the bed to softly moan.

He possessed little patience with this physician, and even less faith. For three days the man had spoken of pestilence and plague, boils and worm-rot, had bled the poor woman until Archer was certain there was not a spare drop of blood to be had from the unfortunate creature. And the only bit of information he'd had to offer was something Archer could have discerned quite ably on his own.

She was lucky to be alive.

He had taken responsibility for the caring of her, feeling that odd and uncomfortable pinch of conscience that forced him to admit he was partly to blame for the mishap. He was, after all, the one who'd insisted upon speed.

As it was, he'd been too late to meet the docking of the

Hebrides, so he concerned himself instead with the placement of the unconscious woman in this small country inn, summoning a physician to care for her. The farmer had been uninjured, had been mollified by a payment that had more than covered the damage to his wagon and its contents. More than that, Archer could not do.

Even so, the fact that she had not woken in three days was disturbing. So much so that he'd banned the physician from using any more of his leeches upon her, thinking she needed her blood now more than they.

One of the inn's maids scurried before him to open the door. She was staying with the unfortunate woman as handmaiden, to brush out her hair, bathe her brow, see to her intimate needs, perhaps say a prayer to summon her to full wakefulness. He silently wished her success in her petition to God.

Archer turned at the door, sent his scowl in the direction of the fawning physician, dampened the look somewhat for the occupant of the bed.

His victim had the brightness of a Eustache Le Sueur painting, hair a shade that mimicked dawn's orange glow, lips too full for proper English standards, a retroussé nose. During the initial examination, the physician had lifted her lids to disclose eyes the color of a verdant forest. She was flamboyantly lovely, instilling in Archer's mind thoughts of emerald green meadows or platters of ripe fruit, neither description apt for this setting or this moment.

Her head twisted upon the pillow, tangled in the webs of her dreams. Archer wondered what nightmare held her within its spell, what incantations her unconscious state brought to the mind's eye.

Her hands were white, with softly rounded nails. On her left hand was a simple unadorned gold band. His luck was holding, then. How much better served he would have been to have struck down a filthy old crone, a gin-ridden beggar. No, his victim was a gentlewoman with voluptuous curves and skin like ivory silk, whose husband was no doubt searching for her now. The irony of the situation did not escape him.

Lost wives.

Did Alice remain senseless just as this woman did, waiting for rescue, for claiming? Or was she sleeping peacefully in a lover's arms, replete, satiated, untroubled by guilt or conscience? Or had she simply hidden herself away, waiting for his sorrow, his penitence?

Where was his wife?

Every day, just as regimented as the sun setting, just as resistant to change, just as stubborn and willful, that question surfaced. No, truth now, Archer. It lay beneath each hour of his existence, awaiting the summons to full, conscious thought.

No.

He wasn't in the mood for truth, he decided. It exacted too dear a penalty.

"She's powerful bruised, sir. She's all blue and green with it." The young maid offered up that information as if he'd needed any further reminding of how close the young woman had come to being trampled to death. "She's a dangerous-looking mark on her lower limb and a bunch of scratches on her chest." That confession yielded a blush and a curtsy. "She's lucky for all that, sir. My sister Sally had a powerful close brush with death once. Mr. Foggin's horse, a mean brute, kicked her, sir, and she was senseless for nearly four days. And all that time, not a word, not a sound . . ."

The sound of female laughter sparkled through the crowd in front of the small stone church. The bride was dressed in jonquil yellow, her blond hair so light it seemed to summon the brightness from the air around her, her beauty enhanced by the simplicity of her dress. Beside her, a man stood, his height topping hers by nearly a foot. She seemed too dainty beside his masculine grace, too delicate next to his form. Where she was blond, he was dark, his features carefully crafted from bone, flesh, muscle. He stood with an attitude of easy grace, a daring look in his eyes that cautioned against trespass, hinted at a dangerous emotion he was careful not to betray.

The bride was surrounded by chattering women, the groom stood silent. While the bride smiled, her newly made husband remained somber. And yet there was emotion between them; what she radiated, he seemed to inhale, leaving the day itself untouched. And leaving them curiously separate and distinct. A couple, but not a pair.

A flash, a moment of time. Gone.

Chapter 3

It was the same face Mary Kate had seen reflected all her life. Green eyes muted with flecks of brown—forest eyes, her brothers had long ago teased, saying that if she were ever lost in the woods, they'd never be able to find her. Orange hair—there was no other shade to describe it—too brazen, too attracting of the kind of attention she'd never sought. Lips too broad as if on the verge of an eternal smile. Freckles across the bridge of a nose she'd always thought too small. A chin too stubborn for her station in life.

Mary Kate didn't know what discoveries she was hoping to find with such an intent perusal. Some sign that she'd truly been insensible for three whole days?

She was lucky to be alive, if she heeded the breathless words of the young maid. Any aches and pains seemed a small price to pay. This homily had been echoed by the physician who companioned her bedside, hovering like a wraith until she'd been able to focus on his wrinkled, wizened face. Every day Dr. Endicott's presence had been accompanied by his noxious tonic, prepared, he'd bragged, with cod-liver oil, honey, Dover's powder, and a touch of fiery ginger. Mary Kate shuddered, thinking of it.

10

She placed the mirror on the bedside table next to the pink roses bunched in the earthenware vase. She didn't think she liked roses, but that might just be another errant memory. Memories?

Good heavens, the dreams.

It was the injury, of course. The shock of the accident, the sleep that lasted three days. Surely that was the only reason for the odd dreams, the snatches of memory recalled. Why, then, did some of these recollections seem disjointed, not quite hers? How silly. To whom could they belong?

And yet they did not seem like her recollections at all. A luxurious wedding. An evermore extravagant trip to Venice, Florence, Rome. Strange visions for a woman wed in a bland civil ceremony, who had suffered her wedding night with great patience and few illusions. Mary Kate's one travel adventure had been to journey to Cornwall with her barrister husband.

Wishful thinking? Dreams once harbored by a naive young girl, resurrected by injury? Odd that these dreams should have such detail. Even more peculiar that they should be peopled by strangers and not images of herself.

She shrugged. It was a mystery, perhaps, that might never be solved.

The young maid had helped her bathe earlier, albeit with Mary Kate sitting on the edge of the bed with her legs dangling down from it. Along with the mirror, she'd also brought news that Mary Kate's benefactor intended a visit prior to his departure. An invitation Mary Kate could hardly decline, since it had been his kindness that had provided for her care. In truth, it was not his fault she had been injured, but simply fate that had caused the accident.

She dangled her legs over the bed again, gathering up

the voluminous folds of her nightgown. It was, like most
of her wardrobe, of good quality but nearly threadbare.
The penury of these past months had not allowed for more
than the barest necessities, and clothing seemed less important than food or paying the rent on her small house.

She had no energy; even the effort of draping her legs
over the bedside seemed enormously difficult. But while
it was true she hurt in places she didn't think possible to
feel pain, the bruising would eventually fade. She would
not let these minor nuisances stop her from reaching her
goal. There was no time for this weakness of limbs. Perhaps she could manage to stand on her own, even walk to
the chair on the other side of the room. It seemed a simple
thing to do, quite easy, really.

She hadn't planned on the pounding of her head, the
sensation that she was moving slower, pushing against air
that had become strangely thick. Her feet appeared to stick
against the cold floorboards, each step so difficult that it
seemed an eternity until she sat heavily on the ladder-
backed chair, her legs collapsing beneath her.

The pain in her head cautioned her against making the
return voyage too quickly. Mary Kate laid her head back,
placed her hands upon the eagles carved into the arms of
the chair, closed her eyes against the onrush of the headache.

Once, as a child, Mary Kate had been racing home
through the fields, caught by a spring storm. Lightning had
struck a tree not ten feet away, terrifying her, leaving behind a scorched trunk, the smell of burnt wood, and an
acrid odor she could not name but would never be able to
forget. It seemed replicated now, in this room far away
from the place where she played as a child.

The pain worsened, seemed to be isolated in the center

of her brow. She pressed the fingers of both hands upon the spot in an effort to alleviate it. Instead, the pain seemed to gather strength as tiny lights floated from the corners of her eyes across her darkened field of vision. It was as if a line formed from above her ears across her face, down to her chin to the back of her head, capturing her in a mesh of pain. She moaned softly, all her concentration fixed upon the hopeful thought that such pain could not last long. Surely it would be gone soon. . . .

Soon he would come again, as much a herald to the night as the sound of the birds settling down for slumber in the woods beyond Sanderhurst.

The solid marquetried door opened with such force that it jarred the painting on the same wall. There were no locks between them; it was only one of his rules. She was not foolish enough to tempt him to immoderate behavior. His moods were difficult enough to gauge, even after a year of marriage. It was as if he prided himself upon remaining a mystery to her, an enigma who frightened her a little.

"M'lord." She sat up in the bed, clutching the sheet to her. It was futile protection against her husband's earnest desires. He was not cruel, but he was persistent. He wished a child, an heir. Something any husband would want. A woman's duty. Her obligation. Responsibility. Such heavy words.

"I would be inordinately pleased if you could but learn my name, Alice. It would be a damn sight better than being referred to as milord in my own bedroom."

He stood in front of her, blatantly naked, uncaring that she scrunched herself up into a ball under the bedclothes as if to avoid him entirely. But then, he was too free with his body, possessing an earthiness that occasionally shocked her.

"I cannot think what you would want of me, milord. Archer," she amended hastily.

"No doubt I've left you in ignorance of the purpose of marriage, wife," he said, a wicked sense of self-deprecating humor shining through his eyes. Alice thought them alight with a devilish look. His humor jarred her; that he could mock himself with such ease seemed an odd trait. She had no more insight into his character than she'd had at their betrothal, nor did she, in truth, wish any additional revelations.

She'd craved a gentle-natured husband, and fate had granted her this man instead. Archer was like a wild wind, swirling up everything in his wake. She felt no more substantial than a leaf in his presence.

On their wedding journey, he'd insisted she welcome him each night, a thoroughly scandalous thing to ask of her. All she'd truly wanted during those interminable six months was to return to her childhood home. He had been determined, however, to prove her fertile. She'd lain beneath him each of those nights, her hands clasping the bedsheets, careful not to move lest doing so incite his passions further. He spent hours touching her, caressing her limbs, licking her skin, suckling breasts that should only know a child's mouth. Each night he seemed satisfied when that humiliating warmth in her lower region, that wetness of which she was so ashamed, lubricated his passage. Then he pushed himself into her, his breath harsh and laboring, an expression of such ferocity on his face that she grew even more frightened. She prayed, insistently, that it would soon be over.

Two months ago, he'd heard her barely whispered prayers.

Since then, she'd been able to forestall his visits by pleading a weakness of the limbs or a megrim. Tonight, one more ruse.

"I am unable to partner you this evening. I've my woman's time." Such frankness embarrassed her, shamed her. Twin spots of color appeared on her pale face. She hoped he did not need further illuminating.

"Then I am once again to be denied the joy of your passion, it seems." She closed her eyes against his crudeness, wishing he would simply go away, leave her alone in this magnificent suite of rooms. It was too much, this chamber, done up in her favorite colors as a wedding gift, all pink and gold and exquisitely lovely. It was too large, too drafty, too filled with shadows. She hated it as much as any room in this monstrous place. She'd married above her, she'd been told. At this moment, and a thousand other moments, she'd have gladly relinquished the title and this place.

Her father said she would be a wife to this earl; her sisters all seemed pleased that the family's wealth was increased by relationship to a countess. But she truly didn't want to be a countess, felt too inadequate to assume those duties everyone said she should fulfill.

Alice huddled beneath the covers, feeling inept, worthless. And feeling, too, the unrelenting bite of shame.

Mary Kate knew she was going to be violently ill.

She made it to the chamber pot barely in time. The physician's tonic and her breakfast writhed out of her stomach. She knelt on the floor, retched over and over, helpless and weak in the grip of the overpowering sickness.

"Here." A wet cloth was offered; a large male hand reached out to brush tendrils of hair away from her damp face. She was too sick to be embarrassed, too ill at that moment to care who witnessed her humiliation.

How long did she kneel huddled there? She didn't know. Nor did she care. All she wanted was for the pain in her head to abate, for her stomach to settle. The wet cloth she held against her face served a dual purpose in that it felt cold and wonderful and it kept her flaming cheeks hidden from the good Samaritan at her side. As her physical discomfort eased, her embarrassment began to surface.

"Are you all right? Shall I summon the physician?"

Her head still hurt, although the pain was not as great as before. Long moments transpired in which she had not required the chamber pot. Satisfied that this, at least, was true, she shook her head, then glanced over at him.

Mary Kate felt as if she'd been put to stone in midbreath. Twice she opened her mouth to speak and twice restrained herself. Her right hand flew up to lie upon her breast. Protection? Or to assure herself that her heart still beat in her chest?

"Are you going to be ill again?" He stood, extended a hand to assist her, but instead of taking it, she remained on her knees, staring up at him.

"You." It was said so softly it was almost an invocation.

He was taller than she'd thought, shoulders broad and perfectly fitted into the deep blue of his waistcoat, sartorially perfect. The room was dim, haloed in gray, an afternoon's grace of shadows. Yet he lost no substance by it. His hands were broad, his long fingers tipped by clean, squared nails. His hair, raven-hued and curling around his ears, fell forward on his brow, bestowing a boyish nonchalance to a face that was neither youthful nor carefree. It was hewn from granite, this face, with strong planes and angles. It was not softened by his full lips, or the slight cleft to his chin. Nor was his appearance muted by the lights in his ebony eyes or the memory of his voice, low and resonant. His bearing was aristocratically stiff, his demeanor that of a man not disposed to cajolery.

He had an eagle's stare.

"I dreamt of you," she said.

He frowned down at her, drew back his hand. "I can only commiserate with you over the content of your nightmares, madam."

"Isn't it strange," she said softly, "that you could look so different attired? But then," she said, looking up at him with a curious look of confusion on her face, "I've never seen a naked man before."

And punctuated that surprising remark by falling into a faint at his feet.

Chapter 4

"**S**he arose too soon, of course. Such a thing would naturally lead to disturbance of the humors."

"The woman was violently ill, Dr. Endicott," St. John said.

"A few doses of my tonic will add vigor to her blood."

Oh, if they would only go away and leave her alone. But they stood above her as if she were a newly made corpse, discussing her endlessly. Such inadvertent eavesdropping was almost as humiliating as the past hour.

Almost.

Who was this strange man who seemed so known to her? So familiar? She forced herself to breathe deeply, not wishing them to know she had surfaced from her faint soon enough. If Mary Kate had her way, she'd remain in this posture for the rest of her life, hands folded over her chest, eyes shut, a living corpse. Embarrassed unto death.

She had dreamt of him. Of being in places she'd only known from books, seeing the flying buttresses of the Cathedral de Notre Dame de Paris, the exquisite delight of Michelangelo's Laurentian Library in Florence, Venice's Church of San Giorgio Maggiore. Such feasts of the eye, delivered to her mind by a fevered wish.

And the other, Mary Kate?

A scene between man and wife? A man's nakedness, candlelit? What explanation could you offer up for that?

Could she have lost her reason? She felt the surge of blood to her cheeks. Could she have once known him, then forgotten everything she'd known? Mary Kate felt a surge of panic at the thought and its accompanying one. Who was real and who the dream?

Mary Kate Bennett, born Mary Kate O'Brien. Orphaned perhaps, or not. Surely left adrift. Married too early, widowed too young. She had milkmaid's hands, strong and capable, favored cherries as a fruit, disliked the chore of feeding chickens as they were as apt to peck her as the ground. She could fend off a man's roaming hands with agility, swipe a tavern full of tables in as quick a time, work from daybreak until the moon rose if the need be there. She'd never stolen and she rarely lied and she'd been taught by circumstance to keep a level head in times of outward despair. If she had a dream, it was to be able to purchase a length of velvet in a green shade that would rival the emerald valleys of Ireland. She'd place the velvet around her shoulders, so that the softest side of it would be next to her skin. Or drape it, perhaps, so that her shoulders peeped through, white and rounded and not marred by work or tanned by the sun. She might pretend, if she could spare a moment or two for the joy of such things, that she was a great lady at a ball, awaiting one of her many suitors, or a woman draped in softness, expecting a lover. Or perhaps a mother, the velvet becoming, through the magical properties of wishes, an infant with a sweet and nuzzling warmth.

No, she knew herself too well to doubt this identity.

And the other? She'd often dreamt of people she did not know. But in such detail?

Stop this, Mary Kate. Too many times the goodwives called you an imaginative child, for leaving a bit of cake beneath a toadstool now and again, for washing your hair with the droplets of dew from the first May morning, for peeling an apple into a long, unbroken strand, the better to determine your true love's initials. But that was long ago, when you were but a child and before you learned that wishes don't work and superstition is just a way to make fools believe. Shame on you for thinking as a child might, or for dreaming as a sinner.

The door closed softly and she let herself sigh a little. Just a gasp of relief. She opened her eyes cautiously a slow peep at a time, to find herself the object of the eagle's stare once again.

She clamped her eyes shut, a mouse rendered motionless with fright.

"It's too late, I'm afraid. I know you're awake." There was a touch of humor in the voice, enough to cause her flush to deepen. That would have given her away if nothing else.

"The physician has gone to make you a dose of his tonic." That information elicited a groan. "Is there anything else I can procure for you?"

"No, thank you." Her face was turned to the wall, making the words a little difficult to understand. He leaned closer.

"Is there someone I can summon for you? Your husband, perhaps?"

"No." There was nothing but silence. Mary Kate felt compelled to add an explanation. "I am a widow, sir."

"A family member, then?"

"There is no one."

"I see."

Mary Kate was quite certain he didn't.

"What did you mean? About dreaming of me?" he asked finally.

Moments ticked by, heavy with silence.

"I cannot explain it to you, sir. It makes no sense to me."

"My name is St. John. You may address me as that or simply as you wish. I do prefer, however, that you not revert to sobriquet. Sinjin reminds me too much of a particularly odious Persian poem."

She smiled, charmed despite herself. "My knowledge of particularly odious Persian poems is limited at the moment."

"As is your explanation."

Silence again.

" 'I have had a most rare vision. I have had a dream past the wit of man to say what dream it was,' " she murmured.

"Your knowledge of Shakespeare is to be congratulated, madam. However, I cannot appreciate the sentiment if you continue with that verse."

" 'Man is but an ass if he go about t'expound this dream'?"

"Exactly. You've taken *A Midsummer Night's Dream* wholly out of context, you know."

She turned and glanced at him. His smile seemed bemused. "It was one of Mrs. Tonkett's favorite plays. I think she believed herself Titania."

"Who is Mrs. Tonkett?"

"My own personal faerie queen. She taught me to

read." There was a smile on those lips, an otherworldly reminiscent smile.

"This conversation has a common center, does it not? That being, of course, confusion. The more perplexed I am, the less curiosity I evince. Is that your aim?"

There was a hesitation before she spoke. "Truly, I have no aims. I simply don't know how to explain."

"One word strung before another would be simple enough."

"Have you ever milked a cow?"

He shook his head as if to dislodge a troublesome fly. "No, I have not."

"It is a singularly boring task. One that seems to last hours, twice per day. Oh, I've known people who talk to their cows while milking them. Words of praise, that sort of thing. But I daydreamed. Of places I'd rather be, things I wished I could do. Sometimes, I pictured myself dancing. I've always wanted to learn to dance, to slide over a brilliant-colored floor with my skirts twirling and my head reeling and my breath so tight that it felt as if I were going to swoon."

"And your dreams of me were like that?"

She turned to him, her smile as bright as a child's, just as mischievous. "Milk dreams?"

"Just so."

His studied insouciance could not dampen the spark in his eyes. Just a small light, like a distant star in a moonless night.

"It began as dreams, really. When I was asleep for so long." She would not look in his direction again, seemingly intent upon plucking the sheet from the area of her right knee. "Then," she said in a voice that betrayed its confusion too well, "I began to dream of you in the day-time."

"And my state of undress? Was this vision summoned while awake or sleeping?"

"I should not have said that." How could she tell him that the words had flown out of her mouth before she could stop them, the sense of wonder upon viewing him deadening all sense of proper deportment?

"It is not my normal greeting, I'll admit." The humor in his tone mocked her, ridiculed her hard-won composure.

Now her attention was all on him, direct and unflinching.

"Why do I feel wanting now? As if the vision was more palatable than the reality?" he asked.

"Perhaps because you did not ridicule me in my dreams?"

"I wonder what's keeping your tonic?" he said, rising. Deft, polite words coated in concern like candied almonds and uttered in the same tone.

She stared after him, absurdly disappointed. He was rigidly polite and exquisitely proper. The person she'd seen in her dreams had been touched by rage and alive with passion.

But still, a hint of the dream him had been there, buried beneath the proper man.

Chapter 5

Mary Kate sat at the window of her borrowed chamber, staring down at the bare trees and dirt road that stretched in front of the inn. It seemed to beckon her, to call her once more upon her journey.

She'd told Archer St. John she'd had no relatives. The bitter truth was that she did not know where they were, hadn't known since that night on the side of the Norwich road.

She'd been asleep in the wagon, having thrown together a nest for herself in the corner, cushioning it with the boys' clothes and her own. It was a crowded place to be, what with all her brothers elbowing for their own resting place. Her mother insisted upon traveling by the light of the moon, despite the dangers, determined to reach the village she'd left upon her marriage to an Irish farmer. Denmouth was to the north, and they were to beg a home from their mother's father, a dour old man, one of her brothers teased her, who feasted on young girls and ate their livers for dessert.

In her sleep she had felt the slowing of the wagon, the jostling of her makeshift mattress, heard voices swirling above her. She mumbled impatiently, wanting to return to

24

her dream, ignoring the drizzle of rain upon her neck, pulling up the cloak until she felt the cloth bristle against her cheek. She'd awakened in the morning, the dampness seeping past the cloak, the sodden garments upon which she'd slept. She'd crept to her feet, brushed her hair out of her eyes, and then raced down the highway and up again, over and over, not believing they had gone and left her behind until one full day had passed.

And now she wanted to know why. Had it been because there were so many mouths to feed? There were ten in all, six younger after her. Or had it been because she was the only girl? Too, she'd been unruly, apt to play pranks on her older brothers, too quick to laugh, to find something of humor in things. His Irish sprite, her da had said. Laughter had been lost that night alongside the road. It had been years until she'd found it again.

She'd become an itinerant worker at the age of ten, earning bed and board as a dairy maid, maid of all work, scullery apprentice. She'd defended herself as best she could, focusing not on the past or the future, but on surviving the present.

Still, there were times, like now, when she couldn't quite forestall the grief, when she found herself pulling excuses from her mind like unripe plums. Except, of course, that nothing she ever fabricated was reason enough to explain leaving a child alone on a raw night, defenseless and fearful.

Two years after she'd been abandoned, old Mrs. Tonkett had hired her to keep her house tidy, then insisted upon teaching her as Mary Kate went about her chores.

For five years she had lived in the empty house with Mrs. Tonkett, one last pupil for the frail, retired governess who was just as used to a fuller home as Mary Kate. Her affection for the old lady grew to be second only to that for her father. If it was true that she'd given Mrs. Tonkett a reason to live, a statement her employer repeated often, then Mrs. Tonkett had given Mary Kate a world to explore.

When Mrs. Tonkett had died, Mary Kate had agreed to marry Edwin Bennett, less for reasons of love and affection than because he had promised her some measure of safety and security in a world that had never been very friendly to half-Irish servant girls. Edwin, in turn, expected to find her grateful and docile, not understanding that a spirit capable of surviving such early desertion could never become wholly tractable again. However, Mary Kate had not found it onerous to be as Edwin wished, outwardly composed, serene. Her husband, who did not believe in an excess of emotion, never concerned himself with thoughts that lay unspoken, or feelings that were never expressed.

She had crafted an existence for herself as a wife, spent her household money on the small store of furniture she'd found, her tiny collection of creamware. She'd kept the house on Bell Street spotless, not only because it was Edwin's wish, but because it was the first home she'd ever had, the first roof under which she'd lived since she was a child that she could call hers.

All of that had ended, of course, the morning she'd discovered Edwin dead in his sleep, so much peace and tranquillity upon his face that she knew what had happened the moment she'd awakened beside him.

"It is with deep regret that I must remind you, Mrs. Bennett, that Edwin made no provision for your future. Although I must confess he was exceedingly generous in his bequests to the firm."

Those were the words Charles Townsende had used, to thrust her back into penury once more. Mary Kate had

wanted to tell her husband's law partner that she was not
unduly surprised. Edwin had made no secret of the fact
that he'd been disappointed in her, as wife, helpmate, con-
fidante, as Galatea to his Pygmalion. He'd not bargained
for her innate stubbornness, a will more often than not
opposed to his own, for all that she'd cloaked it in silence.
Yet leaving her penniless as punishment seemed a bit
much.

Still, there was enough from the sale of her furniture
and her precious creamware to complete her journey, to
finish a quest that had begun the night she'd been abandoned. She was eager to resume what had been interrupted
for too long.

Already she could walk to the end of the hallway and
back again without feeling much pain. She was still breathless, however, a condition caused by her bruised ribs, the
physician informed her. Her healing would be slow, he
warned, if she continued to refuse his tonic. Mary Kate
only leveled a look on him that made him stammer to a
halt and reflect upon his next threat.

The headaches continued, never as debilitating as the
first occurrence. Yet she grew to expect the pain of them,
the strange smell that foretold of their occurrence, and the
dreams that accompanied them, dreams she experienced
even though fully awake.

She didn't tell the physician about those at all. In fact,
she'd told no one but Archer St. John of her dreams, and
he had discounted them as lightly as a parent would a
child's frequent nightmare.

A knock on the door preceded the opening of it by only
seconds. Polly's pert face appeared in the crack.

Mary Kate wanted to tell the young maid that she was
not gentry, had never been granted a maid before, had

herself served farmers' wives and daughters, taken their orders and their insults with feigned humility, and their husbands' groping hands and innuendos with whispered threats. But Polly was taking her job as nursemaid with seriousness. And, too, perhaps her temporary position garnered her some attention belowstairs. For that reason and the fact that she genuinely liked the young girl, Mary Kate allowed herself to be served.

"Cook made these cakes to tempt your appetite, ma'am. Said she didn't want to hear of you refusing one." Polly placed the tray on the table next to the bed.

Beside the teapot was a plate of tiny currant cakes dusted with sugar. Squares of pound cake no larger than the length of her thumb sagged under glistening pastel frosting. Mary Kate would have been tempted to try one, if the pain of the headache had not increased so suddenly and with such power.

It felt as though a band had been placed around her skull and was being dragged tighter each second that passed. She heard Polly's prattling around the small whimper of her own voice, wanted to shut out the bright glint of the sun on the teapot. Every object within sight seemed to be dusted with brilliance and pain.

"Aren't they lovely? Cook calls them lady cakes, all sweet and dainty. . . ."

. . . dainty, he always made her feel, as though his masculinity somehow enhanced her femininity.

She sat at her dressing table, staring into her own eyes. Would the world see something different there? Wasn't there a softening in her expression, where there had only once been sadness? How odd that she should feel such great joy and it not be bubbling from her with the sweet boundless excitement of a spring-fed brook.

She'd feared loving him so. Never known that one day she would embrace the very emotion she'd been so frightened of before. Even Sanderhurst appeared a golden place, a fairy-tale castle, an enchanted land, just the place to be in love, to feel the sense of belonging she despaired of ever feeling after her marriage.

She was so gloriously in love.

She was entranced by his smile, bemused by his laughter. He laughed and she wanted to chuckle in response. He had moments of sadness that made her want to weep. When he was victorious, she yearned to shout the news, and when he failed she leaned her shoulder against him and longed for strength to lend to him. He was so fully alive, this man whose vulnerabilities he allowed her to see as much as his driving ambition and his rapier-sharp mind.

She'd never meant to love him. Not the way she came to love him, of course. Not with her mind, her heart, her body.

He kissed her with such reverence, as if she were a holy icon. Then kissed her again with such power that she could feel the imprint of his lips there, still. His soft inrush of breath awed her with the knowledge that she could make him feel the same way she felt, frightened, powerful, yearning.

He had the most perfect laugh, one that seemed to echo as fulsomely as the bells of Sanderhurst's chapel. His eyes lit up with such grace and fire that her heart almost stood still at his smile, so privileged did she feel to have been the recipient of it.

"I love you." He'd said those words today. In the Sanderhurst chapel, with the soft yellow light from the east window spilling over their faces, he'd murmured those

*words over and over. Soft words, enough to make her close
her eyes against the onrush of feeling.*

Could her heart hold all this joy?

"Have a cuppa, it'll warm the chill of the day."

Polly's soft voice penetrated the odd, soft cocoon that
enveloped Mary Kate. The bedchamber, the faded blue
velvet chair she was sitting in, the golden patina of wood
beneath her feet, all seemed shrouded in a deep, impenetrable fog. Mary Kate took a deep breath, concentrated on
the sound of Polly's voice. Such an anchor was useless,
as feeble as a paper leash restraining a tiger.

Polly passed Mary Kate a cup of tea from the tray she'd
brought in only moments ago. Mary Kate pressed her lips
firmly together, closed her eyes against the room swimming in her vision. It seemed a strange tableau, Mary Kate
thought wildly, trapped inside herself in a way she had
never felt before. She could see Polly standing there, coaxing her to drink from the cup she proffered, see herself
helpless to speak.

Help him. . . . He is in danger. . . .

Her indrawn breath was louder than this sound, yet
Mary Kate still heard it. As frail as a snowflake falling in
the winter air, as tenuous as a spider's web, as daunting
as a shout, it commanded her.

A woman of less restraint would have succumbed to the
shallowness of breath, the light-headed feeling that suffused her at that moment. But she was from farmer's stock,
from a practical station in life that ridiculed such things as
female weakness. She'd helped at lambings and wrung the
necks of chickens she later ate for supper. She'd never
worn a corset until she was seventeen and wed, therefore
had never experienced the chronic shortness of breath so

familiar to others of her sex. Only once had she fainted in her life, and it was here, in this room, that she had done so. Upon viewing Archer St. John.

Wasn't it odd the way things could suddenly slip into place, settle down like an old cat before the fire? Mary Kate could almost hear the click of it, one thought rubbing against the next, easing into position. She recognized not the voice that spoke to her, but the essence of the command. Powerful, demanding, scraping away the veil between life and death.

It was a whisper from a spirit.

"I hope all was satisfactory, my lord."

"Your inn is a marvel of convenience, Mr. Palmerton."

"And your recommendation would be most gladly received, sir." The innkeeper smiled brightly, a practiced fawning, Archer St. John thought. But then, it was no doubt expected by most. For his own sake, he would just as soon the man save his talents for those who craved a little subservient toadying. He wanted to be on his way with all possible speed.

"You may post that I have been exquisitely happy here," St. John said.

"And, if I may beg your pardon, sir, but will the young woman be joining you?" The innkeeper's smile was tact itself.

"The young woman will be recuperating for another day or so, sir, then continuing on her own journey, no doubt."

"I see."

"But I will settle her bill now, if you don't mind."

"Not at all, my lord, not at all."

Why, as he left the inn, did St. John find himself prodded by that imp of integrity, who sat on his shoulder and laughed uproariously as Archer attempted to explain it was for decorum's sake that he did not say farewell to that odd and unsettling woman? Why also did the imp's sardonic voice whisper in his ear that it was less for propriety than an insane longing to stay that prompted his quick retreat?

Seclusion was looking less than palatable lately. Was it that reason he had stayed four days in an inn whose hospitality was generous but whose accommodations were not? Why had he not traveled on to London, leaving word of his address, and funds for her recovery?

The polite thing to do would have been to say something as farewell. If for no other reason than to assure himself that he had been mistaken. She could not captivate him with the ease with which she had done so. What, though, did he say to someone who told him of cows and dancing and milk dreams? Who bragged of viewing his naked body and pronounced him not as vital as his dream persona had been?

He was a man beset by a riddle, his life torn apart by a mystery even more compelling than the one she presented to him. Why, then, did he linger?

Get on with it, Archer. You'll never find Alice this way.

Chapter 6

James Edward Moresham, heir to his father's well-managed horse farm, sat on the edge of the forest that banded the Moresham estate. He'd been awake since midnight monitoring a new foal after a difficult birth, ensuring that its initial problems were corrected, or failing that, that the newest addition to the Moresham stables was put down quickly, without suffering. Samuel Moresham tolerated nothing but the best for his animals, and if that meant his son had to spend the night awake, then so be it.

Yet, it was better than being awake anyway, plagued by his conscience. Despair made a poor bed companion, even worse than loneliness, and loneliness would kill him, he had little doubt.

James sat propped against a huge sycamore, looked up at the sight of the night sky filtered through the branches. This afternoon it had been a pure blue, a color he could not have described any better than to say it reminded him of Alice's eyes. But then, most everything reminded him of Alice these days.

He had been five years old when she was born, a tiny little thing who had squalled and filled their house with baby smells and demands from morning till night. She was his second sister and a disappointment because his step-mother had promised him a brother. He and his father had been disappointed alike, James thought, when Alice was born. He got over it; he didn't think his father ever did.

James had, in the way of boys who would be men, de-cided that babies were too much trouble to bother with, until, of course, he saw Alice all dressed up in baptismal dress, with lace panels down to the floor and a little cap that made her look like a soft white kitten. On that day he'd been allowed to hold her. She'd been fidgety and whimpering and he'd told her to hush in a small, boyish whisper that made her open her eyes wide and decide that it might not be a bad thing to be held in wobbly arms while a smile played down on her face. If it was not love at first sight, it was certainly love early on.

And so they became best friends, the boy five years older and the girl who adored him. Even now James could remember countless times when he and Alice had lain on their backs on this very same hill, looking up at the sky and pointing out clouds that looked suspiciously like Aunt Addy or one of the stable cats or a unicorn perched upon a throne.

They had been friends for so many years. Alice was the one person to whom he'd confided the wish to play the music he heard in his head all day. He wrote it down when he had free time, great glowing symphonies of it, the notes resouncing through his mind the way a concerto trickled over the back of his spine, a brook of music, a sweet spring awakering the senses. It was to Alice he'd played his most cherished compositions, on the pianoforte that had been her mother's only contribution to her marriage other than four daughters.

In the drawing room one night, amidst the gentle light

of the branched candlesticks, he'd known mingled horror and joy to realize that his feelings for Alice were so much more than that of a brother. He knew the moment it had turned to more, held that thought deep in his heart, cherished it like a rare and valuable heirloom.

James swallowed heavily, thinking that the lack of sleep had made him even more susceptible to memory lately. It had been a year since she'd been gone—a year filled with the most anxious of times and the most horrible of thoughts.

He'd not wanted her to marry Archer St. John. There were too many stories about the man; he was rumored to be dissolute even in his youth and reclusive in his adulthood. James had even thought, once, that Alice would refuse his suit, but she had only smiled at him and called him silly and become a bride in the spring.

He'd lost his best friend on that day, and nothing else had ever been the same since.

He often found himself recalling the day she returned from her wedding trip, as if it were a blister he must lance before the healing began. They'd been gone six full months—a tour of the continent being the groom's gift to his bride.

James remembered the day as if it were this morning, the look of Alice all dressed out in her blue-green dress, with the tiny little muff to keep her delicate hands warm, her scent of lavender adding to the spice of early fall.

But she had been changed, had seemed sadder somehow, less vibrant and joyous. Only two months later, his suspicions had become truth, as she cried on his shoulder and revealed the misery of her marriage. He'd held her then, grateful for any excuse to hold Alice in his arms.

James closed his eyes against the memory of it.

* * *

Archer St. John stood beside the carriage, attired in a many-tiered greatcoat and a tall beaver hat, traveler's gear, watching impatiently as Jeremy checked the bridles again, the leads between the horses, the leather fastenings, the silver couplings, the bits, the leather harness. Such concern was one of the reasons he was such a valued employee, an excellent master of horseflesh. Yet it seemed to Archer that he was doing his job with an added bit of obsession.

"If you check the harness once more, Jeremy, I swear that I'll retire you upon our return to Sanderhurst. I've not seen so much moddlecoddling in the last week since my mother left for India."

Both weathered hands stilled on the halter. Archer thought the man winced, but couldn't be sure. "I would not have thought you that flummoxed by an accident, Jeremy. I do not hold you responsible, you know. I was the one who insisted upon such speed."

Jeremy looked up at the sky, down at the ground, then at the sight of his employer standing in front of him. "She made me promise, sir. Swear upon my father's life, she did. That I'd check everything twice to ensure there was no danger."

"And who is so solicitous of my well-being that she would elicit such a promise from you, Jeremy?"

"Mrs. Bennett, sir. Told me at the inn, she did, that she feared for your safety. Had a warning of it and wanted you safe."

"Do you always listen to females so avidly, Jeremy?" Archer had never seen his coachman hesitant before, never seen him almost maidenly in his reticence. Yet the moment should have warned him, being filled as it was with the strange reluctance of speech.

"I did, sir, to this one. She said you were to be protected, sir. That the countess told her so. Alice wanted you safe, she said."

Chapter 7

It took Mary Kate nearly a week to reach the village of Denmouth. Her travels were made slower by the fact that she was still visited by the strange and unwelcome headaches. When they came, she simply sat down on the side of the road and waited them out, experiencing the dreams that came with them with a curious acceptance.

The dreams were almost as odd as the feeling she had that she had forgotten something. Had she left the iron upon the coals? Was the stew pot still hanging where it could boil over? Had the candle wick been trimmed? All these things were nonsensical, since she'd nothing to worry about, nothing to concern her except for the welcome at the end of her journey.

Or lack of it.

Help him . . . Help him. . . .

This time she barely flinched from the sound, knew better than to turn. There would be no one there. Yet the voice was not imaginary; she knew she heard it with an inner ear. The voice was there in her mind, an eternal, vigilant, stubborn entreaty.

She should pretend none of this had happened. Would it not be wiser to deny these odd, unsettling dreams? She was, after all, recuperating from an injury to her head. Except that they weren't her dreams, her emotions, her experiences. Was it simply possible to be two people at once? To feel Alice St. John's emotions, knowing herself to be Mary Kate Bennett?

If that were true, then why was she not more frightened? Oddly enough, the reason embarrassed, perhaps shamed her. It made of her some pitiable creature, a woman so alone in her life she welcomed the presence of a ghost, solely for the company of the haunting. Yet this voice was not spectral or frightening, but soft and gentle. There was no sadness in the words, just determination. No grief, just resolve.

And the images that came to her were not of sorrow, but of joy, a life enriched by a love so strong that Mary Kate could feel the resonance of it even now.

She hadn't the Sight, she'd no patience for tales of folklore and magic. All right, perhaps she was a bit superstitious, but she didn't challenge fate, didn't stick her tongue out at things she didn't understand. She wanted nothing to do with things not of this world, things she could not explain, headaches and visions and whispers in the wind.

She should simply forget this interlude, these days of odd, unsettling dreams, Archer St. John's effect on her. Be about her own business, forget this idiocy of lost wives and foreign places and conversations between Alice St. John and her husband.

Polly had supplied many details of the Earl of Sanderhurst, including his title, his enormous wealth. It had been from Polly she'd learned that Alice St. John had gone missing a year ago. Rumor had her hiding from her husband, or escaping to the continent with another man, or seeking asylum from the church or from her family. It seemed unlikely that any of these stories would be true. Wealthy, titled women did not simply walk away from the benefits of wealth and titles. If they were so idiotic as to do so, Mary Kate reasoned, then they were deserving of their fate.

It was too tempting, this world she'd dreamed. It beckoned like a window slowly opening. Come and look inside. See what you're missing. Archer St. John fascinated her, this man who occupied her dreams. So much so, perhaps, that he also occupied a fair amount of her waking moments. A man to admire, even from a distance.

An earl, Mary Kate. A member of the nobility. A peer of the realm. A man of prosperity and consequence. Not fodder for her dreams. Her marriage might have elevated her in status, but she was still, at heart, a half-Irish dairymaid. It would be foolish to pretend anything else.

Yet she could not help but recall him. He did not possess the aquiline good looks so prized by the upper classes, the sharply etched features and deep-set eyes. His face was too broad for the aesthetically minded, his nose had a bump on the bridge of it, his chin was absurdly squared, and his cheekbones too prominent to satisfy the more romantic ladies. Nor was his physique what women sighed over—he displayed not a good leg in his pantaloons as much as a muscular one. His chest and shoulders were much too large to be considered quite proper. His height alone topped all the men she'd seen squiring the ladies down Bond Street. Nor was his hair the glittery blond so prized, but was black and thick, worn not in the curls that were the rage, but longer and straight. Nor did he sport a chin beard and was otherwise clean-shaven, an oddity when most men waxed eloquent about their facial hair.

Yet it was his eyes she would forever remember about

Archer St. John. They were black, the color of eternity unlit by hope, the deepest ebony, night without a starlit sky. Mary Kate had been transfixed by the sight of those eyes in her dreams, before she'd witnessed the intelligence behind them, the lurking humor, the hint of something else darker, less pronounced.

The last time she had seen him, from the window of the inn, he had looked so utterly alone standing beside his carriage. He should have looked just as he was, a gentleman of noble birth and excellent lineage and possessed of great wealth, about to embark upon a journey. He should not have looked like a child bulked up for winter weather and desirous of a playmate with whom to share the snow.

He should not have touched her heart so.

Oh, Mary Kate, you've never wished for the moon, don't go baying at it now. You'll never see him again, and that's all to the good. You've no business wanting something you cannot have. But he'd touched her somehow, in a way that was oddly endearing, almost painful.

Was that why she had wanted to give him something greater than her simple gratitude, something that would, in some insignificant way, express to him all the feelings she had—appreciation, respect, admiration, and even a touch of longing? Even if she never saw him again, Mary Kate knew she would always think of him; perhaps he would forever inhabit her dreams.

She had nothing of worth to give him, nothing handed down or kept safe, nothing she'd made with her own talent or spun from her hair. Nothing, after all, but the knowledge that had swelled up in her heart and made its presence known an insistent inch at a time.

With any luck, Jeremy would heed her warning. It was

the only gift she had for Archer St. John. His wife's voice, speaking of danger. A warning.

Such a thing was not supposed to happen, was it? Yet the world was filled with incidents that were not supposed to happen. She could attest to that—it was the very reason she was in this place.

The village itself had the deadened look of desertion about it. A few scraggly cottages sat adjacent to the main road; a few more sat huddled around a field located not far away. Mary Kate would have missed the dwellings completely without the aid of an old man who stood hunched against a fence, leaning upon his hoe. At her question, he pointed to the north, grudging aid given without voice.

She knocked on the first of the doors. It was opened by a woman not much older than herself, weighted down by a child perched upon one hip, another clutching her skirts. They were all similarly attired; baby, child, and mother all wore stained butternut-colored smocks; the woman's clothing topped with a brown apron. The three of them, despite their differences in age, all wore the same look—watchful caution. There was poverty in this place, and barely masked despair, for all they looked healthy and pink-cheeked. Mary Kate wanted to tell them there were worse places to be poor than this quiet village. London, for example, where the destitute lived in squalor and filth. But she said nothing, did not even smile, simply inquired of the woman if she knew the address of Eleanor O'Brien. She was given a sharp look and another pointing direction.

A few moments later, Mary Kate found her mother.

Mary Kate stood looking down at the grave marker, a small stone cross with initials carved laboriously into it, no dates to mark her passage. Eleanor O'Brien. This, then, was the answer to her quest, the solution to the mystery? No answer at all, the mystery still obscured in fog.

How long did she stand there? She didn't know. When her legs began to ache, Mary Kate sat at the foot of the grave, her eyes focused upon the cross of stone, lichen covering its surface. It must have taken years for the moss to grow upon unforgiving rock. And all this time, she'd not known.

"So you're Mary Kate, then?"

She turned at the masculine voice, found herself looking up at the tall figure of a man who must be one of her brothers. The likeness to her father was there in the breadth of his shoulders, in the shape of his face. There, however, the resemblance ended. The eyes were unfriendly, the mouth held no smile.

"And you're Daniel." The second oldest of her brothers, he had been nearly a man on that night so long ago. And the least favorite of her brothers. But was a sister supposed to feel such a thing? Or experience the spike of fear she felt now?

"Why have you come, Mary Kate? I've not the funds to support an able-bodied girl."

His belligerence shone in his stance, in the bulldog jaw squared against the world. There was no warmth in his expression, no brotherly affection, nothing that indicated they shared anything but the air they breathed. Their relationship could be no more than accidental, their blood tie no more important to him than if she were a stranger. He stared unblinking at her, a mastiff given legs, his blond hair lit by a watery sun.

She stood and brushed down her skirts. "I've come to find my family. Is that not enough of a reason?"

"You'd be better served by forgetting you were ever an O'Brien, Mary Kate."

"She made that clear enough, Daniel." Mary Kate turned and looked down at the grave again. "Did she hate me so much?"

His laughter shocked her, not that it should come in such a place, but that it should be so mirthless. "Ask why the sky is blue and the grass green, Mary Kate. What does it matter, after all?"

At her look, he laughed again, the expression in his eyes as cold as the sound of it. "You've imagined, then, a tearful reunion with the old harridan? One where she hugs you and says she grieved that you were lost all these years? Count yourself lucky, then, Mary Kate, that you were free of her."

"I was ten, Daniel. Too young to be abandoned, too young to have to learn of the world."

"You survived, didn't you?" His glance encompassed her soft blue cloak and the black silk dress she wore. "Tommy didn't. She near beat him to death. He died of a lung infection, but we all know it was from the beating. She indentured Robert and Alan when they were eight, didn't say a word when her father chained the four youngest to the plow and made them draft horses. She barely knew you were gone, or did you think she longed for you, and cried for her only girl child?"

His smile was sharp, almost cruelly so.

"And the others?" Were all her brothers like this one, then? Hard and as cold as their mother?

"Scattered to the four winds, Mary Kate, as far from this place as they could go."

"And Uncle Michael?"

Michael was her father's youngest brother, the only one

who'd come from Ireland with Da. He'd joined the navy, he said, because he couldn't bear to be away from the sea. Her da used to joke that Michael was safer on the ocean— he was the clumsiest person he'd ever seen on land. Uncle Michael didn't visit often, but it was a celebration when he did.

"Our mother discouraged his visits, Mary Kate. Told him seven years ago never to come back. He didn't. I don't know any more."

Either that, or he would not tell her.

He stepped closer to her. "Go back to the world you've come from, Mary Kate. Dream, if you will, of the mother you should have had, but don't pretend the one you did have was a saint. She was filled with hatred and bitterness and a cruelty you should thank God you escaped."

"She made sure of that."

"No, Mary Kate, she didn't." His look was speculative, his smile a little warmer than it had been, but were there degrees of coldness to ice?

"We all decided she would punish you the most, what with you being so much like Da and being his favorite. You were lost in your dreams, too filled with grief for Da to notice the things you should have. If you would blame anyone, blame us for what happened to you. She thought you'd run away, and that was the only safety we could give you."

Her look must have summoned some deeply hidden brotherly emotion, because he reached out and stroked her cheek with one finger. "So you were forced to grow up a little sooner, Mary Kate. At least you did. You've pinned your hopes on findin' a family to love you. We were never a family after Da died, Mary Kate, so there's no sense looking for one. Make your own life, your own family. *There is no place for you here.''*

And with that, he turned and left the small graveyard.

There is no place for you here.

All this time she'd believed there were people in the world who would want to know where she was, that she still lived, that she had tried to find them.

But they were not here. Not at Denmouth Village.

She sat with her arms around her knees, her shabby portmanteau at her feet. *At least you survived.* But at what cost, Daniel? To have no one, nothing, only a voice in her mind. Something in her chest—was it her heart?—seemed to swell with pain.

The rustle of leaves upon the ground alerted her. Daniel returning, then, to ensure himself that she had gone? ''May I stay the night, at least? It's grown too cold to sleep in the open again tonight, and the only inn I saw was a good four hours away.''

A voice she never expected to hear again answered. ''Such pathos, madam. Such inventive dialogue. However, your plight does not soften one jot of my irritation at this particular moment.''

She turned and Archer St. John stood there, an avenging angel dressed in a black greatcoat, his smile as frosty as her brother's had been, tinged not with disinterest but with rage.

How odd that his appearance seemed almost destined for this moment, his anger no more important than the leaves lying upon the ground. She sighed, as if breathing deeply for the first time in nearly a week, feeling released from some bond of anticipation. Was this, then, what she had been waiting for? His arrival? An end to the feeling that something had been left undone?

"It was absurdly easy to find you, madam. Your ploy would have been more convincing if you had made an effort to hide your destination from others. The little maid at the inn was quite voluble with her information."

"I never expected to see you again."

"Of course you did, madam. It was part of the game. That, I recognize well enough. Lure him closer with little tidbits of information like bread crumbs in a forest. He'll follow the trail, the damn fool, because he's so desperate for information. Well, I've taken the bait. Now, what is my prize?"

Her brows crinkled together in confusion. His frown deepened.

"Was that your lover or simply an accomplice?" he asked, glancing in the direction Daniel had walked. "From the look upon your face, it was not a meeting filled with tenderness. Did you have a lover's quarrel?"

"He is my brother," she said softly.

"I thought you were bereft of family, madam, or is that simply another lie?"

She was silent. What explanation could she give him that would appease his anger? Why, though, should she give him any?

"Come, have you nothing to say?"

Another moment passed, another lesson in silence. A leaf fell to the ground, a squirrel chittered angrily, but no speech passed between them.

"You may keep all your secrets, madam," he said finally, a sentence of conciliation at odds with his look of dislike. "I wish only one thing from you. The whereabouts of my wife."

"What?"

"Do not stumble upon your answer, madam, and your wide-eyed appearance of innocence has no effect on my irritation. Where is Alice?"

Chapter 8

"**Y**ou maintain a muteness which might be endearing, save for the fact that it's to your benefit." His voice was too loud in the closeness of the carriage.

Archer St. John folded his hands over the gold top of his walking stick. Such a pose might have led another person to believe he was relaxed, barely roused to speech. Mary Kate knew better; he'd studied her avidly since he had bundled her into his conveyance.

"What would you have me say?" They had already gone through endless rounds of questioning, Mary Kate unable to supply the answers the earl seemed certain she possessed.

"The truth? An entertaining little tidbit of it would be refreshing. Where is Alice?"

"Must you ask that question again? I've already told you I don't know."

"Then we are at another impasse, are we not? Shall we converse in amiable discourse, or would you prefer another simmering silence?" A small, mirthless smile accompanied that question.

"Have you much experience at abduction? You seem to

have spirited me away with little difficulty.''

"Perhaps I shall grow adept at all sorts of things. You are the first connection I've had with Alice for over a year, madam, the first hint that she has not simply disappeared into the ether. I am not about to allow you to do the same.''

"What would you do if I screamed for a magistrate?''

"If you could find one, tell him that you are under my protection, of course. What interpretation he chooses to make of that is, of course, up to him. But you could wait until we reach Sanderhurst. I am of intimate acquaintance with the magistrate there.''

"Then I shall summon him at the instant of our arrival.''

"Oh, you needn't do that, madam. You are sitting with him.''

At her glare, he smiled.

It was barely past afternoon, yet the winter sky was already growing dim. Mary Kate wished he'd left the carriage lamp unlit, but the faint glow from the lantern was enough to see her abductor quite clearly. The greatcoat had been thrown back, exposing an emerald frock coat, a perfectly folded white linen cravat, and buckskin trousers. His Hessian boots were polished to a sheen, completing the picture of easily acquired elegance, a gentleman of the city out for the country air.

She was hardly the companion for him, with her black dress, stained cloak, and scuffed kid slippers. She felt soiled from being on the road for a week, desirous of the creature comforts as never before—a hot bath and to wash her hair. And then to warm herself. She'd spent the last night huddled beneath a tree, dozing from time to time when the chilly wind subsided.

One finger reached out and touched her with delicacy.

This was true invasion of touch, a finger laid upon her wrist, testing the strength of the pulse beneath. Her wrist quivered ever so slightly beneath his fingertip just before she jerked it free of his touch.

He moved then, sliding down one colored pane over the lantern so that the light emitted from it was barely enough to illuminate the interior of the carriage. Archer leaned back in the corner of the carriage, one elbow propped up on the window ledge, hand curled into a fist near his chin. It was not an indolent pose for all his easy grace.

She'd said nothing when he had led her to his carriage, only turned and looked one last time at the gravestone, then in the direction her brother had disappeared. She'd said nothing to him, and he'd expected no protestations from her.

Mary Kate edged closer to the corner of the seat. A headache was blossoming on the back of her skull, a solemn, implacable warning. She laid her head back against the squabs. Not now, not after all this. It would be the perfect culmination to a hideous day.

"You've grown pale."

"Are you acting as my mirror now?"

"Shall I?"

"Please, do not. I cannot compare with the women of your acquaintance."

"Is this surliness attributable to the fact we've missed dinner? Or are you a naturally poor traveling companion?"

"Please don't."

"Don't be polite? Pleasant? Inquisitive?"

"Don't mention dinner."

"You are ill."

"Yes." This affirmative answer lacked the brittleness of

her former response. It was, in one faint gasp, an admission of weakness, a plea for help. How could one word speak so loudly? She hated it, despised her own frailty.

"Tell me what I can do."

"The light. Extinguish the lantern. Please."

With her conscious will, Mary Kate forced the pain away. But it continued in bursts of sharpness, volleys that radiated from the back of her skull around her face to the corners of her eyes, where they were transformed to long silver strands of lightning.

Mary Kate heard the sounds of metal against metal, the clink of glass, then blessed darkness descended.

"What else?" Archer asked.

"Quiet. Sounds seem to make the headaches worse."

He moved swiftly, almost silently, the brushing aside of her skirts the first indication she had that he sat beside her. The second, more shocking, was that he grasped her shoulders, forced her to move from her wedged position, gently lowered her so that her head rested against one strong, muscled thigh. Thoroughly reprehensible, of course. Daring. Almost certainly forbidden.

Such welcome relief.

Her right hand came up and cupped his knee for balance. Another gesture deserving of rebuke. Archer's hand brushed against her forehead, smoothed the damp tendrils of hair away from her temple. Surely she should protest such impropriety? And she certainly should not be resting against the length of his leg, her cheek becoming familiar with the warmth of him, the movement of muscle, the outline of his body beneath the fabric.

The swaying of the carriage, the body she rested against, the sounds of hushed breathing, the pounding of her head, all these coalesced and became for Mary Kate the essence of these long moments when they traveled through the darkness.

"We've not long to travel. It won't be long now. . . ."

. . . now, he would be there now. Surely such joy was too much to be borne.

Her smile was almost painful, it stretched so wide across her face.

The forest around her sang of spring. Yellow crocus blossoms peered up from shoots of green, noisy hatchlings were being fed by querulous mother birds, the soil beneath her feet was rich and loamy and smelled of wet winters and the sharp fecundity of nature itself.

Alice picked up her skirts and twirled in the grass, feeling as young and as carefree as a child enchanted by the promise of spring. She laughed, thinking herself silly and blessed and utterly in love.

Now he would be waiting for her. She must run to him. Tell him again of her most blessed secret . . .

"Have you no laudanum you can take for the pain?"

"No."

"Did you bring any of that idiotic doctor's tonic?"

"I won't take it," she said, starting to stir. He stopped her by the simple expedient of placing his hand upon her head. Her hair was soft, thick curls that seemed to invite a touch. He extended his fingers through it, palm still pressed against her skull, not realizing that the gesture had become one less of restraint than of caress.

She did, and for a long while allowed herself to experience it, to savor his unconscious touch and not feel the guilt of it. For some time they remained so, trapped in silence, yet neither sought to escape it.

"I'm better now. Truly," she said finally.

He released her and she sat up, moving with deliberate intent to the corner of the carriage.

"Does this happen often?"

"Often enough."

"Which means?" There was a hint of something in his voice, a warning note Mary Kate recognized and obeyed. She wasn't in the mood to taunt him, being weighted down with something that felt like sadness but stung like envy.

"Once a day, sometimes twice."

"And Dr. Endicott had no remedy?"

"I didn't tell the doctor. He would have prescribed another tonic, or some other hideous treatment."

"I don't suppose you had headaches before the accident?" Each word seemed coated with the irritation spiking his voice.

"I'm sure I did."

"But nothing like these?"

"Are you attempting to gauge the degree of your guilt?" She smiled, a watery smile that hurt too much for the effort of it.

"I assume my share of it, madam."

"Not because I require it."

Mary Kate wasn't certain why he was so angry with her. Because he'd been compassionate? Because she'd been in pain and he'd fondled her hair, showed her gentleness?

A flare of flint and the lantern was bright again, harsh enough that she looked away.

"Where is Alice? We've not yet disposed of that question to my satisfaction."

"Are we back to that again? Why do you think I know where your wife is?"

"Because of the warning you spoke to Jeremy, of

course. What danger do you suppose me to be in, madam? Is Alice planning my demise now? Has a member of my illustrious family plotted with her to arrange my death, therefore benefiting the entire St. John family with the wealth I steward?''

She wanted to close her eyes, wait out the residual pain of her headache, but his statement was so idiotic that she had no choice but to reply. ''Then why would she wish me to warn you? Because she changed her mind at the last moment? Hardly credible, don't you think? You cannot make Alice both a villainess and a savior.''

His skin bronzed, the ebony eyes became flat stones. ''What does she want? A bill of divorcement or money? Or both?''

A tense moment more and it seemed the carriage was beginning to slow. A few called commands from the driver indicated that it was so. Mary Kate thought the respite would be welcome, that being somewhere other than in this enclosed space with Archer St. John would be heavenly.

As the carriage stopped, she would have moved to push open the door, not waiting for the footmen to unroll the steps. Archer leaned forward and grasped her forearm with one large hand, forestalling her escape.

''If you tell me now, I'll pay you handsomely. If you divulge the terms of this little plot, I'll reward you far beyond what Alice could have promised you.''

Mary Kate could feel in his grip a violence tightly contained. She rubbed the fingertips of her loose hand against her temple. No, not again. The pain hummed in her head.

Help him. . . .

''You don't understand, do you? I've never met your wife.''

She reached out and with the tips of her fingers touched his coated chest. It was a forbidden thing to do, of course, a gesture frowned upon by etiquette and decorum. It felt to Mary Kate as though she'd stroked a hot stove, the sensation of burning lasting only a second. Still she kept her fingers there, possession and protection at the same time. She wanted to offer him comfort against the words she was going to say, for all she was certain they mirrored the truth.

"I'm sorry, but I'm very much afraid your wife is dead. You see, I believe she's haunting me."

Chapter 9

She didn't look insane, but then Archer wasn't sure he could recognize the face of madness. Unless, of course, it had been in his own reflection this past year. But she wore none of the signs he'd recognized so easily in himself—eyes red-rimmed from days of wakefulness, a trembling in his fingers, a weakness in his limbs. And most especially the wildness of thought, of wondering for a second, a moment, if he could have killed Alice and somehow not known, even this didn't seem mirrored in the woman who stood in front of him, halted by his touch.

She seemed, did Mary Kate Bennett, of estimable poise, her eyes clear and without redness, her limbs steady and without frailty, her face serene while a small smile wreathing full lips. Insanity? Either that, or courage.

"Are you brave enough?" he murmured, the words tossed away in the gentle breeze that seemed to grace their arrival at Sanderhurst. That touch of nature was the only movement in their strange tableau. The carriage, dusty now from its hours upon dirt roads, his coachman crooning words of praise to the tired horses, and he and Mary Kate, somehow trapped in time, his hand gripping her arm, her foot outstretched to take another step, a tendril of hair upon her cheek lifted by the welcoming breeze.

He dropped his hand as she stepped down onto the gravel path that led to the broad granite steps of his home.

If it was rude that he preceded her up the walk, he didn't care. Polite behavior had disappeared the moment she'd announced his wife a ghost. His mind slithered from that thought. Insane, she had to be.

When he heard no movement behind him, he turned back. She had stopped in the middle of the walk, her face turned up, transfixed by the sight of his home. He allowed her that moment. Even kings had been mindful of the beauty of Sanderhurst. Facing east, the great brick house was illuminated by the rising sun, lighting the hundred dark windows like God himself must illuminate a dark soul. The three-story structure had two wings that flanked its main building, always appearing to Archer as solid arms outstretched and welcoming him home.

All in all, Archer St. John thought, houses don't hurt you. They neither disappoint nor promise, and they lack the ability of certain selected mortals to render you confused and without cogent thought.

Sanderhurst, in addition to being incapable of causing him mental anguish and emotional distress, brought to Archer a certain calming influence. From here, the main entrance, he could see the rolling expanse of lawn flanked by woods deliberately left untouched. At the end of the vista, the Fallon River flowed. Sometimes, in the spring, the runoff was so great he could hear the sound of the water gushing over its banks.

When he was a child, Archer had thought Sanderhurst crafted of gold, but Sanderhurst's master mason had only described the fading of the bricks as tingeing rust, or ocher. The man lacked imagination. Or perhaps an only child had had too much of it.

His hands flexed against themselves, fisted. Somehow it seemed the greatest of invasions to have brought Mary Kate Bennett here. This was his haven, his sanctuary. He felt as if he belonged here, as no other place on earth. He did not own Sanderhurst, he was simply privileged to belong to it. Together, he and this immense house were the earldom, the jointure, the legacy of seventeen generations to hopefully as many more. He was its steward, and it was quite possible that Sanderhurst was his salvation.

He had known, even as a child, that he would *be* Sanderhurst for the rest of his life, that what he did now to either protect his estate or lessen its magnificence would be the legacy he left for generations to follow. Even as a young man, concerned more with whoring than conservancy, he'd never put his heritage in jeopardy.

There were times when he stood looking about him, awed as if he'd just recently recognized the surrounding beauty. He relished the pure beauty of its Grecian lines, the serenity of Sanderhurst. Every facet of life here was his responsibility, as paradoxically onerous and joy-filled as being head of the empire his ancestors had created.

And yet, at this moment, he did not see the formal garden with its whimsical fountains, or the rose arbor in full dormancy. He could not have told anyone what color he'd had the eastern paddock fence painted or how many fields were laying fallow. He felt as wobbly as one of the spring lambs, newly born, teetering on legs not yet stable. Because Mary Kate Bennett had uttered words to shatter his mind.

With a restraint for which he congratulated himself, he placed a gentle hand beneath her elbow, cupping it and leading her to the double entrance doors. It was soundlessly opened, to an inviting well-lit hall. He nodded at

Jonathan, not at all surprised to find his butler impeccably dressed. As a child, Archer had decided that Jonathan must never sleep, but watched over Sanderhurst fully attired no matter the hour.

Delicately, tenderly, not because that is how one should treat the mentally deranged, but because she raised his ire to a degree he'd never experienced in his entire life, Archer led Mary Kate Bennett passed his butler, the waiting footman, and up the curving stairs.

He opened the door to the Dawn Room, closed it firmly but quietly behind them. He let his hand drop to his side, surreptitously wiped his palm against his trousers, wondering why he could still feel the warmth of her skin even through many layers of cloth.

He felt something shift inside himself as a door was jarred open, just that. Not a full exposure, but a crack only. What was it that he felt standing there, staring at her as if his own wits had gone wondering? Self-questioning had become such a habit to him that he was not overly concerned with the thrusting imperative. Not anger then. No, that would have been easier to understand. Something else, perhaps, that lured him at the same time it cautioned. A presentment, then? A foretelling of what was to come? Is that what he felt? Had the fates begun to turn, then, to take pity on him somehow and warn him that this woman was a danger if there ever was one.

In the silence, he felt increasingly drawn to her, curious in a way he'd been few times in his life, to discover why her eyes were now shielded from him, why her smile, that small movement of lips and baring of teeth had the ability to stir him in a way that was less provident than lustful.

Perhaps it was the extravagant fullness of her breasts, the tall line of her that hinted of long, lean leg. She was too curved in a way that could not be totally tamed by whalebone, her mouth too full, too beckoning, the skin unbruised, too alabaster dusted with rose. And her hands should not be a focus for his eyes, should they? He should not note the length of fingers, their callused tips, the half moons shining beneath short nails. Working hands.

"You were saying, madam? What exactly do you mean, haunted?" How had he pushed the words past his lips? He didn't know, was only too grateful that he no longer stood gaping at her like a half-wit he'd thought her to be only a moment earlier.

"I should think it perfectly clear." She frowned quite nicely, he thought, as if to frame the idiocy of her words.

"Pretend, if you will, that I am cast adrift on the sea of your logic. Illuminate me, madam. It is my firm belief that Alice is still alive. Therefore, she could not be haunting you. It is indeed a novel game the two of you devised. I do not, however, have the patience for it."

"I do not know your wife, St. John. Nor do I think this is amusing," she said, her gaze as admonitory as the firm set of her lips.

"Oh, indeed it is, madam. It is a delightful bit of whimsy from a woman who intrigues me, unsettles me, and challenges me to remember that I am a gentleman, after all."

"You really must do something about that deplorable habit of speaking about me as if I'm not here."

"I am beginning to believe my life would be so much simpler if I had never seen you."

"As would mine. If you think I am pleased by your wife's appearance in my mind, let me assure you, such is not the case. I've pressing needs of my own that should be addressed."

"And yet you seem to accept being haunted with such grace."

"It is not like that at all."

"Then again, pray illuminate me, the better that I can understand."

"It's not as if I can see her." She looked away, then back at him.

"No? Does she not parade about with chains, or flit into your chamber window equipped with wings? Pray, the next time this occurs, invite me in, then I would have no reason to doubt your story. Until that time occurs, madam, you will remain here."

She was capable of being surprised, he would give her that. Or either she was an accomplished actress. Her eyes seemed to widen with the implication of his words, then just as quickly narrow as she frowned at him.

"Despite the fact that I have neither husband nor relatives willing to protect me, surely such behavior is not commonplace for earls."

"I've a near-perfect memory, madam. Shall I recite my Magna Carta? 'No freeman shall be arrested and imprisoned, or dispossessed, or outlawed, or banished, or in any way molested; nor will we set forth against him, nor send against him, unless by the lawful judgment of his peers, and by the law of the land.' You will please note that the rights granted by King John were to men. English women, however, are still subject to the whims of their protectors. And until you cease to prattle about ghosts and hauntings and tell me where my wife is, I am very much your protector."

He did not believe in specters or fortune-tellers or ghostly apparitions. He believed in things he could feel, the rich earth of Sanderhurst clenched in his fist, a hard ride over fence and through meadow, laughter and port, the small but precious things that marked the days of his life.

Which meant, of course, that either Mary Kate Bennett was a madwoman, or the greatest actress ever born for the stage. She couldn't be telling the truth.

He left her then, locking the door behind him.

Chapter 10

I t was a quiet meal, but then, breakfast always was. It was the only meal Samuel Moresham truly enjoyed, since his wife rarely rose at dawn.

Cecily believed the Almighty was interested in every detail of their lives and proceeded to tell Him about it during grace, prattling on until the gravy cooled and the potatoes were near to ice. Breakfast was blessedly free of talk, just he and James sharing a hot meal.

James was having no trouble putting away his kippers and bacon, but then he always had a ready appetite. Too bad the lad didn't fill out more than he did.

Samuel took a large swig from the tankard at his right, thanking Providence that Cecily had not the courage to lecture him about spirits in his own home. Taken on a bit about religion, she had, especially in the last three or four years. She'd always been devout, but lately, she'd been difficult to live with, so much so that he found ways to avoid his wife.

He couldn't swear, lest she scrabble for that Bible of hers, to unearth some odd Scripture that seemed to pin his ears in place. Even bedding his wife was out of the question lately; all these mumblings about harlotry, sins of the

flesh, seemed too great a price to pay for the doubtful joys
of Mrs. Moresham's participation. He'd rather bed great
lovely Betty in the next village, and pay the price for adultery before his Maker. Divine penance would be less severe than anything Cecily might dole out to him.

James caught his eye again. His hair was streaked by
the sun. Almost blond it was. Enough to remind Samuel
of the boy's mother. He'd loved that girl, with all the hot-
blooded lust he'd been capable of, but still, it hadn't been
enough, had it? She'd wanted to loll about and enjoy being
a baronet's wife, never mind that the title was hereditary
and brought no money with it. She'd tired of all the work
a horse farm demanded, had run away with another man,
only to be found at Cheapside, near dead of the influenza.

Still, it was an odd thing that he could mourn her even
now. Perhaps it was her way of loving and her hot kisses
he remembered, not the fact that she'd left him alone with
a small lad of two.

He remembered the night James was born. It had been
too early for her to have gone to her birthing bed and
Samuel had feared for the child's survival. When the large
baby had been presented to him, all wrinkled and red from
his mother's womb, he's said not a word. He'd kept his
suspicions to himself, even though there was nothing of
the Moreshams about the boy, nothing that reminded Samuel of his own kin.

He'd never said a word, not even after the day he'd
found her, near to death in a cheap room at an inn favored
by rough sailors. She'd told him then that she'd always
loved him, that it wasn't her way, though, to remain with
just one man. And with his question, she'd only looked
into his eyes and then nodded, labeling James a bastard.

He'd decided, that day, that he'd raise her son as his

own and there'd be none to tell him different. So, despite the fact they looked nothing like each other, had none of the same mannerisms, none of the wishes and dreams and hopes father and son sometimes share, Samuel Moresham had taken the child of his wife to son. It had been pride, then, that had labeled James a Moresham.

Too late, he'd realized what a price James had paid for it.

His second wife had been fertile in their marriage and none would say there was a doubt of his daughters' paternity. To the one, they had the Moresham nose, all except Alice. And she had his gestures, she did, and his way of smiling at nothing. He had loved the girl like no other of his children.

Sometimes it seemed to Samuel that he was cursed to love women who were forever leaving him. Alice had simply gone one day and not a word had come since. It seemed that only he and James grieved for her loss.

Ever since James was a lad and Alice a baby, there'd been a special bond between the two of them. Alice didn't talk for the longest time, because James would talk for her. "She wants a biscuit," he would say, when she pointed to the cupboard in the kitchen, or "she wants an up-up," when Alice would raise her arms over her head. There was no sillier sight, or one to more cloud the eyes, as when James would hoist the little girl into his arms, her legs wrapped around his torso, her arms wound around his neck. The two of them would walk off like that, clinging to each other as if there was nothing in the world that could keep them apart.

James and Alice had been closer than any members of the family, always laughing, always together with their fair heads close, whispering, talking, sharing with each other.

Ever since Alice had disappeared, James had seemed subdued, his smiles never quite meeting his eyes, his gaze haunted instead. He appeared almost wan, and had lost flesh.

"You'll join me, then, in the north pasture?" Samuel stood, hitched his trousers up, donned his working coat. That was another thing about mornings, no lectures on manners and what was proper to wear to table.

James nodded, his attention directed at his plate.

"I'd have a look at the foreleg of that new mare if I were you. It looked swollen."

"I'll do it." James glanced up at him, a look that slid away as soon as it made contact.

Samuel wanted to say something, ease the way. But there was nothing he could say, after all. What words would be appropriate? Surely not those of father to son. Nothing fit the moment, no words would pass his lips. If they had been different people, he could have gripped his son's shoulders, eased him into a hug, wiped his own eyes dry of the grief that had never had a chance to breathe. Instead, he walked away, through the dining room, across the oaken floor to the entrance way and beyond, to the hallway that led to the back, to the stables.

It was as well, perhaps, that he would be forever mute.

Instead of sleeping, Archer stood at the window of his library and watched Sanderhurst come alive with morning light. Rest after their night's journey had been rendered impossible by the Bennett woman's announcement. So was peace of mind. No, he could not lay that sin upon his reluctant guest's head. The past year had stripped him of any contentment he might have enjoyed from life.

His marriage to Alice Moresham had long been doomed,

but death was not the agent of separation. Inclination, personality, interests, they had all served their part in dividing what God had joined together.

Archer needed an heir, a point his favorite uncle had hounded him about until the morning he died, still clutching Archer's hand and imploring him with a rheumy-eyed gaze.

Alice was her father's second-oldest daughter, a pretty thing with blond hair curled in ringlets, a small but perfectly formed mouth that reminded him of a child's pursed lips. Her nose was slightly too small, but her cheeks were just rosy enough to claim good health. She was a young woman of seemingly delicate constitution, fanatical loyalty to her family, graced with a timid air that had originally charmed Archer. Her speech was so soft, no more than a whisper, that he was required to bend forward at every utterance in order to hear her. In addition, she had a habit of burying her nose in her reticule, eternally inhaling the noxious scent of her lavender water. It seemed to follow her like a cloud, until the very air that surrounded her seemed rife with the odor.

He had the distinct impression that he frightened the wits out of his new wife, a suspicion that was only reinforced as time passed and Alice seemed no warmer toward him. In fact, she'd taken to clenching her eyes shut and praying whenever he approached her bed, a welcome that had the expected result of rendering him less than willing to complete the marriage act.

He had attempted to talk to her of books he'd read, but Alice claimed that reading hurt her eyes. She disliked plays, admitting that they either bored her or made her melancholic. She did, however, adore musicales, especially those of an insipid nature that caused his skin to crawl and each separate hair on his head to adopt an independent nature as if one by one they wished to indicate their displeasure of such caterwauling.

She was, however, good with children. She seemed to have an affinity to them, and they, in turn, adored her. Archer wanted his children loved, not by a succession of paid companions and nurses, but by their parents. He was prepared to adore his progeny. He wanted that single-minded devotion that Alice spared unceasingly on her siblings and their children to be directed to their offspring. Pity she had not wanted a child of his.

Mary Kate Bennett disturbed him. Why had she entered into Alice's game?

He had not, at first, become alarmed at Alice's failure to return from her visit to her mother. It was a habit of hers to stay as long as she wished at Moresham Farms and advise him later by missive that she was doing so.

If he found his married life difficult, then hell was defined as being confined with Alice's relatives. Although he found Alice's father an amiable man, possessed of a boisterous laugh and the ability to breed the most costly Thoroughbreds in the British Isles, the female side of Alice's family was enough to make him beg off even the shortest visit. Alice's sisters were all equipped with a singular braying laugh, like that of an ass. Although they were all personable women, and attractive in their own way, their voices were high pitched, each sentence ending on a questioning tone. It grated at him, but not as much as their coy expressions and simpering smiles. Alice's mother, however, was the reason he chose to absent himself from the majority of her outings. Her mother was a squat, plump woman with the habit of quoting an endless supply of Bible verses while maintaining the tenacity of a wire terrier while doing so. She was, Archer had realized from his very first courting visit to the Moresham farm, one of those people who, as guests, never know when to leave. He had no doubt she was infinitely effective as a proselytizer. He, himself, would have abjured any religious beliefs but hers if it meant being spared her future presence.

But when a fortnight had passed without any word, he had left to fetch his wife, irked that Alice's antipathy for him had extended to blatant disregard of simple courtesy, but not overly distressed at her absence. The Moresham household, however, had disavowed any knowledge of Alice's visit. His innocent request for his wife's presence created a storm of such magnificent proportions that even today he felt the wind of it.

Alice, it seemed, had vanished.

Archer had, in the first month, alerted their neighbors, the inns that dotted the road to London. He had traveled to the City, calling upon his solicitors, keeping the town house open long after the Season, hoping for word of her.

After a month had passed and still no word had come, the gossip had begun. It was at that point that he had sent handbills the length and breadth of England, offering a reward for information concerning her person or presence. Ships that had been at port at the time of her disappearance were eagerly boarded on their return docking, only to discover that no one matching Alice's appearance was to be found. Nor was any word forthcoming.

He shouldered his burdens in silence, avoiding his wife's hysterical family, while attempting to repair his own aggrieved honor. The increasingly hostile stares of neighbors and servants made it more difficult each passing week to maintain an appearance of equanimity. It was a sad requiem for his reputation.

Archer, you ass. There was nothing left of his reputation, not now.

He found himself like a suicide, whose past was forever wiped clean and rendered invisible by the manner of his parting from this earth. "Oh yes, Richardson, I knew him well. Poor sod, to end it like that." And so the poor sod is forever to be known as bullet-in-the-brain Richardson, never mind that he was a tolerable husband and a good father, minded his properties well and never pinched the barmaids.

Poor St. John, murderer, you know. Killed her and buried the body so deep and so well they'd never find it. Whispered about that she'd run away, but we all know he killed her, poor stupid sod. No doubt buried her body in a bog. Either that or boiled her and ate her in a soup.

Nothing could have been further from the truth. And wasn't that like the devil proclaiming his innocence?

Archer had never believed it truly possible for someone to simply disappear into nothingness. Yet for a year, that is just what Alice had done. What he wanted very much in his life at this moment was not his wife's presence as much as proof that he could not have, had not, murdered her.

Upstairs, in the Dawn Room, slept the only person who might know where Alice was. Who was this woman and what did she want from him? Was she one of the self-proclaimed mystics who seemed to haunt London's society parties? Was she a friend of Alice's? Alice's affection seemed solely visited upon her family.

How perfectly he'd fallen into their trap. He'd wondered at her luck in not being more injured; now he knew the accident had all been staged. A ruse to lure him closer, to inveigle her way into his house, his life.

It was a Machiavellian strategy and one he'd never thought capable of Alice, but then, she must be maddened for money, being unable to tap any of her funds without his approval. That would never be granted until she showed herself at Sanderhurst and took from him the stigma of a man having done away with his wife.

Alice needn't go to such extremes. He was quite willing to agree to a bill of divorcement. He frankly didn't care about the scar upon his name. He had already lived the censure in truth, had he not? For the past year he had been buffeted by rumor, conjecture, and outright suspicion. What was one more disgrace heaped upon his name? At least any social ostracism that resulted would be for divorcing his wife, not murdering her.

But what if it was only money she was after? What if Alice intended to take his money and never come back? He'd be the last of his line, never able to marry again. The heir he'd needed, the children he wanted, would never be born, at least legitimately.

In his home sat the one person who knew where Alice was. Mary Kate's nonsensical story about ghosts and visitations and eerie whispers were just that, a device to lure him into complacency. What was it she wanted?

Alice had, at least, found someone to tempt him, a woman almost too flashy to be quite proper, with her fulsome figure and alluring face, with her odd habit of stroking her fingers through the tendrils of hair at her nape and a scent as elemental as the sun, as expensive as cinnamon.

No, he would keep her conspirator friend at Sanderhurst until he could decide what to do. Or until Mary Kate decided to tell him the truth.

Chapter 11

⌒⌒⌒⌒⌒

Bernadette Aphra St. John, known to her intimate friends and lovers and one or two occasional relatives as Bernie, and to the rest of the world as the Dowager Countess of Sanderhurst, eyed her weary lover with something very much like irritation. Twenty years her junior and gasping like a beached trout. The sounds he was making were quite unlovely, really, and if she hadn't been so replete at this particular moment, she would have shoved him off the bunk and demanded that he leave her cabin. It would not have been an extraordinarily difficult feat, since she outweighed him by at least two stone and topped him by three inches. She was, as her mother had often told her growing up, a rather large girl.

Still, he was a pretty thing, if a bit out of practice. She was quite willing to engage in the act repeatedly so that he might master the skill of it, and therefore his stamina while doing so. It was quite a generous offer, she thought, even though he was the only male passenger left on this St. John ship. The others had departed at Macao, and since there was nothing between their present position and England but a few paltry ports and a long stretch of water, it seemed the most prudent course to give him another opportunity to impress her.

His name was Matthew. That, she had learned before he'd come into her cabin for a glass of brandy. Of his antecedents, she knew little; of his future plans, even less. But he had a warm and golden tan and he seemed quite smitten with her. He was now mumbling something into the feather pillow, in such heartfelt tones that it brought a glow of satisfaction to her face. There was something to be said for experience, after all. Not to mention years of travel. She had picked up a few hints here and there.

She stretched, pulled both arms above her head, wriggled delightfully. She had lived a singularly hedonistic lifestyle, enjoying her food, a glass of good wine, the company of articulate, entertaining people.

She made her temporary homes where the scenery was lovely and the mood was right, and the natives seemed friendly enough, even though India had been frightfully hot. But there had been a dashing colonel, quite an attractive man he was, what with his bright silver hair and his crinkly smile. He was, however, too enamored of her title and the fact that she represented all that lovely St. John money. Pity, if he'd just liked her for being herself, they could have made a go of it. Wasn't it odd the way people kept trying to force her into respectability, when she truly wished to be seen as daring and innovative and odd? It was a little like forcing a square peg into a round hole; too much shaving and shaping had to be done in order to make it happen. She truly didn't want to lose that much of herself. She'd had all the stifling propriety in her childhood, when she'd done exactly what she was told, and in her adulthood, when she'd married someone she didn't like only because it was a good match and her new husband was an earl and rich.

Still and all, it hadn't been that onerous a relationship.

The good man had the sense to die early, leaving her alone with a delightful son to raise. And Archer, thank heavens, only occasionally reminded her of his father.

During the last decade she'd finally obtained a certain liberty of the senses, but otherwise she had remained a relatively staid individual. Well, there was the training with the bow and arrow, a skill she was happy to have mastered, since her instructor was a delightfully athletic-looking man in North America. And the sessions with firearms could not help but come to good use one day. Not to mention the knife strapped to her ankle. She had become quite proficient in the use of that. After all, a lone female did have to protect herself.

The men in her life had been relatively few, until the last year, when she'd finally thrown off the mantle of respectability and done whatever felt comfortable and right. After all, men had been doing it for centuries, it was time for women to engage in the same moral freedom.

All in all, she quite enjoyed her widowhood. There was something to be learned each day, something to be shared each moment, some beauty to be found, some joy to be dispensed. A thoroughly novel attitude that Bernie would have been delighted to share with the world. Except that, of course, in the year 1792, the world was not quite ready for Bernie. Especially England.

She'd left fifteen years ago, determined to find a place, a country, a town, where she belonged, only to discover the most elemental truth of them all. There was no home more suited to her than the one she created, a turtle's self-sufficiency independent of place or location. But the intervening years had not been wasted; they'd exposed her to the cultures of the world, given her a great respect for the dynasty that allowed her such financial freedom. She'd traded the English habit of superior thinking—believing the world bowed willingly at England's doorstep and supped greedily from her spoon—for a more realistic view of the world. The greatest knowledge revealed was that of herself, however, the essence of Bernadette Aphra St. John.

She had learned that bright, vivid colors complemented her, to dress in Indian saris often because the style flattered her large-boned, tall frame. She kept her black hair cut short, to her shoulders, affecting the Japanese adornments she so admired. She was fluent in seven languages, could eat quite adequately with chopsticks, had studied Buddhism, the Koran, the Talmud. The contents of her trunks indicated her eclectic lifestyle and interests. In addition to her wardrobe, she carried home bolts of Cambrai cambric, Laon lawn, Ypres diapered cloth, a well-used hookah, a manuscript of haikus written in her honor by an elderly Japanese admirer, four different types of shallots indigenous to Southwest Asia, and a collection of heavy, black Indian rubber balls she adored because of their bounce.

She was quite aware that she scandalized most of her relatives, some of whom had managed to keep a wary eye on her all these years. What letters had not accomplished, hired watchers had, informing her many and too interested kin of her scandals and her achievements. The former unfortunately outweighed the latter.

Still, she was glad to be returning to the country of her birth. Perhaps it was a function of age, instilling in her a wish for the stability of a life she'd once found staid and uninteresting. She missed the constancy of English life; traditions once taken for granted now seemed almost inestimable: Christmas crackers, plum pudding, rolling hills held captive by mist, a perfectly tended formal garden.

For all that, she didn't regret leaving England. Archer had been grown and utterly independent, and she'd been desperate to become herself, not simply the widowed Countess of Sanderhurst, wealthy, eccentric and deadly bored.

But oh, she did miss her son. Correspondence had kept them close, and they'd been able to meet in a foreign capital or two over the years. But she'd been stuck in some dusty hamlet in India when she'd finally gotten news of his plans for marriage. By the time she could have taken ship and arrived in England, she would have been three months late for the wedding.

Perhaps it was for the best, for all that. She remembered little Alice as a child, dressed in yellow and as sunny as the day was bright. What kind of wife had she made for her son? Not good enough, that was certain. No woman would have been. Another benefit, then, for staying away from England. Archer would not have applauded her behavior as a mother-in-law.

What would her son say if he knew that it was because of him she was returning after all these years? He needed her now, for the first time since he was twenty; she could almost touch the loneliness in his letters, the despair in his search for Alice. She would join her not inconsiderable resources to his and together they would find his missing wife.

Chapter 12

He didn't knock, didn't allow her to bid him enter or deny him leave. There was only the whisk of the key in the lock and Archer St. John was there, dwarfing the doorway with his presence, showing her by his actions and by the implacable mask of his face that he was her jailer.

Mary Kate was seated in a chair before the fire, her legs covered with a silken blanket. In her hands was one of the books he'd sent to relieve her boredom.

"Why are you staring at me in that way?" he asked. "Have I grown horns, or are you measuring the limits of my credulity?" A veneer of politeness was stripped away by his tone.

"I have been trying to think what danger might befall you."

"An earthly guardian angel, charged by a voice from the great beyond? Shouldn't you be demanding payment for this entertainment? Although I must congratulate you, madam. It is an interesting ploy, this talk of whispering voices and visions, but I would have thought you'd put your mind to more productive pursuits, such as admitting your complicity in this little plot of yours and Alice's. After all, truth would be so much easier, don't you think?"

"I've already told you the truth."

"You've divulged a unique version of facts, madam, but I would not necessarily call it the truth. My wife is dead and sending you ghostly dreams. Visions of my life in infinite detail. Now she's sending you warnings of impending doom. Do I have it correct?"

At her slight nod, he smiled. It was a gesture totally lacking in humor.

"Then I am supposed to do what, madam? Be so grateful to you that I part with half my fortune? Pay you off? Why have you concocted a story between you that possesses neither truth nor reason? What could you possibly have to gain?

"You don't have a bevy of spirits in your reticule, waiting to fly forth and speak through you? Pity, think what gullible dupes you could find to finance your living. You could announce yourself as Madame Bennett, Mistress of Cryptaesthesia."

"I don't particularly *want* to be haunted, St. John." She looked at him directly. "It is the first time such a thing has happened to me."

A twist of his lips formed a half smile, something derisive and not at all kind, but then, Mary Kate suspected that Archer St. John was not known for his compassion.

"You and Alice are to be congratulated for your creativity. Such a tale is evident of a mind better suited for children's stories and fables, however. It is wasted on me. Where is my wife, madam?"

"I don't know."

It seemed a parody play they engaged in, the question, the answer, both quick, tight-lipped, uttered by two people who'd grown tired of the necessity for both the question and its rapid response.

Mary Kate decided to go about this differently. It was quite certain that Alice was concerned about her husband's welfare. As concerned about Archer St. John as the earl was desperate for news of his wife. Perhaps if she solved one riddle, she could find the solution to the other.

"Have you any enemies?"

He looked at her as if she'd lost the remainder of her reason. Perhaps she had, to be as honest with him. "I've a score of enemies. None of them would be enriched by my passing. However, they are of a professional, not a personal, nature. Until my wife left me, madam, I have enjoyed a rather benign effect upon people."

"Do you ride?"

He raised one eyebrow.

"An English gentleman rides, of course. But are you competent?"

A second eyebrow joined the first.

"Very well," she said, casting down her eyes. It did not seem quite fair to think him so amusing.

"Do you have any other pursuits that could be considered unhealthy?"

"There is no disturbance in my existence, Mrs. Bennett, but the disappearance of my wife. I don't know how you'll get a message to her, but I'm certain you'll manage. I'd be more than happy to have your letter franked myself. Tell Alice that I want an end to this. Now."

One corner of her lip turned up. She picked up her cup and buried her nose in it.

"Do you find something humorous about that statement?" he asked.

"I shall convey your wishes," she said, unable, finally, to mask the totality of her amusement.

"You *are* laughing at me. Tell me the jest and I'll join you."

She glanced at him. Did he realize that he was so stiffly correct? Yet sometimes she almost saw a glint of humor in those night eyes, and a glimmer of something not proper and certainly not stuffy.

"It's just that we are an odd pair, you and I. You, incensed with your errant wife because she's not present; me, rather grateful because she is."

At his look, she continued.

"I am used to the company of others, St. John. The only people I've seen in the last few days besides you have been the maids, and they stayed no more than a moment or two, performing their duties in such silence that I suspect they were warned not to converse with me. The spirit of your wife has been my only companion."

"You speak of ghosts with such ease, madam. Would it not be more provident to be frightened, if such were the case?"

"If I were of your station, perhaps. But death is nothing new to me, St. John. I've helped at the burial of two of my brothers, prepared my father's body for his shroud. When you're of the working class, death is not a thing to fear as much as a constant presence, almost a friend."

"Even more reason for me not to believe you, presented to me on a platter of lies. You could only profit from this game." He walked to the window, trailed a hand down the fabric of the draperies hung there.

"You expect only lies from me, but all I've given you is the truth."

"And you never lie, of course." He turned and speared her with a glance.

"I've lied," she conceded, placing her cup back upon

the tray. "Not just white lies, either, I'll confess. There were times I've said I'd done something when I hadn't yet completed my task. Label that one a sin if you will, but only of timing."

"And the sin of omission? Are you guilty of that?"

"Not telling all I know? What else would you have me tell you?" Her fingers pleated the edge of the throw that covered her legs.

"Why Alice sent you, instead of returning herself. What you have to gain by pretending she's dead."

"I don't suppose that it would do any good to tell you again that I never knew your wife?" Her look was earnest and somber.

"None."

"Do you only believe in things you can see or touch, St. John?"

"I've found it to be the sanest way of dealing with life, madam." His fingers moved a small and delicate figurine of a shepherdess from the edge of a table.

"And yet you leave no room for faith, or hope, or even coincidence."

"I will not argue religion with you, madam, and coincidence is merely a word to describe inattentiveness. That which links circumstances together can easily be seen by those who pay attention to their surroundings."

Wasn't it odd that her attention was caught by the delicacy of his touch, a brush of finger against a bisque skirt, a slow stroke on a shepherd's crook? "Then I do not suppose you are about to admit that you might come to believe me?"

"There is not a chance of that, madam. I shall only hope you continue to think the accommodations to your liking," he said, ceasing his gentle benediction of touch and bowing slightly.

"I would be a fool to scorn these accommodations. You've given me a magnificent cell." She looked around her, and then smiled at him. "Such ease with wealth amazes me. It also shames me a little because I feel envious, another of my faults too easily illuminated. Or perhaps it is not simply your wealth I envy, but the nonchalance with which you treat it. You will never wonder where the next meal is coming from, or what occupation will allow you to maintain your pride and still garner enough for a small room and one meal a day. Have you ever worried about your future, St. John?"

"So this ploy is punishment for my position?" His smile was not at all friendly. "Is this your idea of deference?"

"Because you're an earl? Or because of your wealth? Neither of these because of your own industry, St. John. As to respect, you lost that the moment you became my jailer. Why should I defer to you, now?"

He strode to the door, opened it with an economy of movement that betrayed his irritation.

"You do not have a servile bone in your body, madam. I suspect you would be cheeky to the King himself."

"Servitude is not a choice I would have made in my life, St. John."

"No, instead you choose to play interpreter for a ghost only you imagine."

"And one who loves you very much."

In that second when he turned, he was changed.

His anger was buried, his irritation flaming out, extinguished, his ebony eyes solid, glowing like agates. There was nothing about his face to indicate that bone and flesh and muscle dwelt within that space, or anything less brittle than hard, carved granite. Even his hands stilled, kept at his sides, his shoulders maintained a military precision, his spine as rigid as if strapped to a saber.

"She loved me? Is that what you call it?" In his voice was an incalculable weariness, emotion that spoke of acceptance, regret, and in a curious and startling way, despair. "Is that why she took a lover? Is that why she labeled herself adulteress? If Alice loved me, I pity the man she hated.

"I propose that you confess your duplicity, thereby ending your imprisonment and allowing me to continue on with my life. Tell Alice that I will give her anything she wishes, including whatever funds she needs, but that I wish my freedom with all due speed. If she wishes a bill of divorcement, I will petition Parliament myself."

It was not his parting rudeness that kept Mary Kate staring after him, but the look upon his face before the door had closed, studied indifference, calculated apathy, rigid and hard as stone. But stone can crack and she'd seen the evidence of it, the glimmer of pain in the blackness of Archer St. John's eyes.

Chapter 13

"**G**ive him an extra measure of mash, Raymond." Archer turned and cast a weary look at the western sky. It was nearly dark and he'd spent most of the day on horseback. A futile and almost desperate search for some type of peace.

"Aye, sir." The groom pulled off his hat one more time, a nervous gesture more than a subservient one. Archer suspected he frightened the liver out of his servants. It was not by reputation that he had managed to assemble the finest servants ever to leave London—the power of his purse did that. Strange, that he did not inspire such fear in Mary Kate Bennett.

He had decided that a day away from Sanderhurst would do him more good than sitting in his library brooding about his reluctant guest. The respite had provided him an opportunity to visit his wife's parents a duty he did not perform as often as he should have, for the simple reason that he could barely tolerate his mother-in-law and found himself treating his wife's father with varying degrees of pity mixed with impatience. But there had been the chance that Alice had sent a missive to her parents, to whom she was devoted.

It had been more than a wasted day; it had reminded him of why he imprisoned Mary Kate Bennett. Moresham Farms was a tidy community of outbuildings surrounding a large stable complex. The house, a stately manor of thirty rooms, was some short distance away, tied to the other buildings by a series of graveled paths. The distance from Sanderhurst was negligible; Archer had covered it in less than fifteen minutes on a fast canter. But the gulf between himself and Alice's parents was measured in more than miles.

His mother-in-law's welcome had been what he'd expected. She had stared at him, arms folded across her chest and lips pursed. Not exactly a look of welcome, but then, he'd been prepared for her antipathy. He had sent a note ahead, asking permission to call upon the two of them. Cecily had responded with a short, terse scribble. A warning of a chill in her hospitality.

Her face was square, her forehead broad; she would have made a passable man, but as a woman she was plain, a fact that Archer found difficult to reconcile with the fact that her daughters were all lovely women. But perhaps the years had added a resoluteness to her features, that stubbornness to her jaw, and beneath the intolerance, a portion of half-buried anger.

He allowed one of the Moresham grooms to lead his horse away, then bowed to his mother-in-law slightly, extending an arm so that he might escort her into the parlor. Except, of course, that she ignored both gestures with disdain.

"I had not hoped to see you so soon again, St. John." He had always been called thus by his wife's mother. No more warmth had ever been expressed between the two of them, and now the frost between them was so thick Archer felt as if he could slice it.

He nodded in reply. He would not stoop to platitudes.

"Have you news of my daughter?" She fixed such an intent gaze on him that he wondered if her aim was to see his insides.

"A question I would ask of you, madam."

"She was always safe within the bosom of her family, St. John. It was only when she became chatelaine of Sanderhurst that she disappeared." It was the opening move to their battle, then, and she'd drawn first blood.

There was a moment, only a hesitation, in which he wondered if he should bother to attempt to warm her, to soften the barrier she'd erected between them. Would she even tell him if she'd heard from Alice? He doubted it. He found himself oddly weary, too tired to attempt to charm Cecily Moresham.

"I shall not inconvenience you with my presence, then, madam."

He executed a perfect bow and turned, heading for the stables, finding Samuel with the aid of one of the ever-present grooms. His father-in-law was engaged in brushing one of his studs, an action that would have been considered odd, if not demeaning, in another man. But Samuel had never considered himself above any occupation, and had bragged to Archer in sunnier days of knowing everything that went on at Moresham Farms, from the exact ration his Thoroughbreds consumed, to exactly what each horse ran on racing day.

Archer stood there a moment until Samuel acknowledged his presence with a short nod. Had he expected anything else? Yes, answered a portion of his mind, that which was occupied by memory. He had always respected Samuel Moresham, had liked the man and envied the talent that had turned a sadly run horse farm into one synonymous with finely bred horses coveted throughout England.

"It's been a while since we've seen you, and a year my Alice has gone missing. Is that why you're here, then?" Samuel bent and gathered up the curry brush, then began to brush Excelsior with long, firm strokes. He glanced at Archer as he stroked the broad nose of his champion with his free hand.

"I have no news to bring you, Samuel. And you? Have you nothing to impart to me?"

The next few minutes were silent ones, the only sounds those of the animal between them, huffing the air, stirring against the harness that tethered him. Somewhere a groom laughed, something metal fell with a jarring chink, a voice called out and was answered.

"I used to think she was an angel, my Alice. A sweet, soft cherub come to life. She was the most beautiful of all the girls, what with her blond hair and sweet blue eyes." Samuel busied himself again, rearranging Excelsior's grooming utensils. He turned his back on both the horse and the earl. "You cannot say she didn't have a charming disposition, Archer, and a compassionate, loving heart."

What good would it do to air his grievances with his wife with her father? He said, instead, the words Samuel asked for, in a tone as gentle as he could muster. "She was a credit to you, Samuel."

"I gave her in marriage to you, Archer, thinking that the union was blessed for all concerned. And aye, I'll not lie to you, Archer, I wanted wealth and position for Alice. But I'd have kept her here a spinster before the day I'd let her near you, if I'd known she'd go missing." Samuel's eyes bore none of the friendliness he'd once expressed, none of the fondness Archer had felt as a young boy grown up fatherless so close to Moresham Farms. "My Alice would not have run away, no matter the provocation. She'd never have left."

A thought that had kept Archer company on his lonely ride. He'd ignored the tenants on his property, the village. He'd been no fit companion for anyone, immersed as he had been in his own thoughts, his own doubts.

How did he reconcile Samuel's vision of his daughter with his own recollection of his wife? It seemed as if they were two different people. Or perhaps it was his own perspective that provided the difference.

He had not loved Alice. The opportunity for warmer feelings between them had been lost in the nights of winter chill, when they'd both sat in the parlor with only the crackle and hiss of the fire to accompany the hours, lost in their own thoughts and feelings, neither able to broach the endless expanse that stretched between them even though it was measured in less than five feet. Or perhaps it was lost in the summer, when he took to spending most of his days outdoors, unwilling to share any room with the unsmiling woman who seemed even more fragile than she had at their wedding, a ghostly wraith of a woman with blond hair and a delicate frame and cursed with silence, eternal silence. Or it could have been in spring, when Alice took little interest in Sanderhurst, only wandering from room to room, her fingers brushing over each piece of furniture as if to test the maids upon their diligence, venturing out of doors to watch the great rugs being beaten upon their frames, the curtains and testers being aired. It was the housekeeper who gave such orders, never the mistress of the house, who looked upon the estate she chatelained as if it were no more than a way station upon a further journey.

No, he had not loved his wife, but he had not hated her, either. That had come later, in autumn, his heretofore favorite time of the year. Archer could almost believe that his emotion for his wife had turned from hopeful expectation to apathy and from there to hatred during that season when Alice had begun to smile and even to hum tunes in his hearing.

She had been happy, truly happy, in her adultery.

It had been years since he had felt even the fleeting expression of joy, let alone a constancy of it. Was that, then, the source of his antipathy? That Alice had been happy while he had never been? Or did it have at its roots his pride, that someone had been able to make Alice smile, when all he was able to accomplish was to cocoon her in silence? Someone had made Alice sparkle and it had not been her husband.

Such innocence, Archer. He hadn't been that naive since his relationship with Milicent. He had only been nineteen when he'd fancied himself in love with Lady Milicent Danworth. She was young, married to a man three decades her senior, insisted she was much put upon and threatened by her husband. He'd believed it all, of course, fell for her much-tried expression of sheltered innocence crushed and broken, found himself rushing to protect her and challenge the monster who would abuse his lovely and delicate wife.

A wiser man would have believed the husband's protests, would have questioned why Sir Gregory had not the slightest intention of defending his much-maligned wife. A wiser man would also have reasoned a little further than he had, gleaning some additional information about the charming Lady Milicent. But he had not. Single-mindedly he had taken it upon himself to dog Sir Gregory's heels, to harass the man until he had no choice but to acquiesce to a confrontation on the field of honor. He'd not deloped as Sir Gregory had done, but had calculatingly shot his rival. The fact that Sir Gregory survived was attributed to his gun's poor sight and not his aim. He would not have minded killing him, and every man on that field that misty morning had known it.

Yet the farce was not yet played out. Rushing to Lady Milicent's house to relay the news that her aging husband would no longer berate her or treat her cruelly, Archer had found her in bed with no fewer than two of his drinking companions, both men still wearing an expression of stunned rapture on their faces when he'd interrupted.

So much for innocence.

He'd thrown both men out the door on their bare backsides, returned to the bedroom to find Lady Milicent screaming for her maid and fumbling for her robe. He'd not waited for her to find suitable garments, but had clamped his hand over her wrist and dragged her to his carriage, half-naked. The journey to the field of honor had taken ten blistering minutes, with Lady Milicent screaming like a depraved banshee the whole journey. He'd pulled her out of the carriage, with her half-falling, stumbling behind him. Only when they reached the end of the field did he stop, flinging her to the ground beside St. George.

"Your husband, madam," he bit out, his disgust for her vying with his own sense of betrayal. She looked a well-used whore, her hair askew, her breasts bare, her petticoat falling down to her knees. She wore nothing to protect her from the scandalized gazes of twenty men, most of whom, he'd discovered later, had already known her in the biblical sense.

He had turned and walked away, leaving her screaming at him, unconcerned about her threats or the hum of shocked voices. He'd learned that she'd left England for Italy, had died there a few years later at the hands of a very determined contessa, who resented her husband choosing an Englishwoman's bed for sport. When he'd learned of her fate, Archer had spared a half moment for a thought of Lady Milicent, but no more. She deserved far less.

Still he'd grown up that day, no longer putting such faith and credence in a woman's tears or weeping words.

Then why had he felt so betrayed by Alice? The pain of it had stunned him. Archer had not known there was any vulnerability left in him, had been startled to find that there were still places in his psyche not scabbed over and rendered tough. But marriage had been a new venture and he had been willing to capitulate to it, bringing to his wife all the damaged and mangled parts of his soul tied together with string, a bouquet of Archer St. John. For the humility of such self-honesty, he'd expected some fidelity, a little kindness, perhaps acceptance as the years passed. Only from his children had he expected love.

Instead, his wife had disappeared, sending him a consolation prize, a woman to serve as hostage to the truth.

Perhaps he was defeating his own best interests by imprisoning Mary Kate Bennett. Perhaps he was better served by allowing her freedom. Only then could he discern her true motives, the next act in this absurd play.

How could anyone that gorgeously flagrant and spectacularly theatrical look so shocked? When he had decried Alice as an adulteress, Mary Kate had looked like someone whose foundations of belief had just been shaken loose, a priest without faith, a child left orphaned. From where had that emotion emerged, from the plenitude of false feelings she kept stowed in her stocking? Did he believe for one moment that it was genuine, or that it had softened to yet another look, one he might even think was compassion? He had wanted to scoff at her, indicate his disgust at her ability to summon forth feelings appropriate to the moment. He had wanted to criticize her blatant near-to-orange hair and her too red lips and the creamy color of her skin and the perfection of her eyes.

It was that one shining tear that had kept him silent. The pure perfection of it. A stranger's empathy. It was as if she *knew* what that statement had cost him.

Chapter 14

H *elp him. . . .*
    The thought surfaced from the abyss of sleep, white-coated and amorphous, sharpening as Mary Kate awakened.

The bed in this room was a deeply luxurious feather mattress topped by chamomile-scented linen sheets and draped in costly curtains. A bowl of hot water and soft towels were constantly changed, as often as the fire was tended. The spacious room was appointed with gold and ivory accents, flocked French paper on the walls, pale yellow damask curtains hanging from the windows. It was luxurious, warm, and utterly welcoming. And at this moment, terrifying.

Mary Kate sat up in the massive four-poster bed, one hand pressed against her chest as if to urge her heart to slow its racing beat. She wondered at the desperate feeling of urgency she felt, this almost insane desire to assure herself that Archer St. John was well.

Her wrapper was a borrowed one, an item of clothing loaned by some unknown personage. Yet at this moment it did not matter how ill fitting it was. It was not her attire that halted her at the doorway, but the fact that circumstances had not altered since she'd slept.

94

She was a prisoner in this room. Her hand grasped the handle, but it didn't turn any easier than it had before. She leaned against the door, huffing out a breath. She flattened her hands against the painted and carved panels of the door as if to press through them, leaned her cheek against the gilded frames.

Help him. . . .

She could not. There was nothing she could do.

She turned, her back to the door, looking at her palatial prison. The resignation that had spread through her at the beginning of her imprisonment had hardened to become something else. Irritation? Anger?

There was a tinge of red on the horizon, like a streak of blood, showing bright and too glaring to her eye. Thunder crashed in the distance, a flick of lightning touched the ground, the air was chilled against her skin.

Help him. . . .

I can't do anything.

Help him. . . .

There is nothing I can do. Please. Go away.

For a second the room was illuminated in a blue-white glow, a perfect nimbus of unearthly brilliance. For an eternity of time measured in slices of seconds, the glare burned itself into her brain. Time stopped, motion ceased, even breathing was halted. Upon the floor, an Oriental rug faded in the glare of a thousand sunny days distilled to one moment. The bed that had cradled her body reflected the luminescence. A second passed, no more, until the sound of thunder exploded in her ears; the walls shuddered and then were still.

She nearly fell, so stunned was she by the experience. The tiny, colorless hairs on her arm bristled; even her eyebrows seemed bushier. The air seemed cleaner, somehow charged, alive.

Mary Kate pressed her hands against her ears, unwilling to admit that she felt the edge of fear, the terrifying tingle of it which made her want to run and hide in the armoire. Yet even there she would not be free of this taunt.

Help him. . . . He is in danger.

There was no duplicity in such a warning, no hesitation in the message. It stood still and gaunt in the morning light, awaiting her action.

Help him. . . .

"I cannot leave the room!" She felt the words rip from her throat.

A crack of thunder was her answer. The building seemed to shake, to tremble in response to the shudder of lightning striking the ground. Mary Kate fell back against the door, both hands outstretched as if for balance.

Help him. . . .

The feeling of desperation was building, a sensation of doom so pervasive that it made her want to cry out. She was silenced only by panic so strong it seemed bedrocked in her soul.

Help him. . . .

The door was solid, immutable. She turned and pounded her fists against the panels etched in gilt, felt the shiver of wood in response. Still it did not give, was not responsive to her sudden, overpowering terror. Both fists slammed against the fragile wood, a door built for privacy, not for defense. The sound was echoed in the thunder, nature's rage coupled with her own alarm.

Help him. . . . She needed no impetus now. The feeling had grown to become a force of its own. She had to get to him. Protect him. Save him. A feeling so great in its urgency that she didn't notice when her clenched hands became embedded with slivers of wood, so wickedly sharp that her skin was pierced. She didn't note the pain, nor the fact that blood dripped red upon the door, down her wrists, dotted the oaken boards beneath her feet.

All she knew was a blinding need to reassure herself he was safe.

When the door swung open, she almost cried in relief, only to find herself colliding with a body, a wall of flesh that stood between her and Archer, a barrier she must cross, defeat, conquer. Seconds later, she realized it was he.

Her hands pressed against his chest, unmindful that it was naked skin she touched, or that droplets of her own blood marked him. Nor was she content with passive reassurance. Her hands darted across his dressing gown, fingertips pressed against the balls of his shoulders as if to judge their strength, against the angle of his chin, down the expanse of his throat.

He would have gripped her wrists, pulled her away, but for the dazed, almost panicked look in her eyes. That, and the fact that silent tears wet her face.

"Tell me you're well," she demanded. Her hands patted his arms, palms flattened against his chest, eyes searched him from toes to tip of nose.

He nodded, then spoke, a link of language between them. "I am well. I promise."

"You're not hurt, then? Nor injured?"

"No. And I am no schoolboy, gone too long from home." Gently he reached out and grasped her roaming hands, a sudden necessary restraint. "And you are not my mother, to inquire as to my health, madam."

Her fingertips seemed to hold sensation trapped in them,

her frantic touch changing to become filled with tenderness, his skin a lure.

Her palms were bloodied, splinters were imbedded in her skin. He was marked by her blood, branded with the intimacy of it. He left her for a moment, went to the ewer, where he moistened a cloth, then returned to her side. He grasped both wrists, and with his fingertips, extracted the splinters. Then, in the absolute silence of the moment, he bathed her hands, wiping them over and over until all traces of the blood were gone.

Her hands trembled. It could be fear. Or something else. Some dark emotion that linked two people of divergent lives and pasts and doubtful futures. A feeling that betrayed its presence in the quivering of limbs and the softening of lips and the breathlessness of lungs. A dangerous emotion surely, but one she'd not felt in a long, long time. If ever, to such a degree.

His fingers traveled from her wrists to her elbows, as if to coax her into serenity, as if his touch had magical properties to heal. And with each stroke upon her skin, his breath grew tighter and hers more relaxed, a juxtaposition she could not help but notice.

He stood so close, a hovering cloud, darkly arresting, attired in nothing more than a deep blue silken dressing gown. She wanted to open it up and walk into its folds, stand against his naked body, rest her cheek upon his chest, place her arms around his waist. Supplicant and victim and penitent.

Instead, she watched him, half-cloaked in shadow, the dawn sky through her open window beginning to fully illuminate the room, sending streaks of watery light into the hallway where they stood, silenced by unbidden emotions and needs neither could voice.

How odd that he'd never frightened her. He was arrogant and quickly angered and capable of whittling wood with the sharpness of his words, yet, she'd never felt in fear of him.

To be this close to him was to sense all those qualities he held within himself, as if the essence of him expanded to allow her inside, to grant her a view of him few were privileged to see. She'd felt his anger, tasted his rebuke, sensed his pain and that one emotion that seemed to link them as they stood suspended between a world bathed in dawn and a house cloaked in night. Loneliness.

She'd been alone forever.

Her hands parted his dressing gown, pressed hard upon his chest as if to imprint the texture of his skin upon her palms. Her fingers combed through the hair of his chest, an intimate gesture more expected of a lover than a woman filled with fear.

Mary Kate blinked and it was as if the world became focused, her look one of confused awareness. Her face was flushed, she could feel the warmth upon her own cheeks.

She stood within the circle of his arms, holding on to his forearms as if for balance. The bed lay only feet from them, the sky was alight with dawn. The lure was there, passion had not disappeared, merely been forced down beneath caution.

She should move, compel her feet to step away. Certainly her hands should drop from their grip upon his arms. She should not ache to lean her head down upon his chest, should not wish to touch her lips to that expanse of hair upon it, riffle her fingers through it again.

She was not wanton, despite what others might say. Only one man had ever touched her, and that loving had left her with no thought to repeat it. Edwin had been a

man of cold disposition but warm inclination, the reason
he'd married her, Mary Kate was certain. Except that none
of his lovemaking had ever tempted her soul, or made her
hungry for it, as she was ravenous now, standing in the
embrace of a man she'd been commanded to guard.

By the ghost of his wife.

His breath was warm, strangely loud, a counterpart to
her heart's beating. She would have stepped back, but he
curled his fist in the fabric of her borrowed wrapper, pulled
her closer until not even a breath separated them. A dark
sensation flowed through her, a taste lingering on the tip
of her tongue, something forbidden and decadently expensive like chocolate. Strange sensations to have when he
stared at her with eyes that glittered with rage. And yet,
below the anger was another emotion, as disturbing and as
powerful. Desire. Potent, heady, as enticing as if he had
been overtly seductive, as if he coaxed her into his arms
with whispers of false promises she pretended to believe.
But he did not entreat, did not cajole, only remained like
a statue of purposeful intent, supremely, confidently male
and frighteningly alluring.

She should have pulled away, not placed both hands
upon his curled fist. Only a fool would smile at his look,
as if in gleeful acknowledgment of her daring.

"Are you my prize, then, for credulity?" His voice was
laced with sardonic amusement, a perfect counterpart to
the small smile that lifted the corners of his lips.

Her hands froze their uncertain movement, the gentle
stroking they'd begun. Archer St. John was not a fractious
kitten.

"Do I get to keep you if only I believe? Come now,"
he said as she pulled away, "don't look at me as if I'd
just murdered your best friend. But even that isn't too

much off the mark, is it, Mary Kate? Murder is exactly what I'm suspected of, and Alice is no doubt reveling in the knowledge that my reputation grows blacker each month she remains hidden.''

He pulled her back into his arms with so much force that Mary Kate nearly stumbled. The statue had come alive, been replaced by a fierce warrior. This man's anger was not coated with civility but was free flowing, unrestrained.

He thrust both hands into the hair at her temples, pressed against her skull as if he would crush her if she did not provide the answers he sought. She should have felt afraid, but she did not even flinch when he bent her back, forcing her into an arc. She reached out and grabbed his forearms for balance.

"It's almost worth the bargain, Mary Kate," he whispered. His lips nuzzled the curve of her ear then dipped to taste the flesh of her throat. She felt the edge of enameled teeth against her pulse, a delicate threat, unspoken warning.

"What is it you want from me?" he asked against her skin; the words seemed tactile, capable of granting sensation. Or was that only the brushing of his lips?

His hand moved to cover her throat, his face obscured her vision, his question buffeted her thoughts.

All she could offer him was the truth, pure, unadorned, perhaps too simplistic in the telling of it.

"Nothing."

The hand still twisted in her hair tightened while the other flattened against her throat. Did he seek to win her compliance by killing her then? For a second, she thought he might; the murderous fury in his eyes was threat enough. Then, slowly, his grip loosened, and he abruptly backed away, leaving her weaving as she stood.

She massaged her throat and glared at him, a remonstrance that seemed to have no effect upon Archer St. John at all. Instead, he reverted to being a statue again, one without remorse or compunction, evidently, to apologize.

"I was incorrect," she said, hating the fact that her voice sounded too timorous, almost feeble. "I do wish something from you." She backed away as a light seemed to glitter in his eyes, a beacon of some odd emotion whose origins she didn't care to explore.

"I very much want my freedom. I fervently wish to never again hear your wife's entreaties. And right this moment, I wish I had never spoken to your coachman."

Then she turned and walked into the Dawn Room, slamming the door in his face.

Chapter 15

"**A**re you all right, boy?"

Samuel Moresham watched as James picked himself off the ground. The bolt of lightning had come too close for comfort. Pinatar was restive this morning; he'd scented the mares, knew what this day would bring. Still, it wasn't like James to make that stupid mistake. The stallion's hooves had to be wrapped in batting, so that he wouldn't injure the mares in his excitement, but anyone who'd been around horses knew the job took three good men. Plus, the oncoming storm should have given him pause, if nothing else. But the lad hadn't his mind on his business. As usual, lately.

The stallion had retaliated by nearly spearing him to the ground with one of his iron-shod hooves. James had rolled just in time to avoid the blow.

"I'm all right." He stood, dusting himself off, out of range of the stallion who eyed him with wildly rolling eyes.

It was as plain as Pinatar's restive movements that the lad wasn't all right. He was as pale as death, with a tenseness about him that spoke of a sleepless night. Again.

It used to be that he'd slip down into the parlor of an

evening, play a bit of a ditty on the spinet. It was a pleasant sound, that, a calming one for a full day. Samuel had grown to expect it. But music had stopped a long time ago, along with James's attention to the details that could get him killed. It was as if the boy really didn't care whether he lived or died. And it was all Samuel's fault, wasn't it?

Samuel wrapped the length of leather around his gloved palm, then slipped it onto the hook mounted on the inside of the fence post. He sighed, heavily, thinking that this day had been coming for too long.

Why now, Samuel? Why, when too much time had passed and too many opportunities had been lost did he feel so compelled to finance the boy's love of music? Had it been those odd dreams he'd had for the past week, the ones that caused him to wake too early in his bed, staring at the ceiling and wondering at the very great grief he felt?

He'd heard Alice sobbing. He could almost see her, sitting beneath her favorite tree, her knees drawn up to her chin, hands clasped around her legs, her gaze fixed on something in the distance, her eyes welling up with tears. It was as if she were telling him that this was the right thing to do.

He'd awakened more than once with tears in his own eyes, certain that he would never see his beloved child again. She may be lost, but Samuel knew with a horrible certainty that she would never be found.

Maybe it was that. Maybe, still, the need for it stared him in the face and he could no longer ignore it. It was a time for reparations.

"Pinatar will wait, James," he said, clamping a hand over the younger man's shoulder. He was of slight build, was James, another trait from his mother. That and the music. How many times had he listened to Caroline sing and wondered why God had given an angel's voice to a woman with a sinner's heart. But then, the workings of God were beyond him. He had enough trouble trying to understand his fellow man.

"I'll not trick you into thinking this is an easy thing to say, boy, but I've been mulling it about long enough."

Samuel began walking to the edge of the paddock to where the pond glistened in the dawn light. The rain had stopped finally.

The two of them leaned against the fence, different men with a shared past. They were dissimilar in spirit, longings, and talents. Yet they were linked by circumstance and by the love of one woman, a secret love by one, a father's love by another.

"I'm willing to have you go and study music, if you will, lad."

Samuel knew that his blessing would have had the power to catapult James into single-minded joy a few years ago. It had been the boy's dream for as long as he could remember, to study as the great composers did. How many times had he heard James say that one of his greatest wishes was to sit in Vienna's Burgtheater, listening to the echoes of symphonies by Mozart or Haydn.

Now, however, his gift seemed oddly empty. Samuel felt like a general standing on a battleground soaked red with blood. A place of smoke and gore and laden with bodies and thick with the stench of death. What did it mean to declare victory when the cost was so great? What did it mean to send James to Vienna now?

Here, at Moresham Farms, the memories of Alice seemed so strong. Down that path, she had toddled as a child. There was the tree whose branches had hid her and

James when Cecily had called them for dinner. On that barn door, the two of them had swung and laughed until the hinges bent. They'd both been punished for that.

Would James feel as though he was being banished? Or that to leave here was to lose her, to banish all those memories he held tight in his heart?

At what price had he given the boy his freedom?

He turned and glanced at the man he'd always acknowledged as his son. Until that day two years ago, when he had been in his cups, flushed with success, pockets filled with winnings from the Derby at Epsom Downs. Then, whiskey had loosened his tongue, and he'd spilled his secrets like the coins he flipped at the barmaid.

In one night James had gone from son to bastard, a nudge from position and birth that Samuel suspected did not disturb him one whit.

"You'll need help in the winter." James smiled. It was a puny gesture at best.

"I can buy the services of men to help me."

"I'll stay for a while."

"You've got a gift lad. Don't let it go to spoil."

"I'll go in a month or two," James said then. Samuel hoped something would make him care by that time.

He wasn't altogether surprised by the reception his gift had inspired. After all, it was a paltry thing he offered James. Reparation for something that could never quite be made right.

Consanguinity. Wasn't that the fancy word that meant what they were? Brother and sister. He'd never worried about it, knowing what he did, but still, maybe he should have told James long before he did. Things might have changed.

Alice might not have married the Earl of Sanderhurst

after all. And then, perhaps she wouldn't have disappeared. And James wouldn't be looking the way he did, as if the life had flowed out of him.

He wished it could be different, but it was a wish he never voiced to another human being. Even now he could not say the words.

How long had James loved Alice? Forever?

And was that why Alice had disappeared?

Chapter 16

She was to be given the freedom of Sanderhurst.

This surprising admission was announced by a sweetly smiling young maid who did not look the least discomposed by stating it, nor did she appear to be rendered awkward by conversing with Archer St. John's prisoner, which led to two immediate conclusions on Mary Kate's part. Either the poor maid was extraordinarily simple, which might explain the curious vacuity of her smile, or this was not the first occasion in which Archer St. John had felt the necessity to imprison innocent females.

Yet if this was imprisonment, it had been kinder than freedom had been to Mary Kate. She'd been fed delicious meals, offered a selection of books from St. John's library, treated like a weary guest expected not to excel at any chore but that of resting. A curious respite for a woman who had always needed to work in order to feed herself, except when she had traded servitude for the chore of being Edwin's wife.

The door stood open, and she just on this side of it, wishing to take the first step to liberation and yet being curiously reluctant to do so. Mary Kate could not account for it, nor the feeling of trepidation as she stepped outside the room. She was the ugliest thing in this house.

Where had her attention been when St. John had dragged her up the stairs, that she couldn't recall the magnificent curved staircase trailing down to the first floor, rising two more floors above her? The walls were clad in silk the palest shade of yellow, like egg yolks frothed and creamy. A hall chest caught her eye; the dark wood was festooned with carvings, and brass handles in the shape of unicorns and dragons. At the end of the hall was mounted a floor-to-ceiling painting of a port, showing rows upon rows of ships and, behind them, the shadows of tall mountain peaks. In the foreground was the most beautiful sailing ship she'd ever seen, its hull painted deep blue, the brass of its rigging seeming to glint in the sun, the white sails puffed proud with wind. On its bow, the name *Fortunatus*.

Mary Kate held on to the banister as she descended the curve of staircase. Upon the landing she stopped, bathed in the wondrous colors of light filtering through a glorious stained-glass rendering of Saint George slaying the dragon. How long did she savor its beauty, stand bathed in the cascade of colors? It was like being showered in a rainbow, one crafted by an artisan's hand. She could have stood there longer, entranced by the craftsmanship that had created this magnificent secular picture, but she was too startled by the feeling that slipped over her, urging her down the remainder of the stairs.

It was a gentle tug, as though a child had grabbed her dress and pulled her onward toward a favorite place, one of games and laughter. So strong was this sensation that Mary Kate looked down at her skirt to ensure herself nothing was there, that it had not caught in the railing, that she had not torn a thread or raveled a hem.

At the foot of the stairs was a rather stiff-necked servant, attired in a severe black frock coat, black trousers, small boots. She would have taken him for an aristocrat had she not seen him when she arrived. She had served under majordomos before, and knew they emulated those they served, some with more autocracy than their employers. Did this rather austere-looking gentleman know her antecedents, suspect that she'd rarely been abovestairs in her position of servant? It seemed so, by his way of looking through her. She only nodded, a gesture that would have been as regal as his had she not been amused by the idiocy of it all. Still, she managed to stifle her laughter, settling instead for a smile.

She turned to the left, not questioning why she felt she must do so, entering a long, wide hallway. There were three doors down this hall. She chose the last one, turned the handle, pushed in the door.

Was this how heaven would look? Indigo blue silk was draped upon the walls, while floor-to-ceiling windows along one side of the room were framed in heavily embroidered blue and gold curtains, tied back by gold figurines of chubby cherubs, each holding flowing gilt ribbons. There was a carpet beneath her feet, an intricate design of fruits and flowers, each thread mellowed to a rich hue, the overall a muted palette of color. Above her head a fresco of blue sky dotted with white clouds made the room appear limitless, a sunlit valley of blue and gold created by man, into which he'd placed his greatest treasures.

Scattered about the room were several mahogany display cases. The first one contained a withered pouch made of leather. Mary Kate frowned at it, trailed her fingers over the hinge in the wood, but didn't lift the glass lid of the case. The second and the third were no more generous with their information, containing a baby's intricate knit cap and an illuminated manuscript that looked old and just as delicate. The fourth, however, contained a large jewel nestled on a blue velvet pillow. It was difficult to ascertain whether the gem was as brilliantly blue as it appeared, or if it simply mimicked the color of its background.

Mary Kate opened the lid of the case and picked up the jewel, holding it at eye level in front of the light streaming in through one window. She had heard of such things, diamonds and sapphires and such, worn by the king. Never had she thought to see such a gem, let alone hold it between two fingers like a child's marble. It glittered playfully, as if it drank in the light and then gave it back reluctantly. Aloft, it seemed simply pure, as the coldest of winter icicles are sometimes tinged blue.

She wiped it clean with the hem of her skirt and laid it back in its nest, a jewel of an egg.

Any other woman, Archer thought, watching her, would bedevil him to learn of its nearly priceless value, or wish it made into a bauble for her adornment. He suspected, however, that Mary Kate would never mention that she had seen it, never covet it.

From the gallery high above the room, he continued to watch her, intrigued by what fascinated her. She seemed less impressed by the leaded crystal bowl than the way its facets split light into iridescent bands of color. Twice he thought she would look up and see him; both times she traced the fragile band of light instead, entranced as a child spying her first rainbow.

He heard her laugh, and the sound of it, low and throaty, rendered him oddly lonely. He braced one shoulder against the wall, folded his arms, and continued to watch her.

Mary Kate. Even her name did not match her. It was

too solemn a name, too proper a name for her. She needed a name as outrageous as that cloud of orange hair, that creamy skin more often than not colored pink. She should have a name that bespoke her sortie into wickedness, the urge he'd seen in her eyes to go further, to dare more, to step outside herself. How odd that such a trait seemed muted beneath her appeal of innocence.

She was no more innocent than he was saintly.

This morning she had been terror-filled one moment, desperate, as frightened as a mother seeking a lost child. The next, a wanton, testing his restraint. He wanted to warn her that it was not safe to play such games with him. He'd been too long alone, too long without a mate, a companion, a lover.

She had been clad in a wrapper Alice had left behind, a garment sewn for a shorter woman of smaller stature, not one with flamboyant curves, whose chin could rest upon his shoulder. Her scent was sultry, something flesh-warmed, a hint of spice.

Did she know how much he had not wanted to heed the voice of warning, the whispers of restraint? Instead, he had allowed himself an instant of pushing against her, as if her softness had been created simply for this moment, and the pliancy of her flesh a pillow existing solely for his comfort. Their bodies touched at several places, bare toes, knees, hands. It was improvident, foolish, but simply, at the last, not enough. Archer wanted to back her against the door until it slammed against the wall. The immediacy of his need had shocked him; the violence of it should have alerted all those restraints put in place by social conditioning.

It had not been the time for lust, nor the place for it. Certainly not the woman. All a series of thoughts that echoed through his brain but were stopped by a wall of lust from reaching his loins. The heel of his hand had forced her jaw up, her mouth to raise to his. He had wanted to inhale her, first, absorb the breath she exhaled, be the air she required. Possession. A curious word to mark so primitive a feeling.

Instead, a breath had halted him. A quick inrush of air, a soft exhalation, a sound no louder than that of a feather dropping to the floor, and yet he heard it. Recognized, too, the excitement of it.

A woman of doubtful virtue.

Alice sent her.

The reminder had had the effect of slicing his skin open. The sharp pain of it, the searing aftertaste had rendered him not as angry as he'd hoped. Instead, he'd felt only tired, fatigued, as if all the sleepless nights he'd spent in the last year had finally made themselves felt.

A strange woman to want desperately. Or maybe not, he countered his own thoughts, watching her skirts furl around her ankles.

There was something about the child in her, a hope not easily doused, a spirit not easily conquered. With that freshness of attitude, she had handed him an impossibility and expected him to accept it. He could not, but he could, and did, appreciate the character that had crafted such a story. He wished, in a thoroughly implausible way, to be like a child with her, to supplant all the many duties he'd assumed over the years, the titles and occupations of a thoroughly adult man, and toss them aside for an hour, maybe more. He would play as a child with a companion, both of them draped in youth and joy as he had never been, even when young.

It was, however, a nicety of thought that would never find fruition in actuality. She was not a child, nor was she

innocent. She was a stranger with a secret purpose; he did
not doubt that it meant softening Alice's return to his life
in some way despite Mary Kate's protestations of ignorance.

"Do you do this often? Study your guests with such
purposeful intent?"

The words jolted him. He looked down at her, she stared
up at him, frozen in that moment by sunlight. She smiled.
It was charmingly done, without malice or ill-will and did
not chastise him for this morning's actions. He could not
help but return it, lured into truce by her openness.

"Who would not stand and stare at a woman playing
with rainbows?"

She didn't answer him, simply smiled that secretive
smile that women have used since the beginning of time
to entrance and warn at the same time.

"I would have thought you would seek the freshness of
a stroll upon the garden paths," he added.

"It looks like rain."

He ignored that lie. The sky was a cloudless blue. "Or
a tour, perhaps of the more public rooms of Sanderhurst."

"Is it a special place, this?"

All the time he'd been talking, he had walked the gallery, to the set of steps along the west wall. He descended
those with easy grace; he'd often hid here as a child, when
his mother had called and he'd not wished to answer, or
his father had beckoned and he had been too afraid to be
found.

Finally he was standing next to her, close enough to
inhale her scent had she been able to afford any. He could
not imagine her handkerchiefs reeking of attar of roses, or
oil of lilac. Perhaps something mixed with sandalwood, a

touch of the Orient, a hint of mystery. Not unlike the woman.

"Have I trespassed?" She looked around her; one hand lifted in the air and then was quickly pressed against her skirt.

"It is a family place, and most miss it. I am surprised you found it so easily." He stepped closer. "It was my favorite place as a child. I was forever lurking in its shadows and playing pirate on the gallery. I cannot tell you how many imaginary miscreants I forced to walk the plank." He looked up at the railing, a small smile wreathing his lips. "Are your hands better?" He extended his hand palm up, and she laid them both upon it. He inspected them carefully. No, other than a scratch or two, there was nothing to indicate they had bled so copiously.

"You are a surprising man, Archer St. John."

"In what way, Mary Kate Bennett?" His smile echoed her own, slightly teasing, infinitely gentle. That he could feel such did not startle him; that he could expose it so easily did.

"You have the fiercest scowl, yet you are blessed with the most gentle touch."

He dropped her hands and turned away. Did she never watch her words?

"Did you have no brothers or sisters with whom to play, that you would pretend to be a solitary pirate?"

He turned and smiled at her, and for all his words, it was not a sad smile. "I was the heir, and had no spare, if you will. My mother told me that she had done her duty to the St. John empire and my father was not welcome in her bed. Of course, she confessed such welcome relief only when I had attained my majority. But as a child, I still hoped for a sister or a brother and rubbed my magic rock and hoped and hoped.''

She remained silent, secrets misting in her eyes, but even the look was veiled from him as she turned away. She took a few steps to the display case holding the Pemberton diamond, but then surprised him as she ignored it for the baby's cap.

"It is said to have belonged to Henry the Eighth," he said easily. "An ancestor was present at his birth and was rumored to have procured many a young maiden for the young Harry." He came and stood beside her again, not crowding her, but not allowing her to remain far from his side. "In turn, he was quite generous to the St. John family."

"And you hold his cap in high esteem." There was that smile again on her lips. He wondered what thought prompted it. "And the pouch? Does that hold a history, too?"

"The first St. John's purse, still rife with the scent of sandalwood. It seemed a fitting thing to honor both the source of our income and our ancestor."

She turned and walked toward another case. He smiled, but did not join her. "You have not asked about the diamond."

"Since you have not believed most of my utterances, St. John, I doubt you would hold much credence in my answer."

"I will suspend my disbelief for the moment."

"I have no love for jewels, or anything so valuable that I must be afraid of losing it."

He opened the display case and fingered the stone she'd earlier held up to the light. "This was the stone I wished upon," he said softly, his voice not that of a man, but of a child, enraptured by the thought of magic. "At least until my father caught me touching it one day."

He said nothing more.

"What did he do?"

He returned the stone to its case, then glanced at her. "Beat me so hard I could not stand for a week. I was not, you see, a favorite of his. But then, I was his only child. I can only wonder what he would have done had he another upon which to practice." The look he slanted her was filled with sardonic humor. "Even my mother could not tolerate him, and she shows an affinity for most people."

"And so you've been taught there is a price to pay for everything."

"How astute of you to realize that. A fellow student, are you, Mary Kate? What or who has taught you so well?"

"You tell me of your childhood, in exchange for a secret of mine, then?" Her smile chastised him at the same time it teased. "Very well. I am the only girl among ten children. You used to wish for a sibling; I wanted simply to be noticed among the ones I had."

"And yet you claim no kin, or had you forgotten that little bit of whimsy?"

There was a look on her face, one closed and shuttered through which he could not see a peek of light. It was as if all her secrets were carefully tucked in and properly buttoned up, hidden.

"You will not tell me, will you? Your aim is to keep me wondering about you, while you cloak yourself in an aura of mystery."

"To what purpose? To elongate my imprisonment here? To appear as an object of pathos? Or to separate you from

your money? I could never hope to be as conniving as you
wish me to be.'' She shook her head, as if to chastise him
for the error of his thoughts. ''My family left me, St. John.
That is all. There is no more of the story but that.''

''And yet you've a brother.''

''Who does not want me in his life.'' The words were
said softly. She lifted her lashes to find him studying her.

''Why do I have the feeling you've taken on a quest?''
he asked softly. ''You will not rest until you've been
spurned by all your kin, is that it?''

''Is wanting a family such a horrible thing?''

''I'd gladly give you part of mine. I doubt they'd want
you, though, as you are without sustenance to support
them. They're a greedy bunch, the St. Johns.'' A smile
brushed his lips and then was gone, leaving only a shadow
of humor, nothing more.

''Then why is this house so silent? You could house
half of London here.''

''I like my quiet, madam, and my life at Sanderhurst.''
He strode to one of the floor-to-ceiling windows, as if to
acquaint himself with a new view, one not seen before.
''You are its first intrusion.''

''Am I? Or was Alice?''

He turned and stared at her as if he could not quite
believe what she had said. ''By God, I was right, you are
too cheeky for servitude. How many times were you
sacked?''

''Never. The men kept me around to paw me if they
could, their wives discovered I worked too hard to dismiss.''

''And did you give them as much grief as you give me,
a starched reprimand and intrusive questions?'' He fisted

the edge of the curtains, turning away from the sight of her dappled by sunlight.

"You would not believe me if I admitted to being quiet and demure, would you?"

His laughter was easily coaxed from him by such an outrageous statement. He walked back to where she stood, alight in a beam of sunlight. "I think that it would be a great pity to dampen your spirit," he said softly. "It's best to try to avoid servitude if that's what it did to you. Is that why you married, or was it for love?"

"If I tell you, will you answer my question? You have not, you know." Her smile joined his. It seemed to Archer that they were doing a little too much of that for a proper prisoner and jailer. But she was not a proper prisoner, Mary Kate Bennett of the servant class, and he was acting far too absorbed for a jailer.

"About Alice? Do you not know everything there is to know? Or has she not whispered into your ear that she was miserable here, that she chose not to be a chatelaine as much as guest?"

She moved beside him, stared down into the case housing the priceless diamond. The glitter in her eyes was no less brilliant.

"How could you not be happy in this place? It is like a magical castle."

"Alas, as far as Alice's thoughts, it was peopled not with a prince, but a troll." Her quick look of compassion seemed too poignant to tolerate. He moved back to the window.

"Some people thought I was a fool to marry a man so much my senior," she said. "But he was kind to me at a time I needed kindness."

"And so you believed yourself in love."

"No." She looked over at him. He wondered how eyes could be so deep they mimicked the great oceans. "I did not believe myself in love. But I found that I could respect him."

"But you never came to love him? Not even for his prosperity and his generosity?"

"How did you know he was prosperous?"

"It is a story of mankind, Mary Kate. The old ones marry the young ones, tempting not with brawn but with bills. And was your aged husband kind and generous?"

A look crossed her face, made shallow the depths of her eyes. Why did he feel as if he could see the edge of her soul captured there? It seemed less manipulative than sad at that moment.

"He was as kind as he knew how to be." Her look changed, became almost accusatory. "But I do not regret my marriage, or wanting to be better than I was born. Is it so terrible to want more out of life than emptying chamber pots all day?"

"Or being pinched by farmers?" He smiled and she seemed bemused by his refusal to be coaxed into argument.

"They never managed more than once," she said, an unholy look of mirth crossing her features.

It was an unsettling notion for Archer to realize he was no better than the besotted cherubs plastered upon the ceiling, eternally enfolded in joy and captured by enchantment.

When she left the room, he didn't bother following her. He'd given her the freedom of Sanderhurst for more than one reason, less compassion about her imprisonment than a test of her intentions. He'd wanted to see if Mary Kate would try to leave. What would she attempt to take as a prize? Both questions had been answered in the way she'd replaced the blue diamond in its case. And even more so, Archer, by the warmth you feel for her?

Don't be an idiot, man. She's a luscious morsel, that's true. And perhaps she does have a winsome sense of humor. And coaxes you into divulging your soul, you daft loon. Strange, he should feel more invaded by her gentle questions, if not his surprising responses. She was insidious. No, too damn charming, Archer.

Still, he went to her room and looked about, certain there was something to prove her false. Instead, there were few personal effects, nothing in her reticule but a balled up handkerchief, and two farthings.

On the table beside her bed was a thin, leather-bound book he'd sent to her, gathered up among the others. She'd not scolded him for his daring, he thought as he opened *Elegies,* but had responded with a gracious note of thanks. Her penmanship was copperplate, correct and flowing in its perfect implementation. He had found himself first entranced by the execution of her *e*'s, the furling of her capitals. Then the only emotion he'd felt was anger that he had allowed himself to fall victim to a woman's simple allure. The book fell open to a much-read page. *License my roving hands, and let them go, Before, behind, between, above, below.* So his guest was a wanton at heart, he thought as he replaced the book as he'd found it.

In the armoire was a small carpetbag, nearly threadbare on the bottom, containing a chemise with yellowing lace, a silver-backed brush that looked to be old, and a pair of stockings carefully folded. On the shelf sat her bonnet, and hanging from the hooks were her nightgown, the wrapper, blue cloak, and two dresses as identically ugly as the one Mary Kate currently wore.

There was nothing in the pitifully few belongings to link her to Alice. Nothing to indicate that her life had been anything but what he'd suspected it to have been, hard work flavored by slices of tragedy.

Money would be reason enough to entice Mary Kate Bennett to play this role, a thought that did not resonate as purely as he'd expected. It was too simple an explanation.

What kind of woman was she, who could dismiss the sight of the rarest of blue diamonds and yet dance with light as if it had been created to be her companion? One who believed in ghosts and spirits and came to protect him.

He found himself wanting to believe her, but being forced upon a precipice at sword point did not mean that the participant truly wished to jump. He would walk as close to the edge as he could, but when she extended her hand and asked him to fly with her, his natural commonsense logic occupied the forefront of his mind. His wish to believe her was a confession he would make to himself but no one else. He had learned over the years to capture his thoughts and errant musings and not divulge them to a soul; it made for less fodder for gossip and less ammunition for those who wished him ill.

But as this quiet moment lengthened, a question stepped forth he'd been pretending not to hear, its stridency insisting, finally, that he pay heed to it. What if she was telling him the truth? And if she truly did not know where Alice was, then what did that mean?

The painting was where anyone would expect it to be, except, of course, that Mary Kate had not known there was such a thing as the Wives' Gallery. Alice was, after all, a St. John wife, the last in a seemingly endless line of good and bad portraiture.

How did she know it was Alice? The same way she had known that walking through this doorway would bring her here, led to this place and this painting. Because she had dreamed of occupying that body while staring full-faced at herself in the mirror, had felt the movement of those hands.

Alice stared out at her from a scene of bucolic beauty. She sat upon a carpet of green grass; behind her, Sanderhurst. The house was a vast sprawling place crafted from bricks faded to the color of old gold. It rose three stories, each floor bedecked with tall, slim windows that reflected the pink and yellow of the eastern sky. Above each window was a heavily carved lintel depicting grinning gargoyles. Beside Alice was a basket of squirming spaniel puppies, one of them trapped forever upon the gentle cushion of her lap.

Pretty ringlets of blond hair framed the sides of a heart-shaped, winsome-looking face. The rest of Alice's hair was caught back in a ribbon adorned with mauve roses and sprigs of greenery. There was a smile on her bow-shaped lips, a comforting, placid type of smile one found in portraits of this type, but there was no answering expression in the azure of Alice's eyes. The absence of emotion revealed either the artist's talent or lack of it.

It was only Mary Kate's imagination that placed Alice standing beside her, of course. Only conjecture that made her note that Alice was much shorter than she was, so much smaller. She seemed ethereal, a loveliness not simply of the flesh, but a goodness of the soul. In a second the impression was gone, and only the portrait remained, a heritage of mystery.

Who are you, Alice? What did you want from life? What dreams did you have? Was living here so horrible for you?

Mary Kate folded her arms around her waist and stared at the portrait. Perhaps if she looked at it long enough, she could reason behind the oils and canvas enough to the soul of the person who stared back at her.

Why did you leave him for a lover? How could you inflict such pain? Did you hate Archer that much? Or love someone else far more? What happened to you?

And perhaps the most important question of them all: *Why me, Alice?*

Chapter 17

Bernie solved the problem of transportation by buying a new coach and four within two days of arriving in London. It truly was a bother having to wait upon a hired hack, and she had never been known for her patience. It was bad enough that it would be days until her things followed her, in the series of wagons needed to transport all the many possessions she'd accumulated over the years.

Still, it was rather nice to be a St. John, even if she'd paid for the privilege of it through nine ghastly years being married to Archer's father. The money was a convenience, even though she could quite well do without the subservience. She'd never understood how some people could acquaint being rich with being good. She was not at all as nice a person as she could be, even though she tried not to be a despot. But she certainly wasn't as kind as some people she knew and she had the devil's own wit when something tickled her and heaven itself knew that she liked her comfits a bit much and the touch of a handsome man more than was seemly. But the way she was bowed and scraped to was almost as if she were a religious icon, or some celestial virgin come down from Mount Olympus.

Did celestial virgins live at Mount Olympus? Never mind, it was a strange and errant thought, but it had managed to take her mind from the toadying of the firm that managed her affairs quite credibly, for all they kowtowed. It gave her a headache.

She obtained a promise that they would not divulge her presence in England to Archer or any of their grasping relatives, and managed to seem decorous and matronly and charming as she bid them a long-awaited good-bye and headed north out of London two days past her tolerance level.

She leaned back against the padded interior of her new coach, tried to ignore the rather noxious scent of lacquer and the even more pungent one of horse, and pretended she was aboard ship, the swaying simply the ebb and flow of tide.

The remainder of her journey had been lonely for the most part. Dear Matthew had left the ship at some port or another and despite her wishing for it, there had been none to take his place. There had been a mother and a daughter, both puny-faced creatures terrified of venturing out of doors, lest they get a touch of the sun, and an old, bearded gentleman who had kept to his cabin for the remainder of the voyage. Lumbago, she'd heard the cook say, as he'd taken a pot of stew to the man.

Another thing about a St. John ship, they were fed well. She pulled the waistband of her skirt loose with one finger. Such inactivity as she was forced to endure did not bode well for the remainder of her dresses.

She would be at Sanderhurst soon, and then she would take walks along the park, enjoy the wintered gardens. Pity, when she'd left the lower hemisphere, it had been winter, and she'd sailed a few months only to reach winter again.

Oh well, she'd just have to find some way to stay warm, she thought, and smiled.

"Is this where you putter about all day, Archer?" Mary Kate's head was tilted back to absorb the wonder of the structure, her eyes wide as she scanned the sunlit expanse of glass. There were thousands of panes arching high overhead, surrounding them on four sides. Walls of clear glass. A house of crystal enveloping all the lovely green plants.

It smelled of the forest after rain, when all the scents seemed to have been lifted into the air, warm, rich earth, decaying leaves, the fecundity of nature. Except that here there was no riotous pattern of leaves on the earthen floor, no dappled sunlight, no chattering forest creatures, not a sound of a babbling brook. There was order and regimen and nature being harnessed by man, a curiously sad place for all its wealth of green, for all its glad profusion of growth.

He did not look happy to see her, she noted, but then, he rarely did. His ominous thundercloud expression had muted over the last few days to a mere frown. Today, however, he had unearthed the expression, and it made him formidable indeed.

Yet some places were meant to be explored, and some people were meant to be bedeviled.

She strolled nonchalantly toward him, admiring the picture he presented standing in a shaft of sunlight. Some men are defined by their clothing while others define themselves regardless of their attire. Even with his shirtsleeves rolled up, black gloves to his elbows, collar undone and discarded, a stained tradesman's apron covering the rest of him, Archer St. John appeared noble, haughty, and at this moment, aristocratically irritated.

"This place is not accessible to you, madam. I have given you the freedom from your room, it does not mean you are allowed to roam at will."

"You act as if my freedom were something for you to grant, Archer. Is this a secret place?" She looked about her, knowing that her very presence discomfited him.

"It is my laboratory, madam."

"A laboratory?"

"Quite so." Was it possible for words to be so sharp they could cut glass? If so, she thought Archer St. John should be wary. The tone of his voice rendered him vulnerable in this place crafted of sparkling panes.

"You dabble in growing things, Archer?"

"I do not 'dabble,' as you would say. Nor is my work in the glasshouse up for speculation or comment."

"Which means, I presume, that you will say nothing further, only go about with that pursed look on your lips, leaving me to either apologize or pretend it did not happen."

"I would appreciate it, in the future, if you would restrict your explorations to the public venues. There is nothing of interest for you here, madam."

"Except for you, Archer. You are perhaps the most fascinating part of Sanderhurst."

She smiled at his look. It was such a combination of startlement and something else, more fierce, more quickly masked, that it piqued both her curiosity and a growing sense of daring.

She'd found the structure quite readily. One of the maids had passed along her query to Jonathan, the lordly-looking majordomo who was responsible, Mary Kate suspected, for

the earl's household running so smoothly. Jonathan had
not demurred at directing her to the earl's laboratory, had
only glanced at her consideringly before leading her here.

Strange, how she'd never thought of plants being considered scientific before. Evidently, however, that's exactly
what they were. As she followed Archer, she passed row
upon row of delicate-looking seedlings, all tagged with
long Latin names. Some were no longer than her thumb,
some had been transplanted to large clay pots sitting beneath something that looked like the nozzle from a watering can. As she walked past one of them, it gurgled, then
emitted a fine spray over the plant.

She closed her eyes, raised her face to the cloud of mist.
It felt as if a thousand little darts were tickling her skin.
She smiled, then opened her eyes, to find Archer St. John
looking at her with more than his usual stoic concern. The
mask had dropped for an instant, to reveal the man behind
the indifference. A man whose look empowered her not to
step back or forward, but to remain trapped in the sheer
web of it.

There was nothing about his stare to indicate indelicacy,
but Mary Kate had the impression of it, nonetheless. A
promise of pleasure, a hint at something enigmatic and
delicious and thoroughly unknown to her. Some emotion,
neither fear nor compassion, lodged at the back of her
throat, slid down into her body where it warmed what it
touched.

And then it was over. Disappeared in the flash of a
smile, a release from a silent bond. The warmth remained
in her body, aching, rendering her breathless, but the real
man lay hidden once again, ensnared behind indifference,
perhaps never glimpsed at all.

"Hardly simple gardening, Mrs. Bennett. I take my work very seriously."

"You may call me Mary Kate, you know. I've already addressed you as Archer."

"I know." Was that disapproval in his voice? What a paradox he was, that he would make her captive on one hand and censure her on manners the next.

"I take it you do not espouse egalitarian principles?"

One eyebrow winged skyward. "Do you often go about saying exactly what you think with such regularity, Mary Kate? I can assure you, while the cows may not mind, you are certain to have difficulty being employed with that habit."

She smiled at the use of her name, recognizing a concession when she heard one. She trailed her fingers over the fronds of a delicate-looking fern, wondering if he wished the truth or a proper type of answer. Undoubtedly the latter, but their relationship had been steeped in an odd sort of honesty from the beginning. What difference did it make now?

"I have hoarded my words for a lifetime, Archer. Been what people expected me to be. I've discovered that the most difficult thing about living has been to find out first who you are and then how to act that way. You feel about for it, like searching for a misplaced shoe in the dark. No one can tell you how to be yourself. It's not written anywhere. And no, I've not often told others what I'm thinking. It's a habit of relatively few days, in fact."

He said nothing to her confession. Instead, he led her into the section he'd apportioned for his work space, for the grafting of new plants, the bifurcation of others. Against one wall was a cage constructed of glass. When it captured her attention, he turned and watched her, explaining its purpose.

"It's the damping-off area. It's for those seedlings that contract a fungus."

"What happens to them?"

"They mostly die," he said.

"But why keep them here?"

"Because they might live."

She turned and watched him, the way he studied his own specimens, with interest and something akin to hope.

"What else do you do here, Archer?"

"I grow things," he answered, the glint in his eye diverting her attention only slightly from his voice. It sounded like wickedness might, if given speech, a ribbon of taffy, colored dark and silky. "Plants that other people say cannot grow in England."

He divested himself of the elbow-length gloves with some degree of difficulty. He opened another door, beckoning her into the damp brightness. Torches lined the high ceiling, scorch marks attesting to their frequent use. The humidity was kept constant by the sprinkling system similar to that used in the adjoining room.

He led her to an odd-looking tree alongside the wall. It had simple leaves and small white flowers arranged in a convex cluster.

"It's the *Pimenta dioica*," he explained, touching one of the leaves with the most delicate of strokes. "When the berries are nearly ripe, they're dried and used as a spice." He opened a glass jar retrieved from an upper shelf and dipped one finger inside. He held his coated finger close to her mouth, watching her face as he did so. *Taste it,* his words said. *Taste me,* the gesture.

"They call it allspice," he said, gently brushing his finger against her bottom lip. A speck of spice clung to her lip, impetus to probe her mouth, push it gently inside.

Her tongue swished against his finger, savored the strong flavor, cinnamon, cloves, something melded together and yet not quite the same. His finger emerged, wet, cleaned, danced around her mouth as if to spread the taste. Where it had been was left numbed, pungent, damp.

"I am experimenting with a species of laurel you might recognize." He uncapped another glass jar, and the odor of cinnamon wafted from it.

She drew back, a smile dusting her face, grateful that he'd chosen not to repeat his earlier action. Her heart still beat so heavily Mary Kate was surprised he did not comment upon the sound.

Another jar opened; this time a viscous liquid, almost an oil, lay inside. He only waved it in front of her. She nearly choked.

"Potent, is it not? It's camphor oil. I've been told that physicians advise their patients to inhale it."

"Why?" Her eyes were still watering.

His grin was almost boyish. "Indeed, why? But that is perhaps the magic of it."

"I'd rather inhale the cinnamon, thank you."

"Or the allspice?" A man's smile this time.

She evaded answering by leaving the room, pretending to study one of the orchids, with its large, papery stem and fragrant blooms.

"That is an acidanthera," he said softly, "one of my imports from Africa. You might consider it another trial of mine, to see if I can induce flowering from something so tropical. I confess that it is most probably an ego-induced experiment, one which has an equal chance of succeeding or failing admirably."

"You have such diverse interests, such strange ones for a landowner."

"Landowner, shipbuilder, silversmith, spice merchant. But surely you knew the extent of my wealth and its headwaters. The St. Johns have been in business since the thirteenth century, Mary Kate. Nearly five centuries of being spice merchants have given us enough wealth that not even the most profligate St. John can spend it all. I should know, I support most of them."

She said nothing as he moved to another strange-looking plant in a room devoted to them, plucked a small, oval fruit from its lower branches.

"*Pouteria campechiana,*" he said, hefting the fruit in one hand. From somewhere he'd acquired a small paring knife. He slit into the fruit, which emitted a musky odor, not unpleasant, simply different. Even that motion was done with grace, an odd thing to think of such a large man.

Yet there was something about Archer St. John that made one think he was beyond such plebeian things as clumsiness and less-than-perfect grace. Who was he, this man so brightly lit by the sun that he appeared luminous, either an infernally simple man or one whose complexities were such that she could never possibly understand him? Which was he?

He handed her a sliver of fruit, most properly, and as she reached out two fingers to slip it from his palm, Mary Kate wondered what she would have done if he'd attempted to feed it to her again.

"It's very sweet," she said, nibbling on the fruit.

"Eggfruit. An odd name, don't you think, for something so sweet? But then again, man labels, nature enables."

"Is this, too, something best grown not in England?"

"New Spain," he said, an almost triumphant look appearing on a face more given to frowns.

She smiled back at him, charmed by his success. Why did she pretend that it was his protection that was so much on her mind? She had not sought him out simply because a whispered voice had entreated her to do so. She had wished his presence because there was something about him that fascinated her, lured her to the edge of propriety.

"So you come from a line of spice merchants?"

"Even pirates, if you wish." He smiled suddenly, and there was something devilish about it, an upturn of lip, a sweet mischief in the glint of an eye. He could charm the elves from behind a toadstool.

"Have you ever heard of the Radanites?" At the shake of her head, he sobered. "They were Jewish traveling merchants, the only avenue of international trade during the eleventh and thirteenth centuries. While the Crusades were pitting Christian against Muslim, the Radanites transported various commodities across both lines. Wool, Frankish swords, furs, all went out toward the Orient, while they returned to Europe with pearls, precious stones, and spices. My ancestor discovered that holy war was not as lucrative as using the Radanites' trade routes. Unfortunately, in addition to those commodities, however, he was rumored to have also dabbled in the white slave trade and providing eunuchs to guard them."

"How absolutely awful."

"You do not look horrified, Mary Kate. Only fascinated. Shall I summon some ancestral trait and measure your worth? I suspect that you would cost a bagful of gold to own. But then, that is, no doubt, what Alice has promised you."

He wiped his hands dry, turned and busied himself with

the arrangement of his tools. A scalpel, such as a surgeon might use, a pegging awl altered for his use with delicate stems, a grafting spreader, an assortment of delicate instruments designed and crafted from his specifications.

"Surely you are not wounded by the truth, Mary Kate," he said, not turning.

"I am merely wondering if now is the time to pose the question I would ask of you."

"What now?" He threw down the toweling he used to dry the last of the instruments, turned.

He was too close, enraged, goaded, devoid of that utterly smooth civility, that politeness of his that had previously tamped down emotion. The man who faced her now was filled with it, brimming over with it, churning with it.

"Why did my wife choose another? Why did she leave me? Why could I not love her enough, or give her enough, or promise her enough to entice her to stay? A title, a fortune she could not spend in a lifetime, yet not enough inducements to remain with her husband. Is that the question you are going to ask?"

A moment passed, then another.

"No, it wasn't. Not really." She toyed with the edge of a leaf, the delicate browning of it something nature meant, not a sign of disease or neglect.

"Then what is it?"

She looked up at him, shyness vying with daring. "Will you kiss me?"

Chapter 18

"**W**ill you kiss me?"
Could she really control her physical responses so adeptly? Or was the blush that grew rosier on her cheeks a true sign of emotion?

"My husband never kissed me. Not the way I think it could be done. No other man has ever touched me."

The words tumbled so reluctantly from her lips that they bore the imprint of truth on their backsides. He did not want truth from her, or to witness the slow blush that crept inexorably over her cheeks. He did not want to experience *her* in the way she offered herself up for his delectation, a redheaded nymph with the soul of a harlot and the naughtiness of a smiling cherub.

He wanted to tell her that her voice should not be that tremulous. It indicated virgins unaware, a maiden's first response, the innocence of spring. She should, instead, if she insisted upon playing a role, emulate the women of the demimonde, lush and experienced and willing.

And yet she offered a dare. Come play with me. A taunt any sane man would accept. Still, there was the feeling that such experimentation would border on danger, a slight slip and he would be falling. Closer and closer into what?

A pit of such confusion that he would forever wallow in it.

Who was she? Erstwhile nymph, playmate, seductress, or something even more elusive? A woman with daring words and longing in her eyes who wanted to play in passion for the sake of it, to taste a kiss and know its power.

He was a fool to think she was that simple. Yet he came closer, drawn by the scent of her, the lulling quietness of her, standing there waiting for his judgment. Would it be no? Adult, wise, restrained, civil. Yes? A child's answer, a promise of delight, if for but a moment, improvident, even slightly wicked.

A smile wreathed his mouth, a look in his eyes of such intent perusal it held Mary Kate in place. "You would experiment, then, with me."

A finger reached out and stroked her lip. There was no spice to lure the taste of her tongue, only the taste of his flesh. He smiled as she flushed again, rendered warm by the look in his eyes, that touch of gaze that lingered and lured and beckoned all at once.

He bent closer, almost brushed his mouth against her lips, but pulled a breath's length away. Gentle fingers trailed against the edge of her chin, traced down her throat, back up again to fondle a tender lobe of ear.

"Did Alice tell you I was so easily coaxed from sanity, then?"

She blinked open her eyes, stared at him. Only the greatest of actresses could mimic that air of confusion, he thought.

"I confess to being adulterous to my wife, Mary Kate," he said, almost lazily, the finger now threading through the tendrils of hair at her temple. What an odd color it was, how bright and glorious. So must the first dawn have appeared, flaming orange light. "But my deed was performed only after my wife demonstrated her preference for another's bed," he whispered, his lips lured closer to the absolute perfection of her skin. Soft, so soft. "And long after she left me for another. Why, though, do I think it would be disastrous to bed you, Mary Kate?"

"I but wished for a kiss." Soft whimper of words. His hands pressed against her skull on either side of her face, his fingers spread through the glorious disarray of her hair. One by one the pins fell free, her hair tumbled loose around his insistent fingers.

"Ah, but, Mary Kate, icing is not a substitute for cake."

In a locked room at the end of the east hall, close to the kitchens, was the spicery, where they kept the household flavorings used for his personal meals. Coriander, cumin, cardamom, pepper, paprika, were all packed in carefully sealed storage jars, side by side with chili powder, curry, turmeric, mace, cinnamon, ginger, nutmeg, cloves. The currency of the St. John empire.

Yet the scent of Mary Kate was something he'd only imagined before, the delicate bouquet of woman, exquisitely gentle yet lingering, some elusive fragrance that imparted knowledge at the same time it hinted of mystery. He breathed it in as he edged closer, victor to the prey, yet feeling curiously defeated by her silence, her tentative eagerness.

Her eyes were open, steady on his, the look in them setting his body on fire. It was as if she kissed him in her mind, her lips pillow-soft and swollen, her tongue dueling with his, his own mouth greedy and voracious and feeding on her.

All this, before he'd touched her.

"Did Alice send you as consolation, then, Mary Kate?

A prize in recompense for the good name she stole from me? Do I get to keep you instead of my faithless wife?'' It was not the first time he'd asked her.

She'd no chance to answer before he laid his lips gently on hers. Gentle intimacy, acquaintance. So might a carnivore bestow a last caress upon his prey before the final killing stroke. She tasted of allspice and Mary Kate.

Her lips were soft and full, slightly moist. It was like sampling the most forbidden fruit; a dart of tongue upon her mouth was hardly enough. He wanted to nibble at her, devour her in a way that was feverishly carnal. He wanted her to be able to taste him on her lips tomorrow.

His thumbs angled beneath her jaw to raise her face more conveniently, offer her as sacrifice to the hot tongue separating her lips. He met her lips with his own, felt hers part immediately, offering haven for his breath, capitulation for his invasion.

She made a low humming sound, a vocal appreciation one might make when being treated to a delectable morsel of sweetmeat, a piquant flavor of cherries in syrup, a bite of rare citrus. Archer would have smiled at the sound of it, had he not been tempted to nibble at her with a little less delicacy and more rapaciousness. She tempted him to the borders of his restraint. Virgin, no; neophyte? He no longer knew or cared.

He came to know her, in the way lovers recognize each other, the startling simplicity of the taste of inner lip, the corner of a mouth, the texture of soft flesh and enameled teeth. He explored her, the way he delved his own conscience. And learned her mouth, her lips, her breath, the way he knew himself.

Finally he drew away, again a breath's distance, enough to measure the dazed look in forest green eyes, yet close enough to stroke a tongue against her lips as if to cool them. She made a sound like a sob, a tiny protesting sound that caused him to shut his eyes and pull her head against his chest.

The strength of his arousal was so great it hurt, pain that both pleasured and demanded. His blood beat in time to its call, his breath sliced through his chest, every muscle readied itself for penetration. He was no rutting animal, no creature of simple needs devoid of intellect. Yet this moment, all his senses were alert; a mating ritual as old as mankind demanded he ease himself in her, unclasp the fists she made upon his shirted chest and place those hands, instead, on his bare skin. She would use her nails upon him; he would mark her with his mouth. She would be warm and wet and welcoming, a fitting vessel for the seed his body ached to disgorge.

Instead, he stepped back. Away.

"Was that all you wanted, Mary Kate? A kiss?"

Her eyes were wide, her lower lip being delightfully restrained by those delicate white teeth. He wanted to place his mouth on hers, tenderly anoint that spot with his tongue, skim her lips. He wanted, in a way so unlike him, to breathe his wants and needs into her, so that his words would be part of her breath, part of her very blood.

He had no doubt this moment was his, because for all the wide and fearful eyes, for all the wonder in those magnificent eyes, she had not run from the room. She did not put her hands up to brace him away from her, not even when he reached out and cupped both her elbows with his palms, drawing her back into his embrace. Only a tiny whimper escaped her lips, but it was not a protest as much as it was a sound of recognition.

He felt like a wolf, starved and lean from a long, famined winter, and she stood docile within his arms, a curvaceous lamb, her blood warm and pounding, rending him almost heady with hunger. He wanted to cover Mary Kate the way a wolf devours its prey. Not with greed or malice, but simply for survival. He felt that if he were denied her, if he could not assuage this ravenous need with her flesh, he would starve. To the death.

He bent and placed his lips on her neck, where the blood beat heavy and strong. She sighed, an open exhalation of surrender, a sound so welcome to his famished body that he smiled at the sound of it. His hands left her elbows, dropping to her waist, carefully corseted and protected by whalebone and lace.

"You are a paradox, Mary Kate," he whispered against her skin. "You have the hair of a strumpet and the boning of a spinster. You are tightly buttoned against sin, and yet your nipples are like tin bullets against my chest. Which is the real you, I wonder?"

He did not give her a chance to answer, swallowing her words in the open cavern of his mouth. It was not a gentle kiss, nor one of domination. It lured and beckoned and promised such sweet joy that it almost burned him.

He pushed her away slightly, holding her arms out oddly with both hands cupped at their elbows. She felt like a rag doll supported by string, a contorted puppet awaiting a master hand.

He studied her as if she were a great work of art, noting the warm flush of her cheeks, the eyes with their confused and helpless expression, as if passion were a strange emotion felt rarely in her life. She looked away as he watched her, her flush deepening, the tendrils of her hair lying mussed around her face an apt match for her blush. He noted, too, her captivation in his hands, the fact she had not moved nor seemingly wished to.

Yet appearances were not to be trusted, especially with Mary Kate Bennett.

"If I led you to my chamber now, would you go? But of course you would. It's part of the game, isn't it?" He stepped back, his smile muted. "The question is, do you go there on your own, or because Alice wished it of you?"

Mary Kate flung open the window, breathed in the cold night air. She felt smothered in the folds of her nightgown. It was as if the air of her bedchamber was too warm, humid, so thick that she could almost feel it as it entered her lungs How silly. It was not the air that felt sluggish, but the beat of her own blood.

She stood at the window for long moments, concentrating on night sounds, the crying of some nocturnal bird, a denuded branch brushing against its neighbor, the sough of winter wind as it raced over the great expanse of manicured grass.

There was nothing there at nighttime that was not present at light of day. Then why did night seem to enhance her emotions, make her feel even lonelier than she'd ever been before? What was there about this night that kept her on edge?

Oh, the answer was there. The texture of cotton against her bare breasts puckered her nipples and caused a flurry in her stomach. Her skin seemed sensitive to each eddy of air, flutter of breath.

She was too restless, too churned in mind and soul and body. The wind invited her, taunted her, urged her to strip off her clothes and be bathed in it, cooling her hot flesh. One example of her insanity. The other had been this

morning, when she had said words she never should have
said. Thought things she never would have believed possible. Asked for a kiss.

She'd wanted to know what a kiss was. She'd not
known that it had the power to invade all of her body. Her
arms had been held straight at her sides, but her fingers
tingled to touch him. Her toes, too, were troubled by sensation, a desire to curl, and rub, and otherwise rid themselves of prickles and a curious warming. His mouth
dusted soft kisses over her lips and she had stood, acqui-
escent and absorbed in all the various sensations flying
through her body.

Even when Edwin had bedded her, Mary Kate had not
felt such a sweeping rush of emotions. A bubble of some
feeling curiously similar to joy had expanded in her chest,
threatened to burst with the fullness of itself. Her hands
reached up and braced themselves upon his shoulders,
found exactly the right spot upon which to rest, as if bones
and muscles and sinew had been created just for such a
purpose. She rose on tiptoe to deepen his kiss, greedy for
more of the feelings that were racing through her body, a
ribbon of fire spreading from hands to feet and back again,
to coalesce somewhere deeper, in the very pit of her.

When his tongue touched hers, she drew back, startled.
But the sensation was eagerly accepted by the rest of her
body. The breath grew tight in her chest, as if she wore a
particularly constrictive corset. Her lips felt as though they
were hot; they, too, tingled, and each time the sensation
was near to unbearable, Archer had seemed to know, to
deepen the kiss.

In some dim, shadowed part of her mind, a portion not
left warm and hollow and pounding with her body's pulse,
Mary Kate recognized that she had been too unworldly,

too curious, for the man and the kiss. She was, perhaps, too receptive, easily conquered. Yet she was also thoroughly, absolutely enchanted.

A star seemed to fall from heaven in response to her unspoken thought. A night bird chittered in derision. Then there was silence again, a deep dark invasive silence.

She should be away from this place.

She had been so hopeful when she had left London a month ago. So certain that her journey would find welcome at its end. Instead, she was now burdened with a resident mind ghost and a longing for something that could never be. A face appeared before her eyes. Not an angelic one, surrounded by blond curls, but one in which black eyes flashed irritation, a mouth reluctantly turned up in humor, a chin defiantly angled out at the world.

No. Please. She shook her head as if to dismiss her longing, as if the vision of Archer could be so easily banished with the toss of her head. Instead, he seemed firmly fixed there, an appendage she'd never noticed before, a presence as resolutely intransigent as that of Alice St. John.

How odd that here, in this place, the echo of her voice was only that, a soft remonstrance, nothing more. Except for that one morning when the panic had nearly torn her apart, it was as if Alice were at peace with her presence at Sanderhurst. As if she'd plotted and planned for such a thing.

What rubbish. There was nothing at Sanderhurst for her, nothing but the lure of Archer St. John. And in that direction lay only trouble and heartache.

Get far from here, Mary Kate. Far enough away that you cannot hear Archer St. John's voice. So far that the memory of him does not lure you to stand at a window and wish to howl at the moon. Perhaps enough time will pass that you will not remember this morning, and the longing you had to walk into his arms.

You begged for a kiss. You would have accepted more.

There is no place for you here.

The truth, at last.

Chapter 19

There was nothing to this business of being a footman, Peter Sullivan thought, even though there were as many rules and regulations as being aboard ship. All to a purpose, he reminded himself, all to a purpose. Still, it was hard to take it all as seriously as that old crust Jonathan would have him do, since there was no danger in him being swept overboard or dying of dysentery. Still, if the majordomo wanted the bloody silver polished, then he'd polish it until heaven itself could be seen in its reflection.

He set the porringer down on the counter and moved to a more comfortable position on the high stool. It was one thing he'd never quite gotten used to, in the five months he'd been away from the sea, the utter quiet of Sanderhurst. The only time it was this quiet aboard ship was in the eye of a squall when all hands seemed to hold their collective breath waiting for the sound of the masts tearing away, or that liver-loosening gush of water that meant there was a serious breach in the hull. Even then, in the silence had come the groan of wood, the creak of timber, the slam of the waves against the side of the ship.

Damn, if he wasn't happy as a clam to be away from that.

He grinned, then began to hum to himself as he grabbed another tray, this one etched with curlicues fashioned just to hold on to the black tarnish. He dipped the rag in vinegar and then a portion of the salt he'd been allotted for this chore and began to swab at the mess.

Maybe it was true that you were born to the sea, or mayhap it was just like his own story, of being too hungry to eat air anymore and being willing to do almost anything in order to survive. Five years aboard one of His Majesty's ships, however, had taught him nothing was worth the fear he'd felt every day of those years. It wasn't that he was a coward; he'd been as brave as the next man. It was that he wanted to be able to predict where the danger came from, and Mother Nature proved to be a fickle bitch, always tossing up a storm in the middle of a calm Mediterranean ocean or a hurricane when they were a day's sail from an island in the Caribbean. No, he wanted his dangers named and labeled, which was why he'd walked away from being bosun of the H.M.S. *Ulysses* and taken his store of carefully hoarded savings and found the first position he could where the floors were nailed down and the only climbing he had to do was stairs, not rigging. Even polishing silver seemed an easy thing, all in all.

It was the quiet that did her in, that and the effort she was making not to be heard. He would probably not have noticed that she passed through the butler's pantry at all if she hadn't been tiptoeing in that fashion that reminded him of one of those Japanese plays he'd seen once.

" 'Tisn't midnight, I'm thinkin', which is the proper time for skulkin', now isn't it?"

She must have jumped a foot at the sound of his voice. Aye, and the scare had done something to her heart, leastways that's what it looked like, with her leaning against the wall, her hand to her chest.

"It's barely dawn. Won't you at least stay for breakfast? Havin' a full stomach makes for an easier farewell."

She just shook her head at him, her eyes wide.

"Suit yourself," he said, turning away from her, still humming a song he'd learned when they'd made port in Spain. Pretty little song it was, about a señorita who'd killed herself for love. He'd rarely had time or opportunity enough for lust, let alone love, but he was willing to wear himself out a bit for the trying.

"Will you tell them that you've seen me?" she asked.

He concentrated on rubbing a particularly odious bouquet of roses, all with little buds and tiny crevices that clung to their tarnish like an old maid her virtue.

"Well?"

"I'd be daft to answer the wind, now wouldn't I? Unless, of course, it whistles up a gale. But no, this is just a little breeze, one of those annoyin' things that whisper in your ear and make you bat your hand at it, like swipin' at a fly."

"Thank you."

"There it goes again, gettin' stronger. I wonder if we're in for a bit of bad weather."

"Are you new here?" she asked from behind him.

"Aye, a week, no more." He didn't turn.

"What were you singing? My uncle Michael used to hum that very same song."

"And did he tell you the words, now?"

"No. I don't think so, I just remember the tune."

"Well, it's a good thing, for all that. It's a sad little song, too sad for a lass's ears, I'm thinkin'. That uncle of yours, would he be a seafarin' man?"

"He would."

"Then you ask him to sing you a song about a mermaid who lost her heart to the king of the sea. That one's got a better endin' all in all. Or there's a ditty about a sailmaker who wants to learn to fly like a bird, that's a pretty tune."

He heard nothing for a moment, then the soft sounds of her kid slippers on the floor.

"Were you a sailor, then?" How soft her voice sounded, like rain upon spring grass. A gentle thing, that. He smiled, thinking that it was a miracle he'd lasted the five years after all, being nearly brought to tears at the thought of fields of green.

"I was, may God forgive the men who lied to me about the sea, and the glory of His Majesty's Navy." His fingertips felt puckered from the mixture he used to polish the silver, but it was a sight better than spending hours scrubbing brine from the deck of a ship only to do it all over again a day later.

"Was it awful?" There was a curious reluctance to that question, and he thought of the uncle she mentioned. His grin softened.

"Not for most. There's men who make the sea their life and would be sad to be in another place. It's a right colorful life for most."

"If you wished to find a man who's chosen the sea, how would you do it?"

He glanced at her, all pretense of being enthralled in the art of polishing gone with the earnestness of her question. "The uncle, now?"

She nodded. She was not the type, being too tall and red-haired and Irish, a sister to his own heritage, but in that moment Peter thought he recognized a tiny woodland creature in her eyes. Something rarely seen in the light of day, perhaps a fox cub, or a baby rabbit, newly born and still pink. Her eyes betrayed the seriousness of her question, a look too innocent, wanting, helpless.

He told himself, later, that it was that look which made him answer her with honesty and something else, a warning, perhaps that she might heed, lest she find more at the end of her search than just an uncle.

"If it were me," he said, turning back to his silver polishing and away from the hopefulness of her eyes, "I'd start with the Admiralty. But I'd be willin' to be disappointed, for all that. His Majesty's Navy sometimes impresses men who've no greater thought than the taste of their next ale, and have no fondness for the sea, and I'm thinkin' they'd have no records for that."

After a long moment, she spoke again. He was grateful that her voice carried only curiosity. "And is that what happened to you?"

He grinned at his face in the silver tray. "Nay, lass, I gave my soul and my body willingly to the cause. But I was a young fool then. The navy made me old, fast."

Sanderhurst was not, for all its huge dimensions, an isolated place. There was a horse farm less than two miles away and, beyond that, a road that looked to be well traveled.

Mary Kate remained at the crossroads until early afternoon. The coachman, Jeremy, had told her that it was a thoroughfare for the public coach system. Other than that, he'd not volunteered another word, nor cautioned her, either, as the footman had done. A few hours past noon, her patience was rewarded as a coach lumbered to a stop in front of her.

The driver took her two last coins willingly, but no one

else in the crowded coach viewed her presence with such welcome. If the rooftop had not been restricted from females, she would have gladly taken a perch there. Instead, she was wedged between two women and a small child, opposite a man and another woman, none of whom spoke or offered so much as a smile.

Mary Kate studied the floor of the swaying carriage, intent not on the footwear of her traveling companions, but on her thoughts. The ease with which she'd been able to leave Sanderhurst was almost anticlimactic. But then, what had she expected? That Archer St. John would care? That he would send a search party after her? Only to find Alice. Not for any other reason. Not because they'd shared a kiss, and a hint of promise in a glasshouse.

Help him. A faint call, a whisper in truth, one she resolutely silenced. She refused to listen to the voice, wanted it gone. She did not want another vision of Alice St. John's life, was too immersed in her own to borrow another woman's feelings, thoughts, wishes.

She would concentrate upon her quest, on what lay before her, not on something that could never be, and someone who would never treat her with more concern than a passing diversion.

She clenched her fists tight in her lap, concentrated on thoughts of the search for Uncle Michael. She'd not thought to look for him before, had reasoned that her brothers knew well enough his destination.

When she found him, would he repudiate her as ably as Daniel had? Or would he welcome her as long-lost kin? Only time would tell. After all, she had nothing to lose. Nothing at all.

Help him. . . .

No. Go away, Alice. Please. Get out of my mind. I do
not want your quest. I have one of my own.

"The only reason I contracted with your partner was
because he guaranteed me his contacts would be discreet
and his expertise would save me valuable time. To date,
Mr. Townsende, neither of you has fulfilled that promise."
Archer St. John sat in his library while his solicitor stood
like a penitent before his massive desk.

"It was hardly my fault that Edwin succumbed to a
brain storm, my lord."

"That excuses Mr. Bennett, but it leaves your failure
glaringly evident, Mr. Townsende."

"I really do not know what you expect of me, my lord.
I cannot simply invent evidence such as you seek." It was
quite evident to Charles Townsende that the gates of good
fortune were swinging ponderously shut upon him. Why
else would he have been summoned to Sanderhurst, put
into the enormous foyer to wait like some sort of tradesman, and only after hours of being cramped and chilly,
finally been escorted to this room, to be stood in front of
the Earl of Sanderhurst's desk like a recalcitrant schoolboy? He wouldn't have been at all surprised if the earl
demanded he strip off his breeches, bend over, and be prepared to be whipped with a birch branch!

"I do not insist upon falsehoods, Mr. Townsende, only
some indication that the enormous sums of money I have
sent you have resulted in some sort of effort on your
part. My agreement with your partner stipulated that you
would interview each incoming vessel's captain, that
you would make inquiries in Scotland and Ireland, and
that you would communicate with your fellow solicitors

on the continent. So far, I am still waiting for a report of any of your activities.''

''What you want, my lord, is not unreasonable,'' Townsende agreed, rubbing his hands together in an effort to chafe some warmth into them. It was physically quite warm enough in this room; in fact, it would have been quite a cheerful place in which to reside had the demeanor of the Earl of Sanderhurst been the slightest bit more hospitable. But no, the look he was receiving was quite forbidding. ''But my firm had undergone severe reversals since Edwin's untimely demise, sir, and in the interim I cannot help but confess to have spent more time than I anticipated in an effort to keep all our clients satisfied.''

''Except for me. Did you think the distance to Sanderhurst insulated you from my irritation, Townsende?''

''No, sir. Not at all. I am, however, rather disappointed that Edwin did not brief me on the completeness of your agreement with him. It is my understanding that you were also using your not inconsiderable contacts to locate the countess. I deemed our firm's involvement to be of a minor matter, and hardly worth mentioning, or even noticing.'' He gave a trilling little laugh.

''While, in fact, I deemed it to be of the gravest consequence, Townsende, enough to have spent a small fortune for your nonexistent expertise. I engaged Mr. Bennett in my search for the sole reason that I had been given reason to believe he would produce results.''

In truth, for all his querulous nature, the ton had chosen to be served by Edwin Bennett. He had a nature for the intricacies of the law, could bargain like a fishmonger, and argue like an Oxford debater, qualities Charles knew quite well he did not possess.

He rubbed his hands together again. Strange, how they

seemed to be growing more chilled instead of warmer. "Indeed, sir, I understand it much better now, and would be more than happy to comply with your original agreement."

"While I see no reason to continue it."

"My firm has been beset by obligations, sir. The death of my partner has affected the firm to its detriment, Lord St. John. I have managed to eke out an existence for myself, and glad I am that I have no wife, no children to support. I cannot but help confess that perhaps Edwin would have been better suited to the duties you'd given him, having been married himself."

"And did his wife disappear, also?" Charles Townsende did not hear the sarcasm in the question.

"I doubt Mary Kate would do anything of the sort, sir. It was a case of the mutton marrying the lamb. And the lamb in this case knew quite well that she was bettering her place in the world."

It would do no good to rub his hands together; the look on Archer St. John's face would have frozen the most hot-blooded creature. Charles Townsende felt acutely uncomfortable, so much so that he prattled onward, aware that he was rambling, but being constrained to do so by the look on the Earl of Sanderhurst's face.

"Mary Kate was significantly younger than Edwin, you know. Quite on my own, dear sir, I investigated the girl. She had, after all, married into the firm. And although it was not that I did not trust Edwin, I have heard how love can ruin a man's mind. I but thought to protect him from such ruination."

The lint on the edge of his cuff seemed of monumental importance to Charles Townsende at this moment. How odd that his new waistcoat should have become so untidy at this early hour. Or perhaps not. He had been forced to rush here after being summoned to the earl's estate.

"She was quite unsuitable, sir. Quite, quite unsuitable. Little more than a scullery maid. Edwin said it did not matter, she had a beauty that overcame her many detrimental qualities.

"Edwin realized his mistake towards the end, I am most assuredly certain. The firm benefited most handsomely from his generosity. But that was nearly a year ago, my lord." Still not a word from the earl, and if he wasn't mistaken, he was certain that Archer St. John had not blinked in the last few minutes.

The smile Charles Townsende proffered him made up in brilliance for what it lacked in sincerity.

"And the widow?"

"Nothing," he said proudly. "Mary Kate O'Brien did not profit by her association, I can assure you. In fact, I'm quite sure the woman was penniless. Absolutely without funds, which should have pointed out to her, as nothing else could have, that she should never have attempted to rise above her class. People like her quite often show their true colors."

"Indeed, Mr. Townsende?" Archer smiled.

Charles Townsende had the oddest notion that a frown might have seemed friendlier.

It took less than ten minutes for Archer to banish his former solicitor from Sanderhurst, the feat being accomplished by the simple expedient of walking out of his library and leaving the man standing there, mouth open. Archer found that he could not bear his company any longer.

Appearance should not matter, he told himself, but it

was not the shortness of Townsende's stature that goaded Archer's irritation, nor even his slicked-down hair, or the way his head tilted to the side like a preening bird. It was that unctuous air about the man, the sidling look, the infernal habit he had of rubbing his hands together in a way that made Archer think of Macbeth.

No, that was not quite true, was it? He did not dislike the man as much as the information he'd divulged.

Archer could almost hear the drip of the icicles melting upon the window ledge. Or perhaps it was the sound of his heart ticking in his chest. No, not that. He was frozen in a hesitation between time, this space of nothingness between seconds, oddly trapped.

It was not, after all, an uncommon name. Bennett. As common as Smith. Had she ever mentioned her husband's occupation? Archer could not recall. Even then, would he have put the pieces together? He had been thinking less of coincidence and puzzles in Mary Kate's presence than the softness of her limbs and the beauty of her hair.

Of course, Mary Kate would know everything Edwin Bennett had known, all the clues and information Archer had given his solicitor in an attempt to find his wife. Of course, she would know details not common knowledge. Evidently Edwin had been eager to impart the tales to his wife, if not his partner, and she, in turn, too eager to use them.

It was quite possible she'd been telling a half-truth all along, that she'd never known Alice at all, had merely taken advantage of her absence to tell a story so ridiculous he could not help but think she was in league with his wife.

This pain in his chest would disappear in a moment.

Strange, that she'd never changed her name, nor lied

about her circumstances, her marriage, her past. Surely someone with guile in her heart would have been more careful. She was simply new to the game, that was all.

Mary Kate's dead husband had been Archer's solicitor. A man whose task had been to find Archer's missi   wife. Mary Kate insisted Alice was dead and haunting her. And into this mix enough whimsical coincidence to blur fact from fiction, truth from fantasy. Enough attraction to wish the whole of it gone, and only the elements remaining. Mary Kate and Archer.

Yet she had not stolen from Sanderhurst, nor had she profited by their association. She had not begged for money, only his belief. And looked upon him with compassion while she pronounced his wife a ghost.

She'd kissed him with the innocence of a virgin; dared him with eyes as wise as a harlot. Intrigued him, despite himself, confused him against his will. The point was, did she know anything about Alice, or had she played him for a fool all along?

Why did he think it would be wiser to leave her alone? And even more troubling, why did he feel this surge of excitement when he realized he had absolutely no intention of doing that?

He couldn't wait to hear her explanations now.

Chapter 20

The stench of fish, the pungent odor of the water slapping against the wharf assaulted her nose long before Mary Kate viewed the sky thick with masts. The schooners lay berthed bow to stern along the pier. Huge nets laden with cargo were being winched up from the holds of two of the closest ships. Mary Kate could not help but wonder what treasure rested inside the crates now laboriously and carefully laid upon the deck. What was its ultimate destination? A merchant's store, a royal gift? A hundred possibilities, a thousand further questions.

She wished she had the coin to take passage on one of those giant schooners. She would stand at the rail and feel the ship skipping over the sea, let the wind, laden with salt and warmth, thread through her hair. She would raise her face to the sun, unmindful of the fact that her skin turned to pink too quickly, and that gentlewomen did not do such things. She would travel the world, explore places she'd only read about, see things she'd only dreamed of, become acquainted with people who lived plain and ordinary lives in exotic locales. She would loosen her corset strings and unlace her bodice, and become as wickedly seductive as the figurehead that stared back at her right now. Larger than life, the red-haired carving seemed on the verge of a smile. An otherworldly chiding smile.

Perhaps it was not the wisest course to have taken, to come to the docks in late afternoon in hopes of meeting with someone. But the Admiralty, while it had proven a wise choice, had not been an encouraging one. There was, indeed, a listing of all sailors, but only if they enlisted in the navy, and only if they shipped out from London. Information concerning other British ports was almost non-existent. Therefore, any question Mary Kate asked about her uncle was met with an obdurate, but civil, silence.

"It will not do any good to ask the location of any of the ships of the line. That information is not forthcoming to anyone, save those with need to know." All this was related to Mary Kate by a gray-bearded clerk, whose look indicated his irritation at both her questions and her insistence.

Help him. No!

Go away, Alice. Please.

Mary Kate pressed her fingers against both temples. A small dot of pain existed there; another spot of it bloomed above her left eyebrow. Not here, not now. No!

She could be as insistent as Alice St. John, as stubborn. The voice had not ceased its imprecation, had accompanied her hours with softly voiced, gently coaxed murmurs. A gentle implacability. A will most stubborn.

It seemed the farther away from Sanderhurst she traveled, the more insistent Alice had become, the louder the voice in Mary Kate's mind. There was no defense against it, nothing she could do but endure the pain of the headaches and listen to the voice as it pleaded and shouted and cajoled with equal ferocity.

She could be as obstinate. Archer St. John did not need

her help. She'd never viewed a man so supremely his own person. To think him in danger would be to render the most majestic of mountains reduced to rubble, the deepest sea a pond.

I don't want to hear you, Alice. I will not.

A few moments later, the pain seemed to subside, although Mary Kate knew it only waited for another time to pounce, catlike. Perhaps she would have a dream when she slept, when her defenses were not so armored. Another vision of Archer? Of Alice's joy? Either one spawned feelings Mary Kate would rather not have—longing and curiosity.

She closed her mind to such thoughts, with the same rigidity that she refused to hear Alice's plea, concentrating instead on the task before her.

She was either an incredibly stupid woman, or she was beyond clever. Surely that was the reason she'd led them a merry chase to London, to the Admiralty and now to the London docks. Archer congratulated himself on the fact that he'd had the sense to take the new footman with him, since it was his information that had alerted them to Mary Kate's ultimate destination. Even so, the fellow hadn't wanted to tell, no doubt effortlessly lured into loyalty by Mary Kate's charm. Well, at least he wasn't the only male similarly affected. As it was, Archer had to regale the man with stories about what could happen to a lone woman in London before he would talk.

Strange, but he hadn't seen the new footman before today, and it seemed an improbable occupation for him. His stature, tanned face and bleached hair indicated a life outdoors, not one of opening doors and standing at attention in odd spots in the hall.

They had slowly been making their way down the pier,

stopping at every bloody ship of the line, it seemed, in an effort to find her. Twice, Archer had thought he'd seen her, only to lose sight of her in the crowded conditions of London's quayside city.

Idiotic woman. Didn't she have the slightest idea of the danger?

It did not matter that she wore mourning garb, or that her hair was concealed beneath a scarf. The whistles and catcalls that preceded Mary Kate's arrival at each one of the ships she visited were both disconcerting and frightening. Still, she had no hope but to remain there, hoping to address one of the officers of the H.M.S. *Argosy*.

"I'm sorry, miss, but the captain has gone ashore." The young man looked to be barely beyond his first shave, but his face was well tanned, and his eyes too worldly wise as they looked her over from top to toe.

"Are you sure it's the captain you want? Can a reefer interest you, darlin'?"

He was barely as tall as her shoulder, not yet fully grown, but he had a leer on his face the match of any of the men who crowded around and laughed at his words.

She had had no choice but to come to the docks and solicit what information she could. Unfortunately, these rough sailors believed she was petitioning for something else entirely.

"Aw, Brian, leave the lass alone. She's for me, can't ye tell?" A burly man who topped her by nearly a foot and was possessed of a beard near as red as her hair stepped beside her, curling one arm around her shoulders. It was not a protective pose, but one of threat. Barely noticeable, but there in the way his hand curved down her arm and too close to the swelling of her breast.

She edged away from him, a simple tactic of bending her knees and scooting beneath his arm before he realized her intent.

"Have you any word of the *Royal George*?" Her uncle's last berth had been on that ship. She could remember his pride on being a foretopman aboard one of the largest vessels in His Majesty's Navy.

It was as if the world silenced in that moment. As one, the men who had gathered at the rail, watching her travel over the plank of wood that stretched between ship and wharf, grew silent. There were noises, the strain of winch, the odd thrumming sound of rope growing tighter, the screech of seabirds. Someone sang a ditty and a pipe played.

But not on the H.M.S. *Argosy*.

"The *Royal George* sank without warning while being repaired at Portsmouth in 1782, my dear. All eight hundred men, including Admiral Kempenfeld, were lost that day."

It was too difficult to separate her emotions at that moment, define them so that she might label each. A horrid sorrow. Acceptance. The spiking of tears. A feeling that *he* was destined to be there, to be standing so aloofly beckoning, a man bathed in power and too strong, finally, to resist.

Archer extended a hand and she put hers in it, allowing him to lead her from this place. Comfort. Security. Protection.

Resignation.

Coincidence?

No, not with Alice St. John's implacable will. There was no coincidence here, no odd set of circumstance set into motion by Fate.

This was destiny.

*   *   *

Archer said nothing as Mary Kate sank back into the coach seat. The tears on her face shocked him. No, not shock, Archer. Concern, yes. Even curiosity. Then what the hell was this other feeling? The one that made him reach out and pull her across the space that divided them, so that she sat next to him, and his arm surrounded her. When he'd seen her being similarly embraced by that seaman, he'd nearly shot the man.

An odd sort of resignation had struck him as he glimpsed a tall woman attired in a soft blue cloak, her titian hair escaping an ugly scarf. He'd wasted no time coming to her aid. Even Mary Kate Bennett was no proof against a mob of leering sailors.

He said nothing as she hiccuped a sob, only pulled her into his lap as he would a small child. Except, of course, that she was not a small child, but a weeping woman. Her tears wet his neck, her fist gripped his cape, he felt the shudders that wracked her as if he, too, sobbed aloud, matching the cadence of her sorrow with his own.

Who, then, did she weep for with such studied grief? Who was the man who was worthy of Mary Kate Bennett's tears? Not a husband. A lover?

He stroked her back, wishing there were fewer layers of clothing between them. Wishing, too, that she did not feel as soft in his arms, nor pliant, nor womanly. Wishing, more than anything else, to know the cause for her sorrow.

"Please. Let me go." Her voice was strained.

"I like holding you."

"It is vastly improper." She laid her head back down upon his shoulder, surrendering then.

"Our entire association has been vastly improper, madam. Plagued by consistent inconsistency, odd coincidence, a flavoring of the bizarre.''

"You do not believe in what you cannot see.'' Why, even coated with tears, did her voice sound chastising?

"And you are eternally believing in such things.''

He glanced down at her, touched not by her solemn look, but the glimmer of a watery smile. Something speared his chest, caused his breath to be compressed. Something dangerously provoking.

"For whom do you weep with such assiduous grief?''

Her fingers toyed with the buttons of his greatcoat, her chin lowered so that he could not see the expression in her eyes. Her soft voice seemed painted with sadness. "My uncle.''

"For a woman with no family, you spend an inordinate amount of time looking for them.''

"And would you not, if you were alone in the world?'' Her chin pointed straight at him. He wanted to nip at it with his teeth.

"Good God, no. I would celebrate, sing hosannas, write odes to my good fortune.'' Why was he trying to tease her out of her grief? Would he not be better served to be demanding the truth from her? Reluctance, Archer? Why? Do you fear the answers to questions that must be posed?

He placed his palm against the side of her cheek, pressing her face back into place against his chest. He did not question his actions; there was, after all, no answer to what he did. Or, if there was one, he did not wish to hear it at this moment. Another inconsistency, then. It would be easier to ignore this strange and novel attraction. Encapsulate it, surround it in glass, watch it grow or mourn its decline. Whatever it was, it needed to be contained, lest it spread to other parts of his mind. Or heart. It was bad enough that his loins were enthusiastically involved.

"We are returning, then, to Sanderhurst?"

"Did you think otherwise? Come, my imprisonment has not been that onerous, surely."

A moment passed, no more.

"You are weeping again." Accusation in his voice, not gentle remonstrance.

"I cannot help it."

"Have I ever told you how I detest a woman's tears?" His voice had softened, become warm. He gave her permission, then, for her grief. She allowed the tears to flow. It seemed she wept a lifetime of them.

His arms encased her in a woolen embrace. He wanted to surround her with himself, protect her from everything that might impinge upon this grief.

How long did he hold her? He didn't know. It was no longer important. Such things as time didn't matter right now, not with Mary Kate's tears dripping over him. A curious baptism, this. An even more curious longing.

"Do you know, I don't believe you were ever a servant. You haven't the comportment for it."

Her skin was pale, pinkened only slightly by the tears she'd shed in the last few minutes. Her eyes were downcast, but they held a sparkle of health. How could she look so utterly lovely when she'd just spent interminable minutes wetting him with grief?

A long moment until she replied, a soft smile preceding her words. "What does it take to be servile enough for you? Should I tug on a lock of my hair, or keep bowing backward out of the room?"

"It might be a pleasant surprise, at least once. And stop gnawing your bottom lip. I find it an extremely irritating habit."

"Is there anything I do well enough to suit you?"

"Indeed, yes. I opine that you will absolutely bedazzle me with your ability to speak the truth." He allowed himself the freedom of anger. It was a blessed release, after all. The questions churned too fiercely in his mind. "You will confess to all manner of things, not the least of which is the fact that your late husband was my solicitor, that you begot this absurd plot because you were destitute and desperate. That you've since seen the error of your ways and will readily divulge that you are a cheat, and the most hideous kind of opportunist. The truth, Mary Kate, you shall excel in it."

He nearly shook her when she grew pale, had to drop his arms and push away from her so that there was a foot at least between them. Damn it, she had no right to look so shocked by his revelations.

"What do you mean, Edwin was your solicitor?"

"I warn you, Mary Kate, I am in no mood to hear any more of your lies, even as inventive as they might be."

"I didn't know." She blinked at him, a startled fawn.

"I met a friend of yours, my dear," he said, his voice as carefully noncommittal as he could make it, no treacherous hills and valleys of emotion there.

She did not seem entranced by such a verbal offering, did not nibble at it as he'd suspected she would.

"A Charles Townsende. He says he was your husband's partner."

He did not add that he'd known her husband quite well, a spare, wizened figure of a man, with sparse and graying hair, long fingers with swollen knuckles, and the distasteful habit of snorting every other breath, as if in dire need for air. It was simply another one of her inconsistencies, that she would have been wed to such a man as this.

"Charles is no friend of mine," she said, her voice clear and without guile. A common enough skill, perhaps, among those who cheat and steal.

"Indeed, he bragged he'd made you penurious. A shameful thing to confess, but he seemed quite proud of it."

She looked at him, a sparrow's inquisitiveness. Direct, unflinching, knowing of her place in the bird world but oddly regal all the same. "Charles thought me a money-grubber, and an opportunist, someone who did not love Edwin the man as much as Edwin the money-maker."

"You confessed yourself that you did not love him."

"I told you I respected him. It was enough for both of us."

"What an idiot you are, Mary Kate, if you believe respect is all a man wants from a wife."

She blinked once, then again, as if the gesture would help her understand his comment more ably. Her smile, when it came, was tinted by a little sadness.

It made him want to kiss her, then have his carriage take her to the farthest corner of the world where she wouldn't be a threat to his peace.

Instead he sank back against the cushioned seat and resigned himself to a long and confusing journey home. It was only later, after they'd reached Sanderhurst and he'd bundled Mary Kate up to the Dawn Room once again, a sense of déjà vu greasing their passage, that he realized she had not answered any of his questions.

Chapter 21

***

Archer opened the stronghold door, withdrew a velvet bag. He dumped the contents of it on his palm. A yellow diamond, unmounted, awaiting the time and inclination to take it to his jeweler, a black pearl whose future he'd not yet decided, his grandmother's ruby-encrusted brooch, the clasp of which needed repair, all these things tumbled free and without onerous memory onto his palm. All these and one more. The cameo brooch lay atop them all, not nearly as expensive a piece as the other jewels, one chosen instead for its likeness to the wearer. The lady of the cameo had Alice's nose, her slight smile. But for the hairstyle, severely Grecian, Archer might have believed himself staring at her portrait in profile.

Instead of sleep, he'd gone to his glass house. But even there he had been unable to concentrate upon the task at hand. So a few minutes near to midnight, he'd found himself in his library obeying an odd compulsion that had caused him to seek out the cameo with Alice's face.

Why? A masochistic urge, surely. One designed to wound, not to heal. He'd given this brooch to Alice on the anniversary of their wedding, a full year of, if not bliss, then at least constancy. She'd rarely worn it, even though he'd searched for months to find just the right engraving, the most delicate of profiles.

Archer had been a solitary child; before him a brother had died in infancy, a sister stillborn. His companions had been, for the most part, adults.

It was not a cruel life, because one accepts what one has, but it was a lonely one. Consequently, when he'd gone off to school, he'd learned some hard lessons and gained some greater joys. One of the lessons had been a difficult one for him. He'd had to learn to share and he hadn't liked it at all.

He discovered that the possessiveness he felt for his belongings was a matter of personality and not early training, a fact that was borne out whenever one of his school chums took something of his without asking for it. He learned, however, to be a team player, to lean upon his friends when a greater goal was at stake. Such school training makes good, obedient British subjects, a thought he'd had many times. But he'd never been required to prove his loyalty to his country. It seemed the St. John heir was more needed as head of his empire than as soldier or sailor.

He was now a man past thirty, with few friends and a lamentable habit of possessiveness that remained with him to this day. A fact his wife had never known.

The brooch lay on his palm, the aristocratic profile seeming to stare at him, accusation in those sightless eyes. He could almost hear Alice's soft whisper.

"Oh, I am sorry. I didn't mean to disturb you."

For a second Archer thought the damn cameo had spoken.

Although it was nearly midnight, Mary Kate was clad in that black monstrosity of a dress. He suspected she felt it kept her safer than her nightclothes.

He should have warned her that he had gained the ability
to see through her garments; imagination had fashioned
anything she wore invisible, veiling her in iridescent nakedness. But he did not speak the words that teetered on
the tip of his tongue, nor did he tell her of his dreams of
late, filled with torrid and amorous adventure, leaving him
hot blooded and stallion-ready at morning.

She slipped a book from its place on the shelf, holding
it close. Archer noted that she was not as calm as she
would have herself appear. Her elbows were locked, her
gaze flitted nervously about, lighting on each separate object in the room.

Once, a sparrow had entered the Yellow Parlor by
means of one of the windows. He'd watched it flutter
around the room in a panic, while the chambermaids swat-
ted at it with their brooms. Strange, how Mary Kate reminded him of that hapless sparrow, dead of fright, his
heart beating so hard it had exploded in his chest. She
trembled in the same way.

You are safer behind locked doors, Mary Kate. Too bad
he'd only thought that warning. It would have been more
honorable to speak the words.

The wind howled outside, a precursor to wintry weather,
to storms out of the north and bent branches laden with
ice. Yet it was a noise like a cautionary sound, a warning
given in nature's voice. Even the fire seemed to know she
was improvident, spitting admonishments at her from its
nest in the hearth.

She clutched the book to her bosom. He wanted to tell
her that *The Dunciad* was frail protection against his
wishes and his wants and an eternity of celibacy visited
upon him. He should warn her that looking as she did, the
firelight making a glowing crown of her hair, her full lips

as alluring as any sweet his cook could conjure up, these were all lures and provocations.

Because Mary Kate was silent, an innocent object of his sudden lustful appetite, and because he was as quickly ashamed of it as he was aware of it, he lowered his defenses just a bit, to equalize their positions.

"You should not be here." There, it was spoken. A warning. Did she come to convince him she was innocent? He did not want to hear what she had to say, prudence guided him to stay away from this woman. What was in question was not that she would try to appear without guile, but how long he would resist her explanations. He suspected he would believe her too quickly.

She looked up, her quick glance less shuttered, as open and wide as an infant's. Someone should tell her she should not be so trusting of others, he thought, irritated, forgetting that he himself should be the one less accepting.

Silence. It had a taste. Dark, thick, it had a tang of rejection, a hint of pain.

It was not a restful silence between them now, but one alight with sparks. He found himself hardening, readying himself, an ancient reaction to man's finding his mate. A totally improvident physical response to a woman diametrically his opposite in all facets of life—station, purpose, past. Yet he could not prevent the reaction in his loins any more than he could the anger she sparked in his mind— that, too, was unwise.

"I did not mean to disturb you."

"Was your husband the one who taught you to speak, who banished the accent from your voice?" He realized he had been making a line of his quills, then, with one finger, he demolished such orderliness.

"My mother did not like to hear the Irish spoken in our house. She would whip us if we did."

"She sounds a veritable paragon, this mother of yours. And the rest? Did she teach you Pope and how to enchant with words, then, Mary Kate?"

There was a flush on her cheek. From his words, or his studied inspection of her?

"Mrs. Tonkett. She was a retired governess, with a penchant for teaching, still. She found a willing pupil in me. I learned my letters from her, learned to cipher and how to add a bill. Most nights I sat by the fire, a branch of candles at my side, while I read aloud the works of Goldsmith, Pope, and Johnson."

"And dreamed of times when you would no longer be a servant." He held a quill too tight between his fingers. It had bent beyond salvaging. He laid it down, steepled his fingers, studied her.

"Is that what you object to the most, that I might wish myself more? Or that I married Edwin and escaped servitude?"

He was too easily irritated by her, by the way she had of standing up to him, by the words she threw back at him. "Why are you here, Mary Kate?"

'Because you thought me guilty of some sin I'd no knowledge of, Archer St. John. Because you followed me and made me prisoner, when all I wished was your wellbeing."

"And yet you speak of Alice as if you know where she is. As if you and she have concocted this plot between you."

"How can I prove I have not done something? It is so much easier to do the opposite. I can provide you with no information that would exonerate me."

"And if I said it does not matter? That I forgive you?" His voice was lazy, deceptively so.

There was silence while she studied him. "I have done nothing to be forgiven for." A smile was her answer.

"What was Edwin like as a husband?"

"You've asked me that before. Do I hold such curiosity for you?"

"I wonder why I feel compelled to answer your lies with honesty. I find that you manage to pique my interest far beyond what is wise. Do you, I wonder, choose to be such an enigma?"

"Another impossible question, Archer."

"Then an easier one. Why did you have no children?"

"I almost bore a child. I lost him before term. The midwife said I would bear another. I never did."

"Did you wish to?"

She linked her fingers together. "My husband did not wish it. He said he was too old to be responsible for another child when he'd already fathered a daughter and a son long dead."

"And so, from that day on, he did not touch you."

"You cannot know that."

"Can't I?" There was a smile upon his lips. She turned away from it, glanced above his head to the open curtains, the night shining black through them.

"My husband was not an unkind man," she said, effortlessly deflecting his curiosity, channeling it into another path. Now he wanted to know what Edwin Bennett had done that would render her so careful of his memory, even now. What was the kindness he had granted her?

"He worked very hard, he was very diligent."

"Yet he was colder than the grave."

"Again, you cannot know that."

"But you did not love him. Why?" He replaced the jewels in their drawstring bag, the cameo, too.

"Is that a question you need answered in order to gauge my innocence?"

"No," he said. "But perhaps in order to satisfy my curiosity."

"You have an overabundance of that emotion. Curiosity between us is a dangerous thing, I suspect. I remember wishing mine satisfied, only to be ridiculed for it."

"Is that why you left, why you preferred the dangers of London to the luxury of Sanderhurst?"

She shook her head.

"Or is it why you're here now, when it would be safer to be tucked into your bed, with your covers drawn up to your chin?"

"Perhaps."

It was the one word she should not have spoken. But, no, she was not content with that, she had to embellish the truth a bit, adorn it with silk ribbons and pressed flowers.

"I find myself oddly reluctant to be alone. Tonight, at least."

He sat frozen, catapulted into disbelief by her invitation, the proof of the similarity of their thoughts.

The fire's glow echoed the color of crimson draperies, was diffused on the silk-covered walls, made mellow the masculine lines of furniture, the mahogany gleam of wood. This room was a place for surreptitious cigarillos, for the sipping of port or brandy, for hearty laughter and pointed discussion of shipping weights and the market's rise. Not a place for confrontation of the basest sort, man against woman.

"Is this the way you would convince me of your innocence, Mary Kate? Blindfold me with lust?"

"I did not know Edwin was your solicitor."

He nodded, as if he had expected the words. "And you were not penniless, and without recourse. Do not forget that part of it."

"I never knew Alice," she snapped, such a harsh sound from a voice he'd grown to think melodious that he smiled, charmed at the sight of Mary Kate drawn to anger.

"That, I am beginning to accept as the truth, madam, perhaps the only part of this that seems plausible." His fingers were occupied in tearing a bit of paper apart, long strands of it as if he would separate the fibers themselves. He wondered if she noticed that his fingers trembled at their chore.

She would be wiser to scramble from this room. It would certainly be safer. Instead, she said the only thing that would loose the reins of anger from his hands.

"And can you not forget, for one night, that you should not believe me? Or pretend, if you will, that I am someone different? Someone you might come to like, to befriend?"

"You have the oddest habit of shocking me, Mary Kate."

He stood and walked toward her. She didn't move, did not retreat, not even when he reached out and touched the curve of her jaw. How utterly perfect she was, all radiant reds and palest ivory, with those green eyes that lulled and beckoned and spoke words her lips never voiced. Hold me. Kiss me. Touch me. Had she said those words, or had he only thought them?

"I do not want a friend of you. Lover, perhaps. Even whore. But not friend. Not charming companion."

He thought she looked like an earnest scholar with her arms around a book, except for that mouth that promised lush kisses and the imploring in her eyes that offered even more—a kitten to his hand, a slave to his mastery, a queen in his kingdom, a woman to his manhood.

Take her.

She was danger and mystery and warmth all in a delectable female package. He'd not felt the warmth for so long.

"If you had any sense at all, you would run from here as if a wolf were on your scent."

"And miss the sweet devouring?"

Her smile hinted at all the answers for all the questions he'd had about her. She expressed longing, she professed ignorance, and yet that smile brought with it all the tenderness of maternal devotion, all the wickedness of Eve, all the excitement of a harlot born and bred for the trade.

He was compelled by lust so strong that it swallowed up all reason and thought and rational discourse, leaving only need and desire like a ticking clock in the foggy uncertainty of his mind. He reached out and gently pulled the book from her grasp. Her eyes were clear, unclouded by any emotion, direct, as serious as any look he'd seen from her.

He did not tell her what he thought, that his wife had offered him legality but no warmth. In her bed he was welcomed with passivity and resignation, not open curiosity and a promise of some mad and wild race to the finish. She had never dared nor challenged him, never questioned or wagered with him. He could not envision Alice ever looking at him this way, as if beseeching him to teach her the strange and wonderful game of love.

He pulled Mary Kate into his embrace, saying nothing until she softened around him, winter taffy growing warm by the fire.

"I'm a fool to offer it, but I'll give you one more chance

to leave this room untouched. After that, my bed will be scented with you.''

''I've no wish to leave,'' she said softly, the words falling between them with almost no sound. It stopped his heart, such sweet surrender, and had the ability to feed the ravenous wolf within, taking the edge off his hunger and leaving him appeased enough for dessert.

He smiled, a particularly raffish grin, comprised of one part victory and two parts anticipation. He bent his head to breathe in her exhalations of breath, in tune with her the way a musician feels the soul of a delicate instrument.

He moved finally, stepping around her to the library door, flinging it open with less than his usual grace. He turned, extended a hand to her, and she stared at it for a long moment until she stepped forward and laid her hand in his.

Chapter 22

He watched her, his face unreadable, the black eyes blazing, the emotion in them too easily read. He did not want a victim, but a partner. Not a subordinate, but a playmate. Not a friend, then, but a lover.

What would he say if she told him her legs were trembling so that she wondered how she could stand? What would he do if she whispered to him that there were places in her body moist and swollen and growing even more so with each breath she took, each slight movement of his fingers now trailing on her back, mocking the thin fabric of her dress and her imprisoned flesh.

She pulled herself away from his arms, but did not move away from his presence. He lured her like a cloud of warmth, affection neither voiced nor expressed but somehow hinted at, and a promise of something she'd never felt but wished for always.

She blessed him for the silence of this seduction. If he forced the words from her, she did not know what she would say. Yes—it would condemn her forever, make of her something her flamboyant appearance had always hinted at, destroy a reputation she'd kept unsullied. No, and she condemned herself to loneliness, not just for this night, but forever.

There was no choice, and yet there was. She did not lie to herself, pretend, did not confuse this feeling in her body, this excitement in her mind, for anything more or anything less than what it was. She may be damned for a sinner tomorrow, but for one night in her life, she would feel something. It may burn and sear and immolate her, but she would walk into the fire gladly, for the sheer joy of being able to remember the flames.

She nodded quickly, a gesture that he seemed to accept, and they left the library hand in hand, twin conspirators in a game neither chose to identify, but each desperately wanted.

He strode up the magnificent curved staircase two treads above her, watching her mount the steps with her left hand holding her skirts, the right tightly held in his. She licked her lips, a nervous gesture, but one that caused him to stop, walk down to where she stood, eyes wide. He bent forward and kissed her, his tongue tasting the wetness of her lips, bathing them as if tasting a delicacy too long left untouched. Just that, a quick kiss, and she was left breathless. He smiled, a gentle smile she'd never seen before, a smile of understanding.

How could he possibly know that she had never felt this way before, that nothing she'd experienced since first seeing him in her mind had been anything similar to the rest of her life?

How could he realize that walking up these steps with him in this magnificent house should have been tantamount to mounting the gallows, and yet it felt as if it was the only act she'd ever performed in her life that was correct and proper? Touching him felt ordained, commanded by a power greater than herself. Receiving a kiss from him seemed the greatest joy. How could he understand that her heart beat so hard that she was breathless from it, that it felt as if just looking at him made her different, stronger, weaker, changed somehow?

The door to the Master's Suite was easily pushed ajar and she was urged forward by his hand and a smile. The door closed behind them, sounding as loud as a church bell pealing in the dawn.

In a matter of minutes, the room was candlelit against the night, bright branches of candles burning without a thought to their cost or the rarity of their sandalwood scent.

He removed his blue waistcoat, his torso clad now only in a white shirt, gathered at the wrists and the neck with precise and delicate stitches. He looked, however, none the less the earl in his shirt and form-fitting trousers. If anything, he looked more predisposed to royalty; a haunting kind of power seemed to envelop him, as if he were capable, at that moment, of performing all kinds of feats of wizardry, not the least of which was luring her here, to this room, to the brilliance of a chamber alight with candles.

He did not smile in triumph; his face was oddly somber, his eyes direct but warm. A lock of hair had fallen onto his brow, but such a minor carelessness could not detract from his perfection, a man in his prime, armed with bold intent and a certain ruthlessness that was evident even in his stance. She should have been frightened by him at this moment, but curiously was not. Excited, perhaps, and certainly questioning, but not of him. He was as he had always been, autocratic, domineering, a man of purpose with hints of tenderness. In this, he was no less.

Archer walked toward the massive four-poster bed where the counterpane was turned down, the pillows plumped. Only then did he turn and hold out his hand again to Mary Kate.

The questioning of herself would come later, when this odd joy was eased, when the pleasure center in her core was satisfied, when she had wept the tears she felt too close to the surface.

"Come here, Mary Kate." Was it possible for a voice to sound so tender and yet so dangerous? Was it command he uttered, or enticement?

She looked from him to the branches of candles scattered about the room. "Are you not going to extinguish the candles?"

His smile was the first upon coming into his room. "No, I'm not going to extinguish the candles. Why should I, when I've wasted valuable moments lighting them?"

She walked the four steps to the edge of the bed, hands clasped in front of her. He loosened one button and then the next and the collar of her dress sagged open.

She did not protest until he reached the last button, her bodice gaping open to expose a serviceable corselet rendered gray from innumerable washings. She placed her hand upon his, forced herself to meet his eyes. There was no amusement there, no cruelty, only some emotion she could not name. She appealed to that expression in his eyes, to the softening she saw there, to latent kindness which was in his person and his character yet only revealed itself grudgingly.

"Please," she asked. It was darkness she craved, the softness of shadows.

He only shook his head, extracted the last button free from its cage, and bent forward, placing a sweet and tender kiss between her breasts. She did not draw away from him, nor make any further protests when he grabbed the hem of her dress and raised it over her head. He did not stop until he'd finished undressing her.

Each article of clothing removed rendered her more naked and more vulnerable, but it was not embarrassment that seemed to fix Mary Kate's feet where he had placed her. It was a feeling she had only felt on dark, lonely nights, when even the air itself seemed to caress her skin, leaving her unfilled and wanting something that had been withheld from her.

Here, and now with his gaze predatory and ravenous and unveering, she would discover what it was that she had always wanted.

His hands reached out and cupped her breasts. She licked her lips, the sight of his dark hands against her body leaving her too warm. It was as if she'd run a great race and could not breathe, but such would not explain the sensation of melting from within. When his thumbs reached out to brush against her nipples, she almost moaned with the sensation. She wanted to press his hands against her breasts. No one but she had ever touched her there. Certainly no one had done what he was doing now, leaning down to suckle upon her as if he were her babe. He held one nipple between his teeth, scraping gently against it, and this time she moaned softly, a sound of entreaty instead of protest.

Archer raised his head, a smile glimmering on his wet lips. The echo of that wetness was on her breast, the nipple tightening and puckering in the air. He slipped an arm around her waist, pulled her closer to him, gently pushing her head against his chest. It was a gesture a longtime lover might make, desire shielded in tenderness.

She had never before been naked in front of a man,

never dreamed of being drenched in candlelight while doing so.

He did nothing but hold her; his clothing felt odd against her skin. She sighed into his shirt, her breath dislodging a tuck around his neck. She inhaled deeply, the smell of him so familiar, so oddly necessary to the sense of rightness she felt at this moment. His hands rested on her shoulders, cupped them in large palms, slid down her back in a waterfall of sensation, then slid to touch her naked buttocks. She ground her forehead into his shoulder, wondering what more he wanted from her. For her to cry surrender? Had she not, standing here naked and uncomplaining, a lamb quite peaceably led to slaughter?

One finger perched under her chin, raised her head. Had he read her thoughts, then? Was he another ghost in her mind? He kissed her then, a kiss unlike any other they'd shared. His lips were hot, his tongue hotter, exploring and demanding and giving no quarter for the license he took. He did not demand her compliance, he expected it. Anticipated, too, she thought, that the sensation would overwhelm her, so much that when he bent down and caught her under the knees and carried her to his massive fourposter bed, she would utter not one word of complaint and protest. Nor did she.

It had never been possible to completely forget the dreams of a nude Archer St. John, but propriety and an odd feeling of shyness had dictated that she try. Yet even if she could recall each separate part of him, Mary Kate could never have anticipated the mind-numbing impact of seeing him naked in candlelight. The curves and hollows of his flesh were both shadow deepened and touched by brightness. He was, quite simply, beautiful. He was crafted of muscle and sun-browned skin, wide shoulders and deep chest, and an arousal that should have terrified her with its proportions but managed only to render her speechless.

Being married to Edwin had not prepared her for this.

Archer stood beside the bed, seemingly unashamed and unabashed by her curiosity. Instead, a smile played about his lips, as if he understood her sudden insatiable desire to watch him move. Mary Kate wanted to ask him to turn, but it was a request she could not quite utter. With his nakedness, he had equalized hers, so that when he sat down on the edge of the bed, she felt less shy than she had before, less exposed. Yet she found a strange and novel thing had occurred in the moments since he had last touched her. It was as if her body thirsted for him, her breasts ached to be touched, her skin needed to be stroked by his large hands.

Still, he did not move.

"I would wish that this night were dawn instead, Mary Kate, and that the light of it was in this room, all rosy and orange, just as you are. Are you a nymph of dawn, then, come to steal away night?"

She shivered, so much that her bottom lip quivered in response. This, then, was anticipation. This heady feeling pooling in her stomach, in her very blood. It was as if she readied herself for him, her nipples pointing, her skin warming, the wetness rendering her open and swollen and receptive. Still, he did nothing but smile softly at her, a tender smile lined along the edges with a hint of rapaciousness.

All the bawdy songs she'd learned at taverns, all the earthy comments she'd heard as a dairymaid, all the advances she'd fought back, and all the nights she'd lain uncomplaining and unprotesting as Edwin took his husbandly rights were as nothing to these moments. This simply could not be the same thing.

The candles lent the room an otherworldly glow. One window was left ajar; enough breeze blew in to tempt the curtains to furl and lend the air a spiced sweetness and chill. Still, it was not atmosphere that made her breathless, or wondering that made her lips part as if they could not contain another full breath. It was the look in Archer's eyes, dark and glittering like the most precious onyx given life.

Circumstance had brought her to him, implausible, impossible, improbable fate. Her own wishes had brought her to this place, this moment, lying upon his bed as if for sacrifice, a willing one if he but knew it.

Or perhaps he did. Why else would he turn her to her side so that her breasts pillowed together, reach out and brush her hair forward so that the curls almost shielded her breasts from his gaze? Why, then, would he palm her skin, trail his hand down from her waist to hip to thigh to long leg to foot, to the tip of her toe, increasing the pressure within her lungs with every soft stroke?

"You are so lovely."

"It is the candlelight. All women look lovely in candlelight."

"And do such women have such lovely skin, soft and white, except where it is pink and glowing?"

"You have, St. John, a greater experience of that than I."

He lay on the bed, stretched out full length beside her, as if they were replete from the act and there was no place he had not stroked, or caressed, or saluted with a kiss. He propped his head on his hand, gazed down into her face. She wondered what he saw as he studied her.

"You seduced me more readily when I was clothed," she said, her lips turned up into a smile. Her eyes, however, did not mirror that smile, they still hinted at confusion, a little hurt, a wondering.

"I admit to being an odd child, in that I savored my vegetables first."

"And is that what I am, a vegetable?"

"You are a most delicious dessert. Certainly a treat to be savored." His fingers trailed from her hip to thigh, as if following an imaginary trail. She shivered.

"Do you grow cold?"

She smiled, a daring smile, he thought, one that matched the sudden sparkle of her eyes. "Too hot, rather."

"You are an improvident woman."

Her smile brightened the room. "I am naked upon your bed. I cannot but admit to such a thing. It seems, however, that I am as safe as if I were in my borrowed chamber."

"Is that what you want to be, safe?"

"If that were so, I wouldn't be here."

One long finger measured the swell of breast. She bit her bottom lip at the touch.

"I am a spice merchant, Mary Kate, for all that I'm earl." His finger trailed up to her shoulder and then down to her neck, tracing an imaginary line to her temple. "I have learned that most people do not understand the essence of spice. Did you know that?"

She shook her head.

"Too much will spoil a dish. It requires only a hint of it, a subtle flavoring. A taste." He bent forward and touched his lips to her temple. "You have a taste all your own. An intoxicating one. Too few people understand that something so rare should be appreciated, relished."

"First I'm a foodstuff, now I'm a spice."

He pulled back, his smile as daring as hers. "Yes. A hint of cinnamon, a taste of nutmeg. Perhaps a dash of pepper." His palm caressed the edge of her chin, cradled her face, supported it as he bent down and placed his lips on hers. It was a soft, pillowy kiss, hinting at restraint.

"What do you want, Mary Kate? Of all the pleasures, what do you want for this moment?" His voice was impatient, hinting that he was not as unaffected as he would pretend.

She was no longer shy. Shyness had disappeared beneath the very great hunger he'd coaxed forth.

"I want you to touch me."

"Where?" His lips brushed against her temple again, his fingers played at the line of her chin. She nipped at one finger, a gesture that made him smile into her hair. She was growing restive, hungry.

Her hands had been folded in front of her, clasped at the juncture of her waist. She'd not explored him, not touched him as she'd wanted, had burrowed all of those hidden needs and wanton responses beneath a prudish temperance. Now she extended one hand and trailed her fingers over his hip.

He jumped at her touch, startled.

"Everywhere." She traced her fingers over his chin, feeling the bristly stubble, feeling wanton and decadent and thoroughly wicked. "Kiss me, please."

"Another demand, Mary Kate?"

"You asked what I wanted."

"Ah, but I did, didn't I?" There was a hint of bemusement in his words.

He did not kiss her as quickly as she wanted, so she grasped his head between her hands and pulled it down to her, her tongue darting across the seam of his lips peremptorily. It was an odd thing, she thought, to want to laugh, to offer up to the gods who knew such things the absolute, utter pleasure of this moment.

"Shall I touch you here?" His smile was as wicked as the gentle intrusion of his finger between her legs, his palm cushioned upon the fiery delta of hair. A delicate invasion, a tender one, so light and tentative that she might have imagined it but for the gleam in his eyes as he watched her. He probed her delicately, as if testing her response to him.

She could only hold on to his shoulders and pull herself closer, wanting something he promised in the glint of his eyes and his knowing smile.

She wanted to pull his head down again for a lusty kiss, to moan, to rub her palms all over his body, kiss him where he thrust so hot and hard against her. A thousand sensations, a hundred impulses. None of them right for this moment, all of them welcomed.

"Here?" Her words, not his. Her touch, intimate and silken, grasping him with slender, tormenting fingers.

He pushed her onto her back, extended a leg between hers, made her his captive in this odd enchantment. She lay as he placed her, eyes wide and unquestioning, mouth tempting, begging for a kiss.

He entered her quickly, but she was ready for him, the arch of her back and soft moan a welcome, an entreaty. He filled her completely, the pressure of his passage ordained by nature itself, the ecstasy of it a gift. His hands slid up her back, gripped her shoulders.

"Forgive me," he whispered, "I could not wait."

She said nothing. There were, after all, no words she could say. Every nuance of intellect was consumed with feeling. Fill me, complete me, end this. All words she might have said had her mind not been focused so deliciously upon what he made her feel.

She sobbed when he moved and clutched him with greedy hands when he stopped. She demanded as well as he, arching up at him, cradling him, offering him delight and torment and sorcery. And the end of the world.

Chapter 23

He had felt his soul splinter.

Archer moved his arm from over his eyes, blinked up at the ceiling, forcing it to come into focus.

Had generations of St. John men and women stared at the canopy above his head? Women in childbirth must have studied the starburst pattern in the center. Perhaps a relative or two, male or female, had been lost in lust or bored enough by the act to stare unseeing at the family crest so artfully embroidered above his head.

He rubbed his hand over the bristle of whiskers on his chin, ground the palms of both hands into his eyes. Sleep should come with great good cheer, a reward for a day spent in honest labor. Instead, he was awake, prodded not by the voice of his conscience, but by something else entirely. A sense of wonder so profound that it made him question what he knew of the world.

He rolled to his side, watched her as she slept. She'd screamed. Not a sound of terror, but one of such fulsome completion that he'd felt himself explode inside of her, reaching a depth of sensation he'd never before experienced.

He'd licked those wondrous lips, crooned words of utter

nonsense between kisses, palmed her breasts, licked her nipples, pretended that he was not victim to this woman's utter sorcery. But that would have been a lie, and Archer St. John prided himself on telling the truth. He'd begun as experienced, proficient, ended feeling as untried as a virgin youth.

What was there about the look in her eyes that made him want to whisper words of praise? What was there about her lips that made him want to kiss her until night turned to morning? Her green eyes had surprising flecks of brown within them, and gold, too, if one looked hard enough. And there was a mole on her shoulder, as if pointing the way to breasts too luscious to avoid sampling. And her nose was straight, quite autocratic, neither too long nor too short for such a patrician face.

Archer had rarely watched anyone sleep before; it seemed an invasion of the basest kind. Even his wife had not allowed him the delicacy of this moment, the open vulnerability of it. Alice had wished him gone the moment his seed was disgorged, the object of his visit being the fertilization of her womb and nothing more. Even his mistress had declined the intimacy of sleep. Did the jowls soften, a snore emerge from lips only known in passion? Questions he'd never asked, never wished to have answered. How odd that he should think of them now. Even odder that this particular moment was ripe with an intimacy he'd never before experienced.

Mary Kate seemed to enjoy a tyranny of possession, her legs spread wide, her arms cast out, she was a Maltese cross upon the plump mattress, but no less charming for her sprawling slumber.

Her pillow was damp, because she'd wept. Another first, then. He'd never caused a woman to weep with fulfillment.

Damn her, that she could make him recall less captivating moments, when he'd cried himself to sleep as a boy. His cheek recalled the feel of scratchy linen, the salty taste of his own tears, the hopelessness that fueled a child's nightmares. It was not a recollection he wished to explore further.

She was not childlike however, more a temptress enjoying a respite. Lush and wanton and urging him to forget she was a messenger, a harbinger of deceit. How odd that he should be entertaining thoughts of tenderness when banishing her from Sanderhurst seemed much the better course.

Archer touched the soft pillow of her lower lip, eased closer and breathed into her mouth, a kiss to incite dreams, to spur her wakefulness. He wanted her again, wanted her awake, to be able to seek in her eyes the answers to all the questions she induced in him.

She moaned softly, and if he hadn't been awake, he would have missed the sound, it was so faint. He placed one hand upon her cheek, smoothing his fingers over her skin.

He made a sound, some crooning nonsense a parent might make to a child in the grip of a nightmare. She turned to him as if seeking warmth and comfort in the long, dark night. He opened his arms and pulled her into his embrace.

Of what did she dream this time? Which scenario could she envision that bared his soul and stripped his spirit clean? It was a strange question to ask of himself, halfway to a point at which he believed her. Barmaid, tavern apprentice, milker of cows, with a countess's insouciance and a duchess's arrogance. Mary Kate Bennett, widow, questioner, sorceress extraordinaire. Why did he think that waking her was a dangerous thing, that he should have her taken sleeping from his room and deposited into a vault with locked doors, a barrier to protect both of them?

She'd been his captive since the first moment he'd seen her. First in injury, then by inclination. When had he become hers? She'd ensnared him just as easily, within the wall of his own mind, the prison of credulity. Who was she? What, truly, did she want of him?

No, he didn't want to know what she dreamed, he only wanted her to wake. He kissed her harder, rubbed his palms upon her arms, gripped her shoulder and pulled her from the mattress into his arms. She lay draped there like some mythical goddess, red hair flaming over his arm. Strange, she was so warm with life, so hot with it that he should have been burned.

Her smile was fraught with tenderness, an odd thing to think when he wanted to kiss it from her face. He wanted to make her scream again, lead her to passion's precipice and lead her off the edge of it, soar with her. Instead, she placed her palm over his cheek, looked into his eyes with a green gaze that peered past the ruination of his soul to the smoking embers beneath. In that look she promised new flames and more, a healing touch. He had not died, then, in her arms, but been reborn to die again. Healing life, that was what this surprising woman brought to him. And something else. It glittered in her eyes, promised him comfort and peace.

Such a look should have frightened him more.

The soft knock on the door pulled him from reverie, released him from utter confusion. He stood, grateful to be pulled from the web of enchantment.

"I beg pardon, sir," Jonathan whispered, "but there is someone who insists upon speaking with you."

"Who is it, Jonathan?"

For once Jonathan's eternal poise slipped a notch. "It's your mother, sir. Come back from China."

St. John the Hermit? Had he ever aspired to such solitary living? He was inundated with women. None of whom offered him peace. Not even his mother, who stood looking at him as if he were one of those odd statues she'd collected from Africa with sagging bosoms and genitalia not as much obscene as to be envied.

Except, of course, that he had donned his dressing gown and restored his hair to some order. It did not seem to matter. He no doubt smelled of sex, of wildness and euphoria, and any other scent her flared nostrils detected.

Still, he loved her with all his heart, however much she judged him at this moment. She'd bathed his skinned knees, sat with him the night his beloved dog, Hamish, had died, watched over him as friend, mentor, and always mother. It was Bernie who had augmented his curiosity about the world by filling his mind with lurid tales of blood and gore, who had played Roundhead with him in the east wing of Sanderhurst and taught him how to hold a saber.

Bernie, the one person in the world he did not wish to see at this moment. When he was twenty, she'd come to him and said that from now on, she would only answer to Bernie, that she was going to see the world, that he was old enough to be a man on his own and that she was not getting any younger. He'd been half-terrified and half-ecstatic to be granted such freedom.

She'd never used artifice when he was a child, and even now disdained the use of powder and paint favored by the older women of the ton, tarting themselves up to resemble absurd ancient dolls. Bernie's face was lined, and her skin was tanned, but there was an energetic robustness about her that reminded him of her athleticism, that she'd taught him to ride using example, not a riding master. It had been Bernie who played with him in the gardens, who fished with him in one of the lakes surrounding Sanderhurst, who hunted with all the skill and avidity of any male he knew. Fondness for this women filled his heart, vying with the irritation he felt.

"I will admit to being absurdly proud of your good looks, my darling son," she said, smiling broadly. "But then, you've shown promise since the day you were born and stared up at me with those black eyes like two lumps of coal in your face. But why on earth do you look as if you've been rousting in the hay all day, dear boy? Not that you have any clinging to you, but you are barefoot, Archer. And although you seem quite dressed, your hair is falling down upon your face. It's quite a thoroughly titillating thing, to have caught you without your composure."

"I'm known as St. John the Hermit, you know. Probably from my dislike of visitors, a reputation I've spread about to discourage our many ancillary relatives from plaguing me for contributions to this or that, or seeking knowledge about the state of my health." His tone was bored, his words almost tinged with sardonic reverie. Except, of course, that his eyes were snapping.

"Well, you're certainly your father's son, my dear. That speech was vintage Earl of Sanderhurst. Is this my welcome, then, Archer?"

He descended the last five steps, stood standing in front of her, shaking his head. Admonition, it was not. Wonderment, quite possibly.

"I suspect the turban is a bit much, Archer, but they are all wearing them now."

"With so many ribbons and bows, Bernie? And an ostrich feather and a ruby in the middle?"

Her headgear, however, was not all that rendered him speechless She was wearing pantaloons. Oh, they were loosely draped, but they were pantaloons nonetheless, in such an odd color green that it looked the shade of pea soup left alone to ferment for a few days. Her jacket was of the same color, but a shawl of splashy flowers topped the affair its fringe almost touching the floor. Her red kid slippers were the most absurd complement to the entire wardrobe selection. Even Archer, having been familiar with his mother's penchant for thumbing her nose at society's strict guidelines for dress, could not restrain a chuckle when he saw those. They were bright red and curled at the toe, like a jester's slippers. At the end of each toe, a silver bell was hung, and his delightfully witty and urbanely charming mother jingled when she walked.

"You have a mind to poke your finger in the eye of the ton, is that it, Mother?" She squinted at him. He only called her Mother when he meant to be particularly irritating.

"Nonsense, Archer. I simply wish to have a little fun. Life is too short to be such a slave to propriety."

"Please, Mother, be more frank with your opinions. You hold too much within," he murmured, bending to give her a kiss.

"No hug? After all, it's been nearly a decade since last we met in Paris."

"You do not look a day past our last meeting."

"And you are as polite as I raised you to be."

"While you are as outrageous as I remember your being."

" I have missed you." Her hand brushed his cheek in

an altogether gentle touch. She smiled up at him with glittering eyes. Twice this night a woman had bestowed such perfect tenderness upon him that it made him wonder if he looked so much in need of it.

He only smiled back at his mother, sincerely grateful she was safe, eternally thankful that she had given him the love he'd needed as a child and had protected him from the almost apathetic cruelty of his father. She had taught him what love was about, that it was conceivable to like one's relatives and to do something that was proper and right and made someone else proud.

"Archer?"

They both turned their heads, looking up at the head of the curving stairs. Mary Kate stood there, hands grasping the overlong folds of one of his unused nightshirts, evidently unearthed from a drawer where his valet kept them. Her hair was in disarray across her shoulders, her lips were bruised from his kisses, her pink toes emerged from beneath the puddling hem. Altogether she had the appearance of a woman well loved. She blinked at both of them. Archer could imagine what they looked like, he nearly naked and his turbaned mother sporting a wide and nearly demonic smile. It was a wonder Mary Kate didn't think herself in the throes of a nightmare. He should have explained before he left the room, but had been, quite frankly, rendered speechless.

Not unlike his current dilemma

"Oh dear, Archer," his insouciant mother replied, evidently relishing the concupiscence that surged through him at the sight of Mary Kate night touseled. "Is that Alice come home?"

He turned and gaped at her.

"And here I returned, just to help find her."

Chapter 24

〜〜∽○○∽〜〜

"**I** am the Dowager Countess of Sanderhurst," Bernie explained, as she mounted the staircase to the accompaniment of tinkling bells on her shoes. "But I am quite positive you cannot be Alice."

Mary Kate stood frozen in place, immobilized by the dawning awareness of the physical resemblance between this surprising woman and the man who stood at the bottom of the stairs glaring up at them.

A mother. Dear God, Archer's mother.

Bernie grasped Mary Kate's hand, held onto it with a grip that was relentless for all its gentleness and propelled her down the stairs. "Alice had such lovely blond hair. Not that yours isn't quite as lovely. But it isn't as if I could mistake you. Unless of course, Alice has changed all that much, and I don't suspect that is true. Besides, she is supposed to be missing." She tossed a glance over her shoulder. "Or has that changed, Archer?"

Archer simply frowned at her.

Mary Kate had no choice but to follow where she led. Archer had the odd thought that it was like watching a dinghy being towed by a merchantman.

"Dear boy, please ring for tea. I've no doubt that your

staff has already taken it upon themselves to do so, despite the hour, but I am quite famished. I have spent the majority of the last week touring England as if I had never been here before. Not that I intended to do so, of course, but the scenery entranced me so much that I simply had to view the lake country. With the end result that I have spent my nights in some truly dreadful hovels. I simply would not do it again. The English must learn a better standard of hospitality."

"You are English, Mother, or have you managed to become an expatriate in your years abroad?"

"I think I am being chastised. Dear Archer, it is not my fault you were caught in flagrante delecto. Do not be such a boor about it." She managed to artfully frown while not accentuating those creases around her eyes. He wondered if she'd practiced that look in the mirror, then recognized the idiocy of that thought. Bernie didn't give a flying farthing what her face looked like; in fact she'd often bragged that she could not wait for old age in order to become a true eccentric. Until then, she'd announced, she would only be considered odd.

"Most mothers would simply swoon," he said now, a reluctant smile softening his answer.

"That is simply the worst kind of insult, to label me as normal."

"God forbid," Archer said dryly, opting to retreat for the instant to the sideboard, where he poured himself a measure of brandy. Perhaps it was a coward's gesture to seek solace in spirits, but it was three o'clock in the morning, he was deadly tired, recuperating from the best sex he'd ever had in his life and all the ramifications that brought to his mind, and intrigued beyond measure to see how his mother and Mary Kate would suit.

Members of the ton were not expected to rear their children. There were nannies for that, or nurses and governesses, tutors for boys. There were riding masters and dance instructors and those whose sole purpose in life was to make miserable the life of one small child, heir to one of the world's great fortunes. Yet his mother had not only taken an interest in his well-being but had overseen every hour of his day, an effortless granting of love and affection for which he'd always be grateful.

He had often thought that perhaps it was not a good thing to have learned of women from one unlike the rest of her sex. His mother was an iconoclast of the first order, eschewing such things as docility and decorum. She spent her money on things like orphanages and the unearthing of obscure artifacts. Each month, in whichever country she was currently residing, she adopted a poor child, spending countless amounts of money on establishing him or her with a family and people who wanted to care for and to love a child. She helped those who would learn obtain skills with which to support themselves, and tossed her hands up in the air and abandoned those who would not.

But she'd never abandoned him.

She had always been there, waiting to welcome him home on school holidays, demanding that he bring what friends he would down to Sanderhurst. She had protected him from the grasping manipulations of those women who cared little about the St. John heir and more about the St. John fortune. Even the horde of relatives he supported had been forced, until his majority, to appeal to his mother first, a state of affairs that proved amenable for all those involved. Bernie, after all, saw nothing wrong with doling out what funds were requested; it seemed there was an inexhaustible supply of it. The petitioners were satisfied,

Archer was pleased because he did not have to suffer through any more of his obscure relatives' whining tales of misfortune, and Bernie enjoyed the power of it.

Even after she'd left England, she'd never abandoned him. Her monthly letters were filled with stories of her exploits, reflections upon life itself. And not uncommon was another lecture upon the error of his ways, the particular sin his mother had chosen that month to assail.

If his greatest wish was for a family, it would not have been the one he was saddled with, who expected him to act as banker for all their demands. It would have been, as "normal" as it sounded, for a wife who quite frankly adored him and children who worshipped him. A fairy tale life, in fact. And a home? Sanderhurst was the greatest of places to found a dynasty. There were hidden rooms and at least three concealed staircases and a large, well-lit library and a thousand places to play. There were lofty ceilings and a storeroom that was located beneath the main floor, dungeonlike. In other words, a ready-made paradise for those children he'd sire. Except of course, that there would be none of those. Alice had, by disappearing, guaranteed that.

He wondered if he'd given Mary Kate a child. It was not for want of trying. He'd sent his seed so deep inside her he wondered she could not taste it. The possession of it had surprised him. No, more than that, surely, Archer. It had given him the single most powerful experience of his life.

What would a child of theirs look like? A dark-haired boy with flashing green eyes? A girl with hair the color of a carrot, with black eyes? A miniature of both of them, temperament to match? He found himself very much wanting to know It was a thought that should have sent him scrambling from the room.

Instead, he leaned back against the sideboard, having fortified his glass once again, and watched two of the most interesting women he'd ever met eye each other with a great deal of trepidation.

"So, I've established the fact that you are not Alice, girl, but have not yet gleaned your true identity."

Mary Kate looked at Archer. He wished, fervently, that his protective impulses were not so easily summoned by such a stricken glance. But he could not help responding to her unspoken plea any more than he could have prevented himself from taking her to bed tonight. Both impulses were likely to have far-reaching consequences.

"Mary Kate is my guest, Mother, that is all that's necessary to know at this juncture."

An eyebrow arched. When had his irrepressible mother become so adept at unvoiced sarcasm?

She turned to Mary Kate, laying a warm hand upon the younger woman's arm. "And how do you find the comforts of Sanderhurst?" There was a gleam of interest in her eyes, or perhaps it was simply speculation, Archer didn't know. All he knew was that the battle of wits was somehow overmatched. Mary Kate was neither noble nor well-traveled, nor so secure in her consequence that she could ignore the dictates of polite society with impunity. Allowing herself to become his mistress was one thing, becoming target for his mother's protective claws was quite another.

He strode to the sofa, extended his hand. Mary Kate placed her fingers across his palm as she stood. It was a delicate gesture, a polite one replicated a thousand times a day between men and women. It should not have struck a cord somewhere deep inside him. An innocent friction that called to mind another stroking, deep inside her.

"It is late," he said, cutting off his mother's questions, silencing with a look the comment she would have made. "There is plenty of time tomorrow for questions."

"And answers, Archer? Will there be time for those?" Bernie didn't smile as she looked up at him, then glanced at Mary Kate. There was something in her eyes he'd seen before, when he'd fallen from his first pony, or been beaten by his father on one of those occasions when he'd been summoned to the library when little more than an infant.

Instead of answering her, he escorted Mary Kate from the room.

Chapter 25

〜◦◦◦〜

"**N**o, no, the elephant's tusk goes on that stand. See, there! And that, my good man, is a fertility goddess, not a good-luck charm. You will do yourself no good fortune by stroking her breasts with such an ardent touch. Oh, there you are, girl," she said, noticing Mary Kate standing in the doorway. "I've heard some interesting tales of you, Mary Kate Bennett."

Mary Kate hesitated at the doorway. "Shall I help you unpack, Countess?"

"Half the fun of resting upon journey's end is unearthing the things one thought so precious at the beginning of the trip. Do you know that I once traversed the Pyrenees with a whole trunk full of Venetian crystal? Sad to say, only about half of it survived the mules, but then again, there are the odds of things to consider. However, you shall attempt to assist me in the placement of these things, now that my furniture is about me."

"Do you always travel with your own bed?"

"My own bed, my own chair, my own mattresses, and the carpets beneath my feet. What good is having so much money if one cannot find a use for it? And before you scrunch up that pretty nose of yours at the frivolity of such expense, girl, just think of the laborers who are so glad to see me arrive and even gladder still of my departure.''

"I was not thinking of such criticism, being one of the people who would have profited by your appearance.''

"Your smile is really too spectacular, my dear girl. Like the sun shining out from behind a dull cloud. So, girl, you're of yeoman class, then?''

"I am from it and of it. Not simply placed here for the pleasure of your son. I have honestly worked most of my life, not simply whored for it.''

The directness of her look would have been hard to escape, had Bernie wished to. Instead, she nodded briskly. "Well, there is that question answered, then. You have magnificent hair, girl, you should let it flow free. Hygeia would have had such looks.''

"Not girl. Mary Kate.''

Bernie squinted at her. "I beg your pardon?''

"I dislike being called girl. I have not been one since the day my monthlies arrived.''

The bluntness of that statement widened Bernadette's eyes and prompted a guffaw of laughter. "I think I shall like you, Mary Kate of the yeoman class. Provided, of course,'' she said, pointing a finger at her, "that you aren't a stupid woman. I cannot abide stupid women. Men, you cannot expect more than average from the lot of them, with a few exceptions. Women, on the other hand, either soar into brilliance or are dumber than an ass's ass.''

"I shall endeavor to blind you with my brilliance.''

"Don't be laughing at me, Mary Kate. I see that look in your eyes. You shall call me Bernie. I dislike Bernadette intensely, and do not answer to Countess, except in such occasions as it is helpful to have a position in the world. It is a singular stupidity, however, to consider those with titles more endowed than those without. Nobility is an accident of birth; being noble quite another thing entirely. Do you not think so?''

It was like being overcome by a giant river, rolling out of its banks. No one expects a flood, especially downstream, where there is no rain. But Bernadette St. John was like the Thames gorged from its tributaries, dangerous to everything in its path. She did not so much converse as she led people into her mind.

"So you think you're being haunted?" This, seemed one of her conversational gambits. Lead the victim into thinking nothing untoward would be said, then thrust the question at her with the agility of a fencer's rapier. ''Well? Do you see spirits, or hear them?''

"Not spirits, no." How could she possibly explain to this woman? It was like being asked to defend yourself, with one word, against the charge of stealing a loaf of bread. Except, of course, that she wasn't a thief, and all she could think of to say was—no. Not spirits.

"He is very attractive, isn't he?" Bernie asked, diverted from her questioning by the sight of one very tall footman. He was blond, with a wicked grin, and most powerful-looking arms.

Mary Kate glanced over at the footman, the same one who had helped her escape to London, then betrayed her to Archer. He was exchanging a meaningful stare with Bernadette. If she didn't know better, a message was implicit in both stares, such a hot-blooded one that Mary Kate turned away, embarrassed. It must run in families, this earthiness.

''It's a natural fact of life, Mary Kate,'' Bernadette said, as if reading her thoughts. ''Making love has been the glue that held society together. Marriages are formed, dynasties created, kings deposed, all for the sake of man wanting a woman. It would, however, be a damn sight better if your own lover were not indisposed by a wife. Even one who's little more than a ghost."

Her look was eagle-sharp, as all-seeing as her son's.

"No ghost," Mary Kate said, interjecting that comment before Bernie could run off again, fueled with nothing more than an errant thought.

"No ghost?"

Mary Kate shook her head.

"No feelings of cold or sounds at midnight? Don't go smiling at me, Mary Kate. That's how it's usually done."

"Not this time."

"Very well, but I'll bet there is a touch of Celtic in you. There'd have to be with that hair."

"And what is wrong with my hair?"

"It's entirely too bright. It is natural, is it not? You don't wash it with henna, do you?" Bernadette asked, inspecting the corner of a teak table one of the footmen had carried in earlier. The change from topic to topic was another trait of Bernadette's, a conversational ploy Mary Kate suspected was to keep the listener unsettled.

"My mother pretended we weren't Irish, when my grandfather was no more than a slave to an absent landlord. Is that Celtic enough?"

"Such a noble race, the Irish. They have long been tied to the land, been able to hear the rumblings of the earth, breathe in the truth of nature itself." She stopped, stood upright, and smiled at the look on Mary Kate's face. "You think I'm daft, don't you?"

Was there a way to answer that?

"Well, I'm not. I'm just interested in a great many things. And I've seen enough to tell me that the world does not always function in the serene way people would have it. I've witnessed rituals which celebrate life by taking it, the scarring of bodies in order to prove the victim's honor and bravery. I've even sat and prayed to the sky, and played a flute to implore the gods to come and sit beside me.''

Another sharp look. "You think yourself haunted, then?"

Mary Kate was beginning to feel like a fox must feel, when trapped by a pack of voracious hounds. "I'm not quite sure."

"Nonsense, of course you're sure. Either something odd is happening to you, or you're making it up. Which one is it?"

"Well, I'm certainly not making it up."

" 'The dread of something after death, the undiscovered country, from whose bourn no traveler returns.' Hamlet said it right, then. But tell me, has nothing odd ever happened to you in your life before? Nothing that would rip the veil asunder?"

"No."

Bernadette plopped down on the edge of a particularly loathsome divan, whose legs resembled the claws of some ancient mythical beast.

"Think, child. Do not dismiss me so quickly."

There was one occasion, only one, in which something odd had happened to her. Should she tell this surprising woman?

"Aha, there is that look upon your face. Something is there. You must tell me. You certainly must."

Mary Kate had been more a child than young woman, still relishing unexpected moments of freedom from her mother. She'd been clad in a yellow smock with her fiercely curling hair tied up in a kerchief. In her pocket was a sturdy cotton handkerchief, a rock prettily shaped like a butterfly, and a pence she'd saved since the day she'd found it on the cobblestone square of Kennelworth Village. She remembered the cloudless day with perfect precision, remembered, too, everything about those moments, trailing along behind her brothers as they guided the cows into the barn. She didn't understand what they were laughing about again, but this time it mattered less what they said than the fact she was near them. They rarely allowed her presence in their august midst, being almost men and not tolerant of nine-year-old girls.

As she trailed a stick in the dust, making patterns with its leafed tip, it felt as though there were a humming passing through the tips of her fingers, causing her knuckles to vibrate, her wrists to tingle, a strange resonant sound traveling by bone through her body. As it seemed to pass through her arms, Mary Kate realized in the way that children sometimes do that something was going to happen.

Her father stood in front of her, his arms outstretched as if wishing to hug her, but as she walked up to him, ready to be enfolded in his embrace, it was as if he took a quick step back, shaking his head. She loved her father, in the single-minded way young girls do. He was a bear of a man, with shoulders that seemed to block out the sun, a large square face, a mustache he occasionally allowed her to tug, and a smile so blinding white that Mary Kate could see it even now, in this bright room far away from the farm of her birth. Except on that day, his face was wreathed in a strangely sad smile, but his eyes glittered with joy.

How well she remembered feeling so confused, as the man she adored had stepped between her and her brothers, and her brothers all unknowing that he had done so. The sun seemed to shine through him, he was nearly transparent, for all that he looked the same, with the look in his eyes, so soft and tender just for her.

"Da?" she'd said, stepping toward him then.

"I love you, lass," he said then, in a soft and curiously sad voice. Her brothers tricked her into making her think that they could not hear him. Even Alan, the oldest, had turned impatiently and yelled at her to keep up, or he would tell their mother she was worthless calling the cows home. None of them saw her father, or pretended not to, a game she had wished they not play.

She was openmouthed yet silent, trapped in an odd sort of horror/wonder as the vision of her father faded from sight. Just like a cloud of dandelion spores cast to the wind, he had disappeared, his smile, his broad and thick mustache, and the lingering voice of him.

She should have known, then, that people would not believe her.

Still, she had tried. She'd rushed ahead of her brothers, racing to the small farmhouse they'd always called home, with only one thought in her mind. To tell her mother what she'd seen, her father's smile so sad, of tingling bones and words that hung on the air and other things she didn't understand.

Her mother said not a word, only plunked down the dinner plate in front of her, grabbing her hair and nearly pulling it out by the roots to gain her attention.

"Go and wash your hands, Mary Kate," she'd commanded in that way of hers that brooked no argument. "And brush your hair," she'd added, never content with only one chore assigned.

Mary Kate had demurred, not due to any sweetness

of nature, but because of the strange look upon her mother's face. Such a look demanded silent obedience.

"I'll not have such silly talk at my table" was all her mother had said then. It was only after the news had come that her father had fallen down and died at market that her mother had spoken of Mary Kate's grandmother, of the whispers of her strangeness, of powers that hinted at witchcraft and Wicca.

That her mother had hurled these accusations at her, Mary Kate flinched at remembering. She'd been crouched over her father's dead body, in the small farmhouse he'd been so proud to own and steward. She'd been too young to understand, but not too young to help prepare her father for his burial.

There had been many things she could have said to her mother then, but such knowledge was only supplied by maturity, and she had been barely a child that night. Hardly able to defend herself against her mother's accusations, buffeted by too many raw emotions, one of which was the sense of strangeness about herself.

Her father had said good-bye, and her mother had hated her for it.

"Very good. I knew it had to be such." Bernie stood, batted her hands together as though carding wool between them.

"Now, tell me everything that's happened to you since you left London, my dear. Every little bit. Well," she amended, seeing the rapidly spreading blush upon Mary Kate's face, "almost all of it."

Chapter 26

"At the risk of offending your vanity, you look as if you're recuperating from a particularly nasty bout of influenza." He grinned at her frown.

"At the risk of offending your lineage, I have just come from your mother. She insisted that I try a curry she concocted. Archer, I do believe it had monkey's brains or something in it." Her look of horrified fascination made him grin again.

"You must only believe about half of what Bernie says, and suspect the rest." He laid the spade down upon the workbench, stepped closer to her. He tipped her chin up so that he could see her eyes. There was no hurt there, no expression of wounded affront, nothing to indicate she'd had her feelings hurt. Odd, the protectiveness he felt. He loved his mother, but his mother loved him. And she would not hesitate to attack anything, or anyone, she saw as an obstacle to his happiness. What would she have done to Alice he wondered, and then resolutely put that thought aside.

"I approve of her gift, by the way."

Mary Kate glanced down at the dress she wore. She'd had no choice in the matter, had tried to decline the countess's generosity with a smile. It had made no difference. "It is supposed to be of the latest style," she said.

"Come," he said softly, holding her hands up away from her. "Let me see you." He twirled her in the room. "You look like the light from a prism, magically splintered into a hundred iridescent colors."

She laughed, charmed by his cajolery. "Your mother waits for me to return, Archer."

He grinned, a perfectly unrepentant grin. "I doubt that. Besides, I do not wish to talk about my mother at this moment, Mary Kate, but only the reason for your newest blush."

"I am not blushing."

In a movement so quick she'd not anticipated it, he lifted her into his arms and strode through the doorway. She gripped his shirtsleeves for balance, hiccuped a surprised gasp, then smiled at the glint of mischief in his eyes.

"What are you about, Archer St. John?"

"Doing something I've always wished to do, Mary Kate, but had no subjects I would willingly test."

"Am I one of your plants now?"

He squinted at her. "Have I not called you a spice? A condiment of exquisite delicacy, Mary Kate."

"I haven't the slightest idea whether you've just insulted me or rendered me a beauteous compliment."

"Must women always be complimented?" His smile offset the stringent quality of his words.

"Must men always be so complaining? After all, it takes but a moment to say something nice."

"I've often found, however, that men are the ones required to say the niceties, while women always receive them."

"Very well. I wanted to thank you, Archer, for last

night, but could not find the words to say."

"A compliment, Mary Kate?"

"A nicety, Archer." She looked down at her fingers, plucked the material from her sleeve.

"Did I bring you pleasure?"

She could not halt the soft inrush of breath. He only smiled at the sound. Her hands grasped one exploring hand. He again extricated them, concentrating upon the small pearl buttons of her bodice.

"Archer!"

"We are alone, Mary Kate, the door is conveniently locked, this portion of the structure is as private as my chamber and everyone knows not to interrupt me when I am engaged in my pursuits."

"And am I considered one of your pursuits, then?" Such a solemn interrogatory from a mouth too wide, lips too full.

"One of my most tantalizing, I will confess."

Her bodice was opened, and he slipped a hand inside. Warmth, curving flesh, and lace. An exquisite combination. Was there ever a more enchanting picture of a woman than Mary Kate bathed in sunlight? The bright crown of her hair, the bodice gently parted, the lace of her chemise hiding her breasts from his gaze, the darkness of her nipples thrusting impatiently against the cloth, peaking it. He drew back and looked into her eyes. There was surprise there, and something else, a touch, perhaps, of desire. Certainly curiosity again.

"I haven't the slightest idea how to treat you, Mary Kate Bennett," he said, brushing his hand against her soft skin. "You are either the most clever woman of my acquaintance, or the most ill treated. An angel or a devil. Which are you?"

"What do you want me to be?"

"Is it that easy?" he mused. His fingers brushed against her flesh, curved beneath a breast. "Are you only what I wish you to be? A wood nymph, perhaps, or an elfin creature, here but for a moment to dazzle me and then, just as quickly, gone?"

She shook her head, the expression in her eyes too difficult to study. He wanted her exposed, not merely her flesh, but her mind. Was that what he truly wanted? How much easier to care less for her motives than for her response.

Her chin tilted in his direction, she brushed back her hair, then clasped her hands before her. It was a strange and touching pose of supplication. It was as if she held all the various pieces of herself together to protect herself from him. He'd seen her ill, embarrassed, bemused, passion-weary. Now he was treated to the sight of her assuming a penitent's posture, utterly serene, a Madonna of flagrant allure.

A look flashed in her eyes, then disappeared as quickly as a falling star. He had not imagined it, had he? A twinkling of fear and something else, a curious pairing of emotions, wonderment and fright.

There was silence in the room, an odd sort of quiet. Not tranquil nor serene, but bubbling with thoughts left unspoken. Words were dangerous things, as sharp as stillettos. It was easier, simply, to be silent in his lust.

He should walk away from her this instant, should he not? How odd that he knew he would not.

He leaned forward, touched her temple with his lips, brushed her skin again, inhaled the scent of her.

How arresting a sight, his tanned hand against cream-colored lace. He did not tease her further, sought out the firmness of her nipple as if it were a lodestone for his fingers, a gentle quest. She sighed, or gasped, either sound one of such sweet surrender that he smiled, tenderly, and kissed her temple again, leading her onward, closer, nearer.

A gentle shake of her head, another soft sound. His other hand, resting on her waist, was drawn up to encompass her other breast, a gentle support, a friendly benediction. She leaned closer to him, willingly solicitous, begging for a kiss.

Instead, he leaned back, looked into her eyes, witnessed the dazed expression, the darkening of her pupils, the dilating of them as her body readied itself for passion. Did she become swollen and moist in places to be invaded with his fingers, his tongue? She sighed, and he extended two fingers, brushed down the edge of lace upon her breast until only an impudent nipple appeared. Like a dawn sun, it peeped over the horizon of lace, eager, curious, tenderly imploring a welcoming suckle.

He could do no less. His hair brushed against her chin, his mouth closed over her left breast. She made some fluttering motion of her hands until they settled upon him, one hand at his cheek, feeling the hollowing of his mouth as he sucked hard and eagerly, the other at the back of his head as if to keep him rooting there. A strange mewling sound escaped her like the cry of an animal in need. A sound that seemed to accompany the tremble of her fingers, the very tremulous nature of her lips.

He gently raised her chin, kissing her with a slow tenderness that paid no heed to the sweeping greediness of her tongue, to the hands that grasped his shoulders, to the eagerness betrayed by the weakness of her limbs.

Last night they'd spiced their loving with words and

laughter, a daring look, a teasing jest. Today they were immersed in silence.

He curved his lips over hers, felt her smile as he kissed her again. His hands left her breast for a moment, returned to the row of buttons on her bodice. One by one he finished unbuttoning them, kissing each inch he exposed by doing so. Only when he finished did he raise his head and look at her, a glance of utter devilment.

He wanted to tell her she was wearing too many clothes, but he had caught the utter stillness of her. Instead of speaking, he reached out and pulled the dress down, baring impossibly white rounded shoulders rendered even more white by the glare of the sun. She trembled in his arms.

He pulled her close, witless at the feel of her quivers, shaken loose from his own needs for a moment, like a dinghy set adrift in a sweeping tide. She did this to him, shocked him without a word spoken.

She was even more beautiful than she had been last night. Today she was his sunlit nymph, white and red and pinked all over from embarrassment, or something else she betrayed artlessly with her shaking fingers.

He extended a hand and she took it, stepping out of her undergarments with the grace of a princess. When he knelt to remove her slippers, he heard her soft, almost painful exhalation.

The sun seemed magnified a thousandfold, its rays upon her skin both illuminated and warmed. He stroked one hand down one curved shoulder to a forearm bathed by a golden light.

He allowed her no modesty as he stared at her. Instead, he lifted her chin with his fingers and forced her to look into his eyes. If he had not been forbidden to speak by some unwritten rule for this moment, he would have told her that she looked insanely proper at this moment, surrounded by greenery, standing naked in a place where nature dwelled and allowed itself to be tamed. She was neither forest creature nor nymph, but rather princess or queen. A regal being who commanded by the sheer power of her beauty.

One hand reached out and snared the opening of his shirt, pulling him closer. He smiled, startled as he heard the material tear. He stripped his clothes off with immoderate haste, baring himself as blatantly as he'd demanded of her.

He left her, went to the wall, turned a lever mounted there. In moments, she was bathed by a mist.

He smiled at her look of wonder, his smile fading as she closed her eyes, turning her face up to allow the mist to bathe her cheeks, forehead, nose. She extended her arms up into the air, her body arching into the soft cloud.

He'd wanted her naked and wet ever since the first time she'd come into his glasshouse. He'd not expected, however, the punch to his gut, the sudden feeling of need so great that he wanted to brand her his.

It did not matter that he thought her an adventuress. It did not matter that he could easily suspect her of underhanded dealings, of being manipulative and cunning. It did not even matter that if she believed in what she said, he could quite possibly call her insane.

At this moment she belonged to him, and that was all that mattered.

The mist bathed their skin, pinpricks of sensation. She opened her eyes to find him staring at her, his face glistening with the mist, his hair wet. And through it all, the sun beat down, warming them.

His gaze slicked down her body just as the water crept,

droplets at a time, down her skin. Her skin was slick, the kiss she gave him voracious. Was it not the lioness who killed the prey? He felt himself swept up in the open-mouthed demand, in her whimpers as if they were shouted commands.

He bit her shoulder, just the tiniest bite, to tame her, teach her who was the master in this game. She retaliated by doing the same, by plucking his nipple between her fingers and then gently biting it, scraping his flesh with her teeth.

What the bloody hell had he started? She was wild, wet from the mist, dappled by the sun, the primordial mate.

Patience, Archer.

Patience, hell.

He turned her, braced her so that her hands rested upon a workbench, stood behind her and drove into her so fast and so hard that she gasped at his entrance.

"Did I hurt you?" he whispered over her shoulder, dotting little kisses upon her neck. Regret and lust vied with each other for dominance. Lust gave a hearty sigh of relief as she shook her head, then reached back with both hands and grabbed his hips.

He should have gone slower, he told himself that. He should have treated her with some gentility, but those words, also, were lost in the mist and the mindlessness of it. He buried his hands between her legs, coaxing her on with soft strokes and intrusive fingers. He heard himself talking in a voice nearly raspy with need, but couldn't decipher the words, had no idea what he said and why.

Nothing mattered at that moment but Mary Kate, and the sobbing cries he heard uttered in a voice lost to pride. He didn't know if they were hers or his.

*   *   *

The glasshouse was attached to the end of the west wing, and through a connecting door Archer could enter the house undetected. It was a convenience he rarely used, but he was grateful for it today, as he strode through the door and into a storeroom with Mary Kate in his arms. He was quite frankly glad of the short distance, of the chair that sat waiting for its ultimate disposition—reupholstery or to be torn asunder for wood and scraps.

Playing Sir Galahad nearly killed him. She was not a delicate female, was Mary Kate, and she was deadweight, having succumbed to that arcane condition the French called so delicately *la petite mort,* and which had given him a bad turn there for several seconds. Now, as he sat upon the abandoned chair with her cradled in his arms, he wondered what the hell was wrong with him that he could be so abjectly contrite on one hand and so pleased as Punch on the other.

It was a gratifying experience for his ego, even though he wasn't sure he could live through too many more of these experiences. Making love with Mary Kate transcended any experience he'd ever had. Oh, he started off slow enough, but he was galloping hell-for-leather at the end, defying gravity, his age, and any rational thought processes that might, God forbid, slow his race to completion. She was damn well wearing him out.

She made a little sound, and he held her closer, her cheek cradled against his naked chest. She was so utterly beautiful, he thought, looking down at her. He was feeling acutely protective at this moment, another sensation of which he was unfamiliar.

Damn, he was a fool. To know so much about a person, to suspect her of the worst subterfuge, and to willingly enter her web of deceit seemed to him to be the most idiotic of actions.

She'd been a barmaid, an occupation she'd easily admitted, yet her voice was softly modulated and unaccented. She'd milked cows with those elegant hands, scrubbed floors with her hair tied up in a kerchief. Why did it not seem to matter? She'd had every opportunity to know his secrets and take advantage of his trust, yet he found reasons to excuse her for it.

He pushed back the tendrils of hair from her face, feeling an absurd sense of tenderness as though she were a child entrusting herself to him. He smiled softly to himself as she half turned, restless. She was more than pretty, she looked like a nymphet, a cherub wafting among the clouds, draped with satin and silk, hair curly and unbound, a creature taken full blown from Guercino's *Virgin and Child*.

Archer, you're an absolute ass.

There was a knock on the door, a discreet tap. Bernie fluffed out her peignoir and then her hair, tilted her chin up, then down.

"Come in," she called softly, thinking that it would not do to seem so eager.

"I've brought the wine you asked for, ma'am." The handsome blond footman stood at attention, which was all very well and good, except that she wasn't his commanding officer and the upper button of his tunic was undone.

"Is it white? I find that red wine gives a headache. But then, perhaps it's because I drank too much of it the last time I partook of it. Could that be it, do you think?"

A grin sliced through the tanned face before it resumed its implacable lines. "I'm certain I don't know, ma'am."

"Your name is Peter."

"Aye."

"And you're new to Sanderhurst."

"Aye, that I am." There was just the most delicious trace of brogue in his voice.

"You needn't look so wary, Peter, I am but trying to be pleasant."

"Is that what it is, now?"

"And what would you call it?"

She should have been scorched by his look. A slow up-and-down perusal of her half-clad body.

"I'd call it seduction, an' I want no part of it," Peter said.

"I beg your pardon?"

"An' right you are. Ashamed of yourself, you should be, Bernadette St. John. Chasin' a man that way. When, and if, we lie down on the sheets, it'll be because I say so, not because you've wiggled your fingers at me."

"Is that right?"

"Aye, it is. An' if you're half the woman I think you are, you'll be willin' to wait for it."

"Will I?"

His smile was a blaze of male satisfaction. She nearly threw something at him. "Aye, Bernie. It'll be worth waitin' for. Until then, I think you'd better have one of the female staff serve you in your room."

She was still staring at the door after he'd closed it.

Chapter 27

Bernie insisted that Mary Kate join her and Archer for dinner in the state dining room, a place Mary Kate had only seen through her exploration of Sanderhurst. Serve there, perhaps. Sup? Never.

She had responded with an earnest desire to have a tray taken in her room. In fact, she would fetch it herself to save the little maid the journey. Even that was vetoed in such a stentorious voice that Mary Kate was certain the entire staff of Sanderhurst, over thirty people, had heard.

"If he thinks you good enough to share his bed, Archer shall not cavil about your sharing his board. Is that not so, Archer?"

It was not enough to have such humiliation heaped upon her, Bernie had to ice the cake even further by involving Archer in this discussion.

She should have stood her ground with Bernie, but experience over the last week had taught her that the Countess of Sanderhurst had an implacable will. Take the matter of her name. She absolutely refused to respond to anything other than Bernie, insisting that she was much more democratic than Mary Kate, else the younger woman would not have such difficulty.

Little did Bernie know that the dilemma of what to call her was the least of her worries. She was more than confused, she was restless and uncertain. The nights were filled with passion laced with humor. The days, with warmth and camaraderie and more comfort than she'd ever known. Still, Mary Kate was mindful that she did not belong here. She did not reside at Sanderhurst because of opportunism or greed, motives she suspected Archer thought her guilty of, even though she lacked the courage to ask him. Instead, she was enchanted and bemused by the range of emotions she felt.

This was not her home and she did not belong here, and these were days of halcyon pleasures that she would never have again. And through it all, the nights when she could not wait to hear his footfalls and the mornings when she awoke to feel him beside her, kissing her neck and leading her to passion's precipice once again, she knew she had to leave. There was a family to find, and loved ones to belong to, and a home, perhaps, that was more rightfully hers.

But for tonight, she would pretend she belonged in this palace, and to its prince. He was exquisitely tailored, the perfection of dress and decorum achieved only by the very rich or those who do nothing all day to occupy themselves but think on their attire. He wore his evening clothes well, even for such a large man. But the twinkle in his eyes did not quite match the severe black of his formal coat, or the snowy lace of his jabot.

'I think, Bernie, that Mary Kate would add just the touch of balance we require for an evening of discussion.''

"There, Mary Kate, did I not tell you? The man is positively democratic in his beliefs, which is but one topic for our dinner this night.''

And it was. That and the slave trade, which Bernie

found reprehensible, an opinion shared by Archer. The high price of food imports was discussed, along with the news Bernie shared that the French revolutionists had turned the grounds of the Tuilleries into a potato field.

"Those fools have made some idiotic law, my dears, that only one pound of meat a week can be eaten, upon pain of death."

"It sounds like something the French would do."

"Your prejudice is showing, Archer."

"What would you have me do, Mother, salute those idiots for slaughtering some of their finest minds, or for developing a revolutionary calendar with such months as Thermidor and Fructidor?"

"He has a French chef only because of me, you see," Bernie said in an aside to Mary Kate. "I hired Alphonse long ago. I think he dislikes the man because Alphonse can outbrood him. Archer does have a habit of melancholia when it rains."

"The sky is perfectly clear, Mother."

"I was being but metaphoric, love. Have you noticed, Mary Kate, that he addresses me as Mother only when he is sorely irritated at me?"

"I am here, you know. I have not absented myself from your midst," Archer said before Mary Kate could answer.

"It would be a shame, my darling, if you do. We women do so like a Homeric hero."

"You have gotten worse with age, Mother, beyond my ability to control you. I should have put that frog into your bed."

"Oh, you did worse things than that to me, Archer. You cried in your sleep. If that did not put the fear of all mothers into me, nothing else would have. Nothing that your feverish little boy's mind could conjure up could possibly have worked as well.''

Mary Kate watched their by-play with fascination. How alike they were, each stubborn and opinionated and determined. How fond they were of each other, that was as plain to see.

"Tell me of India, Bernie. I've heard it is hot and dusty and they worship cows. Is that the truth?'' Mary Kate caught Archer's grateful look from the corner of her eye. She propped her chin upon one fist and gazed imploringly at Bernie, knowing, even from such short acquaintance, that Bernadette St. John was a storyteller, and like most spinners of tales, could not resist a captive audience.

Bernie's voice droned on, and in one ear, Mary Kate heard of the nizam of Hyderabad, and the beginning of the third Mysore War, enough information not to be accused of inattention should Bernie question her. Yet the bulk of her regard was not on her, but on Archer.

Each person held the secret of himself tightly guarded, did he not? Archer St. John. A hermit to all outward appearances. A man of reclusive temperament. A scholar, a spice king, a betrayed husband. All of these descriptions fit him, and yet none singly.

And what did he see when he looked at her? Widow. Gentlewoman only slightly removed from the tavern. Dairymaid, student of Pope, impecunious dreamer.

Mary Kate absently rubbed the back of her neck. The pain was bearable, the anticipation nearly excruciating. Was the onrush of pain another warning? A precursor of yet another vision? And she'd thought herself free of them, having been spared this last week of the soft, insistent voice that impelled her to protect a man who neither wished for her protection nor seemed to require it. And yet she would do so for his own sake now. Perdition. That was what she was headed for; all the innate common sense of which she was so proud rose up in protest. To love Archer St. John was foolish.

I never meant to love him. He was my friend, the one to whom I'd go whenever there was a problem I needed solving, or when the world seemed not to understand me so well. His laughter was the most glorious thing, like the sun sparkling on morning dew, all new and without guilt, or wickedness in any degree.

I remember when we were children together, walking over the fields beside Sanderhurst, entranced with the ancient house of the St. John earls. He and I would fish in the lake to the south of the property, using thread from my petticoat and a whittled hook. He would never catch a fish, he said, because I was forever talking, and fish did not like the sound of a girl's voice. So I would sit on the bank with my knees drawn up and a finger across my lips and a pursed expression on my face evidently so pained that he would finally laugh and release me from the bond of his silence. How like the summer his smiles were, and all I had to do to experience that season was to salt my memory with the recollection of that day.

After all those years of laughter, of confidences, he seemed like my other half, the missing part of me where I stored all the good times, all the wonder tokens of childhood. I like to recall that he was not simply my friend, but that I was his, too. He could coax music from the wind. Once, we had sat beneath a tree and he had bid me be still. We sat there listening to the sound of the spring breeze soughing through the branches, hearing the orchestra of leaves.

It was then I began to realize he could make music from his mind, create it in the basest of places, the most sacred of rooms. He was not simply mine, but with such a great talent, he belonged to the world.

He was my great good friend, my love, my dearest.

One Christmas he bent toward me, offering me a kiss of peace a benediction he'd gifted me for many years. It was a normal gesture between kin and close relatives. When his lips touched my cheek it was as if a stroke of lightning grounded me to the earth. How horrible that knowledge and awful, and how wondrous all at once, as if I knew such a perfect secret but was forbidden to ever entertain it in my mind.

From that moment on, I vowed to become a proper wife to Archer St. John. It was such a sinful thing, to love someone the way I was beginning to love him, so wicked that I tried to forget it.

Instead, he occupied my every thought, my every dream. He was my friend. My love.

Mary Kate blinked, surfacing into a silence that was almost a roar.

Archer sat beside her, rubbing her hands. Bernie sat on her other side, waving a vile mixture of sal volatile beneath her nose.

"Are you very sure you're all right, my dear?"

Mary Kate sat staring at the candles as if fixated by their flicker. In a moment they would tell her that she had not responded to their questions, that they'd had to wave the vile smelling salts in front of her in order to gain her attention. At least she had not fainted again.

It isn't you, Mary Kate thought, looking at Archer, a glance that was filled with enough puzzlement to inspire his own.

But who is it? Whom does Alice want me to protect?

Chapter 28

"It's a breech-loading musket, Mary Kate, not a snake." Bernie rolled her eyes at the way Mary Kate was eyeing her new firearm.

"I truly do not care what it is, Bernie. Why must I even be here?"

It had taken fifteen minutes of walking to pass through the east wing of Sanderhurst. They'd exited through one of the lesser doors, emerging onto a path that led through the adjoining forest. The stark black bark of leafless trees and the gray, smoky sky combined to create a depressing day. Yet there was a hint of warmth in the air, so much so that the constant drip of melting ice was heard.

"Because I truly do not wish to be alone out here in the woods.'

Mary Kate's look was a cross between astonishment and hilarity. "You have a gun, Bernie. A very large and mean-looking gun."

"I do not mean for the sake of safety, Mary Kate. I enjoy concentrating upon more than one task at a time. And I think you should not be so afraid of weapons, my dear. You would do quite well at target shooting, if you could refrain from screaming at the sound of a gun firing."

Bernie had not been prepared for Mary Kate's surprise at the very first shot from her new Nock breechloader.

"While I admire knowledge of any sort, Bernie, I simply must claim willful ignorance. I have no desire to learn."

Bernie sent her a look of such chastisement that Mary Kate resignedly accepted the gun. But the sound of the musket as she fired had her hastily dropping it. Bernie sighed as she retrieved it from the ground.

"Tell me, Mary Kate, have you dreamed lately?"

"Not since that night at dinner."

"And that was, what, a week ago?"

Mary Kate nodded.

Bernie shot a round, necessitating that they wait a moment until their ears stopped ringing and the choking smoke cleared. "It's as if she's growing weaker, then."

"What do you mean?"

"Have you ever given any thought to the notion that Alice is very much alive, Mary Kate?" Bernie frowned down the sight of the musket. "Could it be that you have the ability to hear her thoughts?"

"As much as it would please me to learn why Alice St. John seems intent upon residing in my mind, I find that I do not care why anymore. I simply want her gone."

Bernie only blinked at her.

"It is not an experience I would willingly have had. She is forever there, Bernie. There is much about my own life I would change, not the least of which is Alice St. John's presence."

"Have you ever given any thought as to why you are the only one who seems to have these dreams?"

"No," she said. It seemed to close the subject, yet Bernie could not help but wonder if it was the complete truth.

"Here, hold this," Bernie said, thrusting the musket at her.

Mary Kate made the mistake of gripping it by the barrel, nearly scorching her hand. Bernie jerked it out of her hand and laid it on the ground instead, shaking her head. Then she bent and drew up her skirts past her ankle. There, strapped upon a rather delicate-looking limb, was a length of satin. And within the satin sheath was a very wicked-looking knife.

"You look like a child beholding a rather large sweet-meat, my dear. Your eyes are as round as saucers."

"That is a knife."

"So it is," she said absently, as if just now noticing it. Bernie was tossing the knife from one hand to another. Evidently Mary Kate could not keep her mind on the conversation, seemingly so entranced with the quickness of Bernie's fingers. In a flash the knife was gone, embedded in a tree fifteen feet away, right in the center of a knot.

Bernie walked to the tree, extracted the knife, then proceeded to duplicate the perfect throw. "What is it about your life you would change, my dear?"

"Why do I think your curiosity as pointed as Archer's?"

"Perhaps there is some link between the two of you, something not readily apparent. Why, for example, would Alice have chosen you?"

"Why a half-Irish servant girl, with no pretensions to nobility, few graces, and even less talent, is that what you mean?"

"Oh, pish, Mary Kate. Do you think you aren't good enough because you once milked cows? Or took away chamber pots? Have I led you to believe that? As to your class, you pull such distinction around yourself, Mary

Kate, in an effort to separate yourself from others. You remind me too much of myself. All scratchy with thorns, yet beneath, too vulnerable.''

"I've had to protect myself for too many years, Bernie.''

"And is that what you would change, then?'' she asked, having been earlier told the tale of Mary Kate's early years. "Perhaps your brothers did you a favor by leaving you on the side of the road. A rough type of affection, Mary Kate, but a gesture done with your well-being in mind. Do not forget that.''

"All the more reason to keep searching for them, Bernie. Even though there is no trail to follow.''

"And your uncle dead for ten years. A pity, that. I remember hearing of the sinking of that mighty ship. We St. Johns are not far from the ocean, my dear. It's been our means of fortune, after all. Mary Kate?''

The look on the other woman's face was one of spreading joy. A smile so blinding it could have mimicked the sun was turned on Bernie.

"Uncle Michael could not have been on the *Royal George*, Bernie. Daniel told me that he'd been to see the boys seven years ago! Why did I not reason it out?''

"Still, Mary Kate, this has been a tumultuous decade, and the occupation of sailoring carries its own risks. Do not hold out much hope for him, even if we find he was, indeed, not aboard the *Royal George*.''

"We, Bernie?''

"Of course, my dear. Would you refuse to use the power of the St. John name? It would not be labeled pride, Mary Kate, should you spurn what connections you have. Call it pure stupidity and nothing less.''

"In that case, Bernie," Mary Kate said, "I have no choice, do I?"

"No choice at all, my dear," Bernie responded with a smile.

"We shall, of course, begin in London," Bernie informed her at breakfast.

"Why London?"

Bernie waved her knife in the air. "Because the Admiralty is there, my dear. And before you wrinkle that nose at me, let me reassure you that information concealed from you will almost certainly be revealed to the Dowager Countess of Sanderhurst."

"And Archer? Is he to know, then?"

"Archer concurs with my wish to visit the City, Mary Kate," she said, standing and brushing her skirt of crumbs. It never failed, no matter how diligent she was, there were always specks of what she'd been eating upon her garments. "He does not say so, but I think he means me to acquire suitable fashionable attire." There was a small, victorious smile. "Of course, I shall not illuminate him any further than that. Nor is he aware that you are accompanying me on my journey."

"And you do not think it wiser to inform him?"

"Mary Kate, do you honestly believe Archer would willingly allow you away from his sight, especially if the purpose for which you are going to London is to find your family? He is lamentably possessive, my child, and the presence of an uncle or a few doting brothers is not the sort of thing he would welcome with open arms."

Especially since he has grown so absurdly besotted over the past few weeks. Oh, Bernie had seen the signs, all right, the softening of his gaze, his laughter, the ease with which he comported himself, the inclusion of Mary Kate into his private world, a place heretofore kept sacrosanct and inviolate. No, Archer would not welcome Mary Kate's family. Mary Kate's only response was a slow, burning blush.

In little more than a day they were in London, where speed, blessedly, had to be sacrificed for caution. The speed with which they'd traveled had reminded Mary Kate too much of the accident that had begun her association with Archer St. John. None of her pleas, however, slowed them one whit.

Soon they were caught up in the throng of traffic known as London's streets. Carriages, men on horseback, pony carts and horse-drawn wagons, barrows and rickety push-carts laden with fresh fish, clams, mussels, cheeses, all vied for passage along the same thoroughfare.

If speech were given flavor, it would be a rich and varied stew, a hundred nationalities, dialects, patterns, all melding in the savory broth. Add to that other sounds, the calls of the barrow girls, the sounds of children singing their lessons, the pealing of sext bells. A jangling of noise that seemed to vibrate inside Mary Kate's head and echo against her skull.

Strangely enough, she had not missed it, even though she had enjoyed living in London. Sanderhurst had proven to be as alluring in its way. There was no one in London to whom she might turn; she'd often suspected that Edwin had not been universally liked. There had been no one, other than Charles Townsende, to call him friend, no neighbor he'd wished to cultivate, not one person for whom he'd expressed a fondness. Even his funeral had been scantily attended.

The long coach ride had been made palatable by Bernie's presence, by the stories the older woman told of her travels, of the characters she had met in the years away from England. During the last hour, however, they had each grown quiet, as if the savoring of London required silence.

And in a way, Mary Kate saw a side of the city she'd never seen before, sitting propped against the plush squabs of Archer St. John's carriage. As they approached his London town house, she recognized, again, the great gulf that divided them.

Help him. . . .

Do shut up, Alice.

Bernie's eyes were wide, her look one of startlement.

"I am sorry, did I say that out loud?"

"Well, yes, dear, you did. Is she speaking to you?" Bernie looked not so censorious as fascinated.

"She has not ceased since we left Sanderhurst. She does not wish me far away."

"That in itself could be interesting, my dear. I wonder why."

"I'm sure I do not know, Bernie, any more than I know why she has chosen me to torment." Especially since it was not Archer, but some unknown lover, whom Alice wanted Mary Kate to rescue.

"Have you received any more visions?"

"Not a one, but a constant pain in the back of my head. Almost as if one would be imminent if I allowed it."

"Then, my dear, you must certainly do so." Bernie almost rubbed her hands together in glee.

"It isn't that I don't want to help, please understand that. It's just that I hate losing myself in her. I can barely tolerate it."

"And the longer it's gone on, the less easy it is."

"How did you know?"

"As odd as this might sound, my dear, you've just described my marriage." A chuckle was the response to Mary Kate's expression. "Archer's father was a very domineering sort, who insisted that everyone be exactly what he wanted. I had to dress his way, and speak his way, and only occupy myself in those pursuits which he dictated suitable for his countess. I suppose, in a very strange way, your relationship with Alice is like a union, of sorts, in which there is more power on her side than on yours. Anyone would balk at that, I think, given the circumstances."

"I wish she would find someone else, Bernie. Her presence is rather loathsome."

"But you say at Sanderhurst she does not bother you as much?"

Mary Kate could feel herself flushing, a sure sign that her cheeks were pink. She shook her head, deciding that silence was the most prudent response. Bernie's answer was another chuckle.

The palatial town homes faced each other proudly, as if nodding appreciatively at their counterparts' broad fanlights and cobblestone approaches. Heavy velvet adorned tall, wrought-iron-trimmed windows, as if to shield their occupants. Bright brass knockers adorned each of the black painted doors, but there was no number to identify each residence, no nameplate to announce its owner. It was as if each inhabitant dwelled here in utter secrecy, the possession of money or nobility deserving of some measure of anonymity on these quiet and secluded streets. It was a daunting place to trespass, was Grosvenor Square.

*   *   *

Archer St. John was singularly irritated.

Women kept disappearing from his life with increasing regularity. First his missing wife. Then his mother, and finally Mary Kate, whose position in his life was so tenuous and amorphous that he could not yet decide what to label it.

For a man called hermit, he had spent an inordinate amount of time traveling from one point to another. Even more daunting was the fact that he sought females while doing so. Was he the only man so oppressed by the women in his life?

He was known for his tenacity. It was both his greatest gift and his most formidable weakness. He never gave up easily, often going beyond the bounds of rational behavior to achieve some feat he'd assigned himself. As a child, it had been to learn chess. He'd read everything he could on the subject, practiced with any one of the servants or villagers who knew the game. Only when he could beat every one of his opponents did Archer feel as though he'd accomplished his goal.

He'd also not been content to leave well enough alone with the St. John coffers. The spice trade had brought in millions over the years, a steady, secure source of ever-increasing funds. Archer had expanded the spice line with turpentine and camphor oil.

Yet Mary Kate with her incredible story, her stubborn insistence, her habit of disappearing with regularity, was his match in pertinacity.

Archer rolled the silk shade up for a view of London. Tall spires and angled rooftops vied with a jangle of color here and there. Soot and smoke puffing from innumerable chimneys offered up punctuation marks against the gray winter sky.

She was gallivanting all over England with his mother, for what purpose he did not yet know. Was it to track down his missing wife? Did they honestly think he had not tried to find Alice?

The question was, what would he feel if his wife magically appeared one day? Vindicated? Surely that. Saddened, possibly, by the chasm that stretched between them; memories of desertion would be difficult to breach. And the other? An antediluvian sense of honor dictated that he be faithful, especially if he and Alice were to craft anything from the ruins of their marriage.

Mary Kate. He would have to say farewell to Mary Kate.

"I am more sorry than I can possibly say, my dear. To have raised your hopes so high, only for them to be dashed so cruelly." Bernie placed her hand under Mary Kate's elbow, and together they left the Admiralty building.

They had been greeted by Sir Anthony Pettigrew himself, the great man having learned of Bernie's presence from the same clerk who had refused to grant Mary Kate any information the previous visit.

Anthony Pettigrew wasted no time in formalities, simply planted a rather boisterous kiss on Bernie's open mouth. "Damme, Bernie, it's good to see you. Never thought you'd get back to England. Thought I'd have to run into you in India again."

"Well, as you can see, I am here, hale and hearty."

"And looking as sprightly as ever. The English climate does the very best for you, Bernie. It truly does. Are you here to stay, then?" He lifted her hand and brushed his lips against her gloved knuckles. Bernie only smiled and withdrew her hand as quickly as she could.

"No, just for a few more months. I had a yen for home."

An inquiry for tea was met with the same bemused response, and it was not until an hour later that Bernie felt herself free of the web of Anthony Pettigrew's solicitousness. The head of the Admiralty had been charming, handsome in an elder statesman kind of way, and possessed of the oddest habit of winking at her from time to time, as if they shared a particularly humorous joke at the expense of the rest of the world.

"The fact of the matter is, my dear, I cannot recall one single thing about him. Not where I met him. Not his face. Nor anything about him. Isn't that the oddest thing? From the moment I saw him, I experienced this blank fog. I do hate when that happens."

"Well, you are bound to remember him," Mary Kate said, "at a time when it will not matter."

"Truly, it does not matter now, does it? After all, he has done everything anyone could do. At least we know your uncle was not aboard the *Royal George*. The problem is, we do not know his current berthing."

"Or even if he is still alive."

"Oh, my dear girl, I do realize I told you not to hold out much hope, but sometimes you simply must not listen to me. I am sure your uncle will be found. Quite, quite certain of it. But if we cannot solve one mystery, there is still Alice to consider."

"I do wish, Bernie, that I had never heard that name."

"Then you would have never met Archer. Is that what you truly wish?"

Mary Kate merely closed her eyes, as if this was not the first time the question had been posed.

"Perhaps we should consider cutting our visit to London

short, my dear, and returning to the scene of the accident. Perhaps you will have some sort of vision there, something with which to fine-tune our investigation.''

''I remained at the inn a full week, Bernie, and have told you all my dreams. Besides, I refuse to travel with you, unless you tell the coachman to slow his speed. I would like to arrive at our destination alive.''

''Nonsense, child. Simply close your eyes, hang on to the strap above the window, and think pleasant thoughts.''

''Closing my eyes makes me nauseated, and the only thought I have is that while I may have been lucky during the first occurrence, it is doubtful I shall be so blessed after the second accident.''

''You must begin to show more adventure, my child.''

''And you, Bernie, more moderation.''

''That sentiment is too like something Archer would say. I think the two of you are well matched.''

I think the two of you are well matched. Could it be that simple? How absurd. And how oddly right. Had Alice simply paired the most unlikely of people, from the most improbable of circumstance? And what did that mean? That Alice St. John could not possibly be alive. Living wives do not find companions for their husbands. Their search, therefore, must change direction, and concentrate instead upon Alice's fate, not her willful disappearance.

''What is on your mind now, Bernie?'' Mary Kate interrupted the flurry of thoughts racing through Bernie's mind. ''You have the most unholy look of satisfaction upon your face.''

''I think it time we contact the spirit world, Mary Kate,'' she said. ''Perhaps we've gone about this all wrong. Why not ask Alice where she is?''

Chapter 29

‌"**O**h, thou Phytic oracle, that which sees all, which knows the heart and cleanses the soul of man, aid us in our quest." Bernie's voice was low, the turbaned head tilted back, her eyes closed. The backs of her hands rested upon the table, palms curved up.

The candle flickering in the center of the table seemed to be curiously disposed to follow the tone of Bernie's voice, until Mary Kate noted it was placed so close that any breath from the other woman impacted its flame.

Mary Kate sat opposite Bernie, who sat to the right of Harrellson, the very proper London butler whose face glowed from the effects of St. John port. To Mary Kate's left was an underfootman who claimed to have had spiritual visitations prior to this evening.

While the men were dressed somewhat normally, both women were wearing tunics of buckskin, which smelled as if they hadn't been cured properly. On the top of Mary Kate's head a large bonnet perched, into which at least two dozen crushed feathers had been sewn. Add to that enough silver necklaces to supply a small jewelry establishment. She looked like a living amulet.

It was, all in all, an odd group, rendered even more

bizarre by the ritual in which they were currently participating. Bernie had prepared the room by muttering in Latin, a language none of the rest of them knew, except for those obscure passages taken from liturgical text. *Requiescat in pace* seemed hardly appropriate for this meeting. Or perhaps it was, since the purpose of it was to help Alice St. John rest in peace.

In the middle of the table, upon a silver salver, was a Chinese figurine of a very portly man. In his hands smoked three wands of incense so aromatic that Mary Kate's eyes were watering.

After the purification ceremony, Bernie had had the notion of calling upon the ancient Egyptian wizards, making a pyramid of her hands, which she held above her as she uttered some unintelligible words. She was into Greek oracles when Archer arrived.

"I don't bloody well believe this." The voice was filled with icy contempt.

It had the power to freeze all four occupants of Bernie's bedchamber.

"I chase all over England looking for the two of you, only to find you engaging in this . . ." Words seemed to fail Archer at that point. He simply waved his hands in the air as if pointing at the various accoutrements necessary to such a scene.

"You," he said, pointing one long finger at Harrellson, "get to your quarters." It took a moment for his butler to steady his feet, if not his balance. It was not so much the effect of the ceremony as it was the port.

"You are dismissed." These words were addressed to the underfootman. Mary Kate was not certain if Archer meant forever or just this occasion.

"As to you," he said, glancing at Mary Kate, "get to

your chamber: I'll attend to you later." Where once those words might have instilled in her some anticipation, at this particular moment they rang with warning.

Mary Kate did not bother to protest his rather high-handed dictate. She had not wanted to be included in this foolishness, but she'd discovered that Archer's mother had a single-minded determination that rivaled his. Was it something that ran in the St. John blood? She did not delay in absenting herself from Bernie's room.

"What the hell are you about, Mother?" He turned on his mother the minute the room was cleared.

She ignored him, bent over the circular table, extinguished the remaining candles, then straightened and stared back at him.

"Do you have any idea of how preposterous you look? And what the hell did you do to Mary Kate? Did you give her that damn headdress?"

"Yes, Archer, I gave her the spirit headdress. And the beads, and the moccasins, and the yin and yang coins to hold. I have inculcated many cultures into this ceremony."

"Which is for which purpose, exactly?"

"We are following an ectoplasmic trail, Archer. A transmogrification of souls meeting at midnight."

"What?"

"We're talking to the dead."

"Sometimes, Bernie, I think you're a candle whose wick has long since burned out."

"And sometimes, Archer, I think you a man who cannot see."

"What is there to see, Bernie?" One hand extended toward the table where the joss sticks still smoked. "This? Do you honestly believe you're going to accomplish anything here?"

"At least I am trying, Archer. I but wished to aid Mary Kate, my dear son. I should think you would applaud such motives."

"How, by tossing amulets into the air? By drinking yourself into a stupor to better convince yourself that you hear a visitor from a spirit world?"

There was a silence in which she stared at him, betraying nothing by her gaze or her movements. It was, he thought, a singularly uncomfortable look, one that reminded him of his youth and her interminable lectures about the karma of justice.

"You don't believe her, do you? You truly do not."

"What is there to believe, Mother? That my wife is a ghost, instead of a faithless spouse? Or the most ridiculous idiocy of them all, that Alice cared for me with such deep devotion that she sent Mary Kate Bennett to watch over me? Which of these unbelievable things would you have me believe? One? Two? Or am I to put all my credulity into a handbasket, toss it out the window, and believe it all?"

"So instead, you choose to believe nothing. When did you become such a cynic, Archer?"

"About the same time you became so gullible, Mother."

"Does Mary Kate know?"

"Of course she knows. Did you think I had to cozen her into my bed? Or perhaps pay her to be there?"

It was, Archer thought, a rather unique thing to render his mother speechless. "You look like a mother is supposed to look right now, with your mouth all pursed in disapproval. It won't wash, Bernie. All these years you've taken such great pride in scandalizing the world, in taking the St. John money and creating your own, highly rarefied existence, in behaving in ways designed to shock. I remember your advising me to take my pleasures where I may, because the world was an uncertain place and life itself tenuous.''

"You were thirteen and home from school and pining for a friend's sister,'' she said, removing her turban and fluffing up her hair.

"And what is so different about your advice now?''

"If you do not know the answer to that question, Archer, I am truly disappointed in you.''

"That statement is a tactic women have devised since time began. 'If you don't know . . . ' The poor hapless fool is left dangling and ready to confess to a myriad of sins simply to prevent himself from twisting upon a noose of confusion. It doesn't work with me.''

She planted her hands on her hips and faced him. "Then let me illuminate the situation for you, Archer, since you are so determined not to see it. A young woman has had her life disrupted, her very sanity questioned, her health jeopardized, her reputation ruined, for the sake of one man. You. She sees things in dreams both awake and asleep, but when a voice whispers to her of danger, what does she do? She attempts to protect the object of her concern. And what do you give her in response? You ridicule her and then seduce her.''

"Not that it is any of your business, Mother, because it is not, but the seduction was mutual.'' The solicitation of a kiss the eagerness with which they both entered into their current relationship. Hardly fodder for conversation. It was, he was not altogether surprised to note, something about which he felt intensely personal and private. "Don't interfere in my life. Despite the love I bear you, I will not tolerate it. You are a woman of the world. You know as well as I what happened here.''

She waved her hands in the air. ''Do not try to convince me it's some sort of *droit du seigneur,* Archer, or that Mary Kate surrendered her reputation without a struggle. Even servant girls have to protect themselves in this world ruled by men.''

''And why do I think most men should protect themselves from you?''

''Do not change the subject, Archer.'' There was a flash of anger in her eyes.

''Very well, I shall not change the subject. I simply will not address it with you. My life, my actions, my purpose, are not for comment, not even from you.''

''And Mary Kate?''

''Nor her.''

''And your seduction of her?''

At his silence, she frowned. ''So you'll keep taking advantage of her.''

''She's hardly an innocent, Bernie. She's a woman grown.''

''Who is unaccustomed to such wealth as Sanderhurst boasts. Do you not think that to have some attraction for her?''

''You never stoop to flattery, do you?'' His smile was sardonic. ''Could it be me, and not my gold, perhaps?''

''Only you can answer that question, Archer. What, exactly, does she want? Has she not cozened herself to gain admittance to your life? Does she perhaps not have a nefarious object in mind? I'm surprised you do not send her packing, a jade like that.''

''She could be telling the truth, Mother.''

She rounded on him, her gaze as sharp as Toledo steel. "Exactly, Archer. She could be telling the truth."

He was a man besieged by contradictions. Perhaps that was why he asked the question of Mary Kate, later, in her chamber. "Why do you think it is Alice who speaks to you?"

"Why do you want to know now, Archer?"

She was still attired in that ridiculous garment. She should have looked absurd in it. Yet she did not, nor did she sound like a dairymaid, or resemble any of the servant girls he'd ever caused to be hired at Sanderhurst. She perplexed him and vexed him and caused him to question all those things he'd once thought true and proper and right about his world. And made that world stop with the sheer joy of touching her and listening to her laugh.

"Tell me, Mary Kate."

"How easily you demand, Archer. Speak, Mary Kate, and I'm to divulge everything so that you might ridicule me again."

"Have I? Lately?"

"The price of sharing your bed, Archer?" Her smile was rueful. He found himself wanting to touch her, reassure her through his fingers, lips, embrace, that he would not mock her.

"Please," he said softly, and maybe it was that, only that one word that released her from her silence.

She turned from the window, walked to the fireplace, placed one hand against the mantle. It was a curiously pensive pose, he thought, arrested by the way the light from the fire shone around her, granting her a nimbus of radiance.

"Do you know the feeling you get when you've done

something wrong, and that voice inside reminds you of it?''

"Your conscience?" He smiled slightly. "Some more active than others."

She didn't turn, didn't acknowledge his remark. He had the oddest feeling that this was difficult for her.

"At times it is no louder than the hiss from a teakettle. At others, it feels like a shout." A finger trailed along the edge of the ormolu clock, touched the corner of the marble, smoothed over the carving of grapes, apples, pomegranates. A miniature column was fashioned in gold, the edges of the pediment carving delicate, almost fragile. "Like a reminder, only more insistent. A feeling of danger and a compulsion to ensure that such a feeling is not realized."

"Intuition, then?"

"Are you still attempting to find something rational about this, Archer?" Her eyes flashed irritation. "Do you think I have not tried?"

It was, he thought, a question he'd not pondered. "And how do you know it's Alice?"

"I've seen her."

"You've seen her?"

"In my early dreams, I looked into a pool and saw her face, or a mirror and spied her reflection."

"And you know she is telling you I'm in danger."

She turned and looked at him. It was a direct look, filled with the strangest sort of compassion. "No, Archer, I was wrong. I don't think Alice wants me to protect you at all."

A silence fell, laced not with the strange contentment their silences had been of late, but with emotion bubbling and brewing beneath the surface.

"Another vision, dearest?"

She only nodded.

Archer wasn't quite certain at that moment what he felt. It was such a maelstrom of thoughts that he could barely sort them out, let alone frame a coherent sentence. Above all of the mental clamor was a sense of berayal so foul he ws surprised the air was not tinged with it.

"It is not an original trick, you know," he said, in quite a prosaic tone, he thought. She looked startled at his statemen:, but then he was learning, in lessons drilled into him by ace-bound moments, that he should not trust even her most innocent expression.

"It's played out quite well on the hunting field. The fox changes direction and circles back around, confusing the pack until they're ready to bay at their own mothers. I suppose that is your aim, is it not? To confuse me until I cry off entirely and accept anything you have to say, for the sheer joy of your delectable body?"

She flushed again, a colorful accompaniment to the glare she shot him. Once, a lifetime ago, a moment ago, he would have trusted her. Or at least wanted to. He would have told her that it was quite easy to guess at her thoughts, they were so quickly mirrored in her eyes and in the constant rosiness of her blsuh. Now, he didn't believe the anger and discounted the embarrassment.

"So, I am not to be considered worth saving. Will I be deprived of your company, sweet, while you traipse around England attempting to find yet another gull for your tricks?"

"Don't do this, Archer."

"Don't do what, Mary Kate? Not accept your idiotic story? Again? Who said I ever did?" There, that sounded plausible. Enough to cause a paleness where there had been only blush. She believed him, at least. "Who are you in wait for, sweetling? Who is the next idiot on your agenda? Whose bed, pretending I believe you, does dear, darling Alice want you to warm now?''

He smiled at her silence.

''Come now, Mary Kate, don't tell me you've grown reticent after all this.'' He stepped closer, a stalking motion he recognized even as he measured off the list of emotions warring inside him. Betrayal, remorse, sadness, some strange feeling that made him want to scream at her and shake her and make her cry so that she couldn't tell where her tears ended and his began.

''All I've ever wanted to do was to find my family.''

''Tell me, damn you.''

''I don't know.''

''You don't know.'' He speared a hand through his hair, stared at her, then shook his head. ''I should truly have become used to it, you know. But somehow, you still manage to astound me. Am I such a gullible fool, I wonder? Do I look the part? Did Alice tell you I was capable of being gulled? More fool she, if she believed that. My complicity in her adultery was not by choice, not by a long shot. But I've discovered it's hard to make a marriage when your wife cannot stand the sight of you.''

She stepped away from the mantle, placing more distance between them. He wanted to tell her that it didn't matter; all of England could stand between him and her and if he wanted her, he would have her. Conversely, she could stand naked before him and he'd refuse to touch her if he willed it to be so.

''And you, Archer? How long before you grew to hate Alice?'' How quickly her voice had turned from warmth to ice. Her eyes seemed as cold. Frozen ponds of green. A world of ice.

''You are never content to let something alone, are you,

Mary Kate? You'll worry at it until it unravels, until all the pieces are broken down, until you have a sobbing wretch at your feet. Yes, I suppose I did grow to hate her. Is that confession enough for you?"

She gave him a look, as if he were a slow-witted child. It had the effect of mitigating his hunger, his acute and unwelcome longing, freeing the brunt of his anger.

However, this surprising woman with the flame red hair and flamboyantly extravagant breasts was not content with raising his temper. She voiced the one question no one in the world had the courage to ask to his face.

"Did you kill her?"

A heartbeat in the silence. A few odd and stilted moments in which he closed his eyes, unable to look at her. A moment later, he opened them again, focused his gaze on the roaring fire. How odd that the words felt like glass leaving his mouth, as if ground fine by the effort of passing through his throat. "By God, not even you should have the audacity to ask me that question." Why had she said it? Had she believed it all this time? "It is time for Alice to come home, don't you think? I grow tired of being accused of the murder of a woman we both know is alive."

"You sound so certain, Archer. While I am more sure than ever that she is not."

"If you believe that, then you evidently believe me capable of her murder. I'm surprised you could bear to let me touch you, Mary Kate. Did I soil you in some way?" He strove for a tone of sardonic humor, heard the flatness of his own words. He sounded pitiable. Poor wretch. Betrayed again.

"I am sorry, Archer, the words were improvident."

He glanced at her. "Do not look so contrite now, madam," he said formally, one corner of his lip turning up as if amused. It was nearly a superhuman effort on his part. "You have only said what half the world believes, in any event. I congratulate you on your courage."

"Nonsense. You could not have killed her. I did not mean to say it." She stepped forward, would have touched him, but he moved then.

"How adroit you are. First you accuse and within moments, you pardon. I could only wish that my neighbors and erstwhile friends had taken a page from your book. But then, they do not have the knowledge you and I share, of your complicitous relationship with my errant wife."

She reached out one hand, but it was too late. Because he had left her.

She'd barely been in bed and adjusted her cap before the door opened again and then was shut again as quickly.

Bernie frowned at her guest, whipped off the cap and fluffed up her hair, wishing that she had had the good sense to wear one of her silk peignoirs instead of this damn muslin gown. There wasn't even a bit of lace upon the sleeves, nothing but a rolled French hem.

Damn the man's arrogance. From the look of his smile, it was just exactly what he wanted. She slitted her eyes at him and contemplated throwing the novel she was reading at him. No, bad waste of a good book.

"Well, you've taken your bloody time about it," she said, hearing the surliness of her own voice and recognizing that she wasn't as irritated as she let on. The idiot had led her a merry chase these weeks, always smiling as if he knew something about her, brushing her a kiss when she'd entered or left a carriage. Taming her, he'd even whispered one day, and when she'd nearly thrust her umbrella into his stomach, he'd only neatly sidestepped and grinned that devil's grin.

"Peace, Bernie," Peter Sullivan said, unbuttoning his tunic and eyeing her with a smile. "It's a lonely place, London, I'm thinkin'."

"And a damn cold one," she said, throwing back the covers. She smiled, a warm welcome, and their kiss, when it came, was nearly swallowed by their laughter.

Chapter 30

His smile was a daunting thing to ignore. After a moment, Mary Kate did not try.

"So, you'll not have forgiven me for tellin' them where you were headed," Peter said, as he helped her from the carriage. "I'd wondered, the way you're forever scurrying away from me. You have to understand, the world can be a harsh place for a comely lass as yourself."

She rolled her eyes at his gallantry, then matched his smile with her own. "And you could charm the bees from the hive, Peter Sullivan, a trait I've no doubt Bernie has discovered."

To her amazement, his tanned face turned ruddy. She turned away to hide her amusement. She did not wish to take advantage of his embarrassment. After all, Peter had been the only one of the servants who had been willing to speak to her. The rest acted as though she were neither fish nor fowl, a crossbreed between lower servant and mistress, a category she fit too well in, but an admission she would never make to them. So, for the most part, she spent her days isolated from others, in that peculiar way nobility lived.

Bernie insisted upon visiting every neighbor within traveling distance on their way back to Sanderhurst. An occupation, she explained, that was the only alternative to the boredom of Sanderhurst.

Mary Kate sincerely hoped that this next visit would be better than the last. They had spent an eternal hour with the Misses Hasting, the three sisters who lived a few hours away from Sanderhurst in a drafty old house that looked to be part of an ancient monastery at one time.

The five of them had sat in the dark parlor, rendered so because the sisters had not opened the draperies in the parlor since the day their father had died five years ago. God Bless His Soul. This had been repeated on every utterance of dear departed Papa's name, being unfortunately one of the more favored of the Hasting conversational topics. The three sisters perched upon the opposite sofa like crows upon a bare branch, all dressed in black, all with high foreheads, hair scraped back into tight little buns, all exactly alike save for slight differences of appearance, not personality. The middle one had blue eyes, the other two brown. The one on the left was taller and two years older. The one on the right had once been married.

This visit had been followed by one to the widowed Mrs. Dorset, a quite attractive woman just beyond the first blush of youth. She had spiced the entire conversation with questions about Archer. Mary Kate found herself quite irritated at the constant reference to the St. John fortune, but even more annoyed by the woman's fawning insistence upon repaying the call the next day. "I shall enjoy seeing Lord St. John again. Oh, indeed I shall."

Mary Kate wanted to hit Bernie with something sharp.

Now they were at yet another house, paying yet another call, a uniquely British invention for women of great means and few duties. Such boredom was not, Mary Kate thought, something to envy.

"Straighten your bonnet, Mary Kate."

"I shall. You might note that there is blue icing upon your skirt, Bernie," Mary Kate said with a smile.

"Weren't those cakes absolutely ghastly? At least the topping took the edge off the sweetness, but however did she make it blue? You must admit, however, that the tea was palatable. But that is the last time I shall eat Miriam Dorset's cakes."

"Why do I think you are chattering, Bernie? Is it to prevent me from asking why we've not returned straightaway to Sanderhurst as you promised Archer?" Mary Kate had not spoken to him since the night before, when he'd simply turned and left her chamber. Nor had he visited her later, as she'd half expected. It had been a long and lonely night.

"We are on our way home, child. This is simply an opportunity to meet some people I've not seen in a long while. I'm not a hermit like my son."

"Why does he secrete himself away, Bernie?"

"You haven't experienced any of our relatives, have you, dear girl? Be pleased, then," she said when Mary Kate shook her head. "Bunch of bloodsuckers, forever beseeching Archer for this and that, naming babies after him, planting trees in his honor, all for the sake of a few more pounds per year. He supports over twenty families as it is, and every person in England with a dot of St. John blood in their veins has aspired to tap into the family fortune."

"No wonder he thought me an opportunist. Still, he should not take his family for granted, Bernie. Not everyone is so fortunate."

"There is yearning in your tone, my dear, but let me

assure you, the St. John clan is nowhere near to being familial. Why do you think Sanderhurst is off-limits, and why Archer will only agree to meeting family members in London? They are a yipping litter, the St. Johns. If they would spend half as much energy utilizing their fortunes instead of begging for more, they would be better served. It's what my father did, after all.''

Bernie lifted the brass knocker and rapped sharply on the door.

The woman was placing her needles back into the bag constructed for just such a purpose when Bernie swept into the room with Mary Kate in tow. The smile of welcome on her face froze as she saw who her visitors were.

"Cecily, you're looking well." A bright smile lit Bernie's face. "Come, don't tell me I look as bad as all that? You stare at me as if I'm a ghost come to call."

Bernie began to remove her gloves, one finger at a time, that bright smile still plastered upon her face. "Mary Kate?" She turned and motioned her forward.

"Cecily, I would like you to meet a dear friend of mine, Mary Kate Bennett. From London."

Mary Kate returned her hostess's nod, feeling as though she were in a marionette play and the only person who truly knew what they were doing and why was Bernadette St. John.

"It's been a long time, Bernadette. A great many years."

"Indeed it has, Cecily, but I must tell you that the years have not found you overly changed. And Samuel? Has he weathered with such grace?" Another dazzling smile as she seated herself on the sofa.

"My husband is well. Is that why you've returned, Bernadette St. John? To whore with my husband? In my daughter's house?''

''I'm not quite sure about which part of your question I object to the most, Cecily, referring to Sanderhurst as your daughter's house when it has been in my husband's family for seventeen generations, or calling me a whore.''

Mary Kate stared at Cecily blankly, wondering later if she looked as owlish as she felt at that moment. She sat heavily beside Bernie, any lessons on grace and deportment forgotten in the shock of this moment. Bernie might have warned her upon whom they were calling. She sent a frown in the other woman's direction, but Bernie's attention was focused on Archer's mother-in-law.

''I label you what you are, Bernadette St. John.''

''Even a fool, when he holdeth his peace, is counted wise: and he that shutteth his lips is esteemed a man of understanding.''

''Nothing will be served by blaspheming, Bernadette St. John. God Himself hears you. 'All manner of sin and blasphemy shall be forgiven unto men: but the blasphemy against the Holy Ghost shall not be forgiven unto men.' ''

''I have no intention of engaging in a battle of quotes with you, Cecily. You truly have not changed, then. Somehow I would have thought you softened over the years.''

''To you? Is that why you came? To see if I'd forgiven you? 'Such is the way of an adulterous woman; she eateth, and wipeth her mouth, and saith, I have done no wickedness.' ''

''I came home for one purpose, Cecily. To help Archer find dear Alice. And for that reason alone. I think it's reprehensible that no word has come either from her or about her. Tell me,'' she said, ''have you heard nothing at all from your daughter in all this time?''

Their hostess remained standing, hands gripped tightly together, lips pursed. In her eyes there was no welcome, nor had she offered either woman refreshments, as was customary of afternoon calls.

Altogether, it was quite clear that they were most unwelcome at Moresham Farms.

"Come now, Cecily. Don't tell me she didn't confide in you. Did she perhaps mention a destination she might have gone? Was there nothing about the weeks before her disappearance that seemed to you odd, or unusual?" At her silence, Bernie gritted her teeth and continued. "Will you at least tell me if she was happy at Sanderhurst?"

"I have no intention of talking with you, Bernadette, let alone divulging anything my daughter may have confided in me."

Bernie stood, placed one glove on her hand, toyed with the other. "Is there no way, then, for us to breach our differences, for Alice's sake?"

There was no response to that question. Cecily did not even look in her direction. Instead, she sat at the chair beside the window and extracted her knitting again, studiously ignoring both women.

She sat forward, her spine as inflexible as that of the chair, her starched white cap neither dampened by the humidity nor wilted by the fire. The small bow was tied in a perfectly symmetrical arrangement beneath her chin, her hands now industrious, the clicking of the knitting needles punctuating the silence in an oddly soothing rhythm. It would have been a peaceful tableau, but for the hatred in the air.

Bernie nodded at her, a clipped, almost tense gesture, then sailed through the door. Mary Kate had no choice but to follow in her wake.

* * *

"Excuse me."

Mary Kate blinked, staring up at the young man who solemnly addressed her. He was tall, almost as tall as Archer, but reed-thin, as if never growing the breadth nature had decreed for him. His eyes were hazel, warm, soft, unexpectedly kind.

"I am sorry, but you seemed a bit distracted. I wondered if you knew where you were headed."

Mary Kate glanced around, realized she was almost to the stables to the left of the manor house. She turned and the carriage was still in the front drive, Bernadette chatting with the coachman as if nothing untoward had taken place in the last five minutes, as if the scene in the house had not occurred after all. And how odd she should not remember walking in this direction.

"Not to mention that you should watch your step here." He pointed down at the ground, and only then did Mary Kate realize she had barely missed stepping in a steaming pile of manure.

"Oh dear."

"Shall I help you return to your carriage, then? I'm quite good at avoiding any surprises. We are a horse farm, after all." He extended his arm and Mary Kate placed her hand upon it.

The contact of her palm upon his coat was disconcerting. She seemed to be able to feel the texture of his skin through the cloth, the warmth of his flesh. Mary Kate knew without looking that his hands would be large, the fingers long and slender. The hands of a pianist, a musician.

"You've come to visit my stepmama, then?" He led her to a well-worn path between house and stable.

"I'm afraid I'm acting as companion only."

The arm she held flexed suddenly, muscles tightening. She glanced at him. His gaze was fixed upon the carriage. "That is the carriage from Sanderhurst."

"Yes. It is."

"And you are?"

"A guest there." It seemed the most plausible thing to say, after all.

His eyes seemed infinitely mysterious, as if hiding a thousand secrets, a hundred truths. She felt drawn into the soul exposed by those eyes. There was pain there, resignation and a longing too deep to ever express. And above it all was a sense of loss so profound that it made her breath hitch in shared anguish.

He looked so stricken that Mary Kate wanted, strangely, to go to him, to put her arms around him, to pull his face into her lap. To softly brush back the blond hair that trembled over his brow and sing to him words of comfort, the way a mother would do for a restless child. She would be mother, sister, lover, friend.

Her hand remained outstretched; she stared at it as if surprised by its presence. In truth, she was shocked. What was happening to her?

From somewhere came a voice, masculine and concerned. "Are you all right? Shall I fetch you some water?"

She shook her head from side to side, obeying the impulse to negate the awful strangeness of the past moment. She could not have spoken even if she were able to think the words.

"Would you care to sit down here? You look a bit pale," he was saying, his gentle features etched in concern. That, and a reluctant compassion. "I can summon someone from the house."

"I will be fine in a moment," she said, hoping it was

the truth. She was beginning to feel more herself, more in control of her body's movements, her mind's thoughts.

She pleated the fabric of her skirt between her fingers, wondering what was the correct conversational gambit for a situation such as this. She would move when her knees had stopped shaking, when her stomach no longer felt so unstable. She would not humiliate herself further by becoming ill in front of a perfect stranger.

"My stepmother has some degree of knowledge in the healing arts, madam, if you feel you have need of them."

Mary Kate looked up at the earnest face only inches above hers. "I am certain I will not. I am feeling much better already."

"You were very pale before. There is a spot of color on your face now. You look vastly improved."

"It is, no doubt, embarrassment that makes me flush so."

A sound broke their gaze, a jingle of harness, a muffled voice, the sound of horses restless upon the gravel of the drive, the solid slam of a carriage door. All these things Mary Kate knew and felt and heard, and yet none of them had the power to alter the direction of her gaze or the pull of her heart. With great reluctance, she moved away, toward the carriage and Bernie.

"He has grown into an exceedingly handsome young man, James Moresham."

Mary Kate was still so shaken by her encounter with him that she could only nod. How very odd to have had that reaction. What did it mean? Was she ill? She brought herself back to the conversation with a jolt.

"He and Alice were very close as children. There was never one but the other around. I used to think she could have had no better brother." There were not that many miles separating the Moresham farm from Sanderhurst. An easy canter on horseback, a longer walk.

"Does Archer know about you and Samuel Moresham?"

"My dear, I have been shocking Archer from the moment i dismissed his nurse and took to rearing him myself. Nothing he might hear about me would startle him."

Bernie should have looked subdued by the rudeness with which she had been treated. Instead, her eyes sparkled brightly, her skin was rosy, and there was a broad smile on her face.

"Samuel Moresham was my first love, my dear. We were too young and too silly, and I was just recently widowed. I will confess to stealing a kiss or two from him, yet that is all that ever transpired between us. I fancy, however, that Cecily thinks I left England because of some great unrequited and desperate love I bore Samuel."

"And did you?"

Bernie sighed. "Eleven years is quite a long time to decide to take action against desperation. No, I left England for two reasons, Mary Kate. The first was that Archer was just becoming a young man, the type of man who no longer needed to remain in leading strings. Yet he feels a great sense of obligation toward me. It can be very lowering, my dear. So the only way to free us both from this obligation of love was simply to leave England. The other reason was that I will admit to a certain type of loneliness, but not for a conventional relationship. I wanted to find out what life was about, my dear, and my way of doing that was to see the world."

Since she had experienced the very same kind of curiosity, Mary Kate could say nothing to that confession.

"I admire a great many men, but that does not mean that I bed each and every one of them." At her look, Bernie laughed. "I play cards with Jonathan, my dear, and listen to his woes. He is madly in love with the housekeeper, who will not entertain his suit unless under the influence of a goodly portion of Madeira."

"And Peter?" Mary Kate asked. She had not been blind to the looks between Bernie and the handsome footman.

Bernie had a distinctly cheeky smile, Mary Kate thought. "None of your concern, my dear."

"But why visit the Moreshams?"

"Because frankly, I am running out of suggestions as to where to look for Alice."

"You might have let me know, Bernie."

"Is that a note of censure in your voice, my dear? My only defense is that the idea came to me only moments before we actually stopped. Not that the visit proved to be at all useful."

Mary Kate had not liked Cecily Moresham. Her voice alone, with its twangy nasalness, had grated on her nerves, like the sound a cat will make when scratching his punishing claws against upholstery.

There had been a vicar in the village where she had spent her early childhood. Pastor Gastonby was a wizened old man with twinkly blue eyes, a genial air, and a mouth that looked as though it had smiled its way through life. His mild-mannered face transformed, however, once he was standing behind the rather imposing pediment near the altar of the church. He became a vengeful messenger, promising God's retribution, fire and brimstone and rigid justice, threatening all within his hearing of the punishments meted out for unwed debauchery and unclean thoughts.

He was rarely called upon to usher in death—most terminal penitents were too woefully conscious of just how many sins they were guilty of to be comfortable in Pastor Gastonby's presence. The good reverend, however, never missed the opportunity to say a prayer at the grave site, endless sermons that also included enumerating the departed's many faults, as if annoyed that the sinner was beyond his justice.

This was not the man Mary Kate would have sought out, had she wished a spiritual adviser. She could not imagine telling Pastor Gastonby of hearing Alice St. John's voice, or feeling impelled to aid the woman, for fear that he would denounce her as a tool of Satan.

Cecily Moresham was not unlike the good pastor.

Chapter 31

Sometimes, at night, James could almost hear her call him. It was as if Alice visited him in his mind, the way she had often done when they were children. Once, when he was eight, he'd been helping with loading the hay in the birthing shed placed far away from the house. He'd had a terrible feeling suddenly that Alice was in danger. He'd never been able to explain how he'd known where she would be and how he'd saved her from entering one of the stallions' stalls. She'd been only three, yet he'd felt her peril and had known, somehow, that she needed him. Ever since that day, it was as if there was something binding them together, something wonderful and magical, like an invisible string.

Even now he could feel it. Even now, when she was dead.

When he'd realized it, he couldn't remember. It was as if a brilliance had faded from his life, as if all the music had seeped out of it. Samuel offered him Vienna and he had no music to play.

He didn't think it odd that instead of the melodies, the crescendo of violin and horn, Alice came to him. He almost came to love the night, darkness, quiet, only the sound of her voice, speaking to him with that soft tone as if her words were meant for him alone and not to be overheard by the rest of world. The rest of the world could tumble about on its own, as long as Alice was his.

She would never have left him. Never have denied the love they shared.

What a life they could have had. What joy they could have experienced. She inspired him, empowered him, brought to him something nothing else or no one else ever had. Alice, in the morning, with her face newly washed and her smile dusted with the sun. Alice, with her laughter bubbling freely, with the soft, trusting feel of her hand in his, who smelled of lavender and whose kisses invited him to heaven.

There were times in the last year he'd wanted to die, if dying meant being with her. If he could have, he would have drilled a hole into his heart and let all the pain seep free. Only then could he cope with the world without Alice.

She would have joined him if she could. They had agreed to meet at the crossroads, take the carriage to Plymouth, board a ship there for some other place, the destination not as important as the fact they were going away together.

He would forever remember the day before they were to leave, had rehearsed the memory of it over and over again in his mind. "I wish it could be different, James. I want to begin our new life in the best possible way. I will forever regret hurting him." She had looked like a country daisy, soft and delicate in her yellow lawn dress with matching spencer. Her blond curls were hidden beneath a soft brown bonnet. Her blue eyes had looked so earnest that he could not help but drop a kiss upon her nose, for all they were standing in the crossroads where anyone could see them. It was to have been a last meeting before they left England, for a brighter life where their love did not have to be hidden, their passion did not have to remain muted.

"He has had you for too long, dearest," he said, determined to incite a sparkle of joy in those expressive eyes.

"I would still spare him, if I could." There was earnestness on her face, a somberness he vowed to soften.

"You are too sweet, Alice, too gentle. You would have none of us hurt through all of this. Either Archer St. John is pained, or we shall be. Which is it?"

Her eyes softened, and a smile lit her face. "I cannot leave you now, dearest James. You are my true heart. Heart of my heart. Almost brother."

"If I had not known any different, I would have still loved you, you know."

"And never said a word."

"Such a love is forbidden, Alice darling."

"As ours is."

"No." He held out his hands and she laid hers upon them. They had had this discussion before, but he could not bear to part with her for even an hour without telling her again. "It is no sin when we should have been allowed to marry."

"My father did not know, James, that we loved each other, else I know he would have spoken sooner."

"And told me I was a bastard? That there was no blood link between us? Your mother would have forbidden it regardless."

Her look was sad then, so much that he wanted to take back his words, prevent any grief from coming into her eyes, dimming her smile.

"I will miss her, James, for all her faults. I will miss our family.'

"There is but one word you must say to me, Alice, if you do not wish to leave. One word, and you will feel no guilt, no regret, no longing."

"And forever lose you? Oh, James, I could better tear out my heart."

She had turned away from him, bestowing a last, bright smile upon him, before walking back to Sanderhurst.

She'd never been seen again.

He'd blamed himself for too many months, bearing the burden of his guilt in silence. The morning he was supposed to meet Alice, Samuel had decided to race at Fairhaven. All of the horses entered in the races had to be transported there, a journey of but a few miles, but long enough to delay his return by three hours. When he had finally approached the crossroads, from the east and not the south as he would have had he been coming from Moresham Farms, there was no one there. Only the faint view of a carriage far in the distance.

He had waited for six hours. Waited even longer, until the day turned into night. Had returned home heartsick, because he'd been certain that Alice had simply changed her mind and could not bear to leave the earl. It was only days later that he'd discovered she must have waited for him, that she'd not been seen since that morning.

He knew Alice was dead. And that Archer St. John had killed her. There was no other explanation.

And now another woman was in danger.

"I do not think it proper, Samuel, that that woman is back in our midst." Cecily Moresham emerged from behind the screen draped in a voluminous cotton gown, as impenetrable as a tent over her small, plump frame. Her husband met her on the other side of their bed garbed in a similar fashion, a nightcap the only addition to his wardrobe. He would have preferred to sleep naked, but such an act would have horrified his wife. Together they denuded the bed of its duvet, folded it neatly at the foot. Their movements were identical; years of sharing this chore had made them partners in it.

"Perhaps it would be better if you did not think upon it, Cecily. She seems to upset you."

"She upsets all good people, Samuel. All who would recognize the extent of her evil. Even the Bible states that proper 'women adorn themselves in modest apparel, with shamefacedness and sobriety; not with broided hair, or gold, or pearls, or costly array; but with good works.' "

Samuel, neither long-suffering nor remotely interested in his wife's eternal prattling about good works, held the opinion that Cecily's show of charitable intent was less because she genuinely cared for those less fortunate than that she was concerned about looking the part. His wife was, he had long since decided, an obnoxious servant for the Lord.

"It is my duty to consider the moral climate we live in. Although others would dismiss the harlot for the sake of her fortune. All my life people have excused the St. Johns their behavior, simply because of their rank and their possessions."

"While you covet both."

Her sharp inrush of breath was the only indication of her indignation.

Samuel slipped into their communal bed with such gallantry that not an inch of his skin was shown to distress his wife of twenty-seven years. Conciliation might be the best course. "Perhaps the years have added a matronly

quality to her personality, rendering her less dangerous."
He had extinguished the candle, so there was no way to
see his features.

"I will not have you defending her," she commanded
irritably.

Samuel wanted to tell his wife that someone needed to
defend the targets of her religious zeal, but instead, he
remained mute. Night was the worst time of his marriage.
Once Cecily got a topic between her teeth, she worried at
it until it had been gnawed to the bone. His only desire
was for sleep, not conversation.

Cecily finished her prayers, straightened her gown, re-
aligned the pillow.

"I want to talk to you about James."

Silence. Should he pretend to sleep, or offer protection
for the boy? Curiosity won out, after all. "What about
James?"

"He needs to be directed from his ruinous path, husband."

"And what ruination is that, Cecily?"

"He wants to dabble in music, Samuel, not give his
efforts to following in your footsteps."

"I see nothing wrong with James using his talents, Cecily. It is, after all, not a great legacy I give to him."

"You are a baronet, Samuel. You must not forget your
role in life, to serve as an example for the less fortunate."
Her voice was uncomfortably strident.

"I but wish to tend to my horses, Cecily, and leave the
examples to others."

"That is the reason your son needs guidance. And the
very reason he has not come to worship in the last year."

"I think it has more to do with the services lasting four
hours, and those damn hard benches."

"You show levity where there is no place for it," she said sharply.

"Someone in this family should remember how to smile, Cecily. Since Alice was married, I've not heard laughter in this house."

"You would have me welcome wickedness?"

"Has losing Alice done that to you, my dear? Expunged all your sense of humor?"

"I do not wish to speak of Alice."

Perhaps it was too painful for her, as it was for him.

"Then let us speak of James. I do not know the Bible as well as you, my dear, but isn't there something about a joyful noise to the Lord?"

"The Psalms are ungodly, Samuel. They should not have been included in the true word of God."

"You have a narrow view of what is proper and not, Cecily. I cannot blame James, then, for failing to attend your worship. Your intolerance for the beliefs of others wears thin at times. You're a dour bunch."

She drew herself up and looked down at her husband.

"You will speak to him, then?"

"No, Cecily, I will not. I want him happy, wife, and it's plain he's been unhappy for a long time, now. I've offered him the money to go to Vienna to study, Cecily, and I'll hear no more of it."

"Whatever do you mean, Samuel?"

"Just that. He'll have enough funds to reside there and learn his music. He needs a change of scenery, perhaps, something to divert him from his great grief."

"And what great grief is that, Samuel Moresham?"

He sighed. "You know as well as I, Cecily, even though you've tried to deny it. He grieves for Alice."

"A brother's love."

"A lover's heart."

"You blaspheme. You bring wickedness into this house. Sin. Evil."

"I bring nothing but the truth, my dear. Ugly, perhaps, but the truth, nonetheless. There was nothing before man or God to prevent their union. Except, of course, ill-timing and the Earl of Sanderhurst."

"I do not know what you mean."

"Your voice is trembling, my dear. But come, it can't be that great a shock. Did you never think to yourself that James did not favor me?"

"You label him bastard, then?"

"To my everlasting regret, I wish I always had. It has diminished his consequence none and would have aided his happiness."

"There is more to life than happiness, Samuel Moresham."

Aye, didn't he know it.

Chapter 32

Mary Kate sat upon the second bench of the Sanderhurst chapel, immersed not so much in thought as she was the yellow light from the huge stained glass window at her back. Her thoughts were better saved for another place, one not as blessed and sanctified to glorify God. But they were stubborn things, these thoughts, creeping around her best intentions and slithering beneath the door of her defenses.

The first time she'd come to Sanderhurst had been as a prisoner, in truth. Oh, a little bemused and certainly never coarsely handled, but without much say in her own destiny. The second time she'd returned because she'd been distraught and a bit afraid, and Archer St. John had offered her a haven, one to which she'd grown accustomed. Too, there was the assuagement of a lifetime of curiosity, and a passion she suspected she would never be able to forget.

And this time, Mary Kate? What had he offered this time? There had been no words between them, no coaxing, no dictates, no stern admonishments. She had simply returned to Sanderhurst, as docile as a lamb leading the wolf to a secure and hidden place where there would be few witnesses to view her slaughter. She was no prisoner, unless she was guilty of constructing her own cell, walking into it and slamming the door behind her, then calling out to be praised for the joy with which she'd followed orders never spoken. The cell had somehow become home.

If he were truly hers, she would never leave him. She would be there always, a shadow to his substance, eager to offer company when he wished not to be alone, amusement for his days of worry, eagerness for his hours of teaching. She would be everything he wanted, more than he believed possible, a day of sunshine for his clouds, rain for his parched summer. Such dreams and she was awake.

Was this, then, love? The emotion that made idiots of men and weeping wrecks of women? This longing to be everything for one person? How insidious a feeling this was. It crept up on you unaware, promised impossibilities, led an intelligent person to thoughts of an implausible nature. Stripped away pride and left in its place a passion for life and dreams that could not possibly come true. Was it love? Such an emotion was dangerous to think about, was it not? Such dioramas played in the mind to ruinous results. Scenes of candlelit passion, or those of a family on a picnic. Archer, teaching their child to ride one of the massive St. John horses, together exploring the unused east wing of Sanderhurst. Telling stories in the library, playing snapdragon at Christmas, tasting cookies that the temperamental French cook created from butter and sugar and all manner of St. John spices. Visions to render the watcher starry eyed and unaware of reality.

She must leave, that was certain. She must find a place as secure as this spacious and well-appointed prison, one without a gaoler who captivated her so easily, who spoke words in a voice as smooth and rich as ribbon candy, whose eyes glittered at her in rage or passion or barely banked humor.

She must leave.

It had become, these three words, more than a set of instructions. It was a fervently voiced prayer.

"She used to meet me here, you know," James Moresham said, words that would have jolted her had she not heard the sounds of his footsteps. For a second, a flash of time, she'd thought him Archer, and had prepared herself for the sight of him.

"Alice?"

"Yes." He came around the pew and stood before her, yellow light bathing him in radiance. He looked, she thought, like an angel gone astray. Bernie was right. James Moresham was an exceedingly handsome man; the only detriment to his appearance was the expression in his eyes. And a mouth that looked not to have smiled for an eternity.

He turned and looked up at the round stained glass window that faced east. Rather than having a predominantly rose cast, the east window was lemon colored, allowing the full force of the sun to illuminate the family chapel. Nor was the scene depicted in the window of an overtly religious nature, but merely blooms of something that resembled flowers, but that Mary Kate suspected were spices. How like the St. Johns to have incorporated into their place of worship the source of their great income.

The chapel was not large, but it was superbly appointed. The altar cloth was snowy lace, the chalices and candlesticks looked to be solid gold. Even the small bench upon which she sat was indicative of wealth; a crimson and gold cushion was laced to it and a well-padded kneeling bench lay just beyond her feet. Mary Kate held out one trembling hand before her.

"Did I frighten you? I'm sorry, I did not mean to."

"No, I'm certain you did not." Dare she tell him that she'd almost become inured to being frightened lately? The presence of a resident spirit numbed you to other, ordinary frights. And even though Alice St. John had had the delicacy to limit her appearances over the last few days, Mary Kate doubted it was a permanent absence. Another reason to sit huddled in the chapel? A prayer for absolution, for freedom from a mind ghost whose tenacity was, after all, greater than her own.

"I wanted to speak without the earl present. When I saw you enter the chapel, it seemed the best course."

"Your vigilance was wasted, Mr. Moresham. The earl remains in London." Should she tell him that Archer expanded his search for his wife, that even now he hired people to search the length and breadth of England?

She remained silent, after all, unsolicited loyalty keeping her mute.

He nodded, then came and sat beside her. Together they faced forward, neither speaking, both immersed in their individual thoughts. Mary Kate wondered why she could not feel the presence of Alice more strongly in this sacred place. Together, they'd watched the sun for long moments, content, if not peaceful.

"It was our very favorite place to meet, this chapel. Sitting here, it was almost possible to believe there was a chance for happiness, that our hopes for a future would materialize."

"You loved her very much, didn't you?" Of course he had. And she had loved you as well. Why else that strong reaction when Mary Kate had first met him? It seemed so simple to know these things now, as they sat together much as he and Alice must have.

He turned and his gaze seemed to study her. It was an inspection she'd become used to at Sanderhurst, having been the object of intense curiosity.

"I loved her with all my heart," he said then, before turning and staring at the altar again.

Was it possible for eyes to betray so much emotion? Bleak acceptance, despair, pain so acute that Mary Kate could almost feel it herself.

"The moment she drew breath, it seemed as though she were my shadow. My playmate and my friend. Then my eternal love."

"But she was your sister."

"No. I learned, a little over two years ago, that she and I were not related, Mrs. Bennett."

"And so you told her." If she had known him better, she would have laid her hand upon his sleeve, so much in need of comfort he looked. Instead, she only folded her hands upon themselves and concentrated upon the altar.

"Yes."

"You believe she's dead, don't you?"

He turned surprised eyes to her. "How do you know that?"

Because I think she loved you with all her heart, just as much as you loved her and wanted you protected against harm. Words she could not utter to James Moresham, a certain knowledge she could not share. His stepmother was a zealot who would not hesitate to denounce her as a witch, or worse. And besides, she could not find the words to tell this young man that his worst suspicions were also her own.

"She was going to leave the earl, Mrs. Bennett. We had planned to emigrate. I would teach the pianoforte, Alice would take in sewing. It didn't matter what we did, as long as we were together.'' His eyes mirrored grief and some other emotion it took Mary Kate but a moment to identify. Rage.

''She felt guilty, can you believe it? After all the games Fate had played on us, she felt sad for St. John.''

In the next moments, he told her of their planned meeting. Then a few minutes of silence, during which Mary Kate could hear nothing but the sounds of their breathing.

''And then?'' She could not tolerate the suspense any longer. ''What happened then?''

''Nothing.'' A small shrug, a motion of shoulder beneath cape. ''She never appeared, Mrs. Bennett. Not that whole day.'' There was a pause as he took a deep breath. She should have been prepared for his next words, but somehow was not. ''It is my belief that Archer St. John murdered Alice, Mrs. Bennett.''

''I beg your pardon?''

''I know it sounds fantastic, but I have proof.''

''Proof?'' For weeks she'd been certain Alice St. John was dead. No one had believed her. No one had listened. Now this young man with his soft, earnest voice uttered the words. How odd that her chest seemed frozen, as if her blood had turned to ice.

''She never loved him. She married him because we couldn't wed.''

''Is that your proof?'' A small smile wreathed her lips. An admission, then, of her relief? ''There are thousands of marriages in which one or the other partner does not enthusiastically enter into the arrangement, Mr. Moresham.''

''You do not want to believe him guilty, do you, Mrs. Bennett?'' He turned and studied her, the grief in his gaze muted beneath a sudden and surprising anger. "In your eyes, Archer St. John's innocent."

"I find it almost impossible to believe that he murdered his wife, if that's what you're asking." She remembered too well the stricken look on Archer's face when she had asked him that question. Why had she? Not belief, surely. Pique? Or jealousy? He'd spoken of Alice as his wife and she had not been expecting the pain of that word. It's not as if she'd never heard it. Not as if he had not spoken it before. The question had come in such a rush of feelings, confusion, anger, envy that she'd wanted to hurt him, to punish him in a way that would mimic what she'd felt. The admission was not easy, the truth of it stared her in the face, silent, accusatory. The startling bitter taste of envy had shocked her.

"Alice was carrying my child, Mrs. Bennett." A declaration made with pride and more than a little sadness. "St. John knew that it was not his. Is not pride enough of a reason for St. John to kill her?"

Chapter 33

Archer stood at the window, watching the slash of lightning across the sky. This night storm enhanced his odd mood.

The room had been his father's, a sterile atmosphere of punishment. He'd been summoned here as little more than an infant, to be chastised, to be beaten, to be molded into an earl.

Once this room had become his—the day Sanderhurst and the earldom had become his at the unripe and unready age of eight—he'd closed it off and never entered the room again until he'd become an adult.

Only then had he begun his reform of the place. He'd banished the marble that made of this room a cold and sepulchral tomb, replaced the mantle with a carved Adams work of art, had lined the walls with bookshelves fashioned of mahogany. Upon their shelves resided novels, treatises, and tomes he'd actually read. On the floor lay one of his father's priceless Persian rugs, and on the available wall the art Archer preferred.

From a place of impossible dimensions, he'd scaled it down to human warmth and proportion, creating from his memories something that had never existed, a haven. He'd wanted this refuge so badly he'd invented it in his adulthood to appease the child he had been.

Yet he could never replace his father, and memory refused to soften Gerald St. John's implacable cruelty. All the St. John men were blessed with it, that little gem of distilled wickedness that fed the warped nature of a man born every generation or so. Archer St. John, deprived of his father's love as a child, of belonging as a youth, of acceptance as an adult, would have been one of those men, except for one overriding character attribute.

He was determined not to mimic his father.

The trait was there, however, insidious and lurking, waiting for the propitious moment in which to mature and become full fledged. Over the years it had become more active, this internal monster, feeding on the disappointments of his life, taking sustenance from the bitterness he felt over his wife's defection and wide-eyed, self-admitted adulterous posturing.

For nearly a week, he'd remained in London, encapsulated in his rage and hurt. Feeling that obscene thrust of betrayal. Time had not diminished it. But neither had it lessened his hunger for Mary Kate. A fool. He was a bloody fool. And yet he had returned, soothed and quiescent now that he knew she lay asleep above him. He felt as though he were a starving puppy and she a juicy steak. Feed me, Mary Kate.

The rain lashed against the window. He extended his hand and flattened against the pane, as if to absorb the coldness of the glass.

Was she right? Had he truly hated Alice? Once, perhaps. But still? A thousand times in the last week he'd asked himself that question. The answer was both complex and exquisitely simple.

One night, when Archer could not sleep, he'd heard her crying in her room, adjacent to his. Perhaps a wiser man would have simply doused the sound of her sobs with brandy or a pillow, but he'd found himself compelled by the very real grief in the sound to cross the boundary of the door that separated them. He sat on the edge of her bed, awkwardly patting her back.

"Alice, what is it?" He whispered the question, a gentleness he could not prevent and an empathy that disturbed him too much making his tone soft, an oddly fitting counterpart to her grief.

"Leave me alone." Such directness was not like Alice. She was a creature of soft looks and sweet smiles. She had her maid inform him of her inability to join him for breakfast, sent notes via Jonathan when she was to visit her relatives—visits that he had consistently declined from attending with her. She deliberately avoided confrontation with him. At this moment, however, she did not seem too distressed to issue commands.

He withdrew his hand, but remained where he was, perhaps kept floundering there by a sixth sense that compelled him to stay and offer comfort.

"Go away, Archer. Please."

"I but wished to comfort you, Alice," he said, noting the stiffness of his own voice, hearing it and wishing that he could have sounded less cold and abrupt. This was not the way to comfort crying wives.

"Is there something you wish? Something I could fetch you?"

"Nothing."

"Is there something I could have cook prepare for you to tempt your appetite?"

"No."

"Shall I schedule the dressmaker?"

"I do not worry about my attire, Archer. It is the least of my concerns."

Desperate now, he'd offered her a pet. "One of the hunting dogs has given birth to a healthy litter. Shall I fetch one of the puppies? It might amuse you."

"No."

"Are you hurting anywhere? Shall I summon a physician?"

Perhaps it was because she seemed so disconsolate, perhaps because the hour was late and he was more distressed by her tears than he wished to be. Archer spoke all these blandishments in a voice he would later recognize as that of a fond uncle. To his undying horror, it seemed he was more naive than he had ever believed of Alice.

She had turned and sat up, brushing her golden hair away from her tear-stained face. Her eyes had glistened with moisture—or rage?—her mouth swollen out of their borders, her nose pink. His timid Alice turned on him like a Valkyrie.

"Will you summon my love to me, then, Archer? Tell him how bitterly I regret marrying anyone but him. Tell him that I long for him in my bed each night. Tell him that he's given me a child, who lies nestled in my womb even now. Is that what you'll do for me, my great Earl of Sanderhurst? If so, do it quickly, because I feel as though I'm dying for love."

Archer was a master of verbal dueling, of the artful cut. He'd learned to protect himself by any means necessary and it had been absolutely essential, more often than not, to use his tongue as a swifter sword than any forged by man. He could level with precision anyone who was derisive of him, could smile with a fierce duality while shaming those daring enough to verbally fence with him. His weapons were his quick wit and barely tamed temper, his protection an armor of indifference and an air of ennui.

At that particular moment, however, he could not have framed a complete sentence, let alone cultivated a disinterested air.

His body seemed stiffened by starch, he could feel his eyes blink as they stared at Alice. Yet none of his bodily impulses or compulsions seemed to free him. He had the oddest thought, in that moment—and in subsequent moments when he'd recalled it—that he was being given a rare glimpse into Alice's soul. That who she was and what she wanted were exposed to him in full measure in this moment, as pure as crystal, as brilliant as gold.

And none of that knowledge seemed to fit within his preordained opinion of her. It was as if, quite simply, she'd stepped out of the chrysalis in which she'd metamorphosed and become a new creature, one alien and unknown to the man who remained seated on the side of her bed.

"Will you set me free now, Archer? If you have any decency in your body, you will. If you prize your honor above all things, you will let me go."

Still, he could not speak. Words seemed to be weighted in his throat, upon his tongue, wedged in his brain, yet they did not disgorge themselves easily from his lips.

She watched him as if he were a newly trapped wild animal, dazed and disoriented. He wanted to reassure her that he was not dangerous, but he did not know that to be the truth. The emotions surging through him were unlike anything he'd ever felt before and yet were strangely reminiscent of the times in which he'd stood in front of his father, small and terrified and desirous of his mother's protection.

How softly she had said the words to plummet him into a mind-numbing fog of disbelief. His Alice? The sweet, shy Alice who disliked the deed so much she prayed during it, had willingly gone to another man's bed? Was with child?

He was a man of complexity, a trait he understood about himself. And while it would be no great feat to believe himself justified in hating the fact that his wife was an adulteress, the truth of the matter was that he had been prepared to forgive Alice for that, quite willing to overlook her foray into adultery in order to build a bridge between them. He should have cared, perhaps, about her lover, but found that he could not even summon enough interest for that. He found that he did not want to know, the first time he'd consciously sought oblivion in ignorance.

He had not been, however, able to forestall that one swift knifelike thrust to his heart. Such ventilation was not good for hearts, it left them weak and gasping, but they healed with armorlike rigidity.

At first, perhaps he'd hated her, but then he'd only felt a sense of envy that she'd discovered love and he was still trapped in a limbo created by her disappearance. Given the opportunity, he would have released her from their marriage, wished her well. He had wanted to feel some happiness in his life, some enthusiasm with which to greet each day. Instead, he had been left with regrets, and suspicion, and an odd feeling that there were more acts left to this absurd farce.

Chapter 34

When Mary Kate awoke, it was the deepest part of night, without the moon to lure a sleeper to the windowsill, a dreamer from a nighttime vision. An arm extended to her side, but she found nothing there. She was alone, then. Was that why she'd awakened? No. She'd slept alone often enough.

She turned her head. The pillow smelled of flowers; this dark room held tight with stygian blackness smelled of a field of them. To delight the senses, to entice the dreamer unawares. The sound of the door opening between their two rooms was loud in the darkness. It was as if she'd summoned him here by her longing.

"Forgive me, Archer." It was a humble apology bereft of any flowery sentiments. The night, the blackness, seemed to call for truth without embellishment. Another moment, an eternity of time frozen in an instant. "Please, Archer. You will strangle on the words. Say you release me from my stupidity. Tell me you forgive me."

Were his eyes dark with emotion? Desire or rage?

"I have not spoken to you for a week and yet your first words are ones of entreaty. What man in his right mind would refuse?" He sat next to her on the bed, the mattress sinking beneath his weight. He didn't speak as she moved forward, didn't say a word as she neared him, reached out a hand and touched his where it rested on the sheet.

"A man too stubborn for his own good, perhaps."

"Do not beg with one hand while you swat with the other, Mary Kate." There was a note of humor in his voice.

"Do you wish the candles lit?"

"No, I find my mood enhanced by darkness." He seemed to sigh, a soft sound in the night.

"I'm not without faults, Archer. I freely admit it. I sometimes say exactly what I think before I've reasoned it out."

"What exactly, are you apologizing for, Mary Kate? Alluding to the fact that I've the character to commit murder, or pretending that you can see what mortal eyes cannot?"

"I had no desire to be a party to this," she said. "It has complicated my life more than I can say, coming to Sanderhurst." How much he would never know. "I was simply trying to find my family, Archer. Surely that was not such a grievous sin against heaven. Not enough of one to deserve being haunted."

"Why are you innocent, when you claim the most outlandish circumstances and I immediately guilty when I have done nothing?"

"I remember claiming the same, Archer."

Silence seemed to eat at their thoughts, so much so that they did not speak for long moments. She wanted an end to it, finally.

"Would it matter if I told you I believe you incapable of such an act?" She moved closer, only the stiffening of his body stopped her from enfolding her arms around him.

"Only if it is the truth, and not another momentary expulsion of words. Think on them slowly, then tell me."

"I have thought of them. Ever since the moment I accused you of killing Alice, I've known you could not."

"Besides the fact we both know she is alive, what is it about my character that makes me innocent of all nefarious deeds?"

"Innocent of all nefarious deeds? You are not that pure, Archer. Yet I truly believe that you do not know where Alice is. I simply cannot envision you creating a circumstance in which you are without control."

"It is not my character, then, that acquits me. Nor my charm."

She was grateful for the darkness that shrouded them. He could not see her smile. "All those things you have in abundance, yes. But it was not the deciding factor."

"How damn astute of you, Mary Kate. I dislike feeling powerless."

She reached out one hand and touched him with trembling fingers, feeling the hardness of dormant muscles beneath the fabric of his sleeve.

He didn't speak, didn't move as she started to explore him, with first fingers, than palms, sliding her hands down the length of his chest as if she had never felt or touched, or experienced anything like it before. Finally, he moved, laying down full length upon the bed, pulling her so that she was resting against him, her back to his chest. His right arm reached over her, following the touch of her arm to her hand. He linked his fingers in hers. His left arm braced her head, acting as pillow.

"Why did you stay away so long?" A whisper, an entreaty that did not betray the shyness of the woman who asked the question.

"Is it not enough that I'm here now? Besides, my mother reminded me that you are without protector, privy to my whims, a prisoner."

"Who travels around the countryside in a glorious barouche and sleeps in a bed designed for a princess and wears clothing bartered for in China. I like your way of imprisonment, Archer."

"I should have known you would be just like her. Both of you hoydens."

"Shall I summon one of the footmen to my chamber?"

"Do, and you'll find him dismissed," he said.

"The cook?"

"He's much too temperamental; he should find a post more suitable to his emotions."

"The stable master?"

"He's too heavy-handed with the horses. Let him work for Moresham."

"The earl?"

"A moody sort, given to too much introspection." He twirled a lock of her hair around his finger. "They say he killed his wife. Or failing that, frightened her away."

"They're fools."

"They say he's besotted with an Irish wench, who cozens him out of temper with just a smile." A breath against her cheek. A soft kiss against her temple.

"Can she?"

"Most definitely."

She grabbed his arm with both hands. "Forgive me, Archer, for causing you pain."

He did not speak, did not discount her statement. It was a sign then, just how much she'd hurt him. He said nothing as she leaned into him, turned her head so that her cheek pressed against his chest.

His chin brushed against the top of her head. "You realize, of course, that we are at an impasse, you and I. We have learned to wound each other too well, and cannot go forward. Nor can we go back."

She nodded.

"You have your quest, and I have mine." His embrace seemed to grow tighter, as if to refute the speaking of the words that would separate them.

"Alice was with child." Ever since this afternoon, she'd wanted to speak the words.

"Yes," he acknowledged softly.

"You hadn't told me that."

"No." His breath seemed halted, as if he held it in reserve for her next question.

"Nor was her child yours."

"The gossips have done their work well," he said, his tone resigned.

She didn't correct him, intent, instead, on another point. A question she should not ask.

"Did you mind?"

"Did I mind?"

He pulled away from her, lay flat upon the bed, staring up at the darkened ceiling.

"I have never spoken of Alice's child," he admitted. "I am only certain of its maternal parentage. Perhaps it was pride that prevented me from denouncing Alice, or perhaps some nobler impulse. It was not the child's fault, you see."

She turned, placed her head on his shoulder, extended an arm over his chest. Wordless comfort, it was all she had to give.

"She was proud of it, almost dazzling in her love for her child."

"And you? What did you feel?"

"Like when I was six years old and loved a puppy and my father took it from me and had it killed. It was meant to teach me some odd and perverse lesson, of course, but I never learned what." He reached out his arm and pulled her tightly to him. "To answer your question, Mary Kate, I found I very much minded."

A moment passed, a rearranging of limbs, closer. She wanted to touch every part of him, not as much in passion as in connection. A way to fight the darkness and their own personal demons.

"Was this her chamber?"

"Have you wondered that all along?"

"Yes," she said. "Since the night seems bound for confession, I have."

"She used to occupy the room my mother now romps in, although without footman." He huffed a breath. "Our walls adjoin, and I sometimes wish there was a hallway between us."

She giggled, then caught the sound behind a hand.

"No," he said, taking her hand down. "I do not fault your amusement. We've had little enough of that, you and I. And although I love her dearly, she has become more earthy than I remember."

"Perhaps she takes a page from her son's book."

"Her son sits alone in his room and pines for company, for all that he's been called St. John the Hermit."

"I am here, Archer."

Instead of responding to that barely veiled invitation, he asked, "What will you do when you find your family, Mary Kate? Will you become an aunt to your brothers' children, and tell them tales of your travels?"

"About the gorgon I met, with fierce black eyes, who

imprisoned me in his dungeon and made me eat scraped soup bones?"

She felt the rumble of his laughter against her cheek. It made her smile in response. "I have not thought, honestly, of what I shall do, only that the lure of them is like a signal fire, something I must reach."

"And if you do not find them, what then? Will you become a servant again?"

"It is an honorable occupation, Archer, one with no shame to it."

"I did not say it was, my fierce Mary Kate. Only that I find you oddly unsuited for it. You've the brazenness to be a duchess, and temperament for it, I think."

"Ah, but there are no dukes nearby, who are searching beneath cabbage leaves for me."

"If I were not a knight bound upon a quest, I would upend every cabbage in the land, for all that I'm an insignificant earl."

"You could not be insignificant no matter your station in life, Archer."

"Are you weeping?"

"No."

"Your voice sounds strange."

"Nonsense. You are night blinded."

"I hear very well, Mary Kate."

He bent and bestowed a kiss of such gentleness upon her cheek that she almost confessed the pain of her heart to him. But then, such a statement would have cut through the cloth of darkness that protected them. The night rendered them both inviolate and more vulnerable than daylight. In the darkness, they could share their sorrows, but could not protect against them.

" And you, Archer, what will happen if you cannot find

Alice?'' It was the perfect moment to tell him about her visit from James, about what she knew of their love, of their child. But James, by his own admission, would be far from Sanderhurst in but a matter of days. What good would it do to make matters worse? For that reason, and because she could not bear to cause Archer pain, she did not speak.

"I think," Archer said, his voice but a whisper near her ear, "I shall continue my quest until I am old and too tired to sit upon my horse or hold my lance. And then, perhaps, I will sit in my tower and remember when a red-haired wench coaxed me from my hermitage for a time."

"I hope you are kind in your thoughts of this woman. She did not mean to wound, was only confused and frightened and wishing to help." Mary Kate held on to the arm braced across her with both hands. She wanted to turn in his arms, bury her face in his shirt, cry until all of the tears that welled up in her heart were spent and all that was left was salted air. But she did not, a gift of restraint she granted him without thought of reward or return.

"No," he said gently, "she brought me the greatest of gifts, from Persia and Abyssinia. Oil of laughter and essence of joy. I will treasure them all of my days."

"And take them out and look upon them, I hope, sometimes, and think of her fondly."

"No," he said, his voice so swelling sweet that the tears threatened to spill again. "Some gifts are not meant to be taken from their memory box, but should be put away in a tight place where they will not be spoiled by sunlight or touched upon by age."

Time ticked by, shining minutes of utter perfection, undisturbed by speech.

He held her in his arms, and she lay cradled there, distraught and silent. It was odd, but the night was not spent in love making, but in that simple embrace. A respite from a storm, a quiet time in a place accidentally created just for them.

It was, had anyone thought to ask Mary Kate, a night filled with unbearable pain.

Chapter 35

It was neither his conscience nor his doubts that made Archer leave Sanderhurst for a tour of English ports. Instead, what empowered him was an almost desperate wish to end the suspense of his life, to find a fitting close to his marriage. He felt as if he existed in a cocoon he'd fashioned around himself, composed of wishes and pretense and an almost fervent willingness to ignore the irrefutable.

He could not take one step into the future until he found his wife. If Alice did not wish to come back to Sanderhurst, then he would provide for her wherever she wished. If she had been deserted by her lover, he would set up a residence for herself and the child. In short, he would do anything he could to bring her happiness.

He wished her joy and contentment in life, as if he himself could only attain happiness once he was assured Alice shared in it first.

His coach was readied for the journey; he would visit each one of England's port cities, beginning at Southampton and working himself north. Someone must have seen Alice, and he would not rest until he'd found that one person who could put an end to this.

Running Archer? Perhaps, he acknowledged to himself. Not to the truth, but away from it? Again, perhaps. Mary Kate held too much magnetism for him, too much attraction for the man he knew himself to be. Not the empire builder, not the impatient, hermited titular head of a grasping family, but the young man who'd aged too quickly and the one who ached for the sound of laughter and feel of smiles. She was his lodestone, was Mary Kate Bennett, as finely crafted for him as if she'd studied him and discerned his every wish and waking thought, and then delved beneath the sleeping man and saw the dreams of his soul.

Enough of a reason to fly.

And if he found Alice? What then?

He mounted the carriage steps and settled himself inside, wondering at the loss he felt even now.

The relationship that had formed between him and Mary Kate was so short in duration, so strong in nature. Last night they'd shared a curious kind of empathy, as if a bridge existed between their thoughts. He'd been almost frightened by his need for her, the necessity of her for him. Their stations in life were so dissimilar, their pasts so different. Yet their futures seemed oddly similar, as if both were doomed to act out a loveless existence for honor's sake.

Such a thought was whimsy, unsettling. He was mad with lust. It was the only explanation.

He was either a widower or Mary Kate was the worst of opportunists. So he was trapped between wishes, then, a man married to a woman who had left him and tied to a woman whose motives remained as shadowy as they'd always been, for all that he forgave her, too.

This was a ripe version of hell, then. When had he begun to want to believe her? Alice is dead.

The rumors had accused him of it, but could it be true?

Had he been cursing a dead woman all these many months? Miracles were not, after all, too far from man's collective consciousness, and he supposed there were things to be considered that no man could understand.

What if there was no more to her story than what she'd told? What if it truly was something as implausible as fate? Circumstance so bizarre, a complex contradiction, a puzzle so convoluted that it could only be the truth?

Was it not Socrates who said that by observing objects with his eyes, trying to comprehend them with his other senses, he was afraid he might blind his soul altogether? Had Archer blinded his soul to the truth?

And what the hell *was* the truth?

Cecily Moresham locked the door of the curing shed behind her, dropped the key into her pocket. Not one person of her acquaintance could say that she did not run a proper household.

"Whatsoever thy hand findeth to do, do it with thy might." It was her credo, after all. Some would say that she took on duties others could undertake. But she'd been raised right and proper, with the knowledge that as mistress of Moresham Farms, her duties were to oversee all the details.

Today she'd lit the fire outside the curing shed again, then banked it quickly so that aromatic smoke seeped in through the widely placed floorboards of the small structure. It was important that the fire be refueled once a week with wet tinder and logs, sometimes leaves that had begun to mold, the better to sweeten the taste of the curing pork.

Everyone agreed that Cecily Moresham offered the best ham at market.

She patted the key in her pocket, the only one to the

curing shed. That, too, was her duty, to preserve her husband's money against pilferage and theft or wasteful spending.

Cecily Moresham disliked untidiness in all her dealings. It was, perhaps, one of the reasons she hated the horses her husband bred with such lustiness. Equines were among the most untidy of God's creatures. She would never again be present while a foal was being born. The sight, albeit unwillingly witnessed, had disturbed her in some elemental way.

She had never told Mr. Moresham that she had seen him pull the foal from the mare, nor that she had vomited in the stall near the door. Such things were better never said, and rarely remembered.

The farm dabbled in things of an entirely earthy nature, so disturbing to her that Cecily took to praying aloud on those mornings when the stallions were led to docile-looking mares. Her prayers, however, never quite masked the whinnies and shrieks and screams.

It was not right.

What Samuel was doing for James was not right, either.

And Cecily Moresham held great store in what was right, or should be. Her Calvinist parents had instilled in her a sense of right and wrong that was as immutable as the grave.

"Be sober, be vigilant; because your adversary the devil, as a roaring lion, walketh about, seeking whom he may devour."

She bowed her head as if to hear the words again in her heart. God spoke to her often lately. It was to be expected. He had recognized her greatness, even though she was only a woman.

"Let the woman learn in silence with all subjection. But

suffer not a woman to teach, nor to usurp authority over the man, but to be in silence. For Adam was first formed, then Eve. And Adam was not deceived, but the woman being deceived was in the transgression. Notwithstanding she shall be saved in childbearing, if they continue in faith and charity and holiness with sobriety.''

Cecily clutched both her hands around the knot of her shawl, not bothering to mask or wipe away the tears that trickled down her plump cheeks. Her tears came to her at odd times of late. But that was to be expected, also, since God had raised her up above mere mortals.

For her sacrifice.

She clutched her shawl closer to her chest with one hand, examined the curing-shed fire through the outdoor grate. It was important that the fire be maintained throughout the smoking period, burning not too hot, but kept alive throughout the time needed to properly cure the meat.

It was one of those chores she watched over herself, not quite trusting in the servants to care about the quality of their work.

God expected perfection from her.

Chapter 36

"**S**o you're off then, lad?" Samuel Moresham asked of the man who would always remain his son.

"Tomorrow, sir."

"I've word, then, that the horses fared well on the trip, James. They'll be rested for the race, then. And the grooms left this morning, as arranged?"

"Yes, sir. They should be at Surrey long before you arrive."

"Mrs. Moresham will not attend the races after all, James." He flicked his gloves against his thigh. He had decided not to ride to Surrey, but remain coach-bound. The better to be rested for all the races. Two of his Moresham Farms favorites were featured this week.

"My stepmother has never cared for them, has she?"

"There's a great deal she does not care for, James. I think it a matter of personal preference and not the right and wrong of it." Should he have been that forceful? The look of surprise, and then the quickly masked smile on the younger man's face, told Samuel that such bluntness was perhaps overdue.

"You'll send word of your safe arrival, James?"

He was being as anxious as a mother sending her child off to school. It was a damn sight more misery than he'd wanted to feel.

James would do well. The lad had talent and determination, two things necessary to get on about the world. More than that, perhaps being in Vienna would give him a more hopeful outlook on life. A reason to keep a smile about his face and a tune in his heart.

Even though Samuel Moresham did not believe James would ever recover from Alice's defection. He should know; he'd never quite stopped missing his first wife, James's mother.

"I'll send word, sir." There was a quick smile, a hand outstretched.

Samuel took it in his own. If his palm was a bit sweaty or if he held James's hand for too long, neither spoke of it.

"And you'll let me know if you need any funds? I've put the letter of credit on the hall table. Just take it to the bank in Austria, and they'll draft a marque in your name."

"I appreciate your generosity, sir. More than that. I owe you so much."

"Nothing but money, lad. It doesn't do anything but make things easier. It doesn't solve the real issues of life. If money can fix it, James, it's not a problem. You remember that, lad. And remember, too, that I know I should have made it easier on you."

Another look, another thousand things said.

Samuel mounted the steps and then tapped on the roof. "Grand good luck to you, James," he said, as the carriage drew away.

"And you, sir."

"I'll send word to you if I hear anything of Alice." It

seemed that the wind carried the words away, along with James's response.

"Please, sir, if you would."

A tiny pinprick of hope, then, to be offered as a farewell.

"You and I have not had this time in a while, Archer. I thought you holed up in Sanderhurst for the season." Robert Dunley smiled and passed the decanter of brandy over to his friend.

The soft sway of the stateroom was nothing compared with the pitch and toss of a rolling sea, but Archer was in need of the brandy. It would have been more politic, perhaps, to remember that they were employer and employee, but Robert merely braced his feet apart and grinned at his friend, leaving Archer with no doubt that he was remembering his first visit to the Spice Islands. He had been deplorably seasick.

Rank, wealth, position, had a way of being equalized on the South China Sea. Robert had not deemed that bit of information public knowledge, for which Archer would forever bless him. After all, the St. John empire was based on the sea trade. How idiotic that a St. John grew seasick the moment a ship left port.

The bond had grown from that voyage on, so much so that Robert sent his correspondence not to the St. John clerks, but to Archer himself. Perhaps that was why their friendship had flourished, through the writings of a solitary sea captain and a man equally adrift upon his own ocean.

"I did as you requested, Archer, and sent notices throughout Indonesia and Malaysia. I met with the *Caroline*, and sent the *Shikoku*'s captain the same message. No one has seen or heard anything of the countess."

The stateroom was luxuriously appointed, a signature

treatment of St. John vessels. The larger China and Spice Island ships were all equipped for comfort, especially the captain's quarters, even to the extent that valuable space in the hold was sacrificed. It had taken only one voyage for Archer to realize that eighteen months aboard ship could be made either palatable, or a version of hell. Therefore, he'd given orders that all quarters were to have full-size bunks and a comfortable grouping of chairs and table, all bolted to the floor, of course. There were bookshelves and lanterns that had the safety feature of extinguishing should they be tilted or turned. Large, ported windows held a view of the aft of the ship, while the grate at the top of the cabin allowed light. Thousands of thick glass prisms had been installed in the planking of the deck. The glass magnified sunlight, illuminating places in large ships that had been forever dark.

Archer said nothing as he poured himself another measure of brandy. There were, after all, no words to say. How did one confess that he was not surprised to have received no word of Alice? Such news would have been too easy and thus too suspect.

He wanted, idiotically, to confide in Mary Kate that his initial efforts had not gone well. But he had not even said farewell to her.

No, that was not quite true, was it, Archer? Their parting had been a night's duration. Words could not have made it any more final than the exquisite and painful joy of holding Mary Kate until she'd fallen into an uneasy slumber. For long hours he'd lain there listening to her breathe, occasionally brushing a fingertip against a wrist as if to test the beat of her blood.

She'd made a sound in her sleep that had reminded him too much of a whimper. The sound a puppy might make in pain, too new to the world to trust its goodness, too young to know its cruelty.

He wanted to hold her tighter, but he did not wish to awake her, so he simply looked out over the world turning gold and pink and pretended that he could easily bear a hundred, a thousand, tomorrows without her at his side.

He'd never shared so much of himself with anyone, not even Alice. But then, he'd thought of late that he had not divulged much of himself to his wife, only those parts he'd considered appropriate and washed, near virgin in their innocence. The darkness, he'd never shared, the simmering, always loneliness he seemed to feel, even in the place he loved best of all places.

He did not touch Mary Kate beyond the embrace that sheltered her in her sleep. Not one softening kiss did he bestow on her delightful shoulders, not one caress to her curving waist and the flaring of hip. He could not bear to touch those long, perfect legs, and although his fingers itched to explore the dell of soft red hair cushioning her female secrets, he did not.

What society wished or conveyed or sanctioned of its members had never disturbed or controlled Archer St. John. Instead, he had been forced at an early age to determine what was necessary for his own survival. As a child, it had been his mother and Neddy. The stuffed horse casually gifted him by a friend of his mother had long since rotted; Bernie would be devoted until the day she died. As a young man, it had been food for his mind and women for his libido. Later still, it had been the execution of his responsibilities and the assuagement of certain bodily needs.

During this lifelong search for what appeased him, he'd discovered that he was a creature of sensation. He liked the feel of silk against his skin, loved the texture of Russian sable. He preferred variety among his foods, preferred no cuisine to another but insisted upon greens and light sauces. His wine cellar was chosen for taste, not for popularity, and he especially enjoyed a night spent before a roaring fire, sipping port while granted the companionship of a lovely woman. If the woman was not available, a good book would suffice temporarily. He was offended by other than well-modulated voices—too many times he had watched a beautiful woman open her mouth and destroy the illusion she had so earnestly sought with a few simple sentences. He was sensitive to odors, preferring his own company to that of an ill-washed companion, and some of the members of the peerage still believed that bathing opened up the body to harmful humors. An afternoon walking through Sanderhurst's great parklike vistas was to enliven all his senses, the budding apple trees, the hum of bees, the sound of swallow, nightingale; all these experiences seemed to seep into his very soul.

As had the feel of Mary Kate sleeping in his arms.

She'd come to him with less experience than the most innocent female of the ton. He'd brought to their mating a knowledge crafted from dozens of partners. He had eschewed the company of others; she was too used to being surrounded by crowds. His wealth had insulated him from the world, had made it possible for him to do as he wished, occupying his days with those things of his particular interest. Her poverty had demanded ceaseless employment, her days spent in the service of others in order to provide for herself.

Yet the similarities were there, even if they did not show themselves as readily or as easily as their differences. He had been educated at the finest of schools; she'd been taught nearly the same curriculum by a retired governess with naught to do all day but indulge in her passion for literature and history. He had been taught never to trust, despite the fact that he found himself wishing to. She had been shown that it was better to depend only upon herself, that trust was an emotion with little promise. She had been overlooked because of who she was, rendered invisible by her station in life, her servitude, and yet the person of Archer St. John had been supplanted by the function he occupied, by being head of the St. John empire. Seen not for who he was, but what he could give others. Known not for himself, but what his money could bring.

When had he taken to anticipating the mornings, when she would come and visit him in his glasshouse, attired in one of the garments given to her by his mother, her face scrubbed clean and fresh, her eyes alight with curiosity and mischief?

When had he grown so accustomed to hearing her version of life at Sanderhurst? Sometimes she ventured to the kitchens, pretending she was not pariah there, and sat talking with Peter, only to relate to him all of the gossip of the house, surprising him with knowledge he'd never before learned, along with the feeling that there was more to Sanderhurst than he'd ever known.

When had he become so used to the feelings she aroused in him? Simple lust and complicated need.

Dear God, he wished to be a duke, toppling over cabbages.

Mary Kate's' transition from sleep to wakefulness had been accomplished in a second. There was no sloughing off of sleep, no gray fog in which she surfaced layer upon layer, only this, the sudden wakefulness that had her staring into his eyes with a soft smile.

"Is it morning, then?"

"No," he lied. "Midnight at most. Go back to sleep."

He levered himself up on one elbow and studied her. She brushed back her tangled hair with one hand. She blinked at him, reached up with one hand and touched his cheek tenderly, cradling her palm against it. A drowsy, smile lit upon her lips with the fleeting touch of a butterfly before she fell asleep again.

And that was the last time he'd seen Mary Kate.

"You haven't heard a bloody word I've said, have you?"

Archer blinked, then smiled, a confession in his grin.

"And here I was, dazzling you with my brilliant recitation of all the ports I visited on your behalf."

"I doubt Alice would travel on a St. John ship."

"I've thought the same thing, Archer. Which is why I took the liberty of posting handbills in each port we visited. You are, I hope, prepared to offer a sizable reward?"

"How much did you obligate me for, Robert?" A hand was extended in the air as if to wipe away the words. "Never mind. It does not matter. What is my peace of mind worth, after all?"

"Will you take her back?"

Friendship was an onerous obligation, Archer thought. It required opening one's soul up to scrutiny, one's methods to investigation, one's very thoughts to interpretation. He wasn't sure at that moment how much he wanted to continue this friendship. Enough to answer the question?

In the end he did, not simply because he was low on friends and Robert Dunley had always been a man he admired. Not even because it was an easy question to answer. It was not. No, he answered it because it was something he had long since decided.

''If my wife wishes a bill of divorcement, then I will grant it to her, Robert. And should she be desirous of a reconciliation, I can do no less.''

Robert reached over the table and clinked his glass against Archer's. ''I salute you, then, my friend. You show more perseverance and more forgiveness than ever I could feel.''

''I do not know that it is forgiveness, Robert, as much as it is a certain knowledge of my own grievous faults. How, then can I judge anyone else?''

''Plenty of people try, Archer. The world is filled with hypocrites.''

''And I do believe I am related to a great many of them,'' Archer admitted with a smile.

''Well, I told the pasha that it was frowned upon, abducting His Majesty's subjects, not that I wasn't complimented, of course. He simply declared that the English king had no sovereignty over his country. That he was absolute ruler and as such had decided that I would make a very acceptable wife number one hundred eleven.''

''How on earth did you get out of that situation, Bernie?''

Bernie's eyes twinkled. She folded the last bolt of cloth and placed it on the table.

''Well, the British consul, you see, took a very dim view of an Englishwoman, especially a countess, being paraded through the pasha's district as the newest wife. They told him that it was perfectly acceptable to take me to wife as long as I was confined to the harem. I, on the other hand, refused to be locked up with a group of bored and malevolent women. Therefore, we parted company, quite amicably. I suppose you might call me Her Highness. Unless, of course, he has divorced me, which is quite easily done in Arabia.''

Bernie placed another pile of cloth alongside the white satin. ''You disappoint me, my dear. I quite expected you to be amused. At the very least, you might have been impressed that you were hobnobbing with royalty. Very well, then, but I expect you to be overwhelmed by my generosity. All this lovely fabric can be made into quite proper gowns. I have no intention of your leaving Sanderhurst dressed in that hideous black. In fact,'' she muttered, the argument one of long-standing duration between them, ''I do not see why you feel you should leave at all. We can accomplish by post what you think to do in person.''

She turned and glanced at Mary Kate, the censure of her expression changing to alarm as she viewed her companion.

''Mary Kate?''

A pause as she waited for a response.

''If you do not speak to me, Mary Kate Bennett, I shall summon Jonathan. I shall burn feathers and wave them beneath your nose. I shall unearth my sal volatile from wherever the bloody blazes I've misplaced it and render you nauseous.'' She chafed the younger woman's wrists, patted her gently on the cheeks, but Mary Kate did not cease her wide-eyed stare.

She was lost. Lost in a world colored indigo, white filmy clouds passing over her face, through her as she was led deeper into a place she'd never been before. There was no one here in this space but herself, marooned in a world created from darkness. There was no light, no hint of radiance beyond the line of horizon. Only the blackness beckoned. It was a great and giant fog of nothingness, a place that ate up all that lay before it.

And into this void came terror. A thought at first, it began to take shape, a huge, bloated monster of a feeling, which inhaled the nothingness and ate up the blackness and made her want to cry out. But of course, she could not because she was trapped in this feeling.

"A whimper is not speech, Mary Kate, and I really must insist you talk to me. I am growing quite tired of this eerie little demonstration." Bernie took her by the shoulders and shook her, but Mary Kate could barely feel it. A mewl of terror emerged from her lips.

Now she could faintly hear Bernie bellow for Jonathan. The feeling of dread was growing, the sensation that she was trapped within some horrible vision. The black was being obscured by the red, but in the distance a light was growing. Like a tiny pinprick of hope, Mary Kate concentrated on it, instead of the blackness or the color of blood. Radiant, white, glowing, it seemed to be gaining in size. Help me. How odd that she should feel this emotion, hear the words as if they were shouted instead of thought. An echo trapped within walls. She was so frightened. Then Mary Kate realized it wasn't simply her emotions she was feeling, nor were they solely her thoughts. *Help him . . . please. Help him. . . .*

Alice.

HELP HIM. . . .

The shout of the command was so loud that Mary Kate physically recoiled. She would have fallen from the chair had not Bernie been there to support her, and beside her, Jonathan, who was attempting to revive her with brandy. Only she could not break free of this terrible imprisonment.

The light grew until it was the size of a large ball, a moon of tiny proportions perched above a bleak landscape.

It was the only sensation of hope in this eternity of despair. She focused on it, held tight to the promise of it. Was she dying? Was that what this feeling was, a certainty that she glimpsed death, the utter inability to prevent it, a moment in which she tumbled over the edge and into the pit? On one hand, the suspense was over, the anticipation of it. How odd that we mortals work most of our lives to prevent it, and it is so simply, so ridiculously, easy. But dear God, she did not want to die. Not yet. Please. Not yet. There were too many experiences she wanted to have. Too many words she had not spoken, too much love to feel, not for all humanity, not for all eternity, but for one man.

She felt such grief, such utter impotence. There was nothing she could do, she could not call his name, she could not warn him, there was not enough time. . . .

Help . . . please. . . .

In a moment the light was extinguished, the hope was gone. Only the bleakness remained. In seconds this feeling of being trapped in a wasteland had gone.

Mary Kate blinked, looked around the room, which had regained its commodious dimensions, saw Bernie's concerned face in front of her, felt the arms around her, smelled the pungent aroma of brandy.

Then the terror came. Her blood chilled and seemed to pool. Her eyes widened, her heart beat too hard. Her fingers trembled, her hands shook. She felt so weak she could barely stand, let alone grip Bernie's shoulders.

But she did, impelled by a fear so strong it only mimicked the feeling she'd experienced moments earlier. Mary Kate was nearly incoherent from it. Only once before had she felt such a thing, but even that fright was nothing before this implicit, wordless command.

James Moresham was in mortal danger.

Mary Kate stood, overturning the chair, arms flailing in an effort to rid herself of encumbrances.

"Help me." Each word seemed carved from marble. Chiseled from a mind incapable of functioning against such agony of fear. "Carriage. James." *Please, Bernie, understand*

There was something in this room with them, something that lurked in the corners and had a shadowy face. Terror. It sat on such powerful haunches that it was almost a presence, an emotion capable of being supported without a host.

"Get the bloody carriage ready, Jonathan," Bernie said, not turning away from Mary Kate. "I believe we're about to embark upon a mission."

"Did you say something, Jeremy?" With the top of his walking stick, Archer knocked on the window separating himself from the driver. This particular carriage was equipped with a device that made it possible for it to be opened from either side.

"No, sir. I didn't."

Strange. He thought he'd heard a voice. Archer shook his head. He was tired, that was all. A sleepless night, an excess of emotion. No wonder he was hearing things.

No, it was the feeling in the back of his neck. A twinge that made him turn repeatedly and look behind him as if he were being prodded somehow.

There it was again. That was strange, like a whisper against his neck, except that he felt it from the inside. A breath blown against his inner ear.

It was a fanciful notion that struck him then. An odd thought, totally without basis, without reason.

It felt like a warning.

Chapter 37

⌒◦⌒

His stepmother was a dainty thing, with blond hair that had muted over the years to become rather silver in shade. She was diminutive next to his father, and it struck James as odd that he'd never realized how much Alice resembled her mother. Perhaps, if he had been allowed to grow old with her, he would have looked upon her lovely face one day and seen the same type of wrinkles that he witnessed now upon Cecily's.

Would Alice not have been of warmer temperament, however? Alice was capable of great love and greater understanding. Such warmth of nature had made her gentle with others for the sake of it, not because someone might be watching and approve. He had long decided that there was an edge to Cecily's smile. A coldness that was matched in the blue of her eyes. Sometimes such a look made him wary.

Occasionally he pitied Samuel, especially when Cecily expressed her opinions with such an anger in her voice, or when she quoted eternally from her ever-present Bible. Was there anyone who sparked her admiration? Or anything that prompted her approval? She was perhaps the most unhappy person he'd ever known, but she hid it well beneath the mantle of a martyr. Religious zealots, James had long since decided, were difficult to live with, even more difficult to understand. But after today, there was no reason to see Cecily again, a thought that prompted his tentative smile.

He watched as Cecily came closer, wondering if it had been the music that had summoned her to this room. He had not come here in the last year, too heartsick to play, too numbed by loss to compose anything. The melody he played now helped ease his anguish a little. It had spoken to him last night, between the darkness and the dawn, a perfect crystal sound. As if he poured his tears into a vase, and they became the water of life, tiny distilled drops of pure pain and torment and, yes, joy.

Somehow he would translate his memories of Alice into music, simple notes that would tell of his great lost love and grief. And perhaps, in the creation, grant her immortality. Within his music, Alice would be forever young, a sprite created from wishes and dreams and poignant recollections. The world would know how much he loved her, by listening to one of his compositions, by being stirred, heart and mind and soul. Was not that the most perfect use of music? To speak what could not be said?

"It is a pretty tune."

That confession came from a woman who thought music represented evil and should be punished. He smiled at her, tolerant of her intolerance, knowing that he had only to walk through the door and mount his horse to be away from her forever.

Cecily stood next to the pianoforte, head tilted like an exquisite porcelain bird, the picture of startled delight. Except, of course, that she feigned such an interest. They both knew it, but for the sake of this moment, they each allowed the falsehood.

"You've been here nearly an hour, James. Come, take a rest and share your tea with me." She smiled at him, and the gesture was so like Alice's that all he could do was stare at her, remembering the last time Alice had smiled at him just this way and shared with him the utter beauty of her laughter.

Perhaps that was why his fingers lifted from the keys, silencing the music, why he stood and went to her, giving her his arm. James smiled down at her and escorted Cecily into the parlor, the sunny room she used as hers.

"Can you not make the horses go faster, Peter?" Bernie chafed at Mary Kate's cold hands.

Mary Kate held herself perfectly composed but rigidly stiff, as if she hid all of herself on the inside, where it could not be seen.

"I'm not about to kill myself on this icy road, Bernie. Not in this bloody barouche." He turned and scowled at her from the driver's perch.

"Can you at least put the top up? It's freezing cold."

"Do you want us to get there, or is it comfort you want?" Another scowl.

"Is it too much to ask for both? She's like an icicle."

Once, Bernie had stood in the crowd before a fakir in a Mediterranean market. The wise man had been telling a story of demons and possession when he went into a trance. At first the spectators had laughed and jostled one another, thinking it a well-timed trick. But his expression had been so filled with alarm, his skin pulled tight against his skull, his mouth flaccid and expressionless, that all merriment ceased as the crowd grew silent. Except for the

pulse beat in his neck, it would have been possible to think
him dead. From that moment until nearly an hour had
passed, the fakir remained stiff and unmoving.

Mary Kate was nothing in appearance to that dusty, half-
naked man. Why, then, did the expression upon her face
mirror that same look?

"She looks more like a bloomin' corpse, Bernie."

"Oh, do shut up, Peter."

"It will be all right, Bernie. You'll see."

How did he know that? Was it only because she was so
frightened and he had seen it? She glanced up at him, and
Peter leveled another stare at her, this one warmer than
before, as if he wished to reassure her somehow. The tiniest smile bent her lips.

The journey seemed interminable, and although Peter's
words had been unwelcome, they were not incorrect. Mary
Kate did appear more corpse than living soul. It was as if
everything about her had been coated in a cloak of gray.
Beneath her blue cloak, she was like ice. She didn't speak,
didn't move, her eyes were open and fixed, but on the
distance and not some internal vision. Other than that, she
might as well have been in a trance, so still was she. It
was as if she prepared herself, focused what energies she
had on a coming battle, as a captain might prepare a ship
sailing toward a gale, or a military man might gird himself
upon spying the enemy encamped upon a far hill.

Was it an apt analogy? Was this, then, a battle they were
embarking upon? Good against evil? The thought of it
spawned chills all over Bernie's body, the type of sensation that was a presage to danger, not anticipation.

If she had not believed, she would not be here now. Had
she so completely and absolutely ingested Mary Kate's
terror into herself? Ever since they'd entered the open car-

riage, Mary Kate had remained speechless, a turn of events that had not added to Bernie's feeling of comfort.

She had a strange premonition as she sat beside Mary Kate, bathed in the afternoon sun of a winter day, cloaked against the cold. This journey they were on would lead to something that would change all of their lives, for good or ill. None of them would emerge from this experience without being touched by it. It was a sure and certain knowledge she could not explain to another living soul.

There was that damn noise again.

Archer leaned out the window on both sides of the carriage, inspecting the turning wheels. Nothing. And still he had the distinct impression that the sound was there, whistling in through his ear.

It was the damnedest thing, really. An odd feeling had traveled with him for the last hour. At first he'd thought it was a nudge of memory, something undone, forgotten, left behind. Then, the more time passed, the more irritating a feeling it had become. As if he must do something, act in some way, that the failure to do so would have lasting consequences upon his life.

Help her. . . .

The sound of it made him sit upright.

Help her. . . .

It was not the wheels or the wind or his own imagination. Mary Kate was in danger.

He did not care to investigate the source of this unwelcome knowledge at this particular moment. Nor did he consider that he may be acting in a highly irrational manner. Nothing was as important as the feeling that surged through him, the odd and compelling warning so strong that Archer knocked on the closed window and shouted his instructions to Jeremy.

In Mary Kate's mind sang a song of words. *Help him. . . . Help him. . . . Help him. . . .* A refrain that echoed the turning of the barouche's large wheels. The rush of air against her face kept her upright, from falling into a faint, and the sheer terror in her mind and soul kept her focused on their destination. Otherwise, Mary Kate was certain she would be nothing more than a whimpering child.

It was as if she were in a tunnel, formed with gray, shiny walls. No sound penetrated, only this feeling of being driven forward. Of needing to be somewhere quickly, more rapidly than they were now traveling. She wished that the horses could be spurred to greater speed. There was danger here. Such mortal danger that fear etched into her heart like acid, one damaging drop at a time.

Her hands were clutched tightly together upon her lap, so tightly that she could not feel them anymore.

A sense of danger. A feeling of doom. Alice's voice, soft, entreating, laced with terror. *Help him. . . .*

James Moresham was in danger, of what kind, she did not know. Only that it was swift and deadly and wanted the annihilation of his body, if not the expunging of his soul.

A dark and brooding bird of death hovered wraithlike upon the horizon.

Chapter 38

C ecily had such dainty hands. Odd, that he'd never noticed before now. As she poured his tea, James settled back against the chair, realizing that it had been years since he and Cecily had enjoyed a quiet moment together. It was more often that they sought moments apart than opportunities in which to share silences.

The tea was bitter, so he added extra honey to it, sipping more from a desire not to hurt her feelings than actual enjoyment. But then, most of the rituals he'd engaged in for so long had been done with that in mind. The feelings of others, above his own.

What would it be like to live in Vienna? To walk the streets he'd wanted to see for so long, to experience life among those who talked his language, spoke of orchestration and composition, of tonal melody and contrapuntal rhythms. Who understood the need to express, even as he did.

What would it be like, without Alice?

He sipped at his tea, wondering if this moment was an aberration created so effortlessly by Cecily because he was going away. Was this her way of sending him off with her approval, or simply her way of showing appreciation that he was leaving?

Perhaps he would never know. Cecily did not dabble in truth, only in religion.

"You are packed, then, James?" Her voice seemed the softest of sounds, a cottony thing.

"Yes. I find that I have not as many belongings as I believed. Yet they managed to take up three trunks, nevertheless."

"And your music? Have you packed all those sheets as well?" She smiled, revealing even teeth and a gap on the bottom where one was missing. Strange, he'd never noticed it before now. Or perhaps he'd never shared a smile with her and thus would not have seen such a minor imperfection.

"I have." How had she known of all the sheets he'd covered with his compositions?

"Alice spoke of your music with some fondness, James."

He looked down into his tea. So today was to be a day for firsts, then. She'd never mentioned Alice's name in all these many months. How odd that he'd not noted it before now. Perhaps because he had been so immersed in his own grief that he'd never noticed hers. He wanted to say something to her, some odd comment that would note her grief, or remark upon its presence, or perhaps ease it in a small way. Would it not be the greatest sorrow to lose a child? Especially a child with such sweet goodness as Alice.

And his own child? He mourned that loss, as well.

But he found no words to coax from his mouth, nothing that would ease her pain. Only a look, sent to her without words, one that compelled a soft, bittersweet smile from her.

Odd, that he should feel a kindred spirit in her, this woman he'd never liked, not even on that day his father had brought her home. That moment, like so many others, was frozen in time the way a child's memory sometimes is, complete with all the nuance that adult recollection furnishes to it. He could remember the sky, gray as a squirrel's stomach. The carriage was new; the sound the wheels made upon the gravel mimicked hard rain.

The smell of her seemed to be the first memory he recalled, the scent of her perfume, something too flowery and nearly overpowering. Then her foot as she stepped down from the carriage, white stockings, something a child was not supposed to see, the adult in him cautioned, kid slippers banded across the instep, a skirt of flowered fabric, a coat of coal gray to shelter her from the chill of an early spring day. Cecily, into his life with no more fanfare than that. And the essence of his existence changed forevermore.

It was not that she had been such a severe stepmother. It was mostly that he was simply ignored by her for long stretches, as if beneath her regard. The child in him needed the softness of a mother's touch, but that warmth had never come from Cecily. Instead, he was used as errand boy or object lesson, neither role being much to his way of liking. But when he was twelve, Cecily found religion, grasping piety as if it were a prize handed down for only the most righteous. From that day on, she frowned upon his playing the pianoforte and encouraged his father to limit his free time so that the symphonies he heard in his head would never find fruition upon paper.

He had always suspected she was one of those people who found themselves elevated only upon the descent of others. She spread venomous tales about the most innocent of people, all the while expressing her earnest wish that her prayers for them be answered. Still, he could not hate

Cecily, for one reason. She was Alice's mother. Such an accident of nature was surely worth a few points in heaven.

But even Alice's disappearance had not brought them closer together. James looked at her now, over the rim of his cup, wondering what had brought about the show of affability from his stepmother. He had learned, over the years, that Cecily always had a reason for everything she did. Especially those gestures of charity. They were most often the more suspect.

"You know I've always disagreed with your father about your music, James."

He nodded, surprised again that she would bring their differences to light. So it was to be honesty from Cecily today. "And you know that I have often prayed about it."
Again he nodded, a more cautious gesture now. He did not want Cecily to begin praying over him. Her invocations to God were long and loud and filled with demands. He'd once heard her brag that she was free of the seven deadly sins, but he had the forbearance not to call to her attention the fact that pride was among them.

She folded her hands into a little fisted ball and rested it against her waist. Wasn't it odd that the sun seemed so bright it created a nimbus around her skin, one that appeared as if she glowed? "I told Alice the same thing, of course, when she mentioned that the two of you were going away together."

His hands shook. The cup made a delicate chink of sound against the saucer as he lowered it too quickly. Surprise mixed with hope, but beneath it was an emotion that threatened to overwhelm both, utter confusion. A thousand questions pummeled his brain. Had she seen Alice on that last day? Why had she never told him so? Did she know something of what had happened to his beloved almost-wife? What about his child? His lips trembled with the need to speak all of these questions at once.

A curious throbbing sensation nearly overpowered him, as if his heart were a booming drum, whose sound occupied the entirety of the room. A most bizarre numbness seemed to permeate his feet and hands, an even more strange sensation of his ears tingling, then his nose. And wasn't it strange that his forehead seemed to be made of clay, devoid of feeling, sitting above his features lumplike. And his lips, numb.

Was this, then, the shock of her statement? Had it rendered him insensible?

Her smile seemed oddly bright. Her teeth so white they seemed to catch the glare of the sun. Her hair was too blond; the ribbons of color around Cecily's form seemed to merge into a nimbus of gray. No, black. His field of vision narrowed, compressed, slowly but with definition. It was the one clue he had that it was not shock that caused these unusual feelings. Not surprise nor befuddlement, nor even elation.

He was dying.

His stepmother had killed him, a knowledge that seemed confirmed by the brightness of her smile.

"What is it now, Peter?"

"The bloody wheel's lost a band." He stood frowning at it, his gloved hands clenched into fists and resting on his hips.

"Let's go on without it."

"On what? The iron's what keeps the pieces of wood together, Bernie. Without it you don't have a wheel."

"Bloody hell."

Peter's grin was cut short. "And where the hell do you think she's goin'?"

Bernie turned from her examination of the wheel to see Mary Kate skimming over the grass, her skirts drawn up in her hands, her bonnet hanging down her back. She was running over the snow-covered ground as if to meet a lover.

"You're not thinking of running after her, are you?"

Bernie looked down at her three-inch heels, at her voluminous velvet skirts, at the glitter of frozen blades of grass, then shook her head reluctantly. She was, after all, twenty years older than Mary Kate.

"No, but you'd better get this bloody carriage fixed in record time, my friend."

It was not a request, Peter decided, looking at the expression in his lover's eyes. It was an order.

"With what, Bernie? A prayer and a miracle?"

Bernie looked back at the sight of Mary Kate. She was almost lost among the grove of trees that banded the Moresham Farms from Sanderhurst land, the trail her skirts made in the snow pointing toward her diminishing figure.

"Well, haven't you any tools or something?"

"What we need is a spare wheel. Barring that, we're at the crossroads. Someone's bound to come along sooner or later."

"And what do you propose we do until then, Peter?"

"Stay warm, Bernie. Have you any better ideas?"

Bernie looked to the distance once again. She didn't like being powerless, hated feeling helpless. She was very much afraid that circumstances were conspiring to separate her from Mary Kate. For what reason, she didn't know.

She turned and glanced at Peter. One look at her worried face and he nearly volunteered to race after Mary Kate.

Except, of course, that it would have left Bernie alone.
That, he would not do. He was getting too many strange
feelings about this day to tempt fate even further.

"Very well, Peter, if you can't fix the bloody thing."
She aimed a kick at it, and winced. She wondered, hearing
his chuckle, if she hadn't had the wrong target in mind.

The cold no longer bothered Mary Kate. It seeped in
through her slippers; the sensation of it traveled only as
far as her ankles. Somewhere she'd lost a glove. Or perhaps she'd left it in the carriage. It simply was not important. She ignored the burn of cold against her cheeks, the
fact that her hair had tumbled free of her bonnet.

Ahead, puffs of smoke alerted her to the fact she was
not far from Moresham Farms. Perhaps less than a mile
away. It would have been no distance at all on a bright
summer day. Even in this winter's cold, with the frost of
the morning coloring everything a delicate silver, such distance would be but a stretch of the legs. Now, however, it
loomed as a mirage, ever increasing, so that even after a
hundred steps, Moresham Farms seemed farther away, not
closer.

She should have watched her step, been alerted that this
was not an area cultivated by the plow or fenced for the
horses, but unstewarded land. The open burrow, field
mouse or rabbit or gopher home, ensnared her, and as she
fell, it wasn't the pain from her ankle that made her sob
aloud, or even the jarring impact of the frozen ground beneath her. It was the knowledge that she was so close, but
not near enough.

Not quick enough to save James.

Chapter 39

"**W**asn't it fortuitous that elderly Mrs. Gransted left me her rolling chair? Of course, the old dear hadn't much else to leave. Still, she was grateful for my nursing."

James said nothing. He could not speak. She had incapacitated him with her mushroom tea, a blend of death angel mushrooms and spiced tea.

Cecily finished binding his left hand to the arm of the chair, then stepped back and admired her handiwork. "It's come in quite handy, this chair. And will continue to do so for a matter of months. But of course, you'll have no way of knowing that. You'll stop breathing soon, and then it will be between you and God, all these grievous sins you've accumulated."

She stood behind the high back of the wheeled chair and turned it so that it pointed toward the drawing room door. It was quite difficult, really, what with James being almost a deadweight. Still, God provided the strength for her to propel it through the door.

"I really don't think you realize all your very many sins, James. But I expect that in a matter of minutes, you will be read a litany of them."

She pushed the chair through the doorway, sighing with satisfaction as the tall, narrow wheels cleared easily.

"I don't think, James, that I will ever forgive you for making Alice a party to your evil. She was such a glorious girl, such radiance of form and face. She could have been one of God's angels on earth. Imagine my horror, dear James, when she told me that she was in love with you, her own brother."

She walked around the chair to open the front door, bending and speaking into his wide, staring eyes. "Incest, James. If not of the body, then certainly the soul."

She smiled. "Mr. Moresham confessed to me that you were not his son. But I would have had to kill my darling, anyway, James. Because she was an adulteress, and God never makes angels of those among us who sin."

She pulled the chair through the front door. It slid easily over the threshold.

"How fortuitous that I had been to services that morning. It was cold and my dear Alice was waiting for you, James. And she smiled, with delight and joy. A sinner's smile and a deceitful heart. God gave me the strength to do what I must, just as now."

That morning she'd urged Alice into the pony cart, had warmed her hands within her own. Had coaxed the story from her own child, pretended joy where there was only horror, delight where there had been only revulsion.

"She told me, you know, what the two of you planned. I pretended to wish to help her, which is a sure and certain way to trap Satan in his own web. But I knew, James, that I had to kill that spawn of evil inside of her, that child you gave her."

Cecily pushed the wheeled chair over the first step, then the second. It wobbled, but did not fall.

"Oh, I knew all about the child, James. She told me so. She did not want to, but she was so very frightened by then. She was terrified of death, my glorious angel, which was so silly. Death freed her from her sins."

God had given her the strength to strangle her daughter, using the whip Cecily carried in the pony cart. It had been quite easily done; the fact Alice's mortal soul was in jeopardy added strength to her arms and her mission.

"Alice's greatest transgression was replicating Eve's sin of lust. I punished her for that, as I was told to do. But you cannot be allowed to go and sin even further, James. 'Correct thy son, and he shall give thee rest; yea, he shall give delight unto thy soul.' God forgave you through me once, but if you leave, I cannot save you from God's punishment. I must stop you and save your immortal soul."

The paths between the main house and the outbuildings were designed for foot traffic, not a wheeled conveyance. It was difficult pushing the chair across the gravel, far more difficult than it had been with Alice, perhaps because James weighed so much more. Other than that small detail, the day was not so very different. That morning, too, the farm had been deserted, the men occupied with the race at Fairhaven, the women servants sent to town with lists of supplies to purchase.

God had given her a mission, a duty to perform, and the glory of it fueled Cecily's resolve.

Some might have called it madness.

Mary Kate limped the last few yards, blinked at the sight before her. James Moresham was trundled up in an invalid's chair, bound at wrist, chest, and ankle. Behind him, nearly obscured by the chair's high back, was Cecily, who pushed him down the path toward one of the farthest outbuildings. Mary Kate flattened herself against the stable wall, waited until the creaking of the chair indicated they were past.

She had no weapon, and despite Bernie's encouragement, would not have known how to use one even if so equipped. Nor had she any idea of what to do next, except to follow Cecily and see where this strange journey culminated.

The curing shed. Because of the cold temperature, Mary Kate could see the ribbons of air surrounding the building, indicating the heat escaping from the structure. She crept forward quietly, conscious of the eerie silence that seemed to surround them. There was no noise at Moresham Farms. No horses stamping impatiently in their stalls, no sounds of currying, of iron beating against the anvil. Only the crunch of ice-laden grass beneath her feet, and the puffs of air from her lungs.

The door to the curing shed stood open, a maw of darkness. Hardly an invitation, certainly a warning. Mary Kate stood upon the threshold, empowered not by curiosity, but by a courage fostered from fear. She was desperately afraid to step inside, and even more terrified of not doing so.

She placed her uninjured foot upon the floorboards, took a step inside.

And the world went dark.

"It must be fate, Peter, but is that not Archer's carriage?"

"Aye, Bernie, it is."

They had loosened the horses from their leading strings and remained where they were, reasoning that as close to the crossroads as they were, a carriage was bound to come this way in a few moments. And not five minutes later, Archer arrived.

Was that not fortuitous timing? Or was it Fate again? Archer seemed inclined to think it damnable luck.

"You let her go?"

"I could do nothing else, Archer. She was determined."

"You've written that you have shouted down an entire tribe of aborigines, madam, who were determined to feast upon your flesh. How can one lone woman give you pause?"

"Perhaps my missives were a bit overplayed, Archer. But that is another subject entirely." She placed one foot upon the step and leaned into the carriage. "Can you speed us to the Moreshams'?"

"Is that where she's gone?" There was a look of such stillness on Archer's face that it seemed to chill her even further.

She nodded, but when she opened her mouth to expound upon her answer, Archer simply ignored her, pulled her into the carriage, and shouted something at Jeremy as Peter leapt in.

Speed, it seemed, was more pressing than courtesy.

"Do you not dislike it when people interfere with your plans, James?" Cecily stepped into the doorway, dropped the hook she used to lower the hams from the rafters, the same instrument she'd used to render Mary Kate unconscious. She bent her knees, grabbed twin fistfuls of fabric in her hands, pulling and dragging Mary Kate's body across the wooden floor. She closed the door firmly.

"It makes my job so much more difficult when people will not let me be an instrument of God's will." She retrieved the hook, inserted it into a small metal opening in the wall. With a twist, the panel came free. She slid it against the adjoining wall and turned to James. "The Moreshams have always been resourceful people, James, who planned on protecting their homes and their provisions during political unrest. I doubt even Samuel knows this room is here." There was barely a flicker of life left in his eyes. She would have to be quick, then.

"I am going to show you my most delicious secret now, James. God promised me this would gain me heaven's gates. For this He will award me and reward me. A perfect soul, frozen in time, offered up to my Maker in repentance for sins she and you performed."

She rolled the chair so that it stood balanced over the threshold, half-in, half-out of the small room. The air here, as in the larger room, was permeated with the smell of smoke, but another odor lingered, one sweeter and more ripe with decay. At the end of the narrow space was a makeshift altar, lovingly decorated with a lace cover, once delicate white, now yellowed due to the air of the curing shed. At either side of the altar were candles. A chalice sat in the middle; a Bible lay open as the final adornment.

Alice St. John knelt before it, clad in the dress she'd worn to meet James, her hands clasped together, her swollen stomach sagging below her knees. Rotted rope gouged into her dark, shriveled flesh, at wrists and knee and below her jaw, forcing her body into this position of humility and piety. Her face was upturned, her eyes clouded over and sightless. Her blond hair trailed down her back, almost to the floor.

She was preserved in perfect, abject submissiveness, a parody of faith mummified.

"I brush her dear hair every day, James," Cecily

crooned, pulling the chair out of the doorway so that she could enter the room, then pulling it back again so that he could have a clear view of Alice.

She walked to where her daughter knelt in perfect adoration and smiled beatifically. "She has never looked lovelier, don't you think?"

One hand smoothed over the skull matted with blond hair, not noticing when several long strands clung to her fingers. "I loved her, James, loved her enough to save her from sin. I delivered her from hell, James, as I shall you."

Cecily turned, smiled at the young man her daughter had loved to the cost of her mortal soul, then frowned when she realized that sometime during the last few minutes, James Moresham had quietly, and without protest, died.

Help her....

"Damn it, Jeremy, can't you make them go any faster?"

Bernie didn't bother to question Archer's haste, nor the look on his face, which must have indicated his stark fear. This was terror at its finest, the sheen-coated face, the grip of the bowels. This was death rearing its ugly head and a premonition that was too strong to deny.

"We'll be in time, Archer."

He gave her a sharp look, wondering how she could know. Archer knew something was desperately wrong, wrong in the way a two-headed cat is wrong. An aberration of nature, a mistake, something not meant to be. How he knew it affected Mary Kate so intimately and so vitally, he couldn't say, only that he had to get to her, to shelter her and, if need be, stand between her and this horror.

In all these months, he'd never found himself afraid. Not like now. He'd been concerned for Alice, but had he evinced any more fear for her than for his own reputation?

No. Not like now, when he could feel the soles of his feet go wet and the roof of his mouth become arid.

What was this feeling? Why did it seep into the very marrow of his bones? What did it mean? Why was he so afraid?

And whose voice called him to caution and whispered of danger?

Mary Kate awoke to the sound of praying. Her cheek was flattened against the hard and dusty floor. A muscle on the side of her face jerked spasmodically, and at first she thought it was an insect crawling on her skin. She tried to brush it away, only then realizing that she was bound and gagged. She choked back a moan, but something told her not to move and not to make a sound. She blinked once and a fierce pain welled in one eye.

Her nose smelled the sickening stench of decay before her mind registered what she was seeing. She felt herself begin to tremble as the realization penetrated the dull numbness of pain. Warm, smoky air was sucked into her lungs as she tried not to scream, then realized she could not because of the cloth wedged into her mouth.

Hot bursting blood racing through her veins. A heart muscle clenched and shivering. Nausea, hot, sickly sour, rose in her throat. The sound of Cecily's voice, her prayers to heaven, buffeted against the walls of Mary Kate's mind. Fear rolled through her muscles, clamping those in her neck and chest in spasms. A rictus of a smile spread her lips over dry teeth beneath the gag.

James Moresham sat tied to the rolling chair, quite obviously dead, his eyes vacant and staring. Before him knelt the woman he'd loved, a woman who had been the subject of too much speculation and not enough concern. Alice St.

John. Had she been here all along, kneeling in silent vigil, waiting for someone to rescue her from eternal penitence?

"Will it not be the most perfect sacrifice to our Lord? You cannot cheat me of it, you know. God has promised that He will share in this vengeance."

Mary Kate felt the bile rush to the back of her throat.

The look of venomous dislike from Cecily was not unexpected. Mary Kate stared at the other woman, no anger in her gaze, no strong emotion. Strangely enough, there was no longer fear. That had been burned out of her in those first few seconds upon awakening, by the diorama created by madness, by devotion rendered deadly. And by the sudden and sweeping knowledge that there was no voice within to warn her.

She had failed Alice.

Mary Kate blinked, held her eyes closed against sudden tears. Help him. . . . She had not been able to do that. She had not been in time, or quick enough to prevent James's death. She had not even known of the danger, of the madness that now sparkled so clearly from Cecily's eyes. Would she live with that guilt forever? And how long was forever? Was Cecily going to ensure it was compressed into an hour, even less?

Mary Kate swallowed, wondered if she would be brave in death, wondered how Cecily was going to kill her. Would it be painful, or would it be simply as Mrs. Tonkett had once mused, a step over a threshold, up onto a staircase leading to a world far, far away?

She didn't want to be courageous; she didn't want to die. Yet she was bound and trussed on the floor of the curing shed, with her eyes watering from the incessant smoke and her head still in agony from the first blow Cecily had administered. It did not seem as though there was much hope of survival.

If only she had not raced from the carriage. If only she had reasoned things through. If only she had known what horror awaited her. If only she had not tried to find her family. If only she had not been in the farmer's wagon. If only she'd not found herself entranced by a man with a hint of pain in his eyes. If only she'd not fallen in love with him, his rare laugh, his smile, the teasing look in his eyes. If only, if only, if only.

Was sanity lost one thread of thought at a time?

She felt the echo of the running thud of boots against her cheek before she heard the sound. The opening of the door, the flash of gray light against the candlelit interior, all these sensations flew into her mind like rushing birds just before the scream lanced through the air.

It was a woman's high-pitched screech, an animal's cry of impotent fury. Archer turned toward the sound, unprepared for the attack by the barely recognizable Cecily Moresham.

She came at him with teeth and nails, armed with the grappling iron. The first blow was deflected by his shoulder, the second found the side of his neck, gouging into his skin. He felt the blood flow, wondered at the size of the wound for only a second, until he glanced down and saw Mary Kate, huddled into a corner of the small shed. The sight of her wide, terrified eyes was enough to dismiss any momentary pain as he rounded on Cecily.

Bernie was beside him in an instant, then pushed out of the way by the tall, muscular footman. Peter grabbed Cecily by the arms, had nearly restrained her when she turned her head and like the animal she sounded bit him smartly on the wrist He released her with a bellow of pain. Cecily, impelled by madness, did not stop. She grabbed the meat hook with both hands, raised it above her head, and ran toward Archer.

He glanced past her, his gaze caught and held by the lit candles, by the vision of Alice held captive in eternal piety.

Mary Kate saw Archer freeze into immobility at the tableau he faced. She'd never felt terror as she did at this moment, watching him with fear slicking her blood and harnessing her breath. The gag stopped her from warning him; the screams she made emerged as small squeaks a mouse might make.

"Archer!" A shout of warning from Bernie as the iron hook lowered toward him with violent force. It was a strange, slowed picture of impending disaster. Cecily, armed with madness and determination; Archer, unable to move his limbs or break free of this paralysis of thought and action.

Bernie bent, withdrew the knife she always kept strapped to her ankle, and threw it. It found its target in the bodice of Cecily's proper dress, buried itself hilt-deep into a pulsing, maddened heart. Cecily crumpled to the floor in front of them, her hands still fixed convulsively upon the iron hook.

The most curious look of peace came over her face. A smile wreathed her lips, a strange sort of gurgling laughter emerged from her throat. What she said was lost to the world. It could have been an oath, a blessing, a warning. Nothing emerged but the rattle of death.

Chapter 40

❦

"It was quite a magnanimous thing for you to do, Bernadette," Samuel said. "To allow James to be buried beside Alice in the St. John crypt."

Bernie merely smiled. There was, after all, nothing to say. It had seemed fitting for the mausoleum to house the two lovers, an opinion she had seconded the moment Archer solicited her advice. Just Alice and James, alone for eternity, untainted by Cecily's presence in death. Would future generations look at the inscription carved into the marble and wonder about the story of the two lovers, or would rumors of Cecily's atrocities circle England for months upon years, becoming one of those legends that seemed to flourish on English soil? Only time itself would tell.

She stood beside Samuel on the fringe of mourners, the neighborhood arrayed in brittle black. Whispers seemed to float like smoke, to pool in corners and slither under doorframes. But all those invited to the repast following the ceremony of interment were outwardly respectful, the shine of life dulled from their faces by the presence of death.

Bernie extended her hand toward one of the innumerable

servants and another glass of sherry appeared in it. Magical, effortless hospitality at Sanderhurst. Achieved, however, only after hours of planning.

"How could something that horrible have happened, and I not know?" Samuel asked. "Shouldn't I have seen it or felt it?"

He turned red-rimmed eyes to her. Bernadette St. John laid her hand upon Samuel's sleeve. He looked so much older than she'd imagined he would, but then, the last few days had been filled with aging experiences. Although only an inch or two taller than she, Samuel sported a paunch, a sure sign that too many years had elapsed since she'd made her tearful farewells to him. His muttonchop sideburns were magnificently silver, his eyes lined. The years had not been kind.

"Cecily forgot the basic tenets of any faith, Samuel. Forgiveness. Hope. Atonement. Love."

"But her own child. To have killed her own child. How can I live with myself, Bernadette, that I did not protect Alice?"

"We all have our guilt to bear, Samuel."

"Was it a punishment, Bernie, for not loving her? She was not a woman who believed in such things. She was not an easy woman to love." He looked at her with hope-filled eyes. Did he ask for absolution from her? She didn't have the answers he sought. Did anyone?

There were, after all, no words to speak. At times like this, it was better to remain mute. Silence was her gift to him, a time for Samuel to unburden himself, speak words he would possibly never repeat.

"Do you think she knew that I regretted my marriage?"

Oh, Samuel, will you not leave it alone? "It isn't important anymore, is it?"

"I made a poor decision back then. The world would have changed if I had taken any other woman to wife instead of her. Alice would never have been born, only to die at her mother's hands. And poor James might be a famous man of music."

It was exceedingly difficult to see a proud man crumble before her. He seemed to realize it, because a long moment later he stood straighter, drank deeply from his glass.

"Are you happy, Bernie? Has life treated you well?" The look he gave her was almost speculative, certainly inquiring.

"I have learned to live within my skin, Samuel. I am different from other people, but then, most of us are, in one way or another."

"You always knew yourself, Bernie. I envied that about you."

"It is a skill I've practiced for many years, Samuel. It is not as easy as it seems. There are many things about myself that I would change."

He looked away from her then, to the broad open windows and the vista of the snow-covered lawns of Sanderhurst.

And what would he change? Certainly a wife and two children gone through madness. She would remember the look on Cecily's face until the day she cocked up her toes, Bernie thought. Confusion, then rage, so deep and so black that it seemed capable of eating through the most sturdy metal. And then Cecily's face had simply softened into death, all emotions smoothed away until there was nothing on her features at all. She might have been sleeping.

All wickedness is but little to the wickedness of a woman. How odd that she should remember that quote now. And from the Bible. How absurdly ironic.

"I've the three girls left, Bernie. And my grandchildren. All of whom are at home crying over their mother's grave. What do I tell them?" Again, that look of hopelessness. She wished she had the power to wipe it away. Only time itself would.

"Cecily was their mother. Certainly there was something about her that was good, something fine to remember?"

Then cling to that, my friend, because too many other people will be more than happy to help you remember the worst of it.

"Perhaps you can come to visit them all, Bernie, before they go back to their own homes."

"I'm afraid not, Samuel. I leave for China in but a matter of days."

"Then I wish you well, Bernie."

"And I, you, Samuel."

She bent forward to kiss him on his cheek. Just for a moment he held her, a soft press of body against body until he released her and stepped back. Bernie knew she would probably never see him again.

She strolled away from him then, outwardly serene, inwardly impatient that this day of obligation and ritual be finished. She wanted to be free of the milling people and the mirrors draped in black and the low-voiced humming sounds of voices. Idiotic things people said at such occasions, nothing making much sense. But then, what could be said at such senseless tragedy?

This was not an old man wheezing his last breath in his familial bed, or an ancient crone cackling her last wishes before extending one claw for the hand of Death itself. This was the memorial for two young people, deprived of life because madness had made it so. One a countess, a young woman with a bright smile and a sparkling laugh Bernie remembered from when she was a child. The other a young man of talent and brilliance, who could coax music from his mind and anoint the world with it. And a child never born, never given life, because madness decreed it so. It seemed fitting that they all rested together.

Yet she was more concerned for the living. She'd had only glimpses of Archer in the last few days and had the distinct impression that Mary Kate was avoiding her. Neither looked ready to offer comfort and support to the other. Neither seemed capable of being denied it much longer.

Guilt. A strange word. An even more onerous emotion. They all felt it, did they not? Archer for condemning a victim. Mary Kate for not saving James Moresham. Herself, for killing a madwoman. Even Samuel, for keeping the secret of James's birth too long, for not knowing that he slept beside a madwoman. They were all human beings, all flawed, all destined to writhe a little upon a heavenly spit for the sins they'd committed. But not punished as ably and as permanently as Cecily would have wanted.

As she turned, she caught a glimpse of a cloaked Mary Kate, bonnet pressed down about her face as if to hide her features from the guests. Bernie excused herself, walked into the hallway. Mary Kate gave her a watery smile, a false mimicry of her usual bright greeting. Bernie pressed the young woman's hands between her own, offering wordless comfort. If only there were something else she could have done. Of all of them, she worried about Mary Kate the most. The vivacity of the girl had been muted, as if she resided beneath a heavy, fog-colored cloud.

"Are you sure you wish to walk the grounds now?" Bernie's voice held a great deal of gentle doubt. "It is a very cold place to wish solitude."

"It smells clean and fresh."

Unlike sweet decay. A thought Bernie voiced only in her mind. "Shall I leave you alone, then?"

"I will be fine, Bernie." A resolute smile seemed to promise it.

She pulled open the door, but before exiting the too warm hall, she turned. "Did you know, Bernie? Did you realize Cecily was capable of something like that?"

A moment of thought, as a small and infinitely painful smile appeared on Bernie's face. "Who is to see the face of madness, Mary Kate? Are we not all capable of some horror or another? What keeps any of us just this edge of sanity?"

"That does not hold out much hope for the rest of us, does it, Bernie?" Her hand gripped the door too tightly.

"Oh, my dear, that is all we have, sometimes."

She knew it was not enough of an answer, yet a more complete one might never be found.

Mary Kate sat heavily on one of the rustic benches. In front of her was a small pond that had frozen overnight, to the consternation of several ducks that pecked upon its surface. Tall reeds stiff with ice surrounded half of it; an interesting tree draped its branches along the other half. She was not a gardener, but a lack of proficiency did not prevent her from admiring the work of others. The formal garden of Sanderhurst would be glorious in the spring. Now it lay dormant and brown, carefully shaped and trimmed boxwood hedges peeping from beneath a layer of snow the only spot of color. It was a perfect sight for restful composure, if only she could convince her mind of it.

She needed time alone, unhampered by the demure gentility this day demanded. How odd that she should miss her father so acutely now. Or perhaps not. Her father represented stability, something lacking in her life for years. And love, something she'd not felt since his death until coming to this sprawling castle of a home. But neither stability nor love would be hers for much longer.

Until today, she had not seen Archer since those horrible moments in the curing shed. Mary Kate had never seen anyone undergo such a rapid transformation, from handsome to haggard, from filled with life to almost a cadaver. He'd come and loosened her bonds, freed her mouth of the gag. For a moment he'd stroked his hands over her bruised mouth, but then his attention was turned upon Alice.

Sweet, dainty Alice, shriveled and wizened and bent, nut brown, her skin shiny, leathered by the smoking process. Archer had knelt there in a sad mimicry of his wife's tortured position, his hands stretching out as if to touch her. But at the last moment he could not, just softly withdrew them to rest upon his knees, never noticing when a blond hair fell soundlessly to the floor.

Perhaps Mary Kate could have given him something of comfort in those moments, perhaps said a few words of wisdom, even held him in her arms. Yet it was as if they were all singularly inviolate, separated, kept apart not only by shock, but by the horror of a mind that could have envisioned this tableau and then executed it in perfect detail.

She had not, in the end, touched him. It was Peter who hauled her up into his arms, who planted her in the carriage. Bernie who sat with her during the ride back to Sanderhurst, where the doctor examined her head and ankle and pronounced her assigned to her bed for a fortnight.

Today was the first day she could bear to stand, and today she had indeed stood, while a minister consecrated the new vault in the St. John crypt. After it was over, only she and Archer had remained, staring as the door was slowly closed and sealed. The two people who had loved each other since they were children now lay together in death.

Heaven should have wept for such a loss, and perhaps it did, the tears frozen to become the snowflakes that fell soundlessly around them as they stood there.

And since he had said nothing to her since the moment he'd discovered his wife, Mary Kate said nothing as she left, uncertain of Archer's thoughts or his feelings. There was no voice in her mind, nothing to guide her but a feeling of trespass.

If she felt guilt, it was not of the nature Bernie supposed. She had tried to save James Moresham, despite the ridicule of others. She had tried and failed, but others might not have tried.

No, the guilt she felt was that assumed by those who live when others do not. Death touched a nerve with Mary Kate, a strong and sensuous one that surprised her, then shamed her, then simply amused her. She was radiantly glad to be alive, hysterically gleeful for being pulled back from the brink. She hadn't wanted to die, was not prepared for it, may never be. She had always clung to life with a greedy and confident expectation that things would be brighter, that life would become better, that she herself would experience all those things she'd longed for as a child and a young woman.

Even now, at a time when she should have felt the most saddened, a small flicker of hope breathed like a tiny flame.

Chapter 41

I t was dawn when Mary Kate woke, a scant three hours before she was due to leave Sanderhurst. She had arrived with few belongings; how odd that her portmanteau now bulged at the seams. A book of poetry given to her by Archer, two dresses altered from Bernie's wardrobe, plus the headdress Mary Kate could not bear to part with, it reminded her so much of the odd and iconoclastic countess—all these things rested inside. And at the bottom was a pressed flower from the garden and the most precious treasure of them all, a miniature of Alice St. John as a child, given to her by Samuel Moresham with many tears on her part and a gruff throat clearing on his.

She lay staring up at the ceiling, wondering if she'd have the courage to say good-bye to Archer. Still no words between them, nothing but a stilted silence.

Was it that he had truly not believed her and now was having difficulty coming to terms with it? Or had he loved Alice more than he had admitted even to himself?

She sat up on the side of the bed, then stood. She pulled her nightgown off and spent the next few moments donning her clothes for the journey. The first tinges of light shone upon the horizon, trailing fingers of pink and yellow and rose. Mary Kate chose not to light the candle, but stood at the door of the terrace watching the dawn, feeling the pepper of tears in her eyes.

Only after a few long moments did she leave her room and turn down the hall, turn left at the branch and step toward the Master's Suite. Only once before had she been in Archer's room before, and that journey left a store of memories. She knocked softly on the panel, prepared to turn away if he did not respond to the soft entreaty. She did not wish to waken him.

"Enter."

It was a command given in a fully awake voice. No grogginess or stumbling over words. She bent her head, placed one hand upon the door's lever, then pushed it open with the gentlest of movements.

He was standing at the window, watching the sky lighten as she had, although his view was not of the east as hers had been. The Master's Suite was a huge sprawling room that looked out over the northern expanse of Sanderhurst.

Mary Kate understood why Archer had never thought to guard her, after viewing the sheer size of the landscaped lawn. He needn't worry that she could have escaped; a coach and four would not have been able to travel the manicured expanse in an hour. It was a daunting sight, the massiveness of Sanderhurst, a silent yet overwhelming reminder of the power of the man who had imprisoned her, first in rage, and then in passion. And a goad to remember how different their stations in life were.

She did not belong here.

He turned at her entrance, yet did not seem surprised by her presence. Had he heard her stirring? Or did he know she was about to leave and wished to bid her farewell on his own? Questions she did not feel courageous enough to ask of him. Not now. Not at this moment.

"We have not talked, you and I," he said.

"No."

Her answer seemed to amuse him. A small smile curved his lips. "Are you well?"

"Yes." Why was she finding this so difficult? Why was *farewell* such an onerous word to utter? Say good-bye, Mary Kate, and have an end to this. Of fairy tales and ghosts and wounded eyes. Say good-bye and go back to being of the servant class, where a man looks like what he is, be it ironmonger or fisherman or carpenter. Where pain is from a boil on the arse or a severed thumb, not an agony of the spirit, or a wound of the soul.

"And you? Is your injury better?"

He fingered the bandage on the side of his neck. "Yes. I've been told I heal quickly."

The flesh, perhaps, but the soul? How quickly did the spirit heal?

He looked too tired, as if sleep had been only fleetingly his. Too world-weary, as if he'd seen all that was wicked and evil and hideous about it. Ah, but then, they both had, hadn't they? Was that why they could not talk?

"I've come to say . . ." There it was then, that hitch in her breath. That word, so terribly difficult. *Good-bye.*

"Must you?"

"I'm afraid so."

"Then be gentle, Mary Kate. I'm feeling rather battered and bruised with the truth lately."

"What truth, Archer?"

He looked at her blandly. No, not bland. Nothing about Archer St. John was without emotion, be it good or bad. He seethed with it, anger, disgust, contempt. What would he be like veiled in those emotions of brighter hue—joy, excitement, expectation? Love?

He turned away from her, back to the view of Sanderhurst.

A small laugh broke the silence between them. "That you were right, and I was wrong, of course. Horribly wrong, as it turned out." He turned and watched her, an eagle's stare again. "Was that not what you came to say? Although, I will admit, I'd never thought you the type to gloat."

"Nor am I."

"Forgive me," he said, stepping closer. "I've hurt you. I am doomed to always disappoint you, Mary Kate, first with my doubting, then with my cruelty. Forgive me," he said, reaching her, extending his arms forward and grabbing her shoulders.

She could have easily wrested herself from his grip, but it seemed that he needed the embrace as much as she. She stepped into it, feeling absurdly that she was coming home, nesting in a spot reserved for her in all of nature, Archer St. John's arms.

His chin nuzzled her hair, and of their own volition, her arms crept around his waist, to anchor him there. He was so very warm, easing out all the cold she'd felt for so very long.

"Do you know, since you've come into my life, nothing has been quite the same. Or is it, Mary Kate, that I only see things differently?"

"What things?" Her voice was muffled. She held her cheek against his chest tightly, the way a child would do if frightened or in danger of imminent parting. She never wanted to leave. How terrible, then, that the minutes ticked so stolidly between them.

There was a note of humor in his voice, a rueful acceptance of her insistence. "I had forgiven Alice even before she was found. I no longer thought of her as a perfidious wife, but a woman as trapped as I in our loveless marriage."

"I am so sorry, Archer. For all that I did not do."

He pulled back, studied her with a fierceness that would have denoted anger if she had not seen the fear in his eyes. "You almost died, Mary Kate. You almost died."

He kissed her then, and she kissed him back, surrendering to an unbearable temptation, the feel of his lips. Through the veil of tenderness crept another emotion, one more visceral, more fierce, protection, possession, need. It tore the tenderness to shreds with one swipe of a taloned claw.

Was this what she had wanted, then? One last time to lie in his arms, to feel the strength and the need and the passion he gave her so effortlessly? A memory to last a lifetime. A recollection of bliss to store in an enameled jar and extract on those cold, lonely nights when everything around her was mellow and warm except for the core of her, except for her heart. Then her heart would clench tight in warmth, in recollection. She would extract from her memory jar the feel of his lips on her, the delicate invasion of his tongue, the strength of his hands, the feel of his fingertips as they skated across her skin, eliciting trembles as they passed.

The clothing she had donned only minutes ago was divested quickly. Her hands, or his—it did not matter who—opened laces and slipped buttons from their loops. He helped her with one of her new slippers, sliding it from her foot, his palm cupping her heel in a tender caress.

She had a vague impression of his leading her to the

great state bed, but perhaps he'd lifted her to it instead. Above her head a crest was embroidered; yards and yards of embroidered silk was draped from its large posts. It was sumptuous and ridiculously elegant, sublimely decadent, and she could have been resting on straw for all she cared. His dressing gown was open; the expanse of his chest was graced with shadows. She reached out to touch him, but he stayed her hands, standing beside the bed watching her.

"You are a painting," he whispered, his voice filled with warmth. Perhaps in this memory jar, she would label it tenderness, perhaps she would pretend that much.

He bent to his knees beside the bed, lowered his forehead against the side of the mattress, then reached out and cupped her right breast, the skin of his palm slightly rough and creating a skittering sensation where it touched. It was as if they were new lovers, as if they had never spent hours exploring each other, as if he had not kissed and stroked and trailed a fingertip down each swell and curve of her body.

She felt like a feast of sensation. There, a feather brush of tenderness. Here, a teasing pluck upon her skin. A soft, cajoling bite, the smooth enamel of teeth, a shudder of nerves racing to keep up with the pounding of a heart, a shiver of need.

He lowered himself into her, plunging into her heat with one stroke, as if he reminded her of the sheer physicality of mating, not the mentality of it. He did not simply arouse her, he promised satiation.

"Please." Into the silence she spoke again, the single word lifting his head and causing him to spear her with a glance. It was there in her eyes, there in the grazing of her fingers against his lips, his chin. The mate for his ancient man. The fertility goddess. The victim, staked out and willing.

She surrendered to an emotion she could not name.

He had touched her before, but not like this, not with every inch of his skin being licked by every inch of hers. They were two cats in the morning light, probably making noises like mating animals, but she was insensible to it. He teased her by withdrawing, then entering her with a thrust, no preliminary coaxing, no soft sweet words, only hunger easing the way. He undulated over her; she stretched, feline, beneath him. He nipped at her chin, her shoulder, her tight budded nipples. She clawed at his shoulders, his back, his thighs. Both of his hands held her tight at the waist; she lunged upward with his downward movement. She was tight and hot and wet. He was hard and hot and strong.

He looked fierce and feral and almost animal above her. Was that why her heart beat so loudly and the feelings he aroused in her were so frightening and yet so blessed? It was hunger and desperation so fierce she arched against him in demand.

Such need lasts a lifetime in the mind, but only moments passed before she began to whimper. The sound was an aphrodisiac in the morning, a call to completion, a herald as old as the dawn that streamed into the room.

She bit her bottom lip, he coaxed it free with his fingers, covered it with his own mouth, swallowed the sound of her whimpers as she fell mindless into blackness. Moments later, seconds later, a hundred years later, she cradled him as he did the same.

"Is this all, ma'am?"

"Yes, thank you, Peter," Bernie replied.

He turned half-in and half-out of the doorway, watched her with hooded eyes. "You're really goin', then?"

She straightened from her inspection of the empty armoire, certain that this time she had not left anything behind. She had a habit of doing that, as a mouse might mark its territory, a trinket here, a reticule there, flotsam and jetsam of her life strewn over three continents.

"I've done what I've set out to do, Peter. Why should I remain?"

"I'll not beg, Bernie."

What was there about men that made them so appealing? Was it that they sometimes reminded grown women of their little boys, what with their petulant air and their lower lip all hanging out in brooding silence? And yet Peter did not appear to be a child this moment, not with his muscles bunched up under the weight of her trunk, and his glower.

"You're a good man, Peter. I'm sure there is a woman closer to your own age who would please you as well." Still, there was something to be said for pride, was there not? And the sweet blush of it warmed her face. She would miss him, not only for those nights he'd enlivened her stay at Sanderhurst, but for the surprising good humor of him, for his insightful glimpses into human nature, the laughter they'd shared.

Never mind that. He wasn't for her. He was young and strong and handsome. She was older, slightly worn, and looking for something she'd yet to define.

"I was a seaman afore I came to Sanderhurst, Bernie. I've seen the world and most that's in it. I'm not much more than five years younger than you, but I'm willin' to bet that I've the experience to offset it right enough."

"I'm not one to stay in one place, Peter. Remaining at Sanderhurst would render me as batty as Cecily Moresham."

"I've not asked it of you."

"And the accommodations on even the most luxurious St. John ship are less than commodious, I can assure you."

She ducked her head into the empty armoire once more, less to assure herself she'd left nothing behind than to hide her flaming cheeks. And, perhaps, dampen the rising excitement she felt?

"Is it more than a hammock between decks, Bernie?"

"The voyage to China is very long, Peter, taking months." She emerged from the armoire, the gleam in her eye somewhat subdued, but not as expressionless as she would have wished.

"You look less a matron now, Bernie, or a countess, than a young woman about to set upon a great adventure. Aye, it's a picture that gives my heart a tug."

"It's been a lovely time, Peter. Thank you." There, was that strong and resolved enough? She wasn't a bloody saint, after all.

"I remember it being a boring voyage, Bernie. One in which I'd longed for diversion myself."

"Perhaps it would be nice to have the company of an experienced sailor."

"I was a bosun on my last voyage." He lowered the trunk and advanced on her.

"A credible rank."

"Less than being a St. John, Bernie, a thought you need to give some time to."

"As is my age, Peter."

He grinned then, an utterly lovely gesture that showed his white teeth and tanned skin. "Then, Countess, shall we consider ourselves travelin' companions? You with your great advanced age, and me with my limited prospects?"

"I cannot help but think you've got the lesser of this bargain, Peter. Are you very sure?"

He was nearly upon her. Then he reached out and quite easily lifted her to her toes, bent his head and kissed her soundly, leaving no doubt in her mind that he was quite, quite sure.

"It's a damn long voyage to China, Bernie, my love. I'll make the most of it. By the time we're in Xiamen, we'll see what we think of this bargain of ours."

It was the experience of lying close to a naked male that woke Mary Kate an hour later. The touch of another body, especially one as large and warm as this particular body, was an experience she relished.

He slept beside her, turned to his side, a hand outstretched as if to beseech her to stay. For long moments she studied him in the light of the morning sun.

He had a habit of crossing his middle fingers together, even in sleep. She wondered where that little gesture had originated. A childish wish, forever to be left ungranted? His eyelids danced in his dreams; every few breaths he made a startling sound like a gust of air. Not quite a snore, but nearly so. He slept heavily, as if he had not slept well in the last few days and was making up for such a lack.

Mary Kate felt coward enough to bless this fact, as she stood and silently began dressing. She sat upon the edge of the bed, tempting fate, it seemed, and the sleeping figure on the bed beside her. If he awakes, I will tell him goodbye. If he does not, I will go without a word.

She braided her hair, pinned it to the nape of her neck, all without benefit of a mirror. A nicety not often available for the servant class.

Still, he did not wake.

Another few moments passed, during which she simply studied him, the long, muscled length of him, half-draped by the sheet. He would grow cold, she thought, before she covered him with the thin blanket and then the outer duvet. Still he did not wake.

Finally, when it was evident that Archer St. John was deep in the arms of sleep, Mary Kate stood and looked down upon the bed. In her eyes was a tenderness born of a love unspoken. Just before she left the room, however, she broke her own resolve, returning to the bed, placing a soft and tender kiss upon Archer's forehead. In the smallest of words, so softly spoken they could not possibly disturb him, she whispered her last and most onerous truth of all.

"I love you, Archer."

But there was no place for her here.

Chapter 42

Mary Kate unlaced the black velvet vest and shrugged it off her shoulders, then unbuttoned the white, full-length blouse. She handed both garments to Bessie, the young girl originally hired to be the relief barmaid, but who was more comfortable helping abovestairs. She stepped out of the linen skirt and two petticoats she wore under that, smiling at the effect of her costume, as she called it. It was close enough to a tavern wench's attire to never let her forget, and yet made of richer materials and of a finer cut so that the customers often did.

Still, the clientele of the Golden Eagle were not likely to take advantage, not with a burly ex-seamen stationed at the front doors. He was there to ensure that nothing occurred that would damage the Eagle's reputation, or harm her. Consequently, the small establishment had a growing repute as a tavern where a fair measure of whiskey was traded for a coin, where a man could get a good meal flavored in the way of the French, and talk of politics or women or horses. A customer could work on the docks or in the government, be a soldier or a duke; as long as he knew his manners, he was welcome at the Eagle.

"I thought the Earl of Brighton was going to 'ave a

stroke, ma'am, after you called 'im a knuckle'eaded dunce.''

"He actually thinks the French will settle down into an amicable discourse with England. His words, not mine. The idiot does not see the writing on the wall. We are for war, Bessie. There is little doubt.'' Mary Kate removed her stockings and placed them on the dressing table. "France will declare war on Britain any day. They have already killed their king. What does the idiot think will happen?''

"Still an' all, I don't think 'e liked to 'ear it from you.''

"Stupid man. Just because a woman issues an opinion does not make it wrong.''

"Bloody hell, Mary Kate, tell 'im to let me go. My ears'll never be the same.''

Both women turned at the sound of his voice. Bessie's eyes simply grew wide at the sight of the handsome gentleman in the doorway. Why, he nearly took up all the space, his head nearly touching the lintel. Plus, he had Michael O'Brien's head tucked neatly under one arm, and the man's bull-like shoulders were half-twisted in that position.

Archer only grinned.

"Yes, Mary Kate, do tell me what I'm to do with him. He seems to be of the mind to keep me from you. I tried to tell the gentleman that you and I had business, but he wouldn't take my word for it.''

"Let him go, Archer. Uncle Michael, are you all right?''

The man assigned to be her guard at the front door shook himself free and eyed Archer St. John with a great deal of caution. Still, he edged away from him all the same. He crooked his neck as if to test whether or not his head rested on his shoulders the right way, and then sent a ferocious scowl toward the man who leaned negligently against the doorframe.

"And now, Mary Kate, does a woman professing to be without any kin in the world suddenly possess an uncle? He looks nothing like you. He's a bull of a man and rude, to boot."

"No, Uncle Michael," Mary Kate said, to forestall yet another confrontation. "I'm sure the earl meant no disrespect." She came and stood between them, placing her hands on her uncle's chest, while sending Archer a disdainful look.

"I've six brothers, too, Archer. And a host of nieces and nephews. An entire family, noisy and boisterous." Was it her imagination, or did he flinch?

She turned back to her uncle, her gaze sharp and protective all at once. "Did he hurt you, Uncle Michael?"

Archer's laughter lit the room. "I am flattered that you think me so dangerous, my dear. Your long-lost uncle may be twice my age, but I think he could take on the King's Guards and remain standing."

Uncle Michael looked mollified enough to stop scowling for a moment.

"Should I take him downstairs for you, Mary Kate?"

"No, Uncle Michael. That's all right."

Archer entered the room nonchalantly, as if it had not been nearly a year since she'd seen him, as if every day had not been filled with memories of him. At this moment it was almost too much, the sight of his sardonic smile, the light of something blazing in his eyes, Bessie's stupefied amazement, Uncle Michael's glower.

"Shall we go, ma'am, or call someone?" Bessie asked, handing Mary Kate her dressing gown.

She turned and looked at Bessie and Michael over her

shoulder. "It's all right, truly it is. I'll be fine."

After they left the room, Mary Kate turned back to Archer St. John. In those long seconds she wished for some sort of nonchalance with which to greet him, a detachment with which she could treat his sudden appearance. Such was not an easy thing to accomplish, even less so when she studied him. He was the same, and yet not. There were few physical changes; he was as tall as ever, as broad as a tree trunk, as sartorially perfect. But there were tips of silver upon his black hair, and a few more wrinkles about his eyes. It was as if he had not slept since she'd left him at Sanderhurst, adrift in dreams. How utterly tired he looked.

How long had she waited for him? A thousand years? How many times had she told herself not to think such forbidden thoughts? Earls do not chase servant girls.

And yet he was here now.

"How did you find him?"

"You'll say it didn't happen. That there is no such thing as fate, or coincidence. He came in for a dram of whiskey, Archer. I served him myself." And ended up on his lap, crying, while the whole of the tavern looked to want to tear him limb from limb for making her cry. Michael had told her of the others, of the web of family stretching all over England. Twice they'd met all together, and were planning on another meeting in the spring.

"I would not have thought you gone back to servitude. It seemed I was mistaken, however. It would have made my search a little faster, if not easier."

"You looked for me, then?"

"My dear Mary Kate, I scoured the earth for you. Did you not know?" A small smile played over his lips.

She shook her head.

"I sent one of my ships for Bernie, thinking you were with her. Imagine my surprise when, ten months later, Robert Danley returns, with the tale that my mother is completely smitten with Peter the footman, has made him some sort of tea merchant in China. Did you know they'd married?"

At the shake of her head, he walked closer, still smiling, a gesture of utter benevolence. Why, then, did she feel that he leashed his emotions, kept his anger tightly reined?

'She sent me a four-foot carving of a fertility goddess, accompanied by a scathing letter."

"She did?"

"She did. She lectured me on the St. John habit of autocracy, on the quickness of life, on the fact that I was an idiot to have banished any chance of happiness from my hermitage."

"That sounds a great deal like Bernie." She twisted her hands in front of her.

"Yet she did not divulge where you were."

"She did not?"

"No, she did not." Another small smile.

He walked to the side of the room where her bed lay, a small, narrow mattress covered with a plain, soft blanket. "I awakened to find you gone, Mary Kate, felt as bereft as a child. I inquired of Jonathan what had become of you, and he did not know. Not one servant knew of your ultimate destination. I visited your brother, of all people, Mary Kate. Not a pleasant sort. He is the one for whom the word *hermit* was crafted. Dislikes me intensely, I believe, which is no great loss, since I found myself sharing the sentiment. But you were not with him, either."

He walked to the window, stared full face into the pane of glass, as if he could see the view from it. Only seconds later did she realize that the darkness reflected the interior of the room and he watched her, instead.

"It took ten months to hear from Bernie. Ten months in which to wonder and hope and pray. Do you know what I thought, Mary Kate?"

He turned and watched her. At the shake of her head, he smiled.

"I thought you dead, like Alice. That madness had traveled from the very grave and kept you prisoner."

"Oh, Archer." She had never thought he would think that.

"No note, Mary Kate? No explanation? Was I that severe a jailer?"

"What could I say, Archer?"

He turned again, came closer. Her heart beat in tandem to his closeness. He'd always had that effect on her.

" 'Forgive me, Archer, I cannot stay. I do not like you, nor this way of life. I crave the boisterous noise of my lost companions, the cacophony that is London. I seek another man, who touches me with less haste and more grace, who smiles more, who laughs in immoderate measure.' " He reached out and fingered the tendrils of hair at her temple. "What do you say, Mary Kate? Such a letter would not be that difficult to pen."

"It would not be the truth."

"And what is the truth?"

How easily she had walked into his net of words. What would he say, this earl, to hear what he professed to want? Could she give him that, strip her soul that bare?

"Forgive me, Archer, I cannot stay. I could not live with you one more day and not feel the greatest pain when you severed our association. My habit of self-protection runs too deep, too strong. I love your way of life, I crave nothing more, but I do not belong here.''

There was silence for a moment, while he remained still. His gaze was fixed above her. There was nothing about Archer St. John's face to indicate his thoughts. Nothing for her to be able to discern what he felt.

''And so you left me, to become a barmaid again.''

''No, not quite.'' Her smile was soft, a little melancholic. ''I own the Golden Eagle. Well, half of it now. Your mother owns the rest. It was she who gave me the money for it. But of course, she didn't tell you, did she?''

''Why a tavern, Mary Kate? Why a place where men congregate? Where they can ogle you for the price of an ale?''

''What else do I know, Archer, other than service? I can offer a good meal for a fair price, serve ale and whiskey and a measure of comfort.''

''How far does that measure of comfort take you, Mary Kate?'' His finger stroked the edge of her jaw. She flinched and drew away.

''Is that why you've come, Archer, to accuse me of whoring?''

''And what would you say if I had?''

''That it was none of your concern. That it was my life.''

''And that is all you would say?''

''That is all I would say. And that is all I am saying, Archer, so you can return to your hermitage, satisfied by my answer.'' *Please, do not go, Archer. Do not take my banishment so easily.* It seemed as though he heard her words, if the smile on his face attested to it.

''And what do I tell the voice?''

''What voice?''

"The one that whispers incessantly in my ear. The one that sounds like my dead wife, who implores me to go to you, with such diligence and such demand that I cannot but obey. Do not stare at me so, Mary Kate Bennett. Do you think yourself the only one haunted?"

"You do not believe in such things."

Archer smiled at her look. "Did you never wonder how I came to be with you that day at the curing shed? It was not my vaunted good sense. Not intellect, nor wisdom, but the voice of a ghost, the whisper of a spirit."

"I'd never thought of it before."

"I've had months, my dearest Mary Kate. Months to remember how many times I ridiculed you, and thought you cunning and manipulative. You'd confused me and enraged me. And all that time you were as innocent as you claimed. Coincidence? Strangely, yes. Fate? Maybe that is simply another word for timing so finite that it defies all man's laws.

"Perhaps one day I will tell you of these long, lost months, of the answers I have sought and the questions I asked. Perhaps, if you are patient, I will even tell you that I have realized in these long and dreary months that there is more to life than I can understand. More than I can quantify and measure. There were secrets in the wind, and mysteries of the mind and miracles that only the soul can understand."

"And is that why you're here, because of Alice?"

"It would be enough for most women, wouldn't it?" He took one step closer. "You know as well as I that it is not the full truth. Alice only repeats what my conscience knows full well. Perhaps what I hear is simply my soul given voice, in a sweet and delicate whisper.

"I have missed you, Mary Kate. I need you more than

is wise. I want you more than is favorable to either of us. Come back to Sanderhurst with me.''

''I cannot, Archer.''

In a second he became the Archer St. John he showed the world, shuttered and still, a figure of a man holding incredible vitality inside, yet allowing only coldness and iced fury to be viewed. Here was the man who ran an empire.

''I have been a barmaid, Archer, but it is an honorable vocation. Most of us work hard for our pennies and do not soften the beds of our customers. We serve ale, Archer, not our bodies.''

Her words changed his expression again, seemed to twist something open in his mind.

''You think I want you for my mistress, don't you? Oh, Mary Kate, you seem so wise sometimes that you shock me when you utter something so idiotic. I want you for my wife, my dear dairymaid. Vile temper and all.''

''As flattering as that proposal is,'' she said, irritated, ''I must decline. You are an earl, Archer. You cannot marry just anyone. There is your family to consider, your place in the world.''

''I am an earl, my dearest Mary Kate, because one of my ancestors had the uncanny luck to import sandalwood into the empire, not because of any great feat of my own. Besides, Mary Kate, the world will judge me as it will. I would much rather be happy while they're doing it. And you've forgotten the most compelling reason of all, my love.''

She placed a hand between them, to forbid him to come closer. He only took it and placed a kiss upon the back of it, then rubbed her fingers against his chin, the edge of his smile.

His eyes had softened, become infused with warmth. Her skin seemed brushed with it, her heart seemed to stutter in her chest. Of all the dreams she'd dreamed and all the visions imagined, she'd never envisioned this. Archer St. John, stubborn, intractable, his mouth curved in a gentle smile, decrying society's rules and opinions.

"And what is the most compelling reason, Archer?"

"We've both been taught, Mary Kate, that life is too short for pettiness, for living other than the most complete of existences. My mother would remind us both how fragile we are. And how can we ever forget Alice and James? Should we not grasp love where we find it? Take it and hold it close?

"I love you, Mary Kate. Is that a compelling enough argument?"

Her nod was bemused; her look encouraged his smile.

"Then come with me to Sanderhurst and the world will whisper tales of us, of St. John the Hermit and his fascinating wife, and the spirit which brought them together."

When had he realized that? She had wondered about it ever since that day in the curing shed, all the myriad reasons and questions finally culminating in an odd sort of answer.

He raised her chin and looked down into her eyes, not appearing surprised to see the sheen of tears there.

Had Fate, in the guise of Alice, brought them together? Had it caused the accident, gifted Mary Kate with dreams, placed two lonely people in a situation in which they were forced to recognize their mutual attraction? Peer and commoner, wealthy and poor, they were disparate in all ways that mattered to the world. Yet they had both lacked the trust required to believe in love, both doubted it would ever come to them. And now they stood in wonder, recognizing in the other the degree of love they shared.

How could they not believe?

Epilogue

A melody cushioned her as she slept, a soft trickle of sound that expanded to the complexity of a symphony, with violins and horn, piano and harp. A mixture of glorious noise coming together to form music to stir the heart and soul. It accompanied her journey, this glorious sound, as she rushed alone through the darkness. She was not afraid. She sensed the presence of others, as their spirits reached to touch hers in gentle, encouraging strokes like the most delicate fronds of floating seaweed.

Time was unimportant, a mere device created by man to measure his own fleeting existence. Years, decades, an aeon could pass, and it was only a heartbeat compared with this eternity.

Unguided, she traveled to a distant, unknown place, yet she sensed that the journey was not new, that it had been made before by hundreds, by thousands, by millions who preceded her.

She was spirit, floating and flying toward the radiance that illuminated the shadows. Peace filled her soul and she sensed, rather than felt, the streams of air pushing past her as she grew closer to the brilliance.

Gradually the inky darkness lightened and became

brighter. The air was filled with creamy white circles as if a million fireflies banded together and glowed on the horizon. She was cushioned, gently rocked on waves of luminous light, supremely safe, serenely secure.

If she had arms, she would have stretched them outward, to enfold the peace around her. If she had eyes, they would have been filled with tears of joy. If she had lips, they would have widened in a smile so tremulous, so broad, so ecstatic, that it would have strained the muscles of her flesh.

Instead she was a light herself, the translucent brilliance of a momentary spark, a flash of lightning that darts across a dark summer sky. She could feel her own power and freedom and delighted in being without substance, yet spirit-filled.

Perfect love reached out to her and wrapped around her cocoonlike, warm, comforting, peaceful. She was a channel of that love, the light, and it pulsed through and was reflected from her. She was part of the whole and it was part of her.

The quiet voice that guided her was deep, resonant, and androgynous. She was growing closer. The lights grew larger until she could see that instead of huge circles of brilliance, each circle was comprised of glowing dots. Tiny pinpricks joined together to create one glorious band, intersecting to produce a glittering, pulsating mass of creamy light.

As though a voice had spoken to her, she was led to a smaller circle of glowing luminescence. One of them was Mrs. Tonkett. And then someone else. Mary Kate blinked back tears as she felt her father's soul brush hers in passing, as delicately but as wholly as Alice's did, moments later. Then she felt James, peaceful, serene.

There was no reason to worry or to grieve for any of them anymore. She could not say how she knew this, or why she'd felt it, but it was the most important truth she'd ever experienced.

The sound of a baby's cry summoned her to another world, another existence. Transitory, but so blessed.

She blinked her way from sleep and smiled up at Archer. In his arms he held their daughter, bright red tufts of hair sprouting from the top of her otherwise bald little head. Her hair was the same color as her face, mouth open in a fierce cry. She was hungry, poor mite, and not at all shy about showing it.

"It would have been easier on you had we selected a wet nurse."

"I suppose," she said, opening her bodice and reaching for her daughter. "But I cannot help but think we would be missing something if we had."

"Not sleep." Archer smiled and settled down beside them, watched as his wife suckled their firstborn. A feeling too filled with emotion to call peace always crept over him at moments like this. Gratitude? Of course. Love, certainly. Joy. The purest and most wonderful type of joy.

"You are a greedy little thing, Alicia." Her father's voice held a note of wonderment, his look one of the most tender love. "Your mother is tired. Could you not sleep just this one night through?"

Mary Kate smiled at him, reached out a free hand and cupped his bristly cheek.

"I am never that tired, Archer. And it is you who acted the part of host all day. I am so grateful for your opening up Sanderhurst for my family reunion."

"Well, it was the only way we could show off our

daughter, was it not? Too, it proved to my meddling mother that I've seen the error of my ways."

He had been, much to his mother's delight, enraptured by the thought of a child. And despite his rank and the duty to his earldom, he would not have cared if Mary Kate had borne him a son or a daughter. He had been determined, from the first, that a child of his would not know such agony of loneliness as he had experienced, had planned on filling his nursery with children. He'd interviewed potential wet nurses, renovated the nursery quarters, even chose a gentle pony for their child to ride. He had a set of silver cups sent from the jeweler's, scoured the family Bible for names of worthy ancestors, made himself the talk of the Sanderhurst servants for all his involvement in every hour of Mary Kate's day.

Nor did he show any signs of being less than besotted with his new baby daughter.

"I truly thought Bernie was going to become ill from laughing so hard."

There was a disgruntled look on his face, one that had a great deal to do with his mother, and her reception of his news. "All I said was that it was time the St. Johns had their own family gathering."

He slanted her a look. "Do not start giggling, Mary Kate. Such levity ill becomes a countess."

She chuckled, which set Alicia to whimpering. With tiny fists, she beat upon her mother as if to command her to cease.

"Look, Archer, she has your habit of autocracy even now."

"Nonsense, my love, she's simply hungry."

"Archer?"

He straightened from kissing his daughter on the cheek,

a sign of affection she ignored, being so concerned, instead, with her nourishment.

"Yes, love?"

"I want to tell you about my dream. You may find it difficult to believe."

Her look was so serious that he masked his smile, only reached out one finger and touched her cheek.

"Tell me, darling," he said softly. "I will believe every word of it."

At Avon Books, we know your passion for romance—once you finish one of our novels, you find yourself wanting more.

May we tempt you with . . .

- **Excerpts** from our upcoming releases.

- Entertaining **extras**, including authors' personal photo albums and book lists.

- Behind-the-scenes **scoop** on your favorite characters and series.

- **Sweepstakes** for the chance to win free books, romantic getaways, and other fun prizes.

- Writing **tips** from our authors and editors.

- **Blog** with our authors and find out why they love to write romance.

- **Exclusive content** that's not contained within the pages of our novels.

Join us at
www.avonbooks.com

An Imprint of HarperCollins*Publishers*
www.avonromance.com